"TOUCHING AND WELL-WRITTEN."
—San Francisco Chronicle

"[A] deliciously rich, simmering brew of envy, charity and redemptive love ... Pungent humor and a shrewd eye for human foibles make this latest addition to Hassler's Staggerford saga memorable."
—*Publishers Weekly*

"A journey over the terrain of two real lives ... Hassler's best creations are elementary school teacher Agatha McGee and her soulmate, Father James O'Hannon."
—*The Seattle Times*

"In DEAR JAMES Jon Hassler handles some of the unexpected difficulties of growing older with imagination, insight, and sensitivity; he makes it clear that life is far from predictable at any age.... A thoughtful, wide-ranging novel that is ambitious in its breadth and powerful in its ability to speak to all of us."
—*The Bloomsbury Review*

Please turn the page for more reviews....

"OLD-FASHIONED STORYTELLING AT ITS BEST."
—*Kirkus Reviews*

"If you've seen the Royal Tapestries of France . . . you'll have marveled at the intricate weaving of the strands of colored wool. Jon Hassler weaves words in the same colorful and craftsmanlike way in DEAR JAMES."
— *St. Paul Pioneer Press*

"A perfect blend of character and plot."
— *Detroit Free Press*

"The author uses the universal themes of love, friendship, betrayal and forgiveness, as well as skillfully delineated characters, to show the resilience of the human spirit in the wake of life's unexpected reversals. DEAR JAMES is a truly literate piece of fiction backed by a genuine knowledge of small-town life."
— *Ft. Lauderdale Sun-Sentinel*

"FLAWLESS ...
WONDERFUL ...

Hassler has a great understanding of the importance of friendship."
—*Hopkins Sun Sailor*

"[This] unlikely love story is a pleasure to follow.... It is a rare and skillful writer who can create a setting so convincing that he can return there again and again in his fiction."
—*The Anniston Star*

"DEAR JAMES tells a simple, moving story, but it is in his delineation of character that Jon Hassler excels. The reader comes to understand many of the denizens of Staggerford, but to love Agatha and James, as they reveal themselves to one another at the most profound level of their beings."
—*Levittown Tribune*

"A collection of characters whose relationships succeed in bringing out critical issues of human life: friendship, love, faithfulness, conflict and reconciliation."
—*National Catholic Reporter*

By Jon Hassler
Published by Ballantine Books:

STAGGERFORD
SIMON'S NIGHT
THE LOVE HUNTER
A GREEN JOURNEY
GRAND OPENING
NORTH OF HOPE
DEAR JAMES

Young Adult Novels
FOUR MILES TO PINECONE
JEMMY

DEAR JAMES

Jon Hassler

BALLANTINE BOOKS • NEW YORK

Copyright © 1993 by Jon Hassler

All rights reserved under International and Pan-American Copyright Conventions. Published in the United States of America by Ballantine Books, a division of Random House, Inc., New York, and simultaneously in Canada by Random House of Canada Limited, Toronto.

An episode of this novel (French Lopat as Santa) appeared originally in *Prairie Schooner*, and later as the first annual Winter Book published by the Minnesota Center for the Book Arts. Also, a number of Agatha's observations about Italy bear a striking resemblance to the author's impressions which appeared previously in *Sunday* magazine of the *Minneapolis Star Tribune*.

Library of Congress Catalog Card Number: 92-55068

ISBN 0-345-37708-7

Printed in Canada

First Hardcover Edition: May 1993
First Mass Market Edition: January 1995

10 9 8 7 6 5 4 3 2 1

For Gretchen

PART 1

1

DEAR JAMES, SHE WROTE in blue ink on a page of cream stationery.

It's been snowing all night and my lawn lies deeply buried. There's a round cap of snow on my birdbath, and all I can see of my wheelbarrow is the black rubber handle grips poking out of a mound of white. The snow was a foot deep when I got out of bed, and now at noon it's closer to two. I should have thought to put away the wheelbarrow. My garden hose lies buried until spring.

Agatha McGee wrote these lines at her desk in the sun room, a small room facing south off her dining room. The blanched, unforgiving light falling through the eight close-set windows gave her forearm a chalky appearance as she pushed up the sleeve of her sweater to massage her arthritic right elbow.

Again this year Lillian and I are having a few lonely-hearts in for Thanksgiving—a holiday foreign to you? Lord knows I'm in no mood for entertaining, but I will put on my best hostess face and proceed, not only for Lillian's sake and the others', but also because as far back as I can remember, wisely or unwisely, I've striven to be predictable. Changeableness I've always equated with infancy or a disordered mind.

Agatha carefully blotted her spiky handwriting and turned the page of stationery facedown as Lillian Kite, her lifelong friend, neighbor, and culinary advisor, approached from the kitchen, where both of them had spent most of the morning. Lillian was a stout, red-faced woman of seventy years— Agatha's age exactly. Buttoning her quilted down coat tight to her throat, she came to a halt beside Agatha's desk and said,

3

"I turned the oven way down and put the deviled eggs in the refrigerator. I'm going home and put on my party dress."

"What would I do without you, Lillian?" Agatha capped her fountain pen and watched Lillian wrap her head in a bulky knit scarf of her own creation. The colors were green, gold, and pink.

"Wow, look at it come down, would you!" Lillian drew aside the sheer curtain beside the desk, and the two women silently gazed outside, transfixed by the thickly falling snow, the first serious snow of the year, a soft, windless blur piling itself into deep layers on the angular rooftops and across the shadowless yards.

"Will they come out in this?" asked Lillian.

"The streets ought to be passable as long as the wind doesn't blow."

"Even the congressman—he'll venture out?"

"He'd better. He practically invited himself."

Myron Kleinschmidt, home for the congressional recess, lived down the street in a house as large and old and nearly as attractive as Agatha's. Though not a customary guest at this dinner, he'd turned up yesterday at Agatha's door with a bereft and invitation-expecting look on his face. All of Myron Kleinschmidt's expressions were calculated, in Agatha's opinion; his very posture seemed a pose. Over coffee in her kitchen he'd told her that his wife had stayed in Washington in order to help plan a gigantic prayer breakfast for congressmen's wives. This was quite possibly a lie, thought Agatha; she knew Elena Kleinschmidt to be wholly without spiritual tendencies. He'd also hinted that if she'd care to come out of retirement for a few months, he had an important position to offer her in his next campaign for office. To this she replied as politely as possible that she'd have to wait and see who his opponent was.

"Don't be surprised if he poops out," said Lillian. "He was always the awfulest pantywaist."

Agatha, amused to hear Lillian resurrect this obsolete term, went back in memory nearly forty years and pictured the pantywaist in her classroom. Myron had been a small, round-faced sixth grader constantly seeking her approval for his meticulous penmanship, his arithmetic solutions, his clean fingernails.

This winter marked the midpoint of his seventh term in

Congress. Three times she'd voted for him; four times she'd preferred his opponent. "You must be very proud of him," people habitually said to her, Myron being the only public figure among her former students, and her response to this was a noncommittal smile. She didn't bother explaining that when she was a young woman her father had come away from several terms in the state legislature with a healthy skepticism, not to say cynicism, about politics, which he'd passed on to his daughter. How could you be proud of anyone devoted to a profession founded on compromise?

"Toodle-oo," sang Lillian, letting the curtain drop and tying the woolly scarf tightly under her chin as she departed. "Back in a half hour."

"Don't forget your pickle fork," called Agatha.

She heard the back door close, then the outer door of the enclosed porch. The aroma of turkey drifted through the house. The snow continued to fall. She sat imagining, not for the first time, how gratifying it would have been if Lillian were the sort of friend you could open your heart to. Lillian was a dear and virtuous soul, but she seldom spoke—or listened—from the heart. If I could talk to Lillian, Agatha mused, there'd be no need to write these readerless letters to Ireland.

She uncapped her pen and resumed.

This will surprise you, James—I'm going to Rome. It surprises me, for I'd never foreseen myself as a pilgrim. I always said let others tramp through the Vatican and kiss St. Peter's toe of bronze, I'll make my devotions right here in my dear little church in Staggerford. Let others join the crush in St. Peter's Square watching for the Pope to put his head out the window, I'll draw my nourishment, thank you, from the sacraments as administered by Father Finn. Not that I haven't known pilgrims who found the trip spiritually satisfying, but I've talked to a like number over the years who confessed to being let down. Roman traffic is a threat to life and limb, they've said, and the Italians are loud and demonstrative and pretend not to understand English even while selling you something expensive. If you succeed in seeing the Pope, they've told me, you're too far away to make out his features, and he repeats everything in ten boring languages.

But there's been a change in this old heart of mine, James,

*a change in this old head. Since last June there's been an ill
wind blowing through my life. For forty-eight years, as you
know, St. Isidore's Elementary was my station, my vantage
point, my mooring. Now I have no station. I'm adrift. The days
seem to double in length and the nights are endless. Each
morning I'm out of bed in time for school with no school to go
to. Evenings I feel so useless with no papers to correct that
I've begun watching TV.*

*Have you ever been truly acquainted with gloom, James?
There's a rancid smell in my basement left over from the day
last spring when my foundation sprang a leak and rainwater
spread through the laundry room and storage room, collapsing
cardboard boxes and soaking into the woodwork. The lingering
effect of gloom is like that. It spreads and soaks in. I can't get
it out of my head that the closing of St. Isidore's Elementary
prefigures the shutting down of Christendom. I keep foreseeing
the day when the Church will be reduced to a few wretched old
folks like myself searching for a Mass to go to, and a few
wretched and persecuted old clergymen like you, James, going
around in disguise saying Masses in cellars. There's an ill
wind blowing, as I've said, and the sturdy old vessel of my
faith, afloat for seventy years in the safe harbor of St. Isidore's,
is being tossed about on a sea of despair.*

So I'm going to Rome.

*You see, it was while thinking black thoughts like these one
day last week—an unsettling day of warm winds and continu-
ous thunder and intense self-pity—that the idea came to me.
Hadn't I taught generations of children about the efficacy of
the pilgrimage? Canterbury. Lourdes. Fatima. What right had
I to be disdainful of shrines? A voice from somewhere spoke to
me—the first hopeful voice I'd heard in months—and said I
needed a landmark beyond St. Isidore's steeple. If I could see
St. Peter's tomb and St. Peter's high altar, if I could see St. Peter's successor in the flesh and hear his voice (never mind
what language) and receive his blessing, the vessel of my faith
might be set on course again.*

*But it's not easy putting an idea into effect when you're de-
pressed, and I probably would have done nothing about it if
Father Finn, within twenty-four hours of this impulse, hadn't
suggested that I accompany him on his brother's ten-day tour*

of Italy. His brother is a professor familiar with Italy and tour groups. I demurred at first, but Father Finn was rather insistent (as I secretly hoped he would be), and we're leaving the day after Christmas.

Agatha looked at her watch. It was time to change for dinner. She scanned her wardrobe in her mind's eye and decided to put on her bluish-gray suit with something colorful at her throat. She would wear her silver bracelet and her red enamel pin. She hoped that by the time her guests arrived, she would have somehow called up in herself a holiday kind of happiness.

She waved the sheets of stationery in the air, drying the ink, and then she read what she had written. It met with her approval, the handwriting legible, the phrasing clear. She added her signature, blotted it, and then carefully tore the letter in two, tore the halves into fourths, tore the fourths into eighths, and let the pieces flutter into the wastebasket. Since returning home from Ireland three years earlier, she'd written perhaps a hundred letters to Father James O'Hannon, continuing a habit formed during their days as soulmates, but she never put any of them in the mail.

2

A LATE-MORNING TRICKLE OF hot water gurgled through the rusty radiators of the Morgan Hotel and woke French Lopat out of a bad dream. It was the same old dream about war—babies and young women dead in a village—that French had been dreaming for ten years or more. He uncurled himself from around his pillow, and as he lay on his back, shivering and waiting for the dream to evaporate, he remembered, with an unfamiliar twinge of cheer, that today was Thanksgiving. He'd be warm all afternoon.

He threw off his heavy pile of covers—the top layer was the shag rug off the floor—and pulled on his socks. He crossed the cold, rippling linoleum to the window, raised the tattered shade and looked down on Main Street. Snow had been falling all night apparently, for the ruts of passing cars were deep in the street. He squinted through veils of falling snow and read the digital clock in front of the bank: 11:15.

Searching through the heap of clothing on top of his dresser, he found his best shirt—red and blue flannel—and his best pants—black polyester. He pulled on his pants and carried his towel and his razor down the dim hallway to the bathroom, where he switched on the light and gazed for a minute at the tall, sad-eyed man in the mirror, wondering if people he met on the street sensed the damaged spirit behind the dark, bony face. "Nothing wrong with you a good long rest won't fix," the medics had told him. "Almost a year of duty and not a scratch—thank your lucky stars." Coming up on ten years and still resting, French told himself as he filled the sink for shaving, and because this thought amused him, he smiled at himself in the mirror and opened a painful crack in his chapped lower lip.

8

* * *

Despite his haggard, unlovely appearance, French Lopat was photographed hundreds of times every summer, and his face was featured in countless photo albums across the United States. It was a rare tourist traveling U.S. 71 north to the Minnesota lakes who didn't stop at the information center in Staggerford and there encounter French sitting near the door—outside in good weather, inside in bad—wearing a feathered headdress and a beaded leather vest and permitting himself to be photographed with strangers. DON'T TOUCH THE INDIAN, said the sign on the wall behind him. Small children were his most common companions in these snapshots, but he also posed with fishermen, honeymooners, and retired couples. Never with Indians. Sometimes in the fall there were hunting parties with guns. Now and then a carload of teenagers from Minneapolis with funny haircuts. Once he was photographed with the lieutenant governor and his wife, and another time with an entire wedding party dressed in their gowns and tuxedos. The bride that day was such a beauty that French never forgot her. Nor would he ever forget how drunk the lieutenant governor had been.

French seldom changed his expression for the camera. He'd learned over the years that it was only sentimental old ladies who wanted him to smile. Almost everybody else seemed to prefer—indeed, seemed entranced by—his natural expression of stone-faced seriousness. Some travelers became so absorbed that they actually bent forward and examined his face like a page of fine print, and what they read there they misinterpreted—French was sure of it. How could they possibly know that they were looking upon the dispiriting effect of a war in Southeast Asia? He could tell from their questions that they chose to see instead the silent endurance of the American Indian through seven generations of abuse. "Does the Bureau of Indian Affairs do you more harm than good?" "Is the American Indian Movement still a viable organization?" "Do you live in a tepee?" To these and all other questions, French responded with ten or twelve syllables of a language none of the tourists understood.

Nor did French understand it. Arnold Ulm, executive secretary of the Staggerford Chamber of Commerce, assured French that what he memorized each summer was an authentic Ojibway message, and although French spoke it with conviction, he had no idea what it meant. Further, he held no opinions about the Bureau of Indian Affairs or the American Indian Movement. He'd never lived in a tepee; indeed, he'd never lived among Indians, and was not acquainted with any of the Ojibway people from the nearby reservation who came into Staggerford to shop. He was not even certain of his Indian ancestry, but his skin was dark enough to convince non-Indians. He was unaspiring enough to work for sixty dollars a week from the middle of May until the end of September. During the off-season, when the information center was locked and the windows boarded up, French collected a biweekly unemployment check amounting to half his summer pay.

Having shaved, he carefully combed his thinning hair straight back from his high forehead and then returned to his room. He put on his moccasins, his flannel shirt, and his faded red stocking cap; then he slipped into his snug plaid sport coat and his long black overcoat. The stocking cap he had fished, with permission, from the lost and found box at the Hub Cafe. The sport coat and overcoat came from the Salvation Army store. Every second summer the Chamber of Commerce supplied him with a new pair of moccasins.

Downstairs in the dusty lobby he found Grover, the clerk, arranging a meager display of gum and candy bars on the registration counter.

"Snow," said French.

"Lots of it," croaked Grover, a man so stooped and hollow-chested that his suspenders stood away from the front of his shirt. "And it ain't over."

The lobby was dimly lit by a pair of table lamps. The woodwork was black with age, the flowery colors in the drapes and wallpaper had long ago faded to a uniform gray, and the buffalo head mounted over the radiator had a cobweb hanging from its chin whiskers. Grover was perfectly bald.

"Cold, too," French elaborated.

Without raising his eyes from the candy and gum, Grover told him. "Not so bad—twenty-two." Like French, Grover was a war veteran who had chosen to live out his life in the Morgan Hotel. Grover's war had been against Hitler, his wounds caused by shrapnel. His room was on the ground floor, number 2, behind the stairway.

Bracing himself to go out, French crossed the lobby to the glass-paneled door, but didn't pull it open. Watching a woman in high boots cross the street, he noted her clenched, frozen look as she waded through the snow. Chilled by the sight, he retreated to the radiator to store up some warmth. He said, "Colder tomorrow, I suppose."

"Always colder, the day after snow," replied Grover.

Pressing his backside into the radiator and feeling heat soak into his coat, French said, "Had that dream again."

"Hmmm," said Grover.

"Gets me down."

"Hmmm."

French liked to linger in the lobby when Grover was on duty. A calm, patient man, Grover. As often as you cared to tell it, Grover would listen to the story of the worst twenty-four hours of your life. He seemed to understand how it could happen that between one midnight and the next, in a hot, steamy land halfway around the world, a pall could settle over your days and make nothing but sleep and idleness seem useful anymore.

"I'm invited out to dinner," French said with a humble little chuckle.

"I know it," said Grover. "Miss McGee's."

"How'd you know?"

"It's Thanksgiving, isn't it?"

Grover's memory always amazed French, who never recalled from one year to the next how Grover spent his holidays.

Grover finished arranging his candy display. "They say she ain't herself."

"So I hear."

"You seen her lately?"

"Nope."

"Never changed her storm windows?"

"Not this year. She never called me."

Grover shook his head sadly. "It's the school closing down did it."

"Yup," French agreed.

"Everything's changing."

"Yup."

"Come summer, this here will be all tar, where we're standing."

"I know it," French grumbled, sorry to be reminded that the Morgan was scheduled to be demolished next June to make room for a parking lot. This was one of several developments aimed at keeping downtown Staggerford a viable trading center. Installing public toilets in the basement of the city hall was another. Still another was the renaming of Main Street and Fifth Street, which intersected at the stoplight. The signs at each corner now said Rodeo Drive and Fifth Avenue, though no one called them that.

Grover came out from behind the counter and crossed the lobby to his favorite chair. "I hear she's going to Rome," he said.

"Who?"

"Miss McGee."

"Rome?" French doubted this.

"Rome," Grover insisted. "To see the Pope."

3

*L*ILLIAN KITE RETURNED WEARING a mismatched pair of earrings and carrying a pickle fork. "It's a Christmas card out there," she puffed, entering through the enclosed back porch and stamping snow off her shoes. "It's coming down like feathers and it's an honest-to-goodness Christmas card." In the kitchen she removed her down coat and revealed the same showy violet dress she'd been wearing to this dinner for the past six or eight years, a belted, many-pleated garment she'd made from a mail-order pattern. On her feet she wore a new pair of tan, square-toed ground-grippers.

Agatha's eyes went straight to the earrings, one a gold disk, the other a pendulous creation of blue enamel and rhinestones. "Lillian, your earrings don't match."

"I know it. I've got two sets for dress-up that I just love, so I decided to put on one of each." Tying on a fresh apron, she explained, "Lyle gave me the glittery set our last Christmas together, and Imogene gave me the gold set the last time I was down to St. Paul." Lillian's husband, Lyle, had died many years ago. Imogene, her only child, was employed in the State Department of Education.

"They're very nice," Agatha said as the doorbell sounded, "but they look funny together."

"Look at them one at a time," Lillian suggested.

At the front door Agatha found Father Finn standing on the porch looking sleepy and guarded. "Father, you dear man, why aren't you wearing a hat?" She stepped across the threshold and brushed snow off the shoulders of his coat before inviting him in.

"Pleased to be here, Agatha," said the priest untruthfully. He hung his coat and scarf in the closet and followed her through the living room—dark oak woodwork, creamy lace curtains, ancient furniture highly waxed, embers smoldering in the fireplace—and into the dining room. "Nasty day," he said, rubbing his hands.

"The streets are passable, are they not? I've invited the Jubas and the congressman."

"They'll make it, the plows are out." He looked puzzled. "The congressman?"

"Myron Kleinschmidt."

"I don't recall him at this dinner before."

"My house is open to any lonely-heart, never mind his politics. His wife is spending Thanksgiving in Washington and he's feeling neglected. Are you all right, Father? You look a little peaked."

"Never better," the priest assured her, scanning the table and taking pleasure in the exquisite meal it seemed to promise. The tablecloth was lace, the napkins blue linen, the goblets Waterford, the sterling engraved with an elaborate M. "Nothing wrong with me a turkey dinner won't fix," he added, calling up a smile and a chuckle in an attempt to display a joviality he didn't feel. Having gone to bed very late because of his visit to the bishop's house in Berrington, and having risen at six out of habit, he'd summoned his deepest reserves of willpower in order to give up a nap in favor of Agatha's invitation.

"Promise me you won't step outside this winter without a hat on your head."

"I promise."

Not that a good night's rest ever quite prepared him for Agatha. This woman had a way of putting him on his guard, making him feel somehow less intelligent than he was, less mature, less capable of running a parish. He would turn sixty in the spring, yet in Agatha's presence he often felt clumsy and newly ordained. And today, augmenting his discomfort, he was conveying a letter he wished he'd never read. It contained a message of great delicacy from a man across the sea, a message directed at Agatha's carefully hidden heart.

"You'll have to be more assertive with Sister Judith, Father. You'll have to stand up to the woman and tell her that Jesus never said, 'Our mother who art in heaven.' "

Nodding his head in halfhearted agreement, Father Finn listened for voices, peered into the kitchen and was sorry to find that he'd arrived before everyone else but Lillian. He prayed that the doorbell would soon intervene.

"Or did he?" Agatha chirped sarcastically. She was moving around the table, fussing with the napkins and silver. "Have Bible scholars uncovered some new evidence, Father, that Jesus actually said, 'Our mother who art in heaven'?"

"Not to my knowledge," said Father Finn.

"I thought not."

He watched her line up the butter knife beside the butter plate, poke a spoon into the cranberries. He was sorry to observe that she wore a taut, unhappy expression and looked a little shriveled around the mouth—signs that she was still dogged by depression. Her gray suit was stylish, and the paisley scarf at her throat a cheerful shade of red, but there was obviously nothing festive in her spirit. There were those in the parish who'd predicted this emotional nosedive. They were certain Agatha would fall into despair when, as principal, she lost the fight to keep the school open. After all, they'd said, her time on its staff measured only a little less than half a century—who wouldn't be devastated? Father Finn had told them they'd be surprised—they didn't know Agatha. But he, in the end, was the one surprised.

"Help yourself to a drink, Father, it's a day for a hot brandy, is it not? Would you like me to heat some water?"

"No, thank you, Agatha." Turning to the sideboard to examine the bottles of spirits, the priest recalled how last spring he'd never for a moment doubted that Agatha would avoid despondency, because Agatha in his experience was strict with herself, and resilient, her spirit tougher than the average person's, larger somehow, more forceful. People's spirits, Father Finn liked to think, were vessels of their Creator's breath (this was a favorite image of his, often repeated in the pulpit on Sundays), but the analogy always used to fail him whenever he thought of Agatha's spirit. Her spirit had been more like a wind tunnel.

"And desecrating the Lord's Prayer isn't the worst of it, Father—far from it."

No, it hadn't been despondency he'd feared for Agatha when the parish council, strapped for money and bullied by the bishop, voted six to one in favor of dismantling the school and dispersing the faculty and students. No, what had made him nervous was the prospect of all her pent-up energy turned in his direction. Without the school as her preoccupation, he'd foreseen her becoming the parish's full-time, free-lance troubleshooter. Well, it hadn't happened. Apart from her habitual potshots at Sister Judith, she'd pretty much given up meddling in parish affairs. In fact, she seldom appeared in public anymore, and when she did, she looked unrested and distracted. Neighbors were amazed night after night to see the flickering light of her television. It had been this report of her watching late-night talk shows that alerted Father Finn to the seriousness of her despair and prompted him to invite her along on his brother's tour of Italy.

He suppressed a sneeze, wiped his nose with a dingy gray handkerchief and said, "A month from yesterday, Agatha."

"I'm already packing," she replied flatly, holding a match to one of the candles standing tall in sterling candlesticks.

"And looking forward—as I am?" He was conscious of begging the question, but he had to ask. Given her lack of enthusiasm, he feared she might be regretting her nonrefundable deposit.

"Yes, indeed," she replied evenly, conveying no excitement. "Has your brother met his quota?"

"He needs three more, with less than a week to find them."

"And if he doesn't find them?"

"He'll take us anyhow, pay his own way."

Actually it had not been for Agatha's sake alone that he'd extended the invitation. His brother, Albert Finn, Ph.D., professor of physics at Rookery State College, was an inveterate traveler who this year was touting "Galileo's Italy," a ten-day tour of Rome, Pisa, and Florence during Christmas break. The trip was designed for college students, but having failed to attract the required number of participants, the professor was soliciting travelers not seeking college credit. He had to generate a total of fifteen fares if he, as their leader, was to fly free. Father Finn, due for a vacation, had quickly signed on, and a few days later so had Agatha, bringing the roster to twelve.

"We've heard a lot of piffle over the years from Sister Judith, Father, but lately I've been fearing for her sanity." Agatha held a goblet up to the brilliant hanging lamp and buffed away a fingerprint. "She told her study group the other day that they should think of Creation as God laying an egg."

"No!" said Father Finn, feigning disbelief.

The doorbell sounded.

"Yes, she did." Agatha drilled him with her small blue eyes. "She actually said that."

"Well." The priest suppressed a yawn.

"God laying an egg, just think of it," she said, and left him to chew this over alone in the dining room.

Father Finn, never sorry to be left alone, stood at the sideboard reading the labels. Scotch. Brandy. Two kinds of wine. An expensive bourbon. A rather poor brand of gin. The same half-empty bottle of apricot-flavored vodka he'd seen here at this dinner for at least twelve years. What guest from ages past had drunk apricot-flavored vodka? He scooped ice from a bucket and uncapped the bottle of bourbon, but before filling his glass, he gave himself over to an enormous, eye-watering yawn.

The voices at the front door—a female shriek and the growl of an old man—belonged to the Jubas. Impolite of him, he realized, not to hurry into the living room and allow himself to be fallen upon by Sister Judith and to shake the fat, limp hand of her widowed father, but he didn't have the stamina to face them quite yet, didn't feel quite ready to withstand Sylvester Juba's gloomy complaining, didn't feel up to the relentless chatter that filled any room Sister Judith occupied. Should you have the misfortune to be seated between the Jubas at dinner, you got it from both sides nonstop, dark pessimism pouring into one ear, excited twaddle pouring into the other. You had to be careful which chair you chose.

The priest trickled bourbon over his ice and carried the glass to the table. He pulled out a chair and sat heavily down beside the cranberry dish. Oh, to be home on the couch, drifting pleasantly toward sleep while the Vikings and Lions silently fought it out on TV. He yawned a larger, longer yawn than before and wished he'd had the good sense last night to decline the bishop's invitation to dinner.

Summoned by Bishop Baker on short notice, he'd driven to Berrington and stayed late into the night despite the forecast of snow. He and the bishop had begun their discussion of parish matters over dinner at a place called Ivan Z's (low lights, high prices, tasteless food pretentiously served), and at nine o'clock, when a jazz trio struck up music too loud for conversation, they had sat there for an hour listening to it, the bishop (a jazz nut) obviously enthralled, and Father Finn (a tin ear) unmoved and uncomprehending. Then the bishop had invited him back to his house, where he foolishly stayed until after midnight, sipping a nightcap and discussing Agatha McGee. Agatha's ears must have burned. The bishop entrusted him with secrets about her.

It had taken forever to drive the forty miles back to Staggerford through the dizzying snowfall, and when he got to bed, he couldn't sleep. His brain reeled with all he'd learned about the woman he'd assumed he'd been reading like an open book. Agatha in love? Preposterous. And yet the bishop had shown him the letter, had given it to him and charged him with showing it to Agatha. A man named O'Hannon. A priest, no less, from Ireland. It caused Father Finn to wonder how many other open books he'd been misreading all these years. A lifetime of shepherding your flock in the general direction of their eternal reward while imagining that you understood them heart and soul—but really, what did a priest know?

"It's simply a marvelous, marvelous snowfall," Sister Judith Juba was gushing in the other room. "And your house, Agatha, it sits here looking exactly like a Christmas card, how ingenious of you to set your enameled cream can out there on the porch, I always thought that touch of crimson was perfect in your garden, but wintertime it's simply marvelous on your front porch."

It was Sister Judith who, in her capacity as associate administrator of St. Isidore's, had recently led a prayer for a dead parishioner at the Carlson Case Funeral Home beginning, "Our mother who art in heaven." She'd been doing quite a lot of other novel things as well, thought Father Finn, though "novel" was not the word commonly applied to them. Blasphemous and stupid were adjectives you heard fairly often from the traditionalists, while the more forward-looking parishioners called her innovations liberating and fun. "Novel" was Father Finn's term, he being a tolerant, noncommittal man whose job it was to keep the ship afloat through heavy seas.

He sipped his bourbon. He sneezed softly. He blew his nose. He unwrapped a cigar and wished he could smoke it. Holding it between his fingers and imagining curls of smoke rising from its tip, he wondered whether Agatha had her facts straight, wondered whether Sister Judith had actually described Creation as God laying an egg. He wouldn't put it past her. And when did Agatha ever *not* have her facts straight?

"Oh, there you are!" cried Sister Judith, sweeping into the dining room and patting him on the head. "I knew if I followed my nose I'd find you. Where there's smoke there's clergy, I always say."

True, she'd been saying it forever, every time he unwrapped a cigar in her presence, a presence that had been fairly easy to avoid during the several years when she was teaching at St. Isidore's and living in the convent; but since going off to graduate school and returning to Staggerford with a degree in pastoral ministry and moving in with her widowed father and setting up her office in the parlor of the rectory—all this at Bishop Baker's behest—Father Finn was seeing and hearing altogether too much of her.

Rising to his feet and displaying his unlit cigar, lest she accuse him of violating Agatha's smoking ban, he said, "Let me fix you a drink." Confronted with Sister Judith, a toucher, he liked to be busy with his hands.

"A drink would be lovely," she replied, playfully blocking his way to the bottles and intercepting his cigar on its way to his mouth, snatching it out of his hand and holding it at arm's length. "Horrid, smelly habit, Skipper, lit or unlit." As he reached out to retrieve it, she backed away, which gave him the opening he needed to escape to the sideboard. She joined him there, inserting the cigar into a pocket of his cardigan and linking an arm through his as they surveyed the liquor.

"Scotch and water?"

"Sounds heavenly," she said, releasing his arm.

He made the drink powerful. Alcohol, he knew, ate away at her intensity. He liked her better lit.

"Cheers, Skipper." She raised the glass to eye level, as though inspecting it for impurities, lowered it to nose level, smelled it, then sipped. "Honestly, isn't this dinner a bore? If it weren't for my father—"

"Look at that!" cried Sylvester Juba, waddling into the dining room with Agatha at his side. "Here's the pastor exactly where you'd expect to find him, guarding the booze. Judy, mix me a stiff one—you know what I like."

Sister Judith and her father, who lived together in the massive old Juba house on Juba Street, were the remnants of Staggerford's first and most prosperous lumbering family. To look at them, thought Father Finn, you wouldn't know they were father and daughter. Sylvester was short and stout. Sister Judith was tall and shaped like a stick. She wore, in and out of season, flimsy slit skirts and silky low-neck blouses, as if to display the figure she wished she had. Her blouse today, under her black leather vest, was burgundy and half unbuttoned. She was a tiresomely perky woman in her early forties, though she looked older than that, her bony face deeply etched with the lines of her perpetual smile, and her brown, unruly hair turning gray. Her green eyes, magnified behind thick glasses, had an unsettling effect on Father Finn. They seemed to signify something desperate or unfulfilled in her soul and gave the lie to her cheery demeanor. He'd seen eyes like hers in the faces of abused children and old panhandlers—the large, importunate eyes of those who spend their days begging in vain for kindness or money or love.

"Bring on the bird," ordered her father, whose holiday attire was a lint-collecting wool suit deeply wrinkled at the elbows and behind the knees, and a necktie spotted with food. His lapels were decorated with the tiny metallic emblems of the Rotary Club and the Knights of Columbus. Father Finn was struck by the effect of gravity on the old man's flaccid face— jowls and wattles wagging, bags hanging darkly under the eyes, eyelids drooping, the corners of the mouth turning down. There was the rumor going around, perhaps apocryphal, that the old man watched TV with his eyelids held open with Scotch tape. Another rumor had him sweet on Agatha McGee.

"Nice seeing you, Sylvester." Father Finn extended his hand, which the old man gripped briefly, then cast away.

"Agatha, bring on the bird," Sylvester repeated, leaning

over the table and peering into a bowl. "What's this mushy concoction?"

"We don't eat till everyone's here," Agatha told him. "That's delicious fruit salad—Lillian made it."

He was poking his finger into the creamy dish to snatch out a peach slice when his daughter slapped his hand away and gave him his drink. "Now behave!" she ordered, giggling.

He retreated sulkily to a corner of the room and scowled at his daughter, at the priest, at Lillian Kite, who came in from the kitchen bearing a plate of deviled eggs.

As Lillian explained to the priest and the nun about her earrings, Sylvester Juba settled his eyes on Agatha McGee, his heart's desire, and saw that she was growing old pretty fast this fall. In her white hair he saw only a trace of its former gingery hue. She'd always been small, but now she was scarcely a wisp, and there was a slight hunch in what for a lifetime had been the straightest back in town. Well, it was no wonder she looked down in the mouth. He'd been told (not by her; she never told him anything) that overseeing the breakup of the parochial school had left her up a stump.

Watching her move over to the sideboard and pick up a decanter of her homemade chokecherry wine, he pictured her as Mrs. Sylvester Juba, mistress of his fourteen-room house on Juba Street, joint owner of his stocks and bonds, inheritor (along with his daughter) of his property in town and his acreage out in the country. Every house needed a woman, and his daughter was scheduled to abandon him, because her term at St. Isidore's was a one-year apprenticeship. Soon Judy would be called to some parish in greater need of her pastoral talents, perhaps the cathedral itself in Berrington, and where would that leave Sylvester? Up a stump.

Last June, soon after the school closed, he'd met Agatha coming out of church and asked her to be his bride. She'd laughed and said, "Oh, Sylvester, go on!" as though he'd told her an off-color joke. Did she actually think he was joking? He intended to propose again today, to prove he meant it. With six months to think it over, she might have come to see the wisdom of their union, was likely waiting for a second chance. She could very well be short of money—such a big old house to maintain and pay taxes on. Without students to dote on, she no doubt needed companionship. Throw in with the Jubas and she'd get not only a husband, but a daughter in the bargain. Sell the McGee house and the three of them, even in today's soft real estate market, would be richer by sixty thousand dollars.

Agatha, refilling the wineglass Lillian had been sipping from since mid-morning, and then pouring herself a generous amount, was aware of the old man's bleary eyes upon her. She'd been the object of Sylvester Juba's tiresome attention off and on since the death several years ago of his devoted wife Twyla. One foggy, drizzly morning last June, on the steps of St. Isidore's, he'd gripped her arm roughly and said loud enough for several others to hear, "How about we get married, Agatha?" She dismissed him in a tone meant to convey, despite her embarrassment, a breezy nonchalance. Some of the people on the steps turned and smiled; one or two actually laughed out loud. She had slipped out of his grasp and darted away, hiding behind her umbrella because she felt herself blushing. She knew he wasn't joking, and that's why she was so mortified.

It occurred to her now, sipping wine, that nearly sixty years had probably passed between blushes. In the seventh grade she was one of five pianists performing a Sunday afternoon recital for parents and friends in St. Isidore's gymnasium when she struck an erroneous and ugly chord at the end of a dreamy piece by Debussy. She was so ashamed of herself for this mistake that instead of acknowledging the applause with the curtsy and smile she'd rehearsed, she turned scarlet and shot into the nearest cloakroom, where she hid until everyone was gone. She never went back to lessons. She never touched a keyboard again.

"Cheers," said Lillian, lifting her replenished glass. "Cheers everybody."

The priest and the nun clinked their glasses with hers. The priest said "cheers" and the nun said, "Where's Imogene spending the holiday?"

Lillian drank, smacked her lips and said, "Friends in the city."

"There's a subject for your series," said Agatha, determined to suppress her unsociable feelings by being chatty and helpful.

"Imogene's just the type." Sister Judith wrote an occasional column for the local *Weekly* entitled "Career Women of Staggerford." Agatha had been featured nearly a year ago, the postmistress last spring, Louise Meers of the city council in July, and Marsha Skoog of Marsha's Ready-to-Wear this fall. She was running out of subjects.

"Hey, you're right," said the nun. "Imogene's always been out there on the cutting edge. Exactly what is Imogene's job these days, Lillian?"

"Imogene doesn't live here anymore," answered Lillian in a voice slurred by wine.

"I know she doesn't, but she grew up here. Staggerford informed her."

"She says I should move to St. Paul."

"What does she *do* exactly?"

"She's with the state. She says it's time for me to sell my house and move to St. Paul. She says why wait till I'm too old to enjoy the city."

This was news to Agatha. Bad news. Certain that her neighbor had only the vaguest concept of city life and how she might fit into it, she asked, "But *would* you enjoy the city, Lillian?" She foresaw Lillian's loneliness if she moved. She foresaw her own.

Lillian drained her glass before replying. "Guess how many channels Imogene gets."

"Dozens, I'm sure," said Sister Judith. "Is she in what you'd call a managerial position?"

Lillian, ignoring or not hearing the question, trained her eyes on Agatha. "Guess how many channels."

"Twenty-one," Agatha responded, having been told more than once. It wasn't Lillian's mind she would miss; it was her good heart, her dependability, the light burning in her window whenever she glanced across the alley at night.

Sister Judith gripped Lillian's elbow and gave her a little shake, as though to bring her out of a dream. "Tell me," she insisted, thrusting her toothy smile up close to Lillian's face and narrowing her eyes, "what does your daughter *do* for the state?"

"Library work," replied Lillian placidly. "She's always been in library work."

"But what's her title?"

Lillian, momentarily woozy, pressed her nose flat against her wineglass and smiled vacantly.

"Imogene's called a purchasing coordinator," Agatha explained. "She's in the Department of Education and she works with schools on their book acquisitions."

"She's always reading," Lillian added. "How anybody can read with twenty-one channels is beyond me."

Agatha, already bored with her guests, lowered her eyes and gave herself up to a bit of fantasy. She imagined James in the room. He was mingling with her friends and storing up impressions to be shared with her after they were gone. This was a habit she had, picturing James lifted out of County Kildare and set down in Minnesota and comparing his view of it with hers. *Lillian Kite's a good old shoe,* she imagined him saying, *you're lucky to have her out your back door, Agatha, but don't you wish once in a while she'd come out with a stimulating word or two?*

James, unlike Father Finn, would be wearing his Roman collar (Irish clergymen were seldom caught out of uniform), and of course he'd be the most handsome man in the room, with his steel-gray hair and his sea-blue eyes, and everyone would be struck, as Agatha had been struck in Dublin, by the deep, ringing tones of his voice.

And your so-called nun, Agatha—isn't she repressing a great lot of something or other in that narrow little breast of hers? She strikes me as someone with a need she's trying to ignore by running on about nothing. And her father's a case as well, standing there in a kind of alcoholic stupor. Pardon me for asking, Agatha, but what possessed you to invite the Jubas?

She would explain to him, then, about the bond between the McGees and the Jubas, their friendship going back to the 1890s, when Agatha's father came to town and set up his law office across the street from the sawmill belonging to Sylvester's father and uncles. The Jubas and McGees had been together for Thanksgiving dinner for most of the twentieth century.

James would chuckle then. His retort would be something like, *Ah, the tyranny of tradition.*

"Don't laugh," would be Agatha's response, a statement

directed at James in her imagination but now uttered aloud in her dining room, and attracting—since no one was laughing—a curious glance from each of her guests. She felt her face go red. "The rolls," she said, hurrying into the kitchen, "I forgot to brown the rolls."

4

FRENCH WALKED THROUGH THE snow
with his shoulders hunched, his head bent forward, his eyes on
his moccasins, his hands drawn up in his sleeves. This was
French's wintertime posture. Trying to displace as little cold air
as possible, he contracted his large frame into its smallest possible volume and gave the impression of a man trying to live
inside his coat.

While putting a curve in French's spine, winter also put a
crimp in his thinking. Ever since leaving the warmth of Miss
McGee's house and moving into Room 32 of the Morgan, his
state of mind underwent a change each November when the
snow began to fall. It wasn't depression exactly, because
French's spirit, never high, had nowhere to drop. It was a kind
of hibernation, a surrender to indolence. Between now and
April he would spend long hours reading magazines in bed, lying under two blankets and the rug off the floor. Two or three
times a day he'd go out foraging for heat, most often finding
it at the Hub Cafe, where he liked to drink coffee and read
newspapers at the end of the counter near the steaming
kitchen.

There'd be no heat to soak up at St. Isidore's this winter,
and that was a pity. Whenever her custodian had been over-
worked or out with an illness, Miss McGee used to summon
French to St. Isidore's, where the classrooms and hallways
were wonderfully overheated and the boiler room was posi-
tively torrid. Miss McGee saw to it that the few extra dollars
he earned sweeping floors and emptying wastebaskets were
carefully spread across pay periods so as not to affect his unemployment income.

For most of his life she'd done him favors like this. As far back as his boyhood she'd been strangely solicitous. He felt two ways about this. He valued and was flattered by her kind attentions (who wouldn't be glad to be singled out for special acts of kindness by someone as mighty and discerning as Miss McGee?), and yet along with her acts of kindness was the implication that she was making allowances for shortcomings in his nature that he didn't feel were there, some strain of ignorance or vulnerability that diminished him. True, it gave you a free and easy feeling to have very little expected of you, but it could sometimes be irritating. Now and then his irritation erupted and forced him to say peevish things which he was later ashamed of. He intended to guard against peevishness today.

Snowflakes clung to French's eyelashes. Snow packed itself into his moccasins and soaked through his socks. Leaving Main Street, he trudged along a residential avenue and came up behind a pair of teenage girls far gone in a fit of silliness and laughing themselves weak as they tried to trip and drop each other into the snow. Both girls wore blue jeans, both had auburn hair. The tall girl, whose hair was long and straight, wore a white ski jacket with red stripes. The short girl, whose hair was short and curly and drenched with snow, wore a sky-blue windbreaker. French guessed they were fourteen. As he speeded up to hurry past them, the tall girl, shrieking with laughter, pushed the short girl violently in his direction, which caused him to jerk his head up and jump sideways and throw his hands in the air—it might have been a basketball move—and run frantically away from them. Loping through the snow, his heart racing, he thought of the girl in Saigon who had laughed so happily in the moment before she was blown to pieces.

The girls' laughter died behind him and he came to a halt beside a tree. Leaning against it, he emptied his moccasins of snow and shook his head repeatedly, trying to rid himself of the young woman in his memory. He had touched her intimately as they walked along the dark street, and then she'd broken free of him and run around the corner of a building, teasing him, and was killed by a grenade. From that day to this, French couldn't stand being touched, couldn't stand touching others.

One good thing about winter, thought French, he was hardly

ever touched. It was impossible to avoid being touched in the summer because of his job. He'd tried to talk Arnold Ulm of the Chamber of Commerce into letting him wear a HANDS OFF sign around his neck, but Arnold Ulm said absolutely not—it would take away from the costume. He had to be satisfied with the sign on the wall, DON'T TOUCH THE INDIAN, which hardly anybody noticed.

Approaching Miss McGee's house, French straightened to his full height—six-two—and ran his tongue over his front teeth. Decades had passed since he was a student in her sixth grade at St. Isidore's, yet he clearly remembered how she had never let up about good posture and good dental habits, as well as good grades, good grammar, and good behavior in church. Luckily, she'd never come down as hard on him about his grades, which were seldom very good, as she had on certain other students. She'd never pressed him to his limits, and he'd been fond of her for that. Unlike Sister Mary Sebastian in grade five, who had relentlessly tried to shame him into better scholarship and caused his stomach to ache every morning on his way to school, Miss McGee concentrated on things she knew he could master. "Frederick, sit up straight," she would tell him half a dozen times a day. "Frederick, what's this?" she would ask, pointing to an empty square on his toothbrushing chart. "Class," she would sometimes say, sensing his need for praise, "I want you to notice how Frederick folds his hands in church and follow his example."

To this day she never called him by his nickname, which had grown out of a classroom skit in Sister Mary Sebastian's fifth grade. He'd played a voyageur in the skit, and his only line was "French," uttered three times as three classmates portraying three Indian chiefs inquired about his nationality.

Climbing the porch steps and ringing the doorbell, French recalled the year he'd spent living in comfort in this house. Home from the war, he'd taken the room vacated by Miles Pruitt, a high school teacher who'd been murdered by the deranged mother of a student. This had happened when French was overseas. He remembered Pruitt from his school days, but only vaguely, for Pruitt had been a few years older than French and had made no mark as an athlete. Miss McGee, people said, had been devastated by Pruitt's death, but French saw no evidence of her devastation. Either she'd recovered by the time he moved in, or he was too devastated himself by death on a grand scale to notice.

French, while living here, had got himself a part-time job as a rural mail carrier. It was at Miss McGee's urging that he'd taken the civil service test, and it was in Miss McGee's Plymouth that he'd delivered the mail when the regulars had vacations or days off. For the first few weeks it took him over six hours to drive the routes that the men he was replacing covered in four. He was forever backing up to make sure he hadn't left something in the wrong mailbox.

Nowadays there was a clinical name for French's trouble—he'd read about it in magazines. Doctors were treating it, support groups were formed. Post-traumatic shock syndrome—he liked the term, it sounded important. He liked knowing veterans could get help. Not that he himself would consider treatment at this late date. That year in Miss McGee's house had been a kind of treatment. Abiding by Miss McGee's rules, following her directions, soaking up her praise, listening to her advice, he'd felt his fragmented soul gradually knit itself back together. It was like having a mother again. After several weeks in her spare bedroom, he'd begun to wake up in the morning with something besides dread in his heart. Not happiness exactly, not eagerness for the new day, but a kind of urge to be eager, a longing to be happy.

And his postal job, too, had become easier with time. Perhaps he'd be delivering mail to this day if, in the eleventh month of his employment, the number of Staggerford's rural routes hadn't been reduced. French, last hired, was the first one laid off. And if Miss McGee hadn't kept pressing him to find a new job before he was ready, perhaps he'd still be living in her warm house. Her pushiness was more than he could stand. He needed more rest than she allowed him. He caught on as Staggerford's summertime Indian, but she wasn't satisfied with that. It was too bad, but the only way he could envision remaining on good terms with her was to move out and take a room at the Morgan.

"Frederick, come in. It's been ages. No, don't come in, I'll brush you off on the porch. Turn around." Miss McGee stepped over the threshold with a whisk broom and swept the snow from his shoulders. "Turn," she ordered, and he turned again. "Now come in, I'll take your coat and cap."

Shedding his coat in the entryway and stuffing his cap into one of its pockets, he was surprised by how much the woman had aged since he'd last seen her. Well, it was no wonder. Overseeing the breakup of St. Isidore's must have been an ordeal. And what would she be now—seventy? He wondered if she was losing her memory and the fall chores had slipped her mind. For ten years, fall and spring, he'd been changing her storm windows and screens, but this year she never called him. Maybe he should have come and done it anyway.

But then he noticed how steady she was. Steady of hand as she took his coat. Steady of gaze and steady of voice as she looked up into his eyes and instructed him to go in and find the other guests and help himself to a drink. Her steadiness brought a sudden, queer feeling to his heart—the ache of nostalgia. He was once again seated in desk four, row three, of her classroom and penciling an X in the bedtime column of his toothbrushing chart. He was a little behind, as usual. The others had put away their charts and opened their arithmetic books. There was a problem on the board and Miss McGee was asking for the solution, her steady eyes searching the room for a responsive face. Her eyes rested on French momentarily, and for that moment he was afraid she might reprimand him for his slowness the way Sister Mary Sebastian had always done, but then her eyes moved on and she reprimanded Billy Markell instead, for whispering.

He lingered in the living room, adding a stick of oak to the embers in the fireplace and waiting for Miss McGee to lead him farther into the house, but she insisted that he go ahead on his own—she was keeping an eye out for Congressman Kleinschmidt—and so he braced himself and crossed into the dining room where Sylvester Juba was growling, and his daughter the nun was speaking to Father Finn, and Father Finn seemed to be ignoring her while reading the label on a bottle of wine. He caught sight of Lillian Kite in the kitchen.

"Hello?" said French apologetically, feeling like the misfit he was.

"Hi," said Sister Judith, flying at him with her arms out for a hug. French jumped back a step or two and held her at bay with a stiff-armed handshake, a defense he'd developed when he used to enter her classroom to sweep the floor and empty the wastebasket and she'd come at him like this.

"Cheers," said Sylvester Juba cheerlessly, transferring his drink to his left hand and giving French a brief, ice-cold handshake. The color of the old man's bulbous nose and sunken cheeks gave French the impression—based on a magazine article he'd read recently—of heavy drinking or high blood pressure or both.

"What's your blood pressure?" French asked him. It was all he could think of to say.

"How the hell should I know?" barked the old man.

"Hello, French," said the priest, setting down the wine bottle. "How you been?"

"Not too shabby."

"Glad to see you. Don't know when I saw you last."

"Here. Last year." French shook the priest's hand but avoided his eyes. Priests embarrassed him. Meeting this priest every year on this holiday afternoon, he always expected to be asked why he'd quit going to church. Though he'd quit a long time ago and had never once been asked, not even by Miss McGee, he was still trying to formulate an answer. Sundays, lying late in bed at the Morgan, he would rehearse some irrefutable declaration, something powerful enough to squelch even an old-time nun (he was thinking of the menacing Sister Mary Sebastian in grade five), something like "It's no use praying when I can't keep my mind on my prayers," or "Church makes my conscience act up and my conscience makes me nervous," or something momentous like "I don't believe in God."

But none of these responses was satisfactory. They were all more or less false. He *did* believe in God, sort of. As for his conscience, it wasn't all that active, in or out of church. And while it was true that prayer never failed to set his mind wandering, wasn't the impulse to pray a kind of prayer in itself? So these answers quickly lost their force, and the ones that took their place—the *actual* reasons—didn't sound the least bit powerful: Mass was boring, the church was chilly, and he hated crowds.

"What'll you drink?" asked the priest.

"Shot of brandy," French replied eagerly.

"Ice?"

"Nope."

The priest poured two fingers into a highball glass and handed it to him. "Here's to you."

"Likewise," French replied. He took a big swallow and made a tight face as the brandy burned its way down.

"Quite a snowfall," said Father Finn.

Another swallow, another tight face. "Yup."

"I don't look for this one to melt, not this late in the year." A third swallow, not so hard on the throat. "Nope."

Meanwhile Sylvester Juba turned to his daughter and asked, "What the hell *is* my blood pressure these days?"

"Stroke city," she replied, laughing harshly.

5

T H E   T U R K E Y   H A D   B E E N   basted countless times and Sylvester Juba was finishing his third highball when Congressman Kleinschmidt finally arrived with apologies and a bottle of wine.

"You'll know everyone here," predicted Agatha, delaying his entrance by sweeping snow from his shoes.

"You'll have to forgive me, Agatha, I was on the phone for nearly an hour with a farmer going bankrupt in Hubbard County."

"Stop playing fast and loose with the economy, Myron—the poor farmers are always the first to suffer."

"Don't blame me, I'm laissez-faire." He followed her into the entryway and peered into the living room. "Who's the tall fellow with the slouch?"

"Frederick Lopat? Surely you know Frederick. French, they call him."

"Oh, the Indian. I didn't recognize him without his war bonnet. And there's the good father. How does he do it, I ask myself. How does he live that priestly life all these years and not burn out?"

"He doesn't."

The congressman, hanging his cashmere coat in the closet, shot her a surprised look. "He doesn't live the priestly life?"

"I didn't say that. I mean he doesn't avoid burning out. He's getting lax."

"I don't agree, Agatha. Laid back, not lax. It's his nature. He's always been that way."

This not being a point worth arguing, she said, "Come and meet your constituency," and showed him into the living room, where he was greeted warmly and noisily and asked a dozen

33

questions, not about legislation, but about his wife, his dog, and the Redskins.

Agatha stood apart from the circle of her guests, watching the congressman charm each of them and marveling at his sophistication. Yesterday, alone with her, he'd been glum, but put this man in a crowd and he became glib and bouncy, quick to smile, quick to turn his attention elsewhere if you didn't keep him interested. He was impeccably dressed today in the same striped tie and pristine shirt collar men habitually wore on the evening news from Washington. His gold-rimmed glasses gleamed, and the gray hair receding from his perfectly round forehead was perfectly groomed. He was by far the shortest of her guests, scarcely taller than Agatha herself, and his slightness of build coupled with the beaming smile on his upturned face gave him a boyish appearance—a quality he purposely cultivated, Agatha was sure, as his public and highly reelectable image. In his biennial TV ads he came across as something of a child prodigy—innocent, earnest, idealistic—a man of fifty pretending to be twelve.

She remembered his disdain, at twelve, for the rougher sort of games at recess, and yet he was spared the insults and jeers that twelve-year-old boys ordinarily heaped upon sissies. If not actually liked, he was curiously respected. Boy and man, he'd never been brilliant, warm or especially articulate, and Agatha had been just as puzzled in those days by his power over his classmates as she was now by his popularity among his constituents.

Agatha allowed him ten minutes of chatty fellowship before she called everyone to the table. Lillian Kite and Father Finn were placed side by side with their backs to the kitchen. Sister Judith, flanked by Frederick Lopat and Congressman Kleinschmidt, sat facing them. Sylvester Juba, by longstanding custom, took the chair at the head of the table, where Agatha's father had sat before him. Sylvester was more or less drunk. He squinted at the turkey lying on a platter in front of him and saw with satisfaction that a good bit of its white meat had already been sliced, probably by Lillian. To this end he'd purposely ripped and shredded the bird to bits when last year he'd been asked to carve. Agatha took her place facing Sylvester, the candles burning between them.

Father Finn said grace, Lillian said watch out for the serving dishes because they were hot, Sylvester said the bird looked dried out and tough, and Sister Judith said the table was pretty as a picture. Plates were heaped with turkey, dressing, fruit salad, cranberries, deviled eggs, and baked yams with a brown-sugar sauce. Silence fell on the room while they all savored their first few bites—a silence Congressman Kleinschmidt took advantage of by breaking out in a lengthy and secular thanks-giving. It had to do with Plymouth Rock, the Constitution, the Republican party, President Reagan, priests, nuns, and bankrupt farmers. It included Native Americans as well, and French was embarrassed to be singled out as "our noble Chippewa brother sharing this bounteous meal." The other guests were quite sure there were no Indians in French's ancestry, but no one pointed out the congressman's mistake. To Agatha his words seemed as formless and windy as *Leaves of Grass* by Walt Whitman, the poet largely responsible for cutting American literature loose from its moorings, and she, too, had her moment of em-barrassment when, at the end, she was singled out as "our no-ble hostess with a lifetime of peerless teaching behind her and the golden years of peaceful rest stretching ahead—to her we are more grateful than we can say for this fabulous meal."

"Amen," said Sister Judith.

"I haven't departed this life quite yet," said Agatha.

"I'm about to!" blurted Sylvester, his small, fleshy eyes darting from face to face as he tried to gauge the impact of his words. He added, "Die, that is!" in case anyone missed the point. Shock was registered on only French's face. The others, to Sylvester's chagrin, were ignoring him. "I'll be dead by next Thanksgiving, I promise you."

"These yams are delicious, Agatha," said Father Finn. "I don't know when I last had a yam."

"Thanksgiving a year ago," she replied. "And Lillian gets the credit. Surely by this time you know who's the cook in this partnership."

"My coffin's bought and paid for," Sylvester boomed loudly in French's direction. "It's the finest grade of cherrywood. Brass hinges and handles. Tailored interior."

Sister Judith, laughing, turned to French, sitting on her left, and explained that her father was a joker.

"Who's joking?" her father demanded. "I can take you to the Carlson Case Funeral Home this afternoon and show it to you."

Her laugh rose in pitch and volume. "Oh, you can't either."

"Like hell I can't!" Purple anger came into Sylvester's face. "It's got a rounded top and five coats of varnish so it's smooth as glass, and it's sitting there in the selection room waiting to be my eternal bed. It cost me three thousand, five hundred tomatoes."

His daughter, apparently convinced, stopped laughing.

Agatha, casting about in her mind for a more edifying topic than Sylvester's death and burial, regretted her lifelong obligation to spend Thanksgiving with the Jubas, Sylvester having declined into such an embarrassing wreck and his daughter having been reborn as such a reckless theologian, but how did you break a tradition going back ninety years? James O'Hannon was right—the tyranny of tradition. A tradition instituted by your dear departed father and mother was not something to be lightly cast aside. Losing a tradition like that was like losing a point on your compass. This idea of tradition led her to speculate that perhaps it was true after all that Elena Kleinschmidt, having grown up in Staggerford unattached to any of its churches, *was* organizing a prayer breakfast. Maybe she was trying to introduce a sacred custom of some sort into her life. Agatha turned to the congressman and asked him about it. "I was surprised, Myron. I hadn't thought her the type."

"It takes all types to make a prayer breakfast, Agatha. Elena is known around Washington for her organizational skills. Last summer she organized a flower show." The congressman turned his eyes away from Agatha as he said this, for although stretching or avoiding the truth was second nature to him, he wasn't comfortable doing it in Agatha's presence. While it was true that his wife had helped plan a flower show last August, the prayer breakfast was a lie, a fabrication designed to conceal from his constituents the shabby state his marriage was in. It was Myron's conviction that most Minnesotans, while intolerant of infidelity, were suckers for anything religious.

"Imogene goes to a prayer meeting every second Wednesday," Lillian said of her daughter. "They meet in the basement of some off-brand church in St. Paul."

"Oh, that is so *wonderful*," said Sister Judith, a zealous ecumenist.

French shot an inquiring look at Lillian, hoping she'd go on. He harbored tender feelings toward her daughter. He and Imogene had gone out on a few dates before he went into the army.

Agatha, looking troubled, leaned close to Lillian on her left and half whispered, "You mean Imogene's fallen away?"

"No, nothing like that." Lillian laughed, as though the idea of leaving the Catholic Church were vastly entertaining. "What she does, she prays twice a month with Episcopals and I don't know what-all, and then they have hot-dish."

"That is so *wonderful*," Sister Judith repeated. "So inspiring, so Christian, so . . . *Imogene*."

Lillian, high on wine, continued to quiver with amusement. "Episcopals and Congregationals and all like that," she said.

Agatha, gently patting Lillian's arm as though condoling the bereaved, consulted her pastor. "Are there no restrictions concerning worship anymore, Father? Are we allowed to worship with just anybody, never mind their creed?"

"It's good for us to pray with our separated brethren," said Father Finn, looking into Agatha's worried eyes and thinking how unfair it was that a person as steadfast and respected as Agatha McGee should end up so unhappy in her old age. Because she'd never learned the lifesaving skill of compromise, her steadfastness seemed to be petrifying into a kind of cold and stubborn grudge. New ideas frightened her. Mired in the past, she permitted herself no pleasure in the present. "After centuries of division," he added, "isn't it high time we Christians came together in Christ?"

The congressman, bored by religion, said, "Tell me, French, how do your fellow Indians take to the way you put yourself on display at the tourist bureau? Ever had trouble over that sort of thing?"

"Trouble?" French inquired.

"You know, the cigar-store Indian thing. People treating you like merchandise in a curio shop."

"I've wondered the same thing," said Father Finn. "It seems like such an old-fashioned idea."

"And not very honest," added Sister Judith darkly, referring to French's ancestry.

"In what way not honest?" the congressman asked, but the nun shrugged and filled her mouth with meat, letting him wonder.

"I'm sure it's all very harmless," said Agatha, hoping for French's sake that the talk would move on to something else. She too disapproved of his Indian impersonation, but she chose to blame it on shell shock. The war had left the poor man with an impediment where fruitful labor was concerned.

"Just see to it that my funeral's at St. Isidore's," commanded Sylvester Juba.

"Once," said French.

Having lost track of the question he was responding to, everyone looked at him in wonder.

"Trouble," he explained sadly. "Once there was trouble." Having offered this much, he didn't know where to go with it, so he went on eating.

"I seem to remember," said Father Finn. "Wasn't it in the paper?"

French nodded, chewing.

"I don't remember," said Sister Judith. "Was I away at graduate school?"

"You were cloistered," said her father with distaste. Sylvester Juba had never understood his daughter's attraction to the sisterhood, particularly during her years in the convent. Now that she'd moved home to wait on him, her vocation made more sense.

"What happened?" asked Congressman Kleinschmidt.

"A bunch of Indians carrying signs came and told me they doubted I was an Indian."

"And?"

"They paraded around me. Said I was a mockery."

"And what did you say to that?"

"Nothing. I sort of felt the same way."

"Good for you," said Sister Judith.

The congressman pressed on. "You mean to say you think of yourself as a mockery?"

"Well, sort of."

"Good God, man, you've got to stand up for yourself. You'll never get where you're going in life if you think of yourself as a mockery."

French thought this over and mumbled, "But I'm not going anywhere."

"Oh, Frederick," said Agatha sadly.

Feeling the need for a more energized exchange, Sister Judith stated urgently, "I'd just love to get a group together for prayer breakfasts here in Staggerford. Say the first Saturday of every month in the banquet room of the Hub Cafe. Fellowship and scrambled eggs and maybe a couple of hymns."

"Count me in," said Lillian Kite. "The Hub's sausage patties are the best."

Sister Judith went on in an excited tone, speculating about seating arrangements, appropriate scripture readings, and a system of revolving leadership. She asked, finally, "How many of you will attend?"

The priest and the congressman politely murmured their assent, and her father said he might show up if alive. She didn't expect Agatha or French to respond. She'd long ago given up trying to move Agatha into the modern age, and French was a misfit in any gathering. Lillian said, "If they'll serve sausage patties and baste my eggs, you can count me in."

"I hate eggs," blurted Sylvester. "Especially deviled eggs."

"Speaking of eggs," said his daughter, "it's a lot easier to think about Creation if you imagine it as God laying an egg."

"Heaven help us," said Agatha.

"That concept is in a wonderful book I'm reading, by a wonderful theologian who's derivative of no one. He says original sin is out the window."

"Now wait a minute," said the priest, raising his fork to indicate that he'd have a statement to make as soon as he swallowed.

"He says God in His goodness would never burden His creatures with original sin. He says instead of original sin we were all born with original blessings."

"Now wait a minute," Father Finn repeated, raising a hand to stop her. "If he's derivative of no one, where does he fit into our tradition?" There was an untypical edge of impatience in the priest's tone. He'd listened to a good many lectures on new theology without being particularly unsettled by it, but the topic was somehow harder to swallow today. Served up by Sister Judith across the McGee silver and crystal and lace tablecloth, it struck him as downright sickening.

The nun widened her eyes to display perplexity. "Who says he has to fit into *any* tradition?"

"But what *is* the Church if not an evolving system, derived from earlier times?"

"Oh, Skipper, don't be such a bore," she said, laughing. "Looking backward is exactly what's kept the Church bogged down all these years." She beamed ecstatically at the priest, then at Agatha. "We've been liberated from all that. We're free to think for ourselves."

"Then allow me the freedom to go on thinking as I do," said Agatha hoarsely.

"We are not free to throw out tradition," Father Finn charged. "We're not Unitarians."

"Unitarians!" piped Lillian. "That's the other off-brand religion I couldn't think of. Unitarians," she murmured with satisfaction, "in Imogene's prayer group."

"Get with it, Skipper," the nun ordered happily. "Your whole view of life is colored by that dirty old teaching about original sin. Original sin was a perverse notion dreamed up by the early Fathers, who were all more or less pigheaded."

Agatha sighed and turned away. There was a day—a lifetime—not so long ago when she'd have jumped in on her pastor's side and overpowered Sister Judith with quotations from Scripture, but that was all behind her now. She no longer had the energy or hopefulness to engage in theological strife. True, she still complained to Father Finn about the misconduct of this errant nun, but she'd given up most forms of confrontation. What was the use? The battle was lost, the vitality of the Church draining away, the enemy inside the walls. It was useless to hope one could wait out this new Dark Age. Hundreds of years might pass before the Light renewed itself.

Such was the message in one of her recent letters to James (never mailed), and such was the dreary underside of her thinking in the midst of this holiday dinner. Agatha uttered a sobbing noise in her throat and was startled to have done so. She did it again, and her guests turned to her in alarm. She lowered her head and patted her lips with her napkin, pretending that the sounds had been digestive, and then, simultaneously and by fortunate coincidence, the oven timer rang, indicating that the second batch of brown-and-serve rolls was done, and a snow-plow went by in the street, prompting the priest to excuse himself and go to the front window.

"Are the cars blocked in?" called Agatha, getting up from her chair.

"They are," he said, looking out. "A ridge of snow high as the door handles."

"I'll shovel them out," offered French.

"You will not," said Agatha. "Today you're my dinner guest, not my handyman. I'll phone next door to the Rathmann boys."

French lowered his head submissively. Her condescension made his skin prickle. He'd much prefer shoveling to making after-dinner small talk.

In the kitchen Agatha removed the rolls from the oven and stood for a few moments at the stove with her eyes closed, re-covering her composure. Then she phoned Mrs. Rathmann, who promised to send her sons out to shovel as soon as they finished eating dinner.

Carrying the basket of rolls to the table, Agatha found to her chagrin that Father Finn had broached the subject of travel—chagrin because she had not yet confided in Lillian. "There are three places left," the priest was saying. "My brother will go with the twelve who've already signed up—he's got some re-search to do in Rome—but he's hoping for three more so he can get a free ride."

"Italy," breathed the congressman wistfully. "If it weren't restricted to students, I'd be tempted to go myself."

"Oh, it's open to anyone. Agatha and I are going."

"What?" cried Lillian in disbelief. She turned to Agatha, ac-cusing, "You never told me."

"I haven't been certain about it, Lillian. I've thought of can-celing." This was not exactly a fib. What she meant, and what kept this from being a falsehood, was that she would consider canceling if Lillian signed up. And if her deposit was refundable. And if her logy spirit failed to rise to the occasion. "The Rathmann boys will shovel us out," she said. "They're just finishing dinner."

Lillian lowered her voice and asked piously, "Will you see the Pope?"

"We will," the priest told her. "In his audience hall the day before we come home."

The congressman leaned earnestly forward. "Ten days, you say?"

"Ten days, nine nights. We leave the day after Christmas and fly home the fourth of January."

Sylvester Juba sat with his mouth hanging open. He was hatching a romantic scheme. At length he asked, "How much to sign up?"

The priest set forth the costs, the hotel and meal arrangements, the plans for a side trip to Florence and from there a visit to Pisa—locations significant in Galileo's career. He said an afternoon in Assisi was possible, depending upon the group's wishes.

"Assisi!" exclaimed Sylvester. "Sign me up, my middle name is Francis."

Agatha's heart fell.

"Sign me up, too," echoed Lillian. "My middle name is Dorothy."

It fell further.

"Oh, this is too much," sang Sister Judith with glee, relishing the prospect of ten days unsupervised at home and around the parish.

Agatha steeled herself for the worst. If the nun joined the group, she'd definitely cancel.

"Rome before I die," Sylvester said. "I hear St. Peter's is a hell of a piece of construction."

Disguising her agitation, Agatha rose from her chair and started around the table with the pitcher of ice water. Ten days in close quarters with Sylvester Juba and his daughter—what could be worse? Lillian, dear soul, was merely tiresome, while Sylvester was a crude and drunken ruin and his daughter was an occasion of sinful anger. While refilling Myron

Kleinschmidt's glass, she was further dismayed to hear *him* making speculative noises.

"Ten days, well, I wonder," the congressman was saying under his breath. He had no intention of going, but was mindful of the political return on declaring himself a pilgrim. He felt certain that a press release announcing his intended visits to holy places would greatly enhance his reputation among the stolid old conservatives of his district. At the last minute he could always claim that committee work was keeping him in Washington. Furthermore, by appearing to ally himself with Professor Albert Finn, he might quell the virulent anti-Kleinschmidt feelings among the Rookery State faculty—a mixture of radicals, eggheads, and foreigners who consistently voted for his opponent. "Yes, well," he said to the priest, "I just wonder if I couldn't fit a trip like that into my calendar before Congress reconvenes."

"Wow," said Sister Judith, laughing. "There's your full slate, Skipper."

Agatha, realizing with relief that the nun had no intention of going, moved on with her pitcher to Lillian's glass.

"I'll buy Imogene a rosary and have the Pope bless it," said Lillian.

"I'll call my office first thing in the morning and make sure my calendar's clear," said the congressman.

Sylvester Juba, reaching for the butter and dragging his sleeve through his gravy, said, "A man ought to see the holy places before he checks out." Layering butter on a roll, he lifted his bleary little eyes to Agatha and imagined their ten days of sightseeing together, eating meals together, talking together in trains and hotel lobbies. Ten days of his charm and she'd fall for him like a load of bricks. Today was probably not too early to start softening her up. Watching her approach him with her pitcher of ice water, he searched his mind for something tender to tell her. "Agatha," he murmured as she filled his glass.

"Yes?"

"You look like an angel today."

She stiffened, wondering what this unprecedented compliment signified. Evidently her other guests wondered the same thing, for they were all looking at the two of them, waiting for her reaction. She said, "Thank you."

"But I bet you'd be a little devil in bed."

After a moment of tense silence, all her guests spoke at once about the food they were eating, while Agatha struggled to hold back her tears.

6

T HE GUESTS MOVED INTO the living room
to partake of coffee and sweets, Agatha moving among them,
passing around a plate of caramel and coconut bars. Father
Finn sat down at the front window to watch the Rathmann
brothers toil away at the snowbank left by the plow, Sylvester
Juba sank into the couch complaining of gas pains, and Sister
Judith picked out, one-handed, a Beatles tune on the piano.
Lillian stood at the center of the room engaging French and
Congressman Kleinschmidt in a discussion of food prices.

The congressman had just lifted a coconut bar off Agatha's
plate while assuring Lillian that the President would stop infla-
tion and bring down the price of chopped walnuts, when
Agatha lowered her face into her free hand and allowed her
tears to flow. The startled congressman, as though sorrow were
contagious and lethal, backed quickly away from her, and it
was French who came to her aid, overcoming his reluctance to
touch people and guiding her to a seat on the couch next to
Sylvester Juba. Lillian relieved her of the plate.

The old lumberman, sensing that his remark at the table had
not quite succeeded, decided to cut out the sweet talk. He advised Agatha to buck up because their lives would soon end.
"The sooner you order your coffin, the better you'll feel."

Agatha, shuddering, turned her face away from him, and
discovered Sister Judith kneeling before her, making consoling
noises and asking what the matter was. French stood over
them, scowling fiercely and biting his chapped lower lip.

"I'm sorry, I'm sorry," Agatha said through her tears. "I'm
so sorry."

Lillian, searching down the front of her dress for her scented
lace hankie, handed the plate of bars to Sylvester Juba, who

45

persisted in advising Agatha. "Buy your coffin and make it easy on your survivors. They make just one phone call to the undertaker and you're off to the sweet by and by."

"Ooohhhhh," moaned Agatha, further upset by the mention of survivors. In all the world, she had one blood relative, yet no one but she—not even that relative—knew it. This was a matter that troubled Agatha more and more with each passing year, a dilemma of the most debilitating sort. Either she died without establishing the truth about this survivor and heir, or she drew up a will and brought shame on the family.

"Dry up, Dad," his daughter told the old man gently. "Agatha's got the blues."

Lillian located her hankie down among her underthings. "Here, dry your tears on this, Agatha. It was my birthday present two years ago from Imogene."

Sylvester set about eating the bars off the plate, one after another, while describing his funeral preparations. "My coffin cost me three thousand, five hundred smackeroos. Cherrywood's not cheap."

"Tell us what's the matter," the nun urged Agatha. "Just get it out and you'll feel better."

"I'll be all right," she sobbed, dabbing at her eyes, swallowing, trying to smile and feeling more intensely embarrassed than ever before in her life. She searched for words to explain herself. She considered blaming her tears on some sharp and sudden pain like appendicitis, but of course she couldn't lie. She considered telling the truth, but she didn't know what the truth was, had no idea why tears had been pressing behind her eyes ever since Sylvester's stupid remark at the table, why she hadn't been able to ignore it the way she'd been ignoring his crudeness for years, why she should lose her composure in front of a priest, a congressman, and a few old friends. She considered dashing into her bedroom and remaining there until her siege of sorrow ran its course or until her guests gave up and went home, but her weeping—what little understanding she had of it—felt somehow related to loneliness. It seemed that more urgent than her embarrassment and shame was her unexpected need—indeed, her unprecedented need—not to be alone.

"I'll be fine," she said bravely, "it's just—" She was interrupted by a second fit of shuddering that moved across her narrow shoulders and caused her head to bob up and down. Except for the moist sound of sugary mastication from Sylvester Juba, the room was hushed. Agatha, after this spasm passed, after a sigh and a sob and a strong blow of her nose, explained in a quavery voice that she was over the worst of whatever ailed her, and if everybody would just ignore her for a few minutes they'd be doing her a great favor.

Sister Judith said, "You poor thing you," in a tone so tender and comforting that Agatha was overcome with a new surge of tears and wondered for a ghastly split second if she might someday come to be fond of Sister Judith.

The nun was deeply moved to find Agatha McGee acting vulnerable. She observed how sorrow altered Agatha's face, twisting her features into an expression of pain. She relished this rare opportunity to console her, for although they had been adversaries for much of Sister Judith's life—particularly as teaching colleagues at St. Isidore's—Judith had never been without a certain amount of respect for the old woman (albeit respect tinged with envy), and this respect was deepening with time. Sister Judith, having recently turned forty, was increasingly aware of how few women chose to live out their lives unattached to a partner, and she had begun to look upon Agatha as something of a role model. It was a paradox of the modern age, thought the nun, that in spite of the women's movement, so few women remained perpetually and chastely independent.

"Unnnng," groaned Sylvester Juba, frantically handing the plate of bars to his daughter and pointing to his mouth. "Unnng, unnng," he repeated, indicating that he had sunk his teeth into a cube of caramel and couldn't get them out.

Lillian Kite by this time was shedding tears of her own and drying them on the sleeve of her purple party dress. "I never see anybody cry, but I don't fall apart myself. I'm always a mess from the beginning of 'General Hospital' till the end."

Agatha, smiling weakly up at Lillian, thought, My malaise is catching, Lord, I ought to be quarantined.

"I'm told the Bureau of Indian Affairs has a formula for recompensing Indians for lands wrongly taken away from them," said Myron Kleinschmidt, frightened by emotion of any

kind and thus desperately pretending that Agatha's breakdown
hadn't happened. He buttonholed French and told him what he
knew of the formula—the amount of money per acre, the time-
table of payments—and French, to everyone's astonishment,
including his own, erupted in anger.

"You're always picking on the little people, you jerks in
Washington." Emboldened by brandy, he pursued Myron
Kleinschmidt down the room. "Who did you send to Vietnam?
Us little people, that's who! Who took the Indians' land away
from them in the first place? You cowardly jerks in Washing-
ton, that's who!"

Cornered, the congressman turned and faced him. "Now,
now, now," he repeated over an undertone of nervous laughter.

"Gunnng-onnng" was the sound Sylvester Juba made as he
drew from his mouth and handed to his daughter the gob of
caramel, to which his bridgework was attached.

"Oh, gross!" Sister Judith laughed, getting to her feet and
displaying the gob of caramel with its dripping arc of seven
teeth hanging from it. She carried it off to the kitchen.

Myron Kleinschmidt pointed out to French that his was not
the majority party during Vietnam, that his party was a caring
party, responsible for passing two human rights bills in this
past session alone, but French wasn't buying it. "You're all a
bunch of jerks," he said, trembling with anger and hurrying off
to the dining room to replenish his brandy.

All were affected by Agatha's tears. Perhaps it was the time
and the place—darkness falling with the snow on a warm
house in which everyone was comfortably full of good food
and slightly fuzzy from drink—or perhaps it was the sense of
impermanence instilled in all of them by the sight of a woman
in sorrow who they had thought incapable of tears. Whatever
the cause, a quietness prevailed as they all eased themselves
into a reflective mood, calling up injuries, longings, and worries. It was as though Agatha, by opening her heart, had unlocked theirs as well.

Even Myron Kleinschmidt, since no one was paying any
attention to his political commentary, eventually shut his
mouth, dropped into the chair vacated by Father Finn at the
front window, and permitted the hopeless state of his marriage
to overtake him. Day after day he tried to be too busy to think

about it, but now his heartbreak washed over him, and he wished Sammy March was dead. Sammy March was the son of a bitch from Ohio that Elena was running around with. What a disaster, losing Elena. It could ruin his career. Elena was a spirited, good-looking woman with brains and family money, a star among capital wives. Wednesday mornings she taught rosemaling to a group that included the Vice President's mother-in-law. At a party last summer she had taught the latest South American dance step—a shocking dance, in Myron's opinion—to the Secretary of Defense. That was the night she got drunk and kept telling everyone that there were two things she never wanted to see again as long as she lived. Minnesota was one, and Myron was the other.

The congressman next allowed his mind to dwell on the woman he was linked to in gossipy circles but not in fact, a woman named Naomi Olson, who had worked in Treasury before taking early retirement and going into catering more or less as a hobby. The gossip had come to life on the one and only night Naomi Olson helped him host a party. She was a stout, pushy woman with an insinuating and overdramatic manner of speaking, and he supposed it was Naomi Olson herself who started the rumor. He supposed he'd better not engage her catering service again. Let the slightest hint of an affair get back to the moral watchdogs among his constituency, and after the next election he'd find himself back in his old discouraging job of fifteen years ago—crisscrossing the northwestern quarter of Minnesota trying to sell crop insurance to farmers who couldn't afford it.

French, gulping brandy in the dining room, squirmed with grief as he ran through the events that brought him home from Vietnam. His squad, patrolling the jungle, had come upon a village in ruins. Searching the destruction, they found nothing but dead and dying women and babies. The babies drove French nearly crazy. For hours afterward he heard the gurgling, dying sound one of them made.

It was the following night, during a twelve-hour pass in Saigon, that he met the young woman who promised him intimacy and laughed joyfully as she led him along the dark street toward her room and then was killed by a grenade. That was when his vomiting began. All the way back to camp, all the

next morning, he fought to bring his body under control, but it
kept fighting back.

Then, in the afternoon, needing to be alone with his rebel-
lious body and the horrible images in his head, he stole away
from camp and down into a little green valley where he sat on
a rock beside a stream, listened to the rippling water and
closed his eyes, pretending it was the Badbattle flowing
through Staggerford. Gradually his stomach settled down and
his nausea went away and he grew sleepy. That was when the
sniper fired at him, the bullet passing close behind his ear. He
collapsed from shock, which no doubt saved his life, for the
sniper apparently thought he was dead and didn't fire again.
He woke up in a medic's tent, and that was the end of his duty.
All of this he went over in his mind as he stood staring at the
bottles on Agatha's buffet; then he quickly left the room, went
down the hallway to the bathroom and sat on the toilet and
shook.

Meanwhile, Sylvester Juba, whose face had caved in when
his teeth came out, sat on the couch gumming his gums and
pondering his misgivings about his heartthrob, Agatha McGee.
For one thing, he didn't want a sob sister on his hands. If she
was going to turn on the waterworks every time he said something tender, he'd have to reconsider his proposal. For another
thing, she might be expensive to keep. She liked good clothes,
and she ate quite a lot for her size. And what about her cooking? She was no great shakes as a cook. His wife Twyla had
been very good in the kitchen, a talent not handed down to his
daughter, unfortunately, and he'd been looking forward to being served fine meals once again. Should he forgo the grub and
take the old spinster anyway?

And then there was the matter of her well-known nitpicking.
Mightn't a woman like that turn into a nag? On the other hand,
mightn't a woman like that have a talent for keeping track
of the Juba investments? It was a pain in the neck going
through the mail from his broker and balancing his accounts.
Judy refused to do his accounts. Unholy work, she called it.
Agatha, you just knew, had the skills for precise bookwork. At
this point his musings were interrupted by his daughter, who
reentered the room carrying his rinsed and dripping teeth.

"We're going home," she announced. "The old lumberjack hates to miss the five o'clock news."

He took the teeth from her, dried them on the lapels of his wooly suit coat, and inserted them into his mouth. After tamping them into place with a few little bites and wobbles of his jaw, he countermanded her order. "To hell with the five o'clock news," he growled, "I'm not through talking to Agatha." He then turned to his hostess with as much of a smile as he could muster—a slight lifting of his liverish upper lip—and said, "Sell your house, sugar, and move into mine."

Father Finn, unable to meditate in crowded rooms, had slipped away from the others and stolen into the sun room, where he stood sipping coffee and gazing out at the dying daylight. Snow was no longer falling in curtains and veils. It was zigzagging down in the grainy little flakes that signaled a clearing sky and colder temperatures. A blue jay swooped out of a snow-laden spruce and came to rest on the feeder under the sun-room window. Father Finn watched it peck through the snow for seed that wasn't there. Beyond the feeder, he noticed the handles of Agatha's wheelbarrow protruding from a drift. He noticed, too, that the storm windows had not yet been put up around the sun room, that the screens were still in place. He saw in these neglected chores, so untypical of Agatha, the signs of her weakened spirit, and he pondered whether to withhold the letter until some happier time.

Yet the tone of the letter was urgent. It was not addressed to Agatha directly, but to Bishop Baker. *I'm not asking her for anything so large as forgiveness or understanding,* said the black ink set down in a large, bold hand. *Understanding and forgiveness she already granted me, I like to think, on the day we parted company in St. Stephen's Green. I'm simply asking that she write to me and we resume the exchange which I don't mind admitting was, now I look back on it, the most rewarding experience of my life. There are things I must tell her—and soon, before it's too late. Anything you can manage toward this end will be deeply . . .*

Why the urgency? The letter didn't explain, and Bishop Baker, discussing it last night over drinks in his study, wouldn't hazard a guess. According to the bishop, this man O'Hannon was a priest in the village of Ballybegs, County Kildare. He and Agatha had carried on a lengthy correspondence, which came to an end three years ago when, with Bishop Baker's tour group, she traveled to Ireland to meet the man. Perhaps she had dreams of romance in her heart, said the bishop, for she didn't know O'Hannon was a priest. When she discovered the truth, she returned to Staggerford with an iron resolve to conceal her broken heart. "There's no telling how much grief or anger or undefined emotion she's been living with over the last three years," the bishop had said as he handed the letter to Father Finn near midnight. "All of it compounded, of course, by the closing of the school."

The Irishman had strung her along, it seemed, by allowing her to believe he was a teacher like herself, not a priest. "An absolutely reprehensible thing to do," Father Finn had remarked, assuming the bishop felt the same. A mistaken assumption, as it turned out, for the bishop's response was milder than that. "Maybe reprehensible, Francis, but then again, maybe not. My first reaction was like yours—the man must be a masher—but that was before I confronted him."

"You actually spoke to the man?"

"Oh, yes. I traced him to his parish north of Dublin and walked in on him out of the blue, intending to read him the riot act. But what I discovered instead of a masher was a good enough priest suffering from a pathetic case of loneliness."

"How old a man?"

"Agatha's age, I'd guess. A tall man. A man of intelligence and striking good looks. His face has an aging, James Bond sort of look to it, if you know what I mean. A square-jawed man."

"And he owned up to the deception?"

"Immediately. No beating around the bush. No excuses. He was a priest stumbling through his late sixties regretting that he hadn't shared his life with a woman. I'm well aware of the problem. I've got more than one man like that right here in my diocese." Here the bishop paused and looked thoughtful, as though counting them off in his head. "You're not one of them?"

"No," replied Father Finn, a solitary man by nature as well as choice.

"Well, poor O'Hannon thought he'd solved the problem. In a sense, you see, he *was* sharing his life with a woman, through letters. Their correspondence, I gather, was very fulfilling, very rewarding, on both sides. And where was the harm in it, as long as the woman lived across the ocean?" The bishop paused again, smiling ruefully. "The poor devil never dreamed she'd turn up on his doorstep."

Father Finn, rising from the plush chair in the bishop's study, slipped the letter into his pocket. "So you're saying, for his sake, they ought to be put in touch once again?"

"And for hers."

Father Finn was skeptical, and not eager to carry out his part of this mission. "How well do you know her?"

"Well enough."

"With all due respect, Bishop—"

"Dick."

"With all due respect, Dick, I'm not sure we can be certain what's best for Agatha McGee."

"Love is best for everybody," proclaimed the bishop, helping him on with his coat. He might have been parroting Sister Judith, thought Father Finn; it was her sort of sweeping sentiment.

At the door he asked his final question. "Why is he writing to you and not to Agatha?"

The bishop said he didn't know. They had shaken hands, and Father Finn stepped out into the snowy night.

Darkness invaded the sun room. The priest sipped his cold coffee. He patted his hip pocket, making sure the letter was there. From his sweater pocket he drew out his cigar, rolled it idly in his fingers and fell to musing about how you could go along for years thinking you knew a person's story and then come upon a chapter that knocked your socks off.

"Say, Father." The murmur in his right ear startled the priest out of his thoughts. French had slipped into the room and stood close at his side.

"Ah, French. The snow's letting up."

"Yup."

There was an awkward silence, which the priest tried to fill. "Temperature will be dropping."

"Yup."

Those in the living room had recovered their voices. He heard a growl from Sylvester Juba and a peal of excited laughter from Sister Judith. The congressman was talking about his next campaign.

"Father, about Vietnam," said French.

"Yes?"

"Terrible stuff happened."

"Oh?" Father Finn was trying to hear what the congressman was saying. Evidently his campaign would somehow involve Agatha.

"Babies were killed."

"War," said the priest sadly.

"Women and kids and little babies."

"War," the priest repeated, shaking his head and chewing on his cigar. There was movement in the living room. Coats were brought out of the closet in the entryway.

"Babies," said French weakly. "And then there was this girl." This was as far as French could go without help. He fell silent, waiting for the priest to prompt him or, better yet, to advise him. It was a very long time before the priest spoke.

"Do you want to go to confession?"

French's hope collapsed. This *was* confession. Didn't the priest understand? Was ritual all he had to offer? This was no better than talking to Grover. Grover was a comfort to talk to, but only if you didn't require a response. Today French needed a response.

"No," said French, "I guess not."

They stood in silence, side by side, looking out at the black night, French tied in a tight knot and Father Finn unaware of it. After a minute or so French drifted away.

"Oh, there you are, Skipper," explained Sister Judith, stepping into the sun room and squeezing the priest's upper arm. "The old robber baron and I are taking off. We've put in the required time."

"Yes, I'll be going soon myself," he replied, thinking how typical it was of Sister Judith to swoop in on him at precisely the wrong time and scatter whatever thoughts he was piecing together. She was forever doing it at the rectory, making a beeline from her office to his whenever he'd fallen silent for a few minutes. She was one of those people who couldn't stand repose, a true enemy of wool-gathering. Not a serious character flaw, he supposed, nothing he could put into a formal complaint in order to get her office moved out of the rectory, but it wore you down over the long haul. Pray God she would quickly find another parish when her year was up.

"I'm having the best time picturing you people in Italy. Really, it cracks me up. You've simply *got* to remember each and every detail and tell me all about it the minute you get home." She gave his arm a ferocious two-handed squeeze.

"It cracks you up?"

"Think of it—Myron Kleinschmidt glad-handing strangers, Lillian Kite oohing and aahing over every last relic in the Vatican, and my ancient father chasing skirts. It'll be a circus."

"Surely your father's not serious."

"Oh, he's going all right. He'd follow Agatha to Hell. He's got it in his bonnet that she'd make him a nice little wife in his old age. Didn't you know, he's proposed to her?"

"I thought he was kidding."

"Kidding, hell, he's in heat."

7

T HE CONGRESSMAN, LAST TO arrive, was first to leave, bidding one and all a jolly farewell and offering French a ride home. He could think of no foolproof way of earning the vote of someone as contrary as French, but maybe a ride home would help. In the entryway, he handed French his cashmere coat to hold for him.

"Good-bye, Agatha. Thanks for a superb afternoon."

"You're welcome, Myron. Give Elena my best."

"I will. She'll be sorry she missed it."

"So long, Miss McGee."

"Good-bye, Frederick, I wish we'd had a chance to visit more."

"Yup, me too," he lied, eager to be gone before the old lady cried again. Her tears had unnerved him, caused his own emotional outburst, which he was now ashamed of.

There was a new, deep-winter bite in the chill that fell through the doorway as the two men departed. Agatha drew aside the lace curtain in the door's oval window and made sure that Myron, with Frederick and the Rathmann brothers pushing, got his heavy car away from the curb and out into the pathway cleared by the plow.

Returning to the living room, she wished the Jubas a safe drive home over the snowpacked streets. "I apologize for behaving like a baby," she said. "I don't know what came over me."

"Apologize, nothing," replied Sister Judith, smiling intensely at Agatha as she helped her father on with his coat. "It did me a lot of good to see you cry. It gave me a new perspective on you."

"I won't ask you to explain that."

"No, really, Agatha, we should dialogue about it sometime."

"About what?"

"About letting our hair down. We'd have worlds of things to share, I just know it, once we break the ice."

"What ice? We've known each other all your life."

"Not really, Agatha, not to the point of true understanding."

Agatha weighed this remark, decided it was spurious, and said, "I believe the boys have your car dug out."

Sylvester shook Agatha's hand sideways and up and down and sideways again, declaring loudly that he liked the dressing but the turkey was overdone and dry and he'd never cared for cranberries or deviled eggs, but he'd eaten six hot rolls with lots of butter. "My intake of fat is high as a kite," he said with pride. "The doctor says my arteries are clogged like old lead pipes."

Sister Judith steered her father out into the night, and Agatha quickly shut out the cold. With Lillian at her side, she stood at the oval window watching the Rathmann brothers brush the snow from the Jubas' car and rock it back and forth until it broke free of the snow at the curb. It moved off down the street, leaving only the priest's car under its blanket of snow.

"Where's Father?" Agatha asked.

Lillian shrugged. "In the bathroom maybe."

"Look at the moon," said Agatha, pointing. It was rising pink and enormous over the tree-lined riverbank across the street.

"A Christmas card," breathed Lillian, studying the shadows it cast on the contours of snow.

Agatha let the lace curtain drop. "I'll clear the table."

"I'll start washing."

"If you run low on dish soap, there's more in the pantry."

Lillian went into the kitchen, rolling up her purple sleeves, and Agatha worked at the dining room table, placing bowls and plates on a tray. She did not notice Father Finn sitting in the darkened sun room, watching her.

"Agatha," he said softly.

Startled, she wheeled around, nearly dropping a bowl. He was sitting at her desk, his unlit cigar in his fingers. He seemed to be smiling.

"Father?" She stepped into the sun room and switched on the desk lamp. His smile, she observed, was not the one he usually wore. This was more of a squint, a tense look, a grimace.

"What can I get you?" she asked. "More coffee?"

"Agatha, could we talk for a minute?"

In a flash she knew what was coming. She knew instantly, seeing the familiar brown envelope, that James had entered the room. Indeed, as he handed her the letter, she knew what its message would be. Her heart raced as she drew a chair up beside the desk and sat down. James was the only man she had ever loved in that certain way that women loved men. Her scalp tingled and felt hot.

"It's a letter from Ireland, Agatha."

She nodded, struggling to maintain an impassive expression while picturing herself and James seated on a bench in St. Stephen's Green. She saw the flowers, the walkways, the ducks skimming across the water in pursuit of morsels scattered by a group of little children. Though three summers had passed since that day in Dublin, the smell of junipers came back to her, mixed with the smell of bus fumes. She saw herself and James rising from the bench and saying good-bye, James bestowing a courtly kiss on the back of her hand and asking if their correspondence might be allowed to continue. She was wearing her raincoat. James was dressed in priestly black.

"Seems this man O'Hannon wants to get in touch with you," said Father Finn, carefully moving his cigar around the rim of the ashtray, sculpting ash it didn't have.

She pictured the expression on James's face as they parted. Sadness. Supplication. And something more. Something stark and strained, like fear. His devastation appeared even more acute than hers, and she recalled having to fight off a surge of sympathy for him. She told him perhaps they would continue to write, or perhaps they wouldn't—she couldn't be sure—but that he must not write before hearing from her. Terribly autocratic of her, she realized, but he must grant her that. He must not—after deceiving her—come into her life a second time without an invitation.

"Please read it," urged Father Finn, suppressing a yawn.

Agatha, lowering her eyes to the envelope, was prepared to

be offended by James's breach of their St. Stephen's Green agreement, and yet when she saw that it was addressed to Bishop Baker instead of herself, she was disappointed.

"He seems to indicate some urgency, but he doesn't give the reason," said Father Finn.

She drew out the page of familiar handwriting, hoping her pastor didn't notice her trembling hands. She unfolded it, pressed it flat on the desk and read it with her arms folded—or skimmed it, rather, her eyes darting here and there and picking out the essential phrases—*forgiveness she already granted me ... asking that she write to me ... things I must tell her ... anything you can manage toward this end ... the most rewarding experience of my life ... and soon, before it's too late.*

Her first impulse was to comply—James, her dear soulmate, apparently needed her. Her second impulse was to do nothing—James, her nemesis, had hurt her severely, had stolen her heart at an age when most people had long since put romance behind them, had deceived her and left her in distress. Because this second impulse, fueled by anger and grief and embarrassment, was stronger than the first impulse, which was fueled simply by love, she made up her mind to ignore the letter. Folding the page and slipping it back into the envelope, she said coldly, "You've read this, obviously."

"I have. The bishop asked me to."

"I'm disappointed in the bishop."

"As usual," said Father Finn, testy now from fatigue.

"Well, haven't I a right to be? Breaking a confidence like this?"

The priest nodded and began, "The reason he did it—"

"It isn't a story I wanted told."

"I'll never repeat it, Agatha, you have my word. Now let me explain, please."

"I'm not stopping you," she said curtly.

He shifted in his chair, turning his other cheek to her. "The bishop has flown off to Tacoma to visit his family, you see. He left early this morning."

"The papers are full of it. He's become the journalists' darling."

"And since the letter arrived in yesterday's mail, he had no time to come and see you."

"He could have called."

"Yes, I suppose he could have called. But he thought—the nature of it being delicate—that it required seeing you in person."

"I don't agree. A phone call would have sufficed."

The priest sighed and turned his attention to his cigar, rolling it in his fingers.

"I don't mind admitting this whole thing was the most upsetting experience of my life. I thought I had put it behind me."

The priest slipped the cigar into the pocket of his sweater, then sighed again, but said nothing. He'd come to the end of his patience.

"Thank the bishop, and ask him to put it behind *him*." She smiled at Father Finn—her firm little smile of dismissal.

"I will," he said, rising from the desk. "Thank you for dinner, Agatha. I'll go and say good-bye to Lillian."

He looked into the kitchen and Lillian followed him out, wiping her hands on her apron. Both women trailed after him to the front door. "Good-bye, Father," sang Lillian happily, helping him on with his coat. She seemed not to sense the strain between her friend and her pastor.

"Wonderful dinner, many thanks to both of you."

"Good-bye, come again," said Lillian.

"Get yourself a cap," said Agatha.

"Good-bye," said Lillian again.

Crossing the porch and descending the steps, Father Finn thought it unlikely that Agatha would write to the man O'Hannon. Lucky for O'Hannon, he thought.

8

*L*ILLIAN WASHED AND AGATHA dried.

"I know what Imogene will say. She'll say I should get out of my rut and go."

Agatha harbored a vague and lifelong dislike of Lillian's daughter, an officious crank with her nose in everybody's business. "I suppose we look like bumpkins to Imogene, now she's in the city."

"She's after me to go to Las Vegas with her in the spring. She goes every year."

"I didn't know Imogene gambled."

"Gambles, sees the shows, all like that. There's slot machines right in the hotel. Video slots, she calls them. Last year she lost a bundle. Two years ago she came home a dollar and a quarter ahead."

"A lot of effort for a dollar and a quarter."

"Well, it's the fun of it all. She only goes when she can see Wayne Newton."

"Who's Wayne Newton?"

"He's a singer with the sweetest little mustache. Imogene's got all his records. She says my heart will melt when I see him in person."

They worked in silence then, Lillian imagining the face of Wayne Newton as it appeared on her daughter's record jackets, Agatha picturing the face of James O'Hannon as it appeared in the photo he had sent her early in their correspondence. He was standing between his brother Matt and his sister Marion in front of the O'Hannon family pub in the Midlands—three tall, handsome people squinting in the sunlight, James the tallest. Ever since her trip to Ireland, the picture had been lying facedown, under his letters, in the bottom drawer of her desk.

Lillian, scouring the roasting pan, sang a few bars of "Danke Schoen" in a dim, throaty monotone while Agatha, laying her sterling out on a dry towel, began drafting the response she would write to James if he deserved it—but of course he didn't. She owed him nothing. He'd callously allowed their correspondence to lead them into something perilously close to romance, while withholding the most important fact about himself, the fact of his priesthood. How sly of him. How calculating. Their nearness of heart, he knew, depended on keeping their distance. What a shock it must have been to him when she turned up in Ireland. What nerve, his appealing now for a new exchange of letters. Had he no pride? No conscience? Nothing better to do with his time than to prey on old ladies?

And yet this reprehensible man was only one of the two James O'Hannons continually on her mind. The other James O'Hannon was the soulmate she conjured up a dozen times a day in order to share the routine details of the grim little life she was leading. With no one at hand to share your sadness, you spoke to an apparition. You couldn't very well spill out your heart to people for whom you'd been buttoned up and discreet all your life—they'd think you were cracked.

"Lillian, do you think I'm cracked?" The words were out before she knew it—proof, perhaps, that she was.

"Cracked?" said Lillian, turning from the sink.

"For crying like that, after dinner."

"Nobody's more uncracked than you, Agatha." She turned back to her sudsy roasting pan.

"Not even a little bit daft?"

"Nobody's more undaft, Agatha. We all have our moments."

The scrape of shovels continued after Lillian went home, the Rathmann boys working by moonlight, piling the snow shoulder high beside the driveway and along the sidewalks. When at length they knocked on the back door and told Agatha they were finished, she invited them into the kitchen for cocoa. Slipping out of their enormous insulated boots and their noisy nylon jackets and sitting down at the kitchen table, they exuded so much energy that the room seemed to shrink. Aged nineteen and sixteen, large and muscular, both of the boys were possessed of dark good looks and fairly glistened with good health. They put Agatha in mind of the best horses shown at the county fair—robust, well-cared-for, freshly groomed and larger than life. The younger Rathmann, Tommy, a junior in high school, wore a green twill shirt with the word "Guess" stitched on the pocket. He had rosy cheeks and long eyelashes. His eyes were dark brown, nearly black. This was the talkative brother. "Did you know Dan's got a girlfriend?" he asked.

Agatha, at the stove, stirring their cocoa, said she hadn't heard.

Dan, home from college, blushed. Dan was the shy Rathmann, a muscular hulk sitting at the table with his eyes cast down, a small, self-conscious smile playing on his lips. The words "Grateful Dead" were lettered on his gray sweatshirt. He wore a gold earring.

"He's bringing her home at Christmas," said Tommy.

"Where's she from and what's her name?" Agatha asked the older boy.

"Alissa," said the younger. "She's from Crookston."

His brother turned red.

"A real cute chick."

His brother turned redder.

"Dan," Agatha said, and waited until the older boy raised his eyes. "Tell me about her." He'd been like this in grade six, never speaking unless it was required.

"Alissa Peterson," he said, then carefully weighed his next statement, as though afraid of revealing more than Agatha could stand to hear. "I met her in physics."

"Her dad's into sugar beets," Tommy added.

"Will you introduce me?" she asked.

Dan nodded grimly, lowering his eyes again.

"Her mom's a nurse," said Tommy. "They gave her a car last summer. A Chevy."

"Not new," Dan specified.

Serving them cocoa and two coconut bars apiece, she peered closely at the delicate gold ring in Dan's ear. "Earrings on boys. I've seen them on TV, but not in Staggerford."

"I'm getting my ear pierced at Della's Beauty Shop tomorrow," said Tommy. "They've got a six-dollar deal, ring and all.

My buddies all did their own with needles and a potato, but my folks are making me go to a professional."

"What next?" said Agatha, horrified at the savage choices modern parents were faced with. Allowing or disallowing your son to put a needle through his earlobe and into a potato—life among the aborigines.

"You watch MTV?" Tommy asked her.

"Is that the movie channel?"

"No, videos."

"Videos?"

"You know, Boy George. Twisted Sister. You pay extra."

"I don't pay extra."

"Yeah, it doesn't seem like your bag. I just thought that's where you might have seen earrings on guys."

Agatha returned to the cupboard and put away her pots and pans. "I'll be away for ten days after Christmas, and I'll need someone to watch the house."

"Where you going?" asked Tommy.

"Italy."

"Wow, cool. Dan's going to England in April."

"Are you, Dan?"

Raising his eyes from his cocoa, Dan smiled and said, "Yeah, Alissa's going along."

"You'll be chaperoned, I'm sure."

"It's classes," Dan explained, "at Oxford."

Tommy asked, "What's 'chaperoned' mean?"

"Watched over by an adult," she told him.

"Eighteen's adult now," said Tommy. "Didn't you know?"

She closed the cupboards. "Eighteen used to be more adult than it is now, in the opinion of one old lady."

Tommy drained his cup. "Check me out in two years, and see if you still think that."

When the boys got to their feet, Agatha opened a drawer and drew out her envelope of household cash. "How much do I owe you?" she asked, having already determined that they had earned three dollars apiece.

"That's okay," said Tommy, sliding across the highly waxed floor in his stocking feet and stepping into his boots. "Mom and Dad said not to take your money."

"Whyever not?"

"Because it's Thanksgiving and you're retired and everything."

"Retired, yes, but not destitute." She handed six dollars to Dan, who folded them carefully and pried them into a pocket of his tight jeans.

He said, "Thanks."

"Now, how would one of you boys like to earn ten dollars during Christmas vacation by stepping into my house once a day and making sure my furnace is functioning?"

"We can't," said Tommy. "We're going skiing."

"It will only take you a minute each day. Here, I'll give you a down payment." She removed two more dollars from the envelope.

"No, I mean *skiing*. Montana. Alissa's going along."

Dan smiled sheepishly.

"Montana? My word."

"Me and Dan and Alissa and Mom and Dad. Big-time."

"Big Sky," added Dan.

"During all of vacation?" she asked.

"A week of it," said Dan.

"We're leaving the twenty-sixth."

"Well, have a nice time," she said.

"You too, Miss McGee. Tell the Pope hi."

She tidied up the dining room, folding away the lace tablecloth, picking up crumbs with the carpet sweeper, straightening the chairs and returning the bottles to their place in the buffet, all the while keeping her eyes averted from the sun room, where the letter lay on the desk. When she finished these chores, she turned on the TV and watched without interest an old romantic trifle starring Katharine Hepburn, and then watched the news. A bomb went off in Beirut, killing seven. Jessica Lange had a baby out of wedlock. The Vikings lost to Detroit. The temperature by sunup would be ten degrees.

She went to bed then, feeling exhausted, yet she lay a long time in the dark with her eyes open. The clock struck eleven and eleven-thirty. She got up, slipped into her furry slippers, wrapped herself in her warmest robe and brewed herself a cup of tea, which she carried into the sun room.

She turned on the desk lamp and sat staring at the envelope

from Ireland. Blowing on her tea and sipping it, she felt a great surge of energy spread through her body and brain. Obviously there would be no sleeping as long as this message from James remained in the house. She carried the letter to the kitchen and placed it in a saucepan. She struck a match, set it afire, carried the flaming pan out through the back porch and set it down in the snow. She stood outside in the dark for half a minute, watching the letter curl itself into ash, and then she returned to bed.

The clock struck twelve and twelve-thirty. She got up and returned to the sun room, where she drew from the wastebasket the torn-up letter she had written earlier in the day. After piecing it together, she drew from a drawer a few sheets of fresh stationery and copied it, word for word. Then, without pause, she began another section, labeled "Later," and, writing at high speed, described the dinner, the table talk, the argument about original sin. She admitted to James how extremely disappointed she'd been, and still was, over the prospect of going to Italy with Sylvester Juba, Lillian Kite, and Congressman Kleinschmidt. Maybe they'd wake up in the morning with clear heads and have a change of heart. By this time she was writing with a kind of breathless exhilaration and running out of paper. She drew more stationery from the drawer.

She asked James for his opinion of interdenominational prayer breakfasts. Crossing religious boundaries, she wrote, was not without precedent in the McGee family. Her dear father had attended all sorts of non-Catholic churches, even synagogues, whenever he was in St. Paul for sessions of the legislature. Her father was a gregarious man with a liberal bent and an insatiable curiosity, and while she couldn't very well ask him if he owned up to his errant churchgoing with his confessor (confessions being secret), she had the distinct impression that he never considered it a matter to be confessed. *But of course my father was a law unto himself,* she wrote. *Peter McGee was one of those rare people whose goodwill and force of personality somehow allows them to transcend the restraints that regulate the lives of us lesser mortals.*

She sat back then and considered with amazement what she had written. Transcendent, yes, she'd always regarded her father as peerless—but surely not as living outside the law. Yet wasn't it true? Hadn't Peter McGee, time and again, taken part in heretical rituals in defiance of Church commands? Hadn't he come home on several occasions and told about attending Lutheran services and taking communion from Eastern Orthodox priests? Hadn't he taught her, when she was thirteen or fourteen, the words of a rollicking hymn sung in a Baptist church by people of color? Why had she never been scandalized? Could it be true, as she had just set down in black on white, that a certain few people by their very nature are not bound by the same laws as the majority?

This question led her on to three more pages having to do with her father, particularly his stalwart service to humanity. She felt her metabolism speeding up as she wrote. Her thoughts were flowing, her pen was flying; it must have been the tea. What a shame, she wrote, that making the walleyed pike the Official State Fish of Minnesota was about all that Peter McGee, dead these twenty-five years, was remembered for. Forgotten were the many progressive ideas he conceived and struggled to bring to birth for the good of the people. He met failure on all sides, for he was a man ahead of his time. He served in the legislature from 1925 to 1934, and it wasn't until the 1950s and he was feeble with age that his thinking was shown to be prophetic. He'd foreseen the need for zoning boards. He'd pleaded with his colleagues to expand welfare programs to include the destitute and deprived who were not confined to orphanages and poor farms, people with no source of income and no institution to protect them. He'd campaigned for a new county courthouse, a new highway north from the Twin Cities, and a new statewide system of vocational schools. Expensive ideas, every one of them, and while he succeeded in winning over a fair number of his fellow legislators, he was no match for the Depression. *My dear father was a visionary whose talents were obscured by the murky tides of economics,* she wrote, rather pleased by her phrasing, and picturing James pleased as well.

She counted the pages and was amazed at the number. She read the letter through, and was amazed as well by the energized and headlong quality of the writing. The tone was livelier, less stilted than other letters she'd written James in recent years, and she questioned whether tea alone was responsible.

Was there not another stimulus involved? Yes, there was—she realized this a minute later as she was removing her robe and switching off her bedside lamp. Unlike her other letters to Ireland of the past three years, she'd written this one as though she intended to mail it.

9

*T*HE TELEPHONE WOKE HER. She'd been dreaming she was a little girl again, taking down spelling words dictated by her teacher, and there were a few confusing moments when the ringing phone was the bell marking the end of the schoolday. She slipped into her robe and went to the kitchen, where the clock on the stove told her it was nearly ten.

"Imogene says I gotta get myself together and go."

"Lillian, is it actually ten o'clock?"

"That's what I've got. She says she could've got me a better deal with her travel agent in St. Paul, but Italy's worth whatever you pay. She's glad I'm going with you, she says, because it's a scholarly trip and you're such a scholar."

"A diller a dollar."

"What?"

"Lillian, I haven't slept this late since I was in the crib."

"Yeah, I wondered. I didn't see any light in your kitchen."

"I was dreaming about Sister Rose of Lima—remember her?"

"Sort of. What grade?"

"Third."

"Was she the one made us kneel beside our desks and hold our arms out in a crucified position?"

"I don't remember that. She's the one who taught us 'Trees' by Joyce Kilmer."

"Yeah, that's her. And anybody didn't have it memorized had to kneel beside their desks and hold their arms out. I was never one to memorize. Imogene says this trip will be a tonic for both of us."

"I hope so."

"Agatha, you haven't said—are you glad I'm going?"

"Of course I am." Saying this, Agatha was surprised to realize it was true. She was feeling cheerful and magnanimous this morning, no longer so crabbed and dour. Last night's letter-writing seemed to have transformed her. It would be pleasant having her old friend with her in Italy. "Of course I am," she repeated, and then asked, "Who'll be watching your house for you?"

"Imogene's coming at Christmas to help me pack. She'll stay on a while, two or three days anyway."

"But after that."

"Well, French. Can't we ask French?"

"I'm not sure," said Agatha vaguely.

"Why's that?"

"It's a day at a time with Frederick." Since he'd abruptly moved out ten years ago, she'd been carefully limiting the odd jobs she asked him to do, afraid of pressing him beyond his goodwill.

"Maybe we can get one of the Rathmann boys," suggested Lillian.

"They'll be gone. I asked them."

"Then how about Janet?"

"Yes, I was thinking of Janet. I'll ask her for both of us."

"Agatha, did I drink too much yesterday?"

"Not quite."

"My head feels like I drank too much."

"There were moments when you seemed a little woozy."

"That last batch of chokecherry you made, Agatha, it's too good."

"A little on the sweet side, I think."

"Sweeter the better—goes down like Kool-Aid. Say, Agatha, we won't be memorizing lessons on this trip, will we?"

"We aren't expected to take part in the scholarship. We're only along for the ride."

Lillian was chuckling. "Because I'm too old to be kneeling with my arms out."

Agatha went from the phone to the sun room. It was a cold, radiant morning, sunshine dazzling on the snow, smoke streaming from the neighbors' chimneys. The room was so bright she had to squint as she took up her letter and read it through. It increased her heart rate and made her a bit light-headed. Agitated, unable to sit, she walked from room to room, reading it a second time and realizing she couldn't destroy it. No previous letter to James, sent or unsent, had contained so much of herself. Here was her father set forth in clear and loving sketches. Here were her dinner guests—such an unlikely mix of friends. Here, blended together with her clouded, glum thinking about the Decline of the West, were half a dozen childhood memories, each one precious. Here was Agatha, in other words, whole and entire, and gone was the self-negating impulse that had her tearing up letters for three and a half years. This was a keepsake, a testament, a kind of historical document. She slipped the pages into a folder containing old photographs and newspaper clippings. Then she phoned Father Finn.

"Are we still at fifteen, Father?"

"Fourteen at least," he said. "Sister Judith is seeing to her father's passport, and Lillian called to say she'll be dropping off a check."

"How about the congressman?"

"No word from the congressman. I'll be surprised if he goes."

"Why would you be surprised? He seemed determined."

"No votes in Italy."

"Father, we aren't entirely thrilled to be going with Sylvester, are we?"

"I know what you mean, but I'm betting he'll spend most of his time sitting around the hotel. There's quite a lot of walking on this tour, and I can't see him keeping up."

"Then why is he going at all?" She was afraid of the answer.

"Well . . . who knows?"

"No hedging, Father—why do you think he's going?"

"Because you're going."

"Just as I feared."

She bathed and dressed, and was bundling herself into her long wool scarf and her long wool coat in preparation for the walk downtown for groceries and a visit to Janet Meers when she felt her energy drain suddenly away. She felt the return of the same old heaviness behind her eyes that had been plaguing her for six months, but which she had not awakened with this morning. Her coat weighed heavily on her shoulders, and she wanted to sink into a chair and rest. Where were her high spirits of scarcely an hour ago?

In the drawer of her desk?

Suspecting this to be the case, she returned to the sun room, took out the letter and pictured James reading it. Immediately her excitement returned.

"Lord help me," she said aloud, folding the sheets and slipping them into an envelope. "My highs and lows governed by a man—I must be going haywire." She addressed the envelope, but affixed no postage, uncertain whether she would actually send it. She slipped it into her purse and walked briskly downtown, happily greeting neighbors out clearing their sidewalks and shoppers she met along Main Street. She paused in front of the post office, weighing her choices, and decided she needed more time. She crossed the street to the Morning Star Apartments, where Janet Meers lived.

There were a number of students in Agatha's past who remained or became her friends as they grew older, and Janet Meers, a lithe, brown-haired woman of twenty-seven, was one of them. Janet was the wife of Randy Meers, a realtor, and the mother of two children, a nine-year-old boy and a baby girl. Until last spring they had been constantly in one another's company, Janet serving as Agatha's secretary during her term as principal of St. Isidore's. They'd been an efficient team, and both of them looked back on their time together with fondness, and regret that it was over. Janet had left work in March to have her baby, and returned just in time to pack files into boxes, clean out her desk and lock the office door for the last time.

"Look here, Janet." Agatha set down her coffee cup, removed the thick envelope from her purse and smiled mysteriously as she displayed the address.

"Hey, don't tell me you're starting *that* up again."

"I don't know. I might. He wrote good letters."

Janet laughed. "Honestly, Agatha, you're full of surprises."

The two women were sitting at the wide front window of a second-floor apartment overlooking Main Street. This was the caretaker's apartment. The sixteen-unit Morning Star building was the property of Janet's parents-in-law, and she and her husband Randy were the caretakers. On the table at Agatha's elbow were an insulated pitcher of coffee and a plate of cookies—Agatha's breakfast, though she didn't admit this to Janet. Sara, the baby, slept on Janet's lap. Janet's son Stephen, Agatha's godson, could be heard in another room changing television channels.

Janet spoke as lightly as possible, disguising her concern. "Be careful this time, Agatha. Don't go getting another crush on him."

"Don't be silly. My eyes are open."

Her eyes were actually dancing, Janet noticed, and there was color in the old woman's cheeks. She hadn't seen Agatha looking this animated for ages. "I'm glad," she said. "We all ought to have someone write us interesting letters."

Janet Meers, though more than forty years her junior, was perhaps better acquainted with the interior Agatha McGee than anyone else in town. Janet had accompanied her on that fateful trip to Ireland, had been privy to her heartbreak, had seen her tears, had consoled her. For three and a half years she'd faithfully kept the secret about James O'Hannon, as promised. She hadn't even told her husband.

"Did he write to you or what?"

"Indirectly. He wrote to Bishop Baker claiming he needed to hear from me."

Janet laughed and the baby uttered a gurgling little moan in her sleep. "Which means *he's* got a crush on *you*."

"Will you stop this nonsense about crushes? This is a correspondence between adults, not lovesick teenagers."

"What's in that envelope, your life story?"

"Just a few observations. The weather and so forth. I'm here to ask you if I should mail it." Agatha was not fully cognizant of the fact that Janet's opinion would make no difference. She was here to stall for time until she made up her own mind.

"I guess I'd mail it."

"You understand, the man means nothing to me anymore."
Janet nodded, not believing her.

"It's the diversion of writing and receiving letters. It's a way to fill the time."

"Sure, I can see that."

"And his request that I write. There was some urgency in his tone, which I can't in good conscience ignore."

"Do you suppose he's sick or something?"

"I've wondered. Or maybe it's some family trouble he needs to air out."

"What family?"

"He has a brother."

Janet looked again at the envelope. "I see he's still in Ballybegs."

"He is," Agatha sighed wistfully, and the village on the Irish Sea returned to her, veiled in the hazy and beautiful sunshine of memory. The sun fell on the trees and the shops and the row houses along the street leading to the sea, and it fell on the beach, on the frothy waves creeping ashore. It was a Sunday morning, breezy and warm. She saw herself turning away from the sea, following the wrought-iron fence around the corner of the churchyard and entering with a crowd of parishioners through the gate. She filed into the church of gray stone, ST. BRIGID engraved above the door, and stopped in the vestibule to scan the congregation, intending to surprise James by slipping into the pew beside him, unaware that he was St. Brigid's priest. She heard the tinkling bell over the sacristy door and saw the altar boys step out into the sanctuary. She cut off the memory right there, before James came out, vested to celebrate Mass.

She opened her purse, slipped the letter inside and said, "How's Randy?"

"Busy showing property from morning till night. He sold a farm last week and a house yesterday. We're going to a realtors' convention in Las Vegas after Christmas."

"Right after?"

"The week between Christmas and New Year's. The convention's only two days, but I'm insisting we stay another two or three days. Honestly, he never slows down."

"Such industry."

"Honestly, I sometimes wonder if he's falling in love with money."

Agatha stood up. "Don't disparage ambition, Janet. Remember when he had none."

Janet's response to this was a self-satisfied chuckle. Janet, a poor farm girl, had married well. Agatha had disapproved of the marriage, Randy Meers being at the time an aimless college dropout, but Janet had maintained her faith in him. Now settled into his father's real estate business, Randy was making more money per month than her father the farmer made in a year. In Staggerford as well as in neighboring towns, the market was dominated by the flashy red and yellow yard signs of Meers Realty.

Agatha told her about the Galileo tour of Italy, and Janet responded with enthusiasm. "Oh, Italy, send me cards. I'd love to see Italy."

"It's certain to be a happier trip than the one you and I were on," said Agatha. "Less complicated."

"Unless you go getting a crush on some Roman."

Agatha, politely feigning amusement, stood up and said, "We'll compare travel notes in January."

Janet carefully lifted the baby to her shoulder and got to her feet. "Will you tell me what you hear from Father O'Hannon, what the urgency is all about?"

"You're sworn to secrecy."

"I know."

"Yes, I'll tell you . . . if I mail it."

Janet called her son out of the TV room. "Say good-bye to Agatha, Stephen."

"Good-bye, Agatha," Stephen mumbled obediently, backing slowly toward them, his eyes held by a cartoon. He was a well-built boy with darker hair and a lighter complexion than his mother's. His father, a soldier home on leave, had dropped out of Janet's life the day after Stephen was conceived. Janet was seventeen then, unmarried.

Agatha bent and kissed the top of his head. "Do you like days off, or would you rather be in school?"

Stephen shrugged, his eyes on the screen.

"Go back to your program," she said, patting his head. She was not dismayed by his lack of interest in her. He had been fond of her when he was little and he'd be fond of her again.

"We'll talk when we're both a little older," she said to him as he was returned to his cartoon.

"Do you watch Twisted Sister?" she asked Janet.

"Pardon me?" Janet thought she misunderstood.

"Do you get the channel where boys wear earrings? The Rathmann brothers were telling me about it."

"MTV." Janet laughed. "No, Randy wants it, but I don't think it's something Stephen ought to watch."

"Dan Rathmann wears an earring."

"So does Randy."

"Heaven help us."

"He had his ear pierced for his birthday," said Janet unashamedly. Indeed, rather proudly, Agatha thought.

Again putting off her decision, Agatha passed up the post office and entered Druppers' Grocery, a small enterprise half in and half out of the modern age. The cash register was electronic and the vegetables were sealed in plastic, but you ground your own coffee by turning a crank and you could point to a loin and specify the chops you wanted.

"Agatha, what's this about you and Sylvester?" asked Theodore Druppers from behind his meat counter. He was a squat, bright-eyed man nearly Agatha's age, a trustee of St. Isidore's and a former mayor of Staggerford. He wore a fresh white apron and a black bow tie.

"What have you heard?"

"You two were going to Italy together."

"Along with a dozen others. It's a group."

"And if everything goes good, you'll get engaged over there."

"Lord God, what—where—who told you that?"

"Sylvester. He was just in."

She hissed angrily. "Not in my wildest nightmares have I imagined myself married to Sylvester Juba."

"And you'll sell your house."

"Ridiculous."

"And be his wife and keep his books."

"Asinine. Give me a lean pork chop and a half a pound of thickly sliced bacon."

Trembling with wrath, she stood waiting for her order. She

wanted to weep. She did weep. She drew her scarf up to her eyes and turned to face a shelf containing soups and spices. She hated Sylvester Juba for being a stupid ass, and Theodore Druppers for being such a callous tale bearer, and most of all she hated weeping. After a lifetime of stability, what was she doing on this emotional roller coaster? No wonder she'd been feeling so reclusive these last several months—go shopping and have a nervous breakdown.

"Thank you, Agatha," the butcher said, handing her the two packages. He was about to remark on the weather, but when he saw the state she was in, he quickly busied himself at his chopping block, abashed to think that he might have caused her tears.

She paid the girl at the checkout counter and stepped outside feeling the need for a quiet few minutes in a warm corner to gather herself before she made another run at the post office. She hurried along the street—her vision impaired by ice forming on her eyelashes—and turned in at the Hub Cafe, where she sat at the table in the window and ordered tea and prune whip. Facing away from the other patrons, including Frederick Lopat on a stool at the far end of the counter, she carefully dried her eyes with paper napkins and asked herself why, on two successive days, she should weep.

The answer, she decided, was men. Men were to blame for her tears, and a great deal more. Oh, the serenity if half the human race weren't men. Why were men so much on her mind? James O'Hannon. Sylvester Juba. Peter McGee. Why was so much of the letter in her purse devoted to her father? Rereading the letter this morning, she'd felt guilty for slighting her mother.

Was it possible that James O'Hannon, the foremost man in her present-day life, had opened up a channel of memory going back to the foremost man in her past? Yes, she thought, this seemed likely. Her fondness for James, like her fondness for her father, made her nostalgic and sad. And having reached this conclusion, she felt a little better. If you couldn't cure what ailed you, at least it helped to know the nature of your ailment.

The waitress came with her order. Nibbling prune whip and absently watching the cars and pedestrians pass along Main Street, Agatha wondered if in some ways James O'Hannon and Peter McGee weren't the same man. Both were bright and affable Irishmen. Both were sensitive and idealistic and served the public in professions of the greatest trust. Was it too much to say, as well, that they'd both stolen her heart? No, she decided, not both of them. Her father certainly, and forever, but not James. Well, yes, perhaps James, but only temporarily. She wouldn't be considering a renewal of letters if the least bit of love were involved.

Finishing her prune whip and sipping her tea, she allowed Sylvester Juba back into her thoughts, and she understood why he brought tears to her eyes. It had to do with his being so far inferior to James and her father. If you needed a man in your life and had to settle for a disaster like Sylvester Juba, who wouldn't weep? How fortunate, she told herself proudly, that I really don't need a man in my life.

"Hi, Miss McGee," said a man, jolting her out of her thoughts. She turned and saw Frederick Lopat standing near her table, tucking his ears into his stocking cap.

"Good morning, Frederick. Sit down."

"I was just going."

"Sit down anyway." She would risk proposing that he watched her house.

He obeyed, removing his cap and patting down his hair. He asked if it was cold enough for her.

"Yes, I detest the cold."

"Me too." He sat forward in his chair, as though awaiting orders.

"Frederick, I'm going to Italy for ten days, as you know."

He nodded, running his fingertips over his whiskers and wishing he'd shaved. She'd think he'd developed sloppy habits. Which he had.

"Would it be too much trouble for you to check my house once a day while I'm gone?"

"No trouble," he said.

"Just to make sure the furnace is running, so the pipes don't freeze."

"Can do," he said almost unctuously, enjoying the prospect of lounging around her warm house.

"Remember the winter the Jerrods went to see their daughter in Texas and their pipes burst? Water down the walls and sheets of ice across the floors. They had to redo every room."

He wagged his head sympathetically. "That can happen."

"And the plants, of course. I have a few plants to water."

"No problem," he said happily, picturing her couch with its unobstructed sightline to the TV.

"And bring in the mail."

"Sure thing."

"What would be fair, a dollar each time?"

"Plenty fair," he said. A dollar was peanuts, of course, but he'd profit in other ways. He'd bathe in her bathtub. He'd maybe fix himself a meal in her kitchen.

"If you'll stop over one day, I'll give you a key."

"Will do." He sat at attention for a few more moments, and when it became apparent that her instructions were over, he put on his stocking cap.

"Frederick," she said, "I'm thinking of calling off next year's Thanksgiving dinner."

He removed his cap and made a face: mild disappointment. "How come?"

"Yesterday's gathering was not a success."

"I thought it was just fine, same as always."

"Do I need to remind you that the hostess fell apart in front of her guests?"

He made another face: so what?

"That group goes back a long time together, but it's changing."

He nodded. "One jerk can ruin it for everybody. Don't call off the dinner—just don't invite Sylvester."

"Oh, I would never single him out. He's been a friend of the family all his life."

"What family?"

"My family. You have to make allowances for old family friends."

"You haven't got no family, Miss McGee. You're all there is to your family."

She drew in her breath, as though insulted or shocked. She did not point out the error in his statement. She carefully formed her response. "The Jubas were particular friends of my parents, Frederick. I can't very well banish them from my parents' table."

"That's not your parents' table," he said with emotion, for

the dead Vietnamese babies were suddenly crowding into his mind. "The dead don't own nothing."

"The silver, the crystal, the lace tablecloth—all of it was acquired by my father and mother."

French didn't hear this because there were two babies and a young woman lying on the floor of the first hut he looked into. The woman and one of the babies were dead. The other baby, the smaller one, was lying on its back looking up at him with an innocent smile. What had the squad done about this baby? He couldn't remember.

Agatha patted French's hand. "You're a thousand miles away."

He came to, smiled and said, "Twelve thousand."

"The war?"

"Yup."

"It still comes back?"

"Not quite so often." He put on his stocking cap. "Often enough."

"You can get help for it now."

"I know, I read about it. It's even got a name."

"You really should ask for help."

He shrugged. "I'm okay."

She was careful not to insist. Losing Frederick as a lodger was a wound that wouldn't heal. He'd been so undemanding, so quiet, so considerate. He'd also been argumentative at times, but only to the exact degree she happened to favor. He'd present the case for the other side—as now, concerning Sylvester Juba—but never insist on having the last word.

"Frederick, I saw a job in the paper."

Oh, no, not this again.

"The bakery."

He nodded. "Nights."

"You'd learn a trade."

"I'm pretty happy with the job I got."

"But so many months of idleness."

He smiled at her. "I can handle it."

"How is it possible? I'm having a horrible time trying to fill my days."

"It just takes practice. You'll get the hang of it."

10

*D*EAR AGATHA,

I cannot tell you how overjoyed I am to have your letter, so generously full of the life you're leading and the thoughts you're thinking. I will try my best to respond in kind, but at the moment I'm off to Dublin for an appointment and my bus is about to pull out. This is simply to say that you'll be hearing from me at greater length, and that by answering my letter you have answered my prayers.

Fondly and gratefully,
James

This note arrived on a temperate, silvery morning in mid-December, twenty days after Agatha mailed her letter. They had been, for her, twenty days of anticipation, second-guessing, and looking down the street for the mailman. She read the note half a dozen times before placing it with his other messages in the bottom drawer of her desk, and she went back to it several times in the afternoon, pondering its disappointing brevity and granting finally that it was probably the best a man could do while running to catch a bus. As for the postal delay, she recalled that while some letters used to speed between Staggerford and Ballybegs in six days, it hadn't been unusual for others to take seven or eight. Not surprising, therefore, that this exchange required ten days each way, considering the bureaucratic breakdown you expected in advance of the Dark Ages.

The note put Agatha to work. Besides failing to plan and pack for her trip to Rome, she'd been neglecting her Christmas cards and any number of household duties, but the day the note arrived, she washed slipcovers, cleaned the oven, and summoned French from the Morgan Hotel to help with certain other chores. While waiting for him to arrive, she wrote and addressed seven Christmas cards.

French's first job was to climb into the attic and bring down her suitcases. He came down sneezing.

"Is that a cold, Frederick?"

"I guess so," he lied. Actually it was attic dust, to which he was loath to draw her attention because she might send him up there with her feather duster and vacuum. He drew the line at housekeeping.

"Now please go out and start the car and let it warm up. Lillian and I are going downtown." Handing him her key ring, she added, "Check the oil and the tires and all the belts and the hoses."

Promising to do so, French went out the back door and crossed the yard to the old horse barn, the last remaining garage in this town with a manger and a hayloft. Parked inside was Staggerford's oldest car in running order, a finny Plymouth Belvedere with a shiny plum-blue finish and scratchy woven-rush seat covers. French read the dipstick and found the oil not far off the mark. He tugged on the fan belt, then shut the hood and kicked two of the tires. He got in behind the wheel, started the engine and listened to it rumble and pop for half a minute before backing out. Leaving the car growling in the alley, he carried a storm window across the yard to the sun room, guessing what his next chore would be.

He guessed wrong.

"Frederick," Agatha said, lifting a window and speaking through the screen. "You'll have to do the windows on a day when it thaws. They need to be washed."

Happy to put off the windows, he didn't point out to her that the temperature had risen into the high thirties and water was trickling along the street. He nodded and carried the storm window back to the garage.

While Agatha and Lillian were gone, he strung Christmas lights along the eaves over the front porch, dug the wheelbarrow and the garden hose out of the snow, and chipped ice off the back steps. He was widening the path between the house and the garbage cans when the Plymouth came creeping down the alley and stopped at the barn door. Protruding from the trunk was a long-needled pine.

"Frederick, please help Lillian with her tree."

He did so, crossing the alley with Lillian and asking if Imogene would be home for Christmas.

"She'll be home Christmas Eve. If she wasn't coming, I wouldn't put up a tree, but Imogene likes a tree. Agatha's not putting up a tree—first time ever. We're leaving the day after Christmas, so what's the use of a tree, she says. 'I see what you're saying,' I said to her, 'but Imogene likes a tree.' "

Trailing needles, French dragged the tree through Lillian's bright blue kitchen and lemon-yellow dining room and into her peach living room. This was a smaller house than Agatha's, the rooms overfurnished, the walls overdecorated.

"We'll put it in the front window. I'm not going to trim it because Imogene likes to do the trimming herself. She likes to pick it out, for that matter, but if I wait till she comes home Christmas Eve, they'll all be picked over and scraggly. Personally, I'm partial to spruce and so was Lyle, but Imogene likes these long-needle jobs. Now just a minute, I'll go down and get the stand."

Waiting for Lillian to come up from the basement, French surveyed the room, imagining where Imogene might have sat while writing him her three letters in wartime. Did she sit over there at the card table, which was now covered with knitting and newspapers, or in the overstuffed chair with the gold metallic thread running through the fabric? Or possibly she sat on the blue couch with her feet up on the red vinyl hassock.

The three letters had caught up with him all at once in the psych ward in Hawaii. They came as a complete surprise. She hadn't seemed all that enamored of him when they dated. The first letter consisted of a single sentence: *Staggerford is proud of you.* He was pleased but skeptical. The second convinced him of her sincerity: *A lot of us have come to the conclusion that this war should never have been fought, but that doesn't detract from the honor you do us by fighting it. In fact there's something of the classic tragedy in your going off with no choice in the matter to sacrifice your life in a wrongheaded cause. "The Charge of the Light Brigade" and all that. Well, this is just to let you know you haven't been forgotten.*

How consoling. How kind of her. He thought of writing back, but he never did, partly because he wasn't equipped—he lacked stationery and stamps and a facility with language—and partly because he was too listless from medication. But from that day forward he had a new way to think of his military service, indeed of his entire life. Classic tragedy—wow, it sounded like a really good movie.

Imogene's first two letters he carelessly lost, but the third, which contained an amusing reminiscence from his high school days, he kept to this day with his socks in the top drawer of his bureau. He still took it out and read it once in a while.

I'll never forget the day report cards were handed out, and Mr. Lastrup was such an erratic grader he always had a bunch of students coming in after school to ask why they got what they got, and you and I were there among several others in his math room—I was a senior when you were a sophomore, right?—and everybody was asking him to justify their low grade, but when it was your turn you said, "How come I got an A?" Well, everybody was stunned to think French Lopat got an A in geometry or algebra or whatever it was you were taking from Mr. Lastrup that year, and he looked in his grade book and found that he'd made a mistake and changed it on the spot to something low, like a D or an F. What made you ask? Were you really that honest? Are you still?

French, moving around Lillian's living room, chuckled happily at the memory. He hadn't suspected the A was a mistake. He actually thought he'd earned it, and he wanted to know what he'd done right so he could excel once again during the next marking period. Mr. Lastrup promptly gave him an F. Soon the tale was told out of school, and when Miss McGee heard it, she praised him for owning up to his lack of talent in math. He didn't tell her that his ignorance was so abysmal that he hadn't known how untalented he was.

His eye fell on Lillian's various keepsakes. Beside the front door hung two stitched samplers, one proclaiming HOME SWEET HOME in red and white, and the other RISE AND SHINE in orange and gray. Over the couch was a framed print of a bearded, radiant Jesus knocking at a door, and a larger print of the Holy

Family and their donkey fleeing into Egypt. Glued here and there to the wall in tight bunches were several bottle caps covered with pink and yellow yarn meant to resemble blossoms; they stood on green leafy stems painted thickly over the wallpaper by an amateurish hand.

Standing on a table under a frilly-shaded lamp were two large photographs, one of a young bride and groom, no doubt Lillian and her husband Lyle, she slim and pretty and looking supremely satisfied, he tall and handsome and looking apprehensive. They were standing outdoors on a bright day, under a flowering tree. Beside it was Imogene's high school graduation photo, obviously taken in Herbert Ahrens's studio in the days when Mrs. Herbert Ahrens, who had gone to school for the purpose, tinted pictures by hand and made everybody look like an overcosmeticized corpse, lips too red, cheeks too pink. Imogene in particular looked unwell, her mouth set in that rather sour expression caused in certain women (French observed) by too much of a good thing. Too much motherhood or too much money, for example; or, in Imogene's case, too much study. Though this picture predated her return to town with her degree in library science, it seemed to French to have *Pipe down, this is a library!* written all over it.

Lillian came puffing up the cellar stairs with the stand and held the tree upright while French got down on his knees and tightened the bolts at its base. "Did you know Imogene wrote to me in the army?" he asked.

"She did?"

"Was it something she did a lot of in those days—writing to soldiers?" He'd developed this fantasy wherein she'd singled him out because she truly cared for him.

"Whoops," said Lillian, "it's leaning your direction."

"I mean I just wondered if she wrote to quite a few guys." Out of high school and before going into the army, he'd taken Imogene to a few movies, bought her a few malts. After returning home from the army, he'd timidly gone into the library to thank her for the letters and see if her looks had improved— she'd always been gawky—and was told she'd taken a library job in Berrington.

"She used to fire off letters to Washington every time you

turned around," said her mother, "but I don't remember soldiers. Now it's leaning towards me."

"I needed cheering up and the letters helped. I was in a hospital in Hawaii and down in the dumps. I just wondered if she
wrote to a lot of guys."

"Ask her when she comes for Christmas, why don't you?
She was a great one for writing to authors and senators, but I
don't remember soldiers."

"I might do that."

At noon, eating egg salad sandwiches with the two women
in Agatha's kitchen, French brought up the letters again, relat-
ing the incident in Mr. Lastrup's classroom. With a self-
disparaging chuckle, he said, "I never knew if Imogene was
impressed with how honest I was, or how dumb I was."

Dumb, Lillian guessed. "Imogene can be hard on stupid
people."

Honest, thought Agatha. "You were always very scrupulous,
Frederick. I remember the pains you would take with your hy-
giene chart."

"But asking why he got an A," said Lillian. "Isn't that
pretty stupid?"

"Yeah," French agreed, smiling timidly. "Who else would
do a thing like that?"

"Being out of step with the world is not stupid," said
Agatha. "It's integrity of the highest order. And the beauty of
it is, you haven't changed in all these years, Frederick. You'd
do the same today."

He looked surprised. "I would?"

"People don't change. The deceitful among my twelve-year-
olds grew up to be more or less shady in adult life. The trustworthy have always remained trustworthy."

After some thought, he said unhappily, "No, I think people
change." He was pondering not only his summertime make-
believe as Staggerford's Indian, but also a certain dishonest ritual that took place every two weeks at the employment office.
In order to receive his unemployment check, he had to declare
that he had looked for work and found none. This was a fed-
eral regulation. Nobody looked for work, yet everybody
claimed to.

"The die is cast by the sixth grade," Agatha declared.

He pondered this, then looked to Lillian for confirmation.

"Some people change, and some people don't—that's what Imogene says."

"No," said Agatha softly, confidently. "Take Imogene, for example." Seeing Lillian smile with satisfaction at this, Agatha allowed her to go on believing it was a compliment.

Feeling the need to move Miss McGee into the modern world, as well as the need to confess, French shifted uneasily in his chair and unloaded his guilt. "Sometimes the system *makes* you change," he said, and he went on to explain how the unemployment procedure worked. "Mr. Steffanson says, 'Did you look for work this week?' and you say, 'Yup,' and he makes a note of that on your card and hands you your check."

"And you don't actually look for work?" asked Agatha, her eyes wide with discovery.

He shrugged. "No jobs."

"No jobs is no reason to lie."

"Unemployment pays your rent, buys your meals—that's the reason."

"How long has this been going on?"

"Ever since I been on unemployment. Probably a lot longer. It's how it works."

"Lillian, did you know about this?"

Lillian did not know, nor did she like to admit to complete ignorance. "Imogene might have told me."

"Look, it's not really lying," said French. "It's what you call blowing smoke. It's just a way of getting around the rules."

"A statement is either true or false, Frederick."

"But, see, Mr. Steffanson knows everybody's blowing smoke. If you tell somebody yes and he knows it's no, then how can it be lying?"

"The person lied to is in no way responsible." Agatha's face took on a hard, narrow look. "You know what you must do, don't you, Frederick?"

He sighed, regretting he'd brought it up. "Look for work."

"Exactly."

"There isn't any. Not around here. Not in the winter."

"If you're going to say you've looked for work, then you must look for work."

He exchanged a meaningful glance with Lillian. Its meaning was that there was no moving Miss McGee into the modern age.

11

T $_{W O}$ $_{D A Y S}$ $_{L A T E R}$ $—A$ sunny, thawing day—the promised letter arrived. Agatha treated it ceremoniously, carrying it into the sun room and carefully slitting the envelope with her grandmother's opener of ivory, unfolding the pages and pressing them flat on her desk before going into the kitchen to brew a pot of tea. French's shadow fell across the letter as he climbed the stepladder, replacing a screen with a storm window.

Dear Agatha,

Apologies for letting a day and a half pass before getting around to this reply. I had to remain in Dublin overnight and only got back here to the rectory this very minute—ten minutes before six, to be exact, on a dark afternoon of wind and drizzle.

My dear Agatha, how do I begin? Perhaps by assuring you of my sincerity when, in yesterday's note, I said that you had answered my prayers. You cannot know how timely, inspiring, and crucial to my well-being your letter was. Is.

Or perhaps I should begin by confessing that I have been writing you the occasional letter all along. Every now and then, full of something to say but with no one to say it to, I've taken out a sheet of paper, written your name at the top, and unburdened myself. A drawer of my desk is full of such letters, one of which I intend to enclose with this one, because it concerns the death of my mother. While the smaller sorrows of my recent past have pretty well diminished or disappeared, as ordinary sorrows are wont to do, this one lingers. It's a sorrow that needs to be conveyed to you before I can let it go.

Or perhaps I should begin by announcing to you that I'm retiring from the active priesthood. My bishop has declared seventy the mandatory retirement age, and I can't say I'm sorry. The duties of a parish priest grow more and more complex at a time in my life when I am more and more inclined to avoid complexity. Is it the same with you, Agatha, or am I alone in my need for simplicity? As I walk along the seafront these days, I find my gaze drawn to the distant headlands because their shapes are strong and simple. Sometimes I don't even notice the people I meet on the pier.

And strong and simple as well are the headlines in the Independent and Times. The headlines are all I read, the news underneath being such an ungodly mess, particularly on the Ulster page, where every day there's a new story of my countrymen in the North wallowing in blood.

But no, I'll not begin with troubles, neither my own nor my nation's. I'll begin with congratulations. Anyone setting off for Italy ought to be congratulated. You'll move through the landscapes of history, Agatha, through architectural wonders, through museums packed full of the greatest sculptures and paintings in the world. And of course you'll be stirred to your soul in Vatican City, you'll come away with your faith refreshed. Though not a great traveler myself, I have been three times to Italy and loved it more each time. Besides the history and art and the Pope, there's the everlasting sunshine. The pleasure I take in the Mediterranean sunlight warming these old Irish bones is almost sinful.

She was interrupted in her reading by the ringing phone and by French coming in for a fresh pail of hot water.

"Agatha, there's been a bomb," said Lillian on the phone.

"What? What are you talking about?"

"A terrorist bomb in Italy, it was just on the news. I'm calling Imogene right away. I'll call you back and let you know if we should cancel."

"Where was it?"

"They said Italy. On a train."

"I mean what city?"

"They said, but I don't remember."

"Was it Rome?"

"I don't think it was Rome. There were people hurt. Seven, I think they said."

The twinge of fear that ran down Agatha's spine was immediately followed by a twinge of disgust—standards of behavior breaking down all over the place. "Lillian, I won't cancel no matter what Imogene says."

"You won't?"

"Our chances of being terrorized are very small, I'm sure."

"I'll call Imogene, and then I'll call Father."

"Furthermore, the terrorist's aim is intimidation. We must not be intimidated."

"I'll let you know what they say."

Hanging up the phone, Agatha repeated Lillian's news to French, who was filling his pail at the sink.

"A bomb," said French thoughtfully.

"Lillian's afraid we'll be targets, but you have to ignore people who try to scare you. You have to pretend they're having no effect."

French nodded and went outside with his pail, and Agatha returned to the letter.

There was a bombing in Ulster last week—an innocent family destroyed when their car blew up on their way to Mass in Derry. I didn't know the family personally, but I have in my parish a cousin of the dead, an elderly man who went north for the funeral and reported seeing so much hate and suspicion mixed with everyone's grief that he feared for his own safety, he being a virtual stranger among them, and hurried home right after the burial. I tell you, Agatha, I am so sick of the Troubles I don't know where to turn. They haunt me. They cast a dark shadow over all I look upon.

On a happier note, there's a general refurbishing going on in Dublin, in preparation for its millennium. Lots of new paint and varnish and a new community spirit the likes of which I've never sensed in the city before. The entire length of Grafton Street is now off limits to cars—foot traffic only, and that on splendid new paving stones. A new statue is planned for O'Connell Street.

This was followed by news of people in Ballybegs, whose names meant nothing to Agatha. Who was Langtry the fisherman that his stormy courtship of a woman up the coast deserved a page and a half? Who were the Connellys that the names of their eight children should be listed along with their ages and accomplishments in school? Agatha might have recognized these people if she'd read his old letters in recent years, but she hadn't. Last summer, cleaning her desk, she'd taken the letters out and counted them—seventy-seven—and returned them to the bottom drawer, facedown, without reading a line.

Today's letter concluded with a weather report and, as usual, a gracious farewell. *It's with a happy heart, Agatha, that I seal this and send it off to you, and it's with an eager heart that I look for your reply.*

Fondly,
James

Well.

Her head swam. There was so much to respond to. So much to question. The man who wrote this letter resembled the man she'd been carrying around in her head for three years, but there were differences. Her old James O'Hannon never dealt in meaningless flattery. To claim that her letter was "timely, inspiring, and crucial to my well-being" was the most awful sort of cajolery. She'd have to tell him, if she replied, that she suspected him of blowing smoke.

Furthermore, her old James O'Hannon had always been fatalistic about the Troubles in the North. "Die and let die," he'd once said to her, reacting to a shooting in Belfast. She'd been stunned by his harsh tone, and yet understood the reason for it: in an earlier siege of Troubles, when James was a small boy, his father had died of a burst appendix because the British forces had imposed a curfew on their town and restrained the family from going for the doctor. Consequently, James, like a good many of his countrymen in the Republic, preferred not to be drawn into discussions about their brothers in the North. But here his tone was very sad, almost desperate, his view of life apparently darkened by the new clouds piling up over Ulster.

And another thing, her old James O'Hannon had no appetite for eating his heart out. Hadn't he lost both his mother and sister long before she met him in Ireland? Yes, she distinctly recalled their conversation in a restaurant in Dublin, he telling her how both of them had died, and how his careless brother, left alone, was permitting the O'Hannon public house to go

into decline. Was it self-pity or senility drawing him back to
his mother's death after all this time?

She was unfolding the five-page enclosure about his mother
when the phone rang again.

"Agatha, we might kick the bucket in Italy. There was a
bomb on a train." This was Sylvester Juba, wheezy and loud.

"Don't be ridiculous. It wasn't in Rome."

"I don't know, Agatha, we could walk into killers over there."

"Call Father and ask what he thinks."

"Not that I'd mind dying. It's the rest of you I worry about."

"That's generous of you. Call Father."

"You got his number?"

Agatha recited it.

"Not that I'd mind dying, Agatha. It's dying among wops
that bothers me."

"Good-bye, Sylvester."

She was scarcely out of the kitchen when the phone rang
again. Sylvester again.

"Judy, put Father on."

"Sylvester, you've got the wrong number."

"Who is this?"

"Agatha. Call the number I gave you."

"I did."

"No, you didn't." She gave him the number again.

"Agatha, there's a sperm bank in Minneapolis."

"What?"

"What do you think—if my life's in danger?"

"Good-bye, Sylvester."

The pages concerning Mrs. O'Hannon were mostly random
scenes from James's boyhood. She was taking him on the train
to Galway. She was altering his father's suit to fit his brother
for Confirmation, and three years later to fit James. She was
defending James against the troublesome woman next door
who claimed he cut in front of her in the confession line.
Though she tried to hide it, and his brother and sister never
brought it up, it was evident to James growing up that he,
youngest of the three, was her pet. Widowed, she made the
pub a thriving business with her good sense and her congenial
manner. But in her last years she was odd. Her gregarious na-

ture disappeared. She sat silent before the fire for hours at a time. It bothered James a great deal that she'd scarcely acknowledge him when he went home on a Sunday afternoon for a visit. They sat in the room like strangers.

This enclosure, two years older than the letter it came with, was written on yellowing paper in a bolder hand. Comparing the pages, Agatha detected a striking difference in the penmanship. The new formation of letters was not so uniform as the old. Here and there in the new letter the pen wobbled and shook. Here a line went downhill at the end, there it rose. What premature infirmity ailed the man?—he was only seventy. And what was this repellent smudge on page four—something he'd been eating? She folded both letters and sat for a time watching French work with the windows.

Lillian, needing help turning mattresses, invited French and Agatha across the alley for lunch. Pacified by phone by her daughter and her pastor, Lillian spoke of the bomb in Milan with pride, as though she'd survived it by strength of character. "Blew a man's hand off, the radio said. An outfit called the Red Guards is taking the credit."

"That's China," said Agatha. "The Red Guards are in China."

"Think of it, all that distance."

"It can't be the Red Guard. It must be the Red Brigade."

"Red something, anyhow," said Lillian.

"Your fridge looks like it needs straightening," said French, eager for the conversation to move beyond bombs. "It looks like it leans toward the stove."

"No, it's the stove that's crooked because of the floor. It slopes."

"Bombs in Italy, bombs in Ireland," mused Agatha ruefully. "And both of them Catholic."

French could have added that Vietnam had a lot of Catholics too, but the thought of bombs was making him queasy. He pushed away his bowl of soup and stood up. "Your faucet drips." He went to the sink and turned the hot and cold water on and off. "Need new washers."

"Lyle was always so good about fixing things around the house," Lillian said.

"What would my father have done?" Agatha mused.

"Oh, your father wasn't handy around the house," Lillian replied. "Don't you remember, he called in a repairman every time the least little thing was out of whack."

"No, I'm talking about the fighting in Ireland. If he hadn't emigrated as a child, he'd no doubt have been on the Home Rule side."

Lillian smiled fondly. "A scrappy little man, Lyle used to call him."

"But not violent, Lillian. Surely he wouldn't have condoned violence."

"No, scrappy with his mouth, Lyle meant."

"Yes, his weapon was language. But once the bombs and bullets started up, I can't picture him on either side. He was a peaceful man at heart." She fell silent for a few moments, as her mental picture of Peter McGee became outlined, not for the first time, by the larger frame of James O'Hannon. What poor Ireland needed was the talents of men like that, pointing out the error of bloodshed. What a shame James wasn't young enough to make a difference, what a shame her father was dead.

"I can put you in a couple new washers," said French.

"There might be washers in Lyle's toolbox."

"Where's it at?"

"On the basement landing. Here, I'll show you."

Agatha, left alone with her soup, thought about the bomb in Ulster and about James's despairing reaction to it. She thought about his inability to put his mother's death behind him. She thought about his less than perfect handwriting. Whereas upon reading the letter these had seemed the traits of a stranger, she now saw them as perhaps belonging to James after all. Perhaps some people *did* change. Mulling this over in Lillian's bright blue kitchen, she came to realize that the real James O'Hannon was capable of surprising turns of mind, while the James O'Hannon she'd been harboring in her thoughts all this time had no more life to him than a portrait, a statue, a corpse. It was at once sobering and daunting—and downright exciting—to realize that when she took up her pen this afternoon, it would be a living, breathing man she would write to, and not merely her memory of such a man.

12

F R E N C H   W O K E   U P   I N his cold room with his head blessedly empty of dreams. He heard "Deck the Halls" blaring from scratchy loudspeakers on lampposts beneath his window, and this reminded him that tomorrow, Sunday, would be Christmas Eve, the day Imogene Kite arrived home from St. Paul. He burrowed deeper under his four blankets and his shag rug, hugging himself for warmth and imagining Imogene answering his knock on her mother's back door and his proposing a date and her accepting and setting a day and time and his leaving her with a word or two about the letters she wrote him years ago, how consoling they'd been, how he still read the one about his A in math from time to time, and how it always made him laugh.

What if she turned him down? How bad would that hurt? Bad enough, probably, to make him wish he hadn't asked her, but he was ready to risk rejection. Nothing against Grover, his old companion downstairs, but French felt ready to start talking to women. Nothing against Miss McGee, but he was ready to talk to a *young* woman. He hoped Imogene wasn't a toucher like Sister Judith. He didn't think he was ready for touching quite yet.

What if she accepted? Where would they go? He had no car. Unless Imogene offered to drive, they'd be confined to Staggerford and its limited possibilities—the movies and dinner at the Hub.

Computing the cost, French suddenly realized that if he didn't pick up his unemployment check today, Saturday, before noon, he'd be penniless for over a week, because Steffanson, the employment officer, suspended his twice-weekly visits to Staggerford between Christmas and New Year's. He threw off his covers and climbed out of bed. He went to the window and raised the shade. Below him a line of cars waited at the stoplight, the exhaust from each car engulfing the car behind it. When the light changed and the line moved, he heard the squeak of tires on the hard-packed snow, the sort of brittle sound tires never made unless it was at least ten below zero. The clouds of exhaust cleared, revealing a brown cat gingerly crossing the street, keeping its tail and as many feet as possible high off the icy ground. The clock on the bank said eleven-twenty. "We Three Kings" was now playing on the loudspeakers. He hummed the melody as he dressed.

Downstairs in the lobby, Grover mumbled, "French," greeting him without looking up from his newspaper.

"Cold out," said French, pulling on his stocking cap.

"Eighteen below. Up from twenty-one."

"Coldest day yet."

"Thursday was colder."

"Feels colder than Thursday in my room," said French.

"A damp cold," Grover agreed.

"Going for my check."

"Mmmmm," said Grover, turning a page.

French was bracing himself to step out into the cold when the door swung open and two boys burst in from the street, followed by a stream of frigid air that chilled French's ankles. The boys, wearing light jackets and jeans and tennis shoes, were ten or eleven years old. They went straight to the radiator and held their hands out to its meager warmth.

"What's your business here?" Grover demanded sternly, letting his newspaper sink to his lap. "See that?" He pointed to a faded sign on the wall behind the registration counter. NO LOITERING.

"We need to get warm," said the taller boy, whose hair was long and tangled, and whose wrists had grown out of his sleeves. He and his friend, a chubby boy with food on his face, turned around and pressed their backsides against the radiator and studied the other signs on the wall. LEAVE YOUR KEY. NO PETS. NO CREDIT. They studied the gum and candy display on the counter.

"Only for a minute, then," said Grover. "We're not a warming house here at the Morgan."

"What a spooky dump," exclaimed the tall boy, crossing the lobby and peering up the dark staircase. "Do people really stay here?"

"All right," said Grover, insulted and angry, struggling up out of his low chair. "That's enough out of you. Out you go."

"Is that real?" asked the chubby boy, gazing up at the buffalo head over the radiator. He jumped, trying to grab its beard, but came down with only a wisp of cobweb.

The tall boy climbed half a dozen steps, stopped, craned his neck to see around the landing and said, "Spooky dooky."

Grover, raising his voice and waving his newspaper as though scaring off birds, said, "Why aren't you kids at the free show? Go on now. Skedaddle."

Moving swiftly across the lobby, the chubby boy snatched a pack of gum off the counter, the tall boy a candy bar, and they ran past French and out the door. French heard them laughing as the door swung shut, saw them dodging cars on their way across the street.

"Why didn't you stop those goddamn thieves?" demanded Grover.

French, watching them dash into the Orpheum Theater, said nothing.

"Kids," muttered Grover, joining him at the window. "Every kid in the county's in town today. The Chamber is paying for two free movies—ten-thirty and twelve-thirty. It's a gimmick to get their parents to shop here instead of spending their money in Berrington. Why didn't you stop them?" he asked again.

French, ashamed, left the hotel asking himself the same question. He crossed the street and read the schedule of movies posted in front of the Orpheum. He thought it fortunate that *Out of Africa* should be playing while Imogene was home, women being nuts about Robert Redford. Dinner at the Hub, then the movies. An enchanted evening.

He walked briskly along the icy sidewalk, past Druppers' Grocery, Meers Realty, and Ahlgrens' Variety Store. He passed the Chamber of Commerce office and saw Arnold Ulm, his summertime boss, sitting at his desk. French waved, but Arnold Ulm, holding a phone to his ear with one hand and twirling the left wing of his waxed mustache with the other, didn't notice him.

The building next door, formerly a pizza parlor and before that a hardware store, housed government offices, both local and state. French pulled open the door and entered an enormous, high-ceilinged room with dividers of brown and orange fabric standing at various angles and forming baffles or cubicles around the several desks.

Only the employment desk was occupied this morning. A woman and two men stood before it in single file, facing Steffanson, who drove in from Berrington on Tuesdays and Saturdays. French joined the line. The man in front of him he knew to be a bricklayer, but he didn't know his name. He tried to get a conversation started by commenting on the cold, but the bricklayer didn't respond.

Steffanson was a youngish man with close-cropped hair and long ears. Sitting with a manila folder before him, he glanced up at the woman and asked, "Have you looked for work since your last check?" The woman said she had. Steffanson marked the yes box on a card clipped to the folder, then drew from the folder the envelope containing her check. "Here you are, now bear in mind—"

The woman snatched the envelope from him and walked speedily out the door.

As the next person stepped up to the desk and Steffanson shuffled his pile of manila folders, a woman with a Christmas corsage pinned to her coat came in and took her place behind French. She asked if he had the correct time.

"I'd guess twenty to twelve," he said, showing her his wrist with no watch.

"Did you know it was twenty-two below this morning?" she asked.

"I heard twenty-one."

"Twenty-two and my car froze up." The woman was short and very round, and her corsage—a collection of silver bells, spruce twigs, and holly—was so large and spiny she seemed to be standing behind a hedge. "Probably busted the block," she continued. "It's the gas station's fault. The kid at the gas station told me I was good down to forty below. Who can you trust now-days? Who's honest?"

"I know what you mean," said French. "I saw a couple kids stealing candy at the hotel this morning."

"Kids! Aren't they the limit these days?"

"Ten, eleven years old. Out and out thieves."

"What can you do?"

"I tried to catch them, but they were too fast for me."

The woman made a face of disgust. "Kids."

The man at the desk left with his check, and the bricklayer moved into his place. French, watching Steffanson sort through his folders, was profoundly sorry that he'd lied to the woman, sorry that he hadn't blocked the hotel door until the kids gave up the gum and candy and apologized to Grover. What had happened to the instincts Miss McGee had praised him for as a child? *You'll never set the world on fire with your brainpower, Frederick, but you've got good instincts.*

"Have you looked for work since your last check?" Steffanson asked the bricklayer.

The bricklayer nodded.

Steffanson checked the yes box, drew an envelope from the folder and held it out of the man's reach. "This is already your ninth check, you know."

The bricklayer nodded. "I was laid off early this year."

"You realize the limit is twenty-six weeks of unemployment. That's thirteen checks." Steffanson's weary voice was low and solemn.

The bricklayer nodded again, edging closer to snatch the check.

"You have four checks to go, and four checks won't even take you past February. There's no bricklaying around here till summer, so you better look for other work. You might try the paper mill."

"Look for work?" The man sounded angry.

"By the end of February, or go on welfare."

"Listen, I'd rather go on welfare than work at the mill. I'm a bricklayer." He swept the envelope from Steffanson's hand and stalked out, muttering.

Steffanson, sighing, closed one folder and opened another. "All right, French, have you looked for work since your last check?"

French, surprising himself, said "No."

"What?" Steffanson, his eyes on his desk, cocked his head.

"No," French repeated, again surprised, and quite pleased with himself.

Steffanson slowly raised his eyes. "French, we've been through this a hundred times, you know how it works. Now once more—have you looked for work?"

"No." French was smiling broadly, hatching a little scheme. He would go next door and ask Arnold Ulm for work—no chance—and come back with a clean conscience.

Steffanson hung his head. "Get out of here, you're wasting my time. Go look for work if you must, then come back. Next."

French, chuckling to himself, went next door. Arnold Ulm was still on the phone, still twirling his mustache. French put his head in at the door and said, "Any work for me here?" Arnold Ulm gave him scarcely a glance. He withdrew his head and turned back to the employment office with a high heart and a light step. It was a game, of course, but putting the question to an employer made him feel quite satisfied with himself. Why not do this every two weeks, inquire at some place of business on his way to the employment office—the jewelry store, say, or Kaylene's Boutique, places a bewhiskered man with scabby lips and cast-off clothes wasn't welcome inside the door, much less behind the counter?

As he reentered the employment office and noticed that two men had slipped into line ahead of him, a hand gripped French's wrist and pulled him back outside so fast that he nearly fell over. It was Arnold Ulm in his shirtsleeves.

"You're just the man, French. We haven't much time." Ulm pulled him next door. French tried to resist but could gain no traction on the icy sidewalk. He skidded into the Chamber office and Ulm shut the door.

"What the hell's going on?" He wrenched himself free of Ulm's grip.

"Quick, take off your coat," ordered Ulm, unbuttoning it. "We need a Santa Claus at the free movie. Our regular Santa's sick. The movie's about over and there's no Santa."

French, a head taller than Ulm, glared down at him and folded his arms tightly in an attempt to keep his coat on.

"Look, it's a ten-minute job at the most," pleaded Ulm,

pulling the coat off his right shoulder. "The kids come out of the movie and you hand out bags of candy. Less than ten minutes. I'll give you five dollars."

"Quit pulling on my coat!" French shouted desperately. "I don't want a job. I was kidding. I was just qualifying for unemployment. Get your hands off me."

"All right, ten dollars." With a fresh grip on the collar of the coat, Ulm stripped it off and came at him with Santa's red coat.

"Stop it!" French cried hysterically, backing away.

Ulm scooted around him and stood with his back to the door, blocking it. "Don't fight it, French, I need a Santa bad. Just remember who butters your bread in the summertime. You think Indians are hard to find around here? You think I couldn't replace you in those feathers in five minutes if I took a mind to? You think there aren't a dozen Indians—*real* Indians—waiting for that job of yours at the tourist center?"

"I don't believe it," said French, believing it.

"They think you're a phony Indian, French. They've told me so. I tell them they're wrong. I tell them we've got papers on you. But really, how do I know you're an Indian when *you* don't even know?"

French capitulated, less frightened by the prospect of losing his job than by the pushing and shoving he'd have to endure in order to get past Ulm in the doorway. He said "Okay," and Ulm handed him the red coat together with the red pants, the red suspenders, and the long red cap with the tuft at the end. He directed him into a tiny bathroom to change.

"Wash your face while you're in there, French. You never look very clean."

"Go to hell."

He came out dressed in red and white and wiping his face with a paper towel. The white collar of Santa's coat had turned his skin, by contrast, dark olive.

"Not bad," said Ulm, "but your face is showing." He reached up and pasted Santa's beard high on his face, running the mustache over the bridge of his nose.

French swatted him away, shouting, "Damn it, leave me room to breathe."

"Breathe under the beard, we've got to hide as much of your face as possible. There's nothing jolly in your face."

French tore off the beard and took it into the bathroom, where he carefully pasted it on in the mirror. "Ten minutes, ten dollars," he called to Ulm.

"It's a deal."

The heels of Santa's loose boots were high, tipping French forward so that he could hardly walk, and outside on the ice he was helpless without Ulm's aid. Attracting notice, they scurried along the sidewalk to the Orpheum, French gingerly touching the cold storefronts for support and Ulm leading him along by Santa's loose belt buckle.

The manager of the Orpheum, a certain Mr. Harrington, was all business—show business. A man in his sixties who wore expensive suits and colorful bow ties, he'd been in town only a few months, sent by an exhibitors' corporation to draw the old Orpheum back from the verge of bankruptcy.

"Holy Christ," said Mr. Harrington as French and Arnold Ulm came stumbling into the lobby. "Don't tell me that's Santa Claus."

"It's the best I could do on short notice," said Ulm, leaning French against a mirrored wall. "The real Santa's sick." He laughed to indicate he had made a joke.

"This is no Santa! Where's his fat belly? And what's wrong with his face?"

"What's that supposed to mean?" asked French, injured.

"That's his natural color," Ulm explained. "He's usually an Indian."

Balancing himself on his high heels without support, French followed Ulm to a table at the center of the lobby heaped high with small plastic bags of candy.

"I've seen scarecrows look more like Santa than that," said Mr. Harrington, taking a handkerchief from his pocket and wiping smudges from the mirrored wall where French had touched it.

With a swelling of young voices, a pair of padded doors swung open at the far end of the lobby and a mob of children dashed to the candy table. It took the manager and his ushers a minute or more to organize them into two lines; then at a signal from Ulm, French began to hand out the bags.

"Have you been good?" he asked the first girl in the left-hand line. The girl was tiny, and breathless with fear of him. "Yes," she whimpered and ran with her bag.

"Have you been good?" he asked the boy at the head of the right-hand line. The question seemed to French an important and justifiable part of the ritual. If parents and teachers weren't calling kids to account these days, at least Santa ought to be doing so. "Sure," said the boy, grabbing the bag.

"Don't ask them if they've been good," pleaded Mr. Harrington, wringing his hands. He turned to Ulm. "Why is he asking if they've been good?"

"Just give out the candy," ordered Ulm.

"And hurry it up," Mr. Harrington added. "There's another show to get ready for."

The next boy French recognized as one of those who had stolen candy at the hotel. This was the heavier of the two, the one with smudges of food on his face. "Have you been good?" he asked him.

"Yeah," said the boy, pulling at the bag in French's hand.

"Like hell you have!" French tried to withhold the bag, but the boy had a firm grip, and they both tugged. As the manager and Ulm stepped forward to help the boy, French twisted the boy's arm and freed the bag. In retaliation the boy leaped at his face and ripped off Santa's beard, causing French acute pain, the dried paste tearing at his whiskers. Lunging at the boy, intending to slap him—his first voluntary touch in years—French lost his balance on his high heels and fell to the floor. The children broke rank and crowded—cheering—around the table, struggling against the ushers and one another and helping themselves to as many bags as they could get away with, and rushing outside with their loot. In fifteen seconds the candy was gone, and only a small knot of troubled little boys and girls—believers—remained in the lobby, watching French crawl out from under the table with his beard and one of his boots missing.

"Throw him out!" commanded Harrington, directing his ushers frantically. They escorted French to the door and left him standing on the sidewalk in one boot. He stepped out of it and ran back to the Chamber office in his stocking feet. Ulm came running along behind him, carrying the boots and the beard.

Examining his face in the mirror, French tenderly patted a streak of inflamed flesh along his jawline. Ulm stood in the bathroom doorway, addressing French's back. "Would you please explain that?" he fumed. "Were you trying to lose my job for me? Ruin me?"

"I knew the little pup," said French, feeling energized and strangely happy. "He's a thief. I did what I had to do."

"Since when did you start passing judgment on children?"

"Since I became Santa Claus."

"And next summer, if you're still at the tourist center? I suppose you'll pass judgment on the tourist children."

French smiled at himself in the mirror. "An Indian doesn't pass judgment—that's Santa's job." He shut the door in Ulm's face and changed his pants.

"You really screwed up," shouted Ulm through the door. "You put me in a hell of a bad light. Harrington's going to bring this up at the next Chamber meeting and I'm going to be the goat."

French emerged from the bathroom, handed Santa's outfit to Ulm and put on his long black coat. "Ten bucks," he said, holding out his hand.

"Don't be funny," said Ulm.

French left the office chuckling and rehearsing his line to Steffanson: "I looked for work."

Next door the employment office was locked. At first French thought the door was merely stuck, and he wrestled with the latch; then he peered through the window and saw no one inside, no lights burning. He backed away, bewildered—surely it wasn't noon yet—and bumped into a woman carrying two shopping bags. "I beg your pardon," said the woman sarcastically, expecting an apology.

Standing in her path with his head acutely tilted, he read the clock in front of the bank. Ten after twelve.

"Are you drunk?" she asked disdainfully.

"I'm broke till New Year's," he groaned.

The woman hurried away. French remained there for a few moments, shaking his head vigorously, as though ridding himself of water in the ear; then he moved off down the street, his eyes on his feet, his hands drawn up in his sleeves, his thoughts on his dashed plans for Imogene. He checked his pocket for coins and found enough for coffee.

On a stool in the Hub, warming his hands on his hot cup and picturing the astonished look on the boy's face when Santa withheld the bag of candy, French burst out in a snorting laugh that caused the man next to him—a stranger eating pie—to move to a farther stool. Then he called to mind Steffanson's astonishment when he said no instead of yes, and his laughter came out in such an odd, convulsive noise that the stranger put still another stool between them. Oh, the elation of acting on something you believed in. He'd be living off his friends for a week or more—but, oh, the consolations of integrity.

Then, his elation waning, he wondered who those friends might be. He added up his friends. They totaled three. This astonished him. Surrounded most of his life by the familiar faces of his hometown, he'd naturally assumed that he lived among multitudes of friends, and so it came as a shock to realize there were only three people he knew well enough to ask for money. He could ask Arnold Ulm after he cooled down. Arnold Ulm had lent him the odd dollar in the past. He could ask Grover, and he'd get nothing, Grover being such a penny-pincher, but that made him no less a friend. And then, just as he was calling his third friend to mind, she walked in the door and took her customary place at the window.

Needing a dose of approval, he carried his cup to her table and told her the story of his morning. He explained everything except the part Imogene played in his motivation. He said he was broke until after New Year's.

"Here's your ten dollars in advance," said Agatha, counting out ones from her purse. "You can't eat on that for a week, I realize, but you're welcome to make meals in my kitchen while I'm away. My pantry's well-stocked."

"It seemed like the right thing to do," he said, fishing for a little more praise. "I couldn't go on lying like that."

"Of course it was right, Frederick. I'm very proud of you." She patted his hand, and he was twelve years old again.

13

THE PILGRIMAGE BEGAN BY car, with Father Finn at the wheel and Sylvester Juba sitting at his side trembling and coughing and criticizing the priest's manner of driving. Riding in the backseat were Agatha McGee and Lillian Kite. There were seven suitcases in the trunk and two more bound to the roof with ropes.

Ten miles out of Staggerford, urged by Sylvester to drive faster, the highway being clear of ice and snow, the priest reset his cruise control at a slightly higher speed. Five miles farther on, urged by Agatha to drive slower, certain stretches of this highway known to be narrow and dangerous, he brought his speed back down.

"We've got to hold her at sixty-five to make Rookery in two hours," instructed Sylvester Juba, throwing his voice over his shoulder at the women. "We can't be dawdling along and miss our plane."

"We've allowed ourselves sufficient time, haven't we, Father?"

"Plenty of time," the priest assured her.

"Then there's no need to risk our lives."

Sylvester spoke crossly. "You have to get there early to get a seat on the aisle. All of a sudden you need to pee, you want to be on the aisle."

"I'm afraid we may not have our choice of seats," cautioned Father Finn. "Sometimes with tour groups the seats are assigned ahead of time."

"Listen, at the price we're paying, we ought to be able to sit in the cockpit if we want to. If I'm not on the aisle, I'm not going."

If only, thought Agatha.

"If you're not on the aisle, we'll talk to my brother," advised the priest. "He can maybe get somebody to switch with you."

"Imogene always likes a window seat," said Lillian. "She carries an atlas with her, so she can tell the names of the rivers and towns."

"Such a fact-finder, your Imogene." This was the closest thing to a compliment Agatha could bring herself to apply to Lillian's daughter. She recalled Imogene as a sixth grader with an elongated body and a short temper, her nose in a book, her head full of memorized lists, her grades superb, her personality chilly. Now, turning forty, Imogene was still gawky and chilly and full of mostly useless information.

Agatha had spent Christmas Eve with Mother and Daughter Kite, an evening marked by Lillian's delicious halibut dinner and Imogene's lecture on Galileo—inclined planes, the heliocentric universe, the telescope. Imogene, having prepared for this tour of Italy as if she were going herself, had presented the two old friends with a paperback guide of Italy, instructing them what to look for at each stop. "Climb the Tower of Pisa and imagine Galileo experimenting with the velocity of falling objects," she told them. "At the History of Science Museum in Florence you'll see one of Galileo's fingers preserved under glass."

"One of his fingers?" Agatha and Lillian had exclaimed in unison.

"Yes, I kid you not, one of his fingers. Italians have this grisly habit of preserving human relics. Then when you're in Venice, you'll see the tower where Galileo demonstrated the telescope to the Doge. He showed him how it could pick out enemy ships farther off than the naked eye can see."

When Agatha reminded her that Venice wasn't on the tour, Imogene had been outraged. "You're not going to Venice? You have to go to Venice, that's where the telescope came into its own as a means of civil defense. It's fair to say Venice was the birthplace of modern technological warfare. You're not getting your money's worth if you're not going to Venice."

Lillian had chortled admiringly—her daughter was so brilliant—and deferred to Agatha for a reply.

"Galileo is not our primary interest, Imogene."

"But it's a Galileo tour."

"Galileo is our means of getting to Italy. Father Finn promises there will be a great deal more to it than science."

"Like what?"

"Why, art, architecture, cathedrals, hill towns, the Vatican, the Colosseum." Agatha quoted the promises Father Finn had made. "The Trevi Fountain, Michelangelo's *David*, Michelangelo's tomb, perhaps Assisi with its shrines of St. Francis and St. Clare. And of course the Mediterranean Sea."

Imogene looked pained. Imogene was a prober, a digger, a tireless follower of thin streams to their remote sources. Her tunnel vision kept her from taking in views as broad as Agatha described. There was perhaps no single thing in Agatha's list that Imogene was incapable of understanding and possibly even appreciating, but only if it remained just that—a single thing. In other words, she could not allow herself to take up the study of the Colosseum until she finished the books she had yet to read on Galileo.

But her intensely narrow focus was hardly a character flaw, and Agatha reminded herself that she must overlook it. Other features, however, were impossible to overlook. Imogene was nosy, pushy, and gruff. She was strident in her opinions. Moreover it annoyed Agatha, a student of inherited family traits, that Imogene should be so unlike her parents. Her mother was the easygoing type, her father had been a reticent man, and both of them had been good-looking in their youth and middle age. Imogene was tense, loud, and unattractive. Agatha, despite her conviction that physical appearance was no basis for judging people, seemed to have been born with an aversion to tall, horse-faced women with rough edges.

The highway wound through the Chippewa National Forest, and Agatha was struck as never before by the beauty of the snow-laden trees. Mile after mile she gazed with wonder at the sparkling, untrammeled snow where the morning sun fell across it, particularly where it contrasted with the deep blue snow lying in the shadows of the dark blue spruce. It was as though her aesthetic sense, sharpened for Italy, was putting itself through a trial run before leaving home. "Have you ever in your life seen anything so beautiful?" she asked.

Father Finn responded with a purr of appreciation, Sylvester

Juba said the forest ought to be opened up to lumbering—he'd spoken to Congressman Kleinschmidt about it—and Lillian, laying a hand on Agatha's arm and smiling blissfully, said, "I'll come home to a perfectly clean house. Imogene's going through it from top to bottom while I'm gone."

Agatha waited until the landscape became less attractive before responding. "You're lucky, Lillian, there's no telling what my house will look like with Frederick making his meals in my kitchen."

"Is he rooming with you again?" asked the priest.

"No, no, just taking a few meals until his unemployment check comes through. It was delayed for some reason."

"Why doesn't he make an honest living?" questioned Sylvester, who then supplied the answer. "He's lazy, that's why."

Agatha held her tongue.

"Dead wood," growled Sylvester. "Freeloaders like him ought to work or go hungry."

"French is not emotionally stable," explained the priest.

"Put him to work—that'll stabilize him." Sylvester was trembling quite noticeably. The loose flesh of his face rippled and wobbled, and his hands shook in his lap. His mid-morning dose of liquor would have brought this under control, but he'd promised his daughter and his pastor that he'd abstain for the duration of the trip.

"French is so nice," said Lillian. "I don't see why some woman doesn't marry him."

"Oh, my," said Agatha, fascinated by the thought. She'd never imagined Frederick Lopat married, and couldn't now imagine a suitable wife. "Who'd have him, Lillian?"

"Well, there must be some nice woman about his speed— you know, not too swift—who'd like to make him a nice home and give him a nice little baby or two."

"I don't know if he'd be a reliable father," said the priest.

"I'd worry about his being a good provider," said Agatha.

"My guess is he's a homo," said Sylvester.

Father Finn turned on the radio.

At the airport in Rookery, Father Finn turned his car over to a priest friend to keep in his garage for ten days. In the terminal, a gleaming new facility of varnished logs and red carpet, the Staggerford delegation was introduced to Professor Albert Finn, Ph.D. The professor's appearance, particularly his manner of dress, fell far short of Agatha's expectations. He was shorter and chunkier than his brother the priest. His gray hair had receded far back on his head, turning his brow into a wrinkled pink dome, and under his nose hung a ragged gray mustache. She thought it a scandal that he should be traveling to Europe in a purple sweatshirt and soiled tennis shoes. She knew him to be in his early fifties, younger than his brother, but he looked older—worn down like herself, she supposed, by his years in the classroom. He carried his clothes in an old GI duffle bag with A. FINN and a serial number stenciled on the side.

But despite his appearance and his getting her name wrong, Agatha was pleased to find him warm and solicitous. Warmer, in fact, than his brother, and quicker to smile. "I'm so pleased, Mrs. McKee, to have you along. I know, being the teacher you are, that you'll like my students—they're the cream of the crop."

"Miss McGee," she corrected him.

"Oh, pardon me, of course, Miss McKee. Now remember, I'm at your service throughout the tour. Let me know your needs and I'll do whatever I can."

"Mc*Gee*," she corrected him.

"McGee, of course, of course, I'll get it right yet. I knew a McKee family one time, and I guess the name stuck. Please let my students take care of your luggage—I've assigned two of them the job of getting our bags on and off planes and buses."

As the professor moved on to shake hands with Lillian, Agatha was approached by a blue denim jacket and earphones. "Tell me which are your bags, Miss McGee, and I'll take them over to the check-in counter. My name is Darrin."

Darrin was tall and lean, and Agatha thought him very handsome in a pale-skinned, blue-eyed, Scandinavian way. She asked him, "Is that Twisted Sister you're listening to?"

"The Doors," he said, removing his earphones. "Want to borrow them till the plane comes?"

"No, please spare me." She laughed, and was amazed to detect a trace of injury in his expression—was he completely without humor? "The black and the gray are mine," she said, pointing to her bags. "You're a godsend, the black one weighs tons."

They crossed to the ticket counter, where Agatha's request for a window seat near the front of the plane was honored, and Lillian's preference, the seat next to Agatha, was honored as well. These seats, they were told, would be theirs on both the short hop to Chicago and the connecting flight to Europe. With boarding passes in hand, both women were introduced to the other student aide, a dark-haired young woman named Trish.

"Did you people draw lots?" Agatha asked.

"No, we volunteered," Trish replied happily.

Darrin explained, "Dr. Finn says us who help you old folks don't have to do the Galileo paper he's assigning the rest of the class."

"Darrin, shut up," ordered Trish. "You aren't supposed to tell them that."

"Don't worry, I understand," Agatha assured her. "In my own college days I abhorred writing papers."

"You went to college?" asked Darrin.

"I did."

"Wow," he said softly.

A flash camera lit up the terminal as Congressman Myron Kleinschmidt arrived, looking polished and jolly. He was here not to fly with the group, but to make a public display of seeing them off. He had alerted the news-starved editor of the *Rookery Morning Call*, who had sent a cameraman and a reporter. Gathering the Galileo group around him, and standing between the priest and the professor, he answered at length all the questions he told the reporter to ask; then he delivered a convoluted statement on pending tax legislation. Following that, he posed for several photos, his arm draped first over the priest's shoulders, next over the professor's, and finally there was a shot of him standing amidst the ten students.

When the posing was over, he shook Agatha's hand and wished her safe passage. "Promise you'll say a prayer for me at St. Peter's."

"Don't worry, you're on my list, you and Elena."

His expression suddenly darkened. "Why, what have you heard?"

"About what?"

"Me and Elena."

"Nothing," she said, reading trouble in his scowl.

He brightened, but not enough to dispel her suspicions. "That's fine, then. Pray for us both. We can always use your prayers, Agatha. You're one of Elena's favorite people—she's often told me so—and of course you know where you stand with me. I've decided that you're definitely my choice to run my campaign office."

They were interrupted by Trish, who thought Myron was joining the tour group. She introduced herself and asked, "Are you interested in Galileo?"

"Yes, indeed, a giant in his field," said Myron; then he fled across the terminal to shake hands with a group of travelers arriving on a flight from Fargo.

Trish turned to Agatha. "Are you interested in Galileo?"

"Only vaguely."

"I know, I couldn't care less. My parents said I should go. I won't get many chances to go overseas once I graduate. I'll be taking over my parents' restaurant."

"And where is that?"

"Minneapolis. Corelli's on Nicollet. Maybe you've heard of it."

"I've eaten there."

"Oh, you have?" Trish squealed.

"During a teacher's convention a number of years ago."

"Oh, that is so *neat.*"

Darrin returned to Trish's side, and Agatha asked him, "And your parents—where do they live?"

Darrin removed his Walkman from his shirt pocket and reduced the volume. "Huh?"

"Tell me about your parents."

"They live in Bemidji. My dad's a doctor."

"And your mother?"

He shrugged. "She's just my mother."

"Are you interested in Galileo?" she asked.

He pondered the question a moment, then said, "Who?"

They rose into the blue sky over Rookery and descended into the clouds over Chicago, where their scheduled two-hour

layover, despite the complaints to airline officials by Sylvester
Juba, grew to nearly four hours. Agatha passed part of the time
discussing American education with the professor, whose dim
view of the future corresponded with her own, but whose reaction to it was far different. Instead of taking up arms against
the powers of darkness, Professor Finn had decided not to resist. This became apparent when she challenged him on the
question of student papers. "Don't get me wrong, Dr. Finn, I
appreciate Trish and Darrin's help—it comes as a pleasant
surprise—but why in the world does that excuse them from
writing the course paper?"

The professor wearily rubbed his eyes. "It's Christmas, Miss
McGee. Waiving the course paper is my gift to the less ambitious among my students."

"It's no gift whatsoever. By lowering standards you cheat
them out of learning."

"Ah, Miss McGee, I've conducted this tour seven times,
and I assure you they'll learn more in Italy by simple osmosis
than they will by writing papers."

"Then why assign papers to the others?" She distrusted osmosis as an educational method.

"The others feel as you do—short-changed without doing
papers." He smoothed down his wiry mustache with the fingertips of both hands. "But to tell the truth, I dread reading them.
I've seen far too many student papers in my day. I've lost any
eagerness I had for correcting them."

"Well, I'm not telling you how to teach, Professor, but I always found that whenever I helped my students with their
early drafts, there wasn't much in the final draft that needed
correcting."

Professor Finn's laugh was a cackle. "Miss McGee, if I
can't stand to read the final draft, how could I possibly stand
to read the earlier ones?"

A look of wistful pleasure came into her eyes. "Oh, but to
be in on the paper from the start, Dr. Finn—that's where the
real satisfaction lies. Helping students order their thoughts, witnessing their discoveries . . ." She was picturing her sixth graders as they filled their notebooks with observations on any
number of topics—the weather, current events, birds, family
history—and then, under her direction, shaped their conclu-

sions to fit a tightly written essay. She recalled from nearly forty years ago Myron Kleinschmidt engrossed in a paper on the Truman-Dewey election. From twenty-five years ago Imogene Kite's exhaustive study of the gypsy moth came to mind.

"If you honestly believe that, Miss McGee . . ." The professor lifted his shaggy eyebrows expectantly. "Then maybe you wouldn't mind terribly if my students came to you for help with their first draft. They're supposed to be writing as they travel."

"I'd be honored."

At this point the professor was called away by his brother the priest. Agatha watched the two of them conferring next to a bank of telephones; then she saw the professor place a call. While he spoke on the phone, she saw Father Finn directing his gaze at a row of seats facing a wall of windows, and there she saw Sylvester Juba, silhouetted against the light. He sat with his chin on his chest, his eyes closed, his coat collar turned up around his ears. He was shaking violently. Was he sick? Angry? Demented? Should she go and investigate? She rose from her seat, but then hesitated. Aiding Sylvester was a risk. He'd take her help as a sign of her love. He'd give a romantic twist to anything tender she said. It was alarming to think of the trail of difficulties this obtuse boor was bound to leave in his wake from here to Rome and back. Sister Judith should have foreseen this, should have insisted he stay home.

Agatha sat down next to Lillian and said, "What's going on with Sylvester?"

Lillian looked up from a newspaper with an enormous photo of Elvis on the front page under the headline, SPOTTED IN THE ROCKIES.

"Over there." Agatha tipped her head.

Lillian took off her reading glasses and squinted against the light.

They watched the professor hurry from the phone to a seat beside Sylvester. Both brothers spoke to him, making earnest gestures. Then Father Finn went to a phone and dialed a number, apparently from memory. When he finished his call, they coaxed Sylvester to his feet. The three men approached

Agatha and Lillian. There was something almost ceremonious in their formation, in their deliberate pace.

"Agatha," said Sylvester, coming to a halt before her, "I need to tell you something." He seemed dazed, washed out, palsied.

She stood up and led him to an empty row of seats. "You're not looking your best, Sylvester. What's wrong?"

He sank to a seat and sighed. "I'm turning back before I get any farther from home. There's a return flight leaving soon." He took a few deep, sour breaths, then continued. "They got me a refund on my ticket to Italy. Not a total refund, but most of it. They called Judy, and she's driving to Rookery to meet my plane. I have to tell you something, Agatha, before we part company. I'm not really sick, I'm just feeling sick, if you know what I mean."

Agatha said she didn't.

"I mean my head and my stomach feel sick but I'm not really sick. It's just that I don't feel good enough to fly all the way to Rome, and when I get there, who would my doctor be? Some wop."

"Is it the flu?"

"It's not the flu, it's just a sick feeling. But that's not what I want to tell you. What I want to tell you is this. I want you to take this time away from home to think about us getting married."

Agatha sighed. Her shoulders slumped.

"I mean, Judy will be leaving home pretty soon, and we're each of us living in a goddamn ark, and doesn't it make perfect sense to get married and cut our expenses?"

She said nothing.

"That way we could feel like we belong to somebody instead of being at loose ends." She saw an anguished expression cross his face, saw it quickly replaced by a calculating look. "When it comes to stocks and bonds, I've got more to offer than any man in Staggerford. You'd be on easy street."

"You look terribly sick, Sylvester—what is it?"

"You'll outlive me, Agatha. My arteries are full of gunk and my ticker could stop any time. I've bought my coffin already. You'd be my well-off widow."

"Is it your heart? Maybe we should call a doctor right here and now."

"It's not my heart, it's just a sick feeling. What I'm saying is this: Go to Rome, think it over, pray about it. Then come home with your answer." Through all this he had not been looking her directly in the eye—his eyes had been moving between the buttons on her coat and the snowflakes flying past the wall of glass—but now he trained his bloodshot gaze on her face and said, with emotion, "I really wanted to go with you, Agatha. I wanted to be there when you saw the Pope."

She was moved to pity, his flaccid countenance so pasty and unhealthy-looking, his breath imbued with the stale aroma of yesterday's spirits, his acute loneliness apparent in his weak, watery eyes. Examining his face for traces of his former self, she saw nothing of the younger Sylvester Juba. How was it possible that this palsied old misfit could have swallowed up the shrewd and confident man who used to manage Juba Lumber? Did even one cell or corpuscle of the handsome, blue-eyed ladies' man of generation ago still exist inside this wasted hulk?

"You've always been a better Catholic than me, Agatha, and I thought if the Pope saw me and you together . . . he'd think I was a better man than I am."

She was further moved by his simple eloquence. She put her hand out to him, patted his arm. She'd never before heard him admit to any sort of inferiority. "I'll pray for you at St. Peter's, Sylvester."

"I wanted to be included in the blessing he gives you."

"You will be." She patted his sleeve. "You'll be there in spirit." She rose to her feet, and Professor Finn came forward.

Watching them move away down the concourse, she put a question to Father Finn. "Is he really sick, or has he just lost his nerve?"

"Both," said the priest. "He's sick for lack of liquor, and he's lost his nerve for the same reason."

"Is that why he's shaking—lack of liquor?"

The priest nodded. "I told him he couldn't travel with us if he continued to drink, and he promised to stay dry throughout."

"The poor man—he's an addict?"

"Surely you knew that."

"Isn't it curious? I never once thought of him as an alcoholic. How could I *not* have known?"

Father Finn's reply was lost under an amplified voice calling for passengers to Rome to begin boarding. With a final glance down the concourse, Agatha and the priest saw Professor Finn hurrying back to the gate area, and saw, behind him, Sylvester disappear into a doorway labeled BAR.

"How pitiful," she said, though she felt her pity fading.

"A shame," the priest agreed.

Replacing her pity, she realized, was a vast sense of relief.

14

F R E N C H ,   M E A N W H I L E ,   L A Y   O N Miss McGee's couch wishing she owned a remote device for switching channels. Sated with soap operas, he was ready for a game show or two, but too indolent to rise up from under her warm, forest-green afghan. He had arrived at noon, brought in the mail, watered the plants, and prepared himself a larger lunch than he'd eaten in ages—a glass of prune juice, a glass of orange juice, a plate of ravioli from a can, three slices of toast, a dish of sherbet, two cookies, and several cups of coffee. Twice during the afternoon the phone had rung, and he'd let it go on ringing until the caller got the message—Miss McGee wasn't home.

Now it rang again, and he wondered if it might be Grover trying to reach him with a message. He tried to imagine the message, and failed. He never got messages. Next he imagined Miss McGee calling from an airport somewhere with a last-minute bit of instruction. This possibility drew him up off the couch and into the kitchen. He picked up the phone on the seventh or eighth ring and said hello.

"French, what's up?" A woman's voice.

"Not much. Who's this?"

"Imogene."

"Oh, hi, Imogene." His voice went small and tight. For all his plans concerning Imogene, he felt suddenly defensive and afraid.

"So what are you doing?"

"Not much. Watching television."

"You moved in over there, or what?"

"No—just, you know, watching television."

"So would you like to come over for supper?"

His first impulse was to say no. So was his second. Stalling, he said, "You mean over there?"

"Over here, with me."

A long pause. "What are you having?"

"Good Christ, what kind of a question is that? What are you, on a diet?"

Her tone was harsh, and he hung up in self-defense. He'd forgotten how hard-edged Imogene could be. He left the kitchen in a state of nerves, convinced all over again that lying low was the best policy. He'd been lying low for ten years, avoiding engagements with people who threatened to complicate the simple routine of his days. Lying low was his habit and his salvation. He switched channels, returned to the couch and tried to recover his tranquility by giving himself up to "Jeopardy!"

The phone rang again, but he didn't get up. How could he possibly eat a meal with someone as abrasive as Imogene? What a lucky thing he hadn't got his unemployment check and squandered it on a date. He let the phone ring eighteen times.

A few minutes later he heard a pounding on the back door. He couldn't very well pretend he wasn't in the house; she knew he was. She'd come around the house and peer in the front window; she was that type. Getting to his feet, he wished he'd given her a definite no on the phone. Now he'd have to say no to her face.

He unlocked the kitchen door and the porch door and found her standing on the back step wearing a thick blue coat fastened with frogs and a pink knit scarf wound tightly around her neck. He was struck by how old she looked. The years seemed to have lengthened and coarsened her face. Meeting her on the street, he might not have immediately recognized her.

"Hi, Imogene."

"So what do you like, steak?"

"Well . . ." He stalled. He was fascinated by her looks. He hadn't remembered her nose this long, nor her eyes this big. In her senior yearbook she had been called Joan Crawford's double (extravagant high school flattery), and now, twenty-five years later, she was aging the way Joan Crawford had—the eyes larger, the expression more defiant and threatening. But her mouth was exactly the same as before—a small slit of a mouth above a shallow chin. Her forehead, too, was the same—very high because that's where her brains were.

"Listen, you're alone, I'm alone, it's Christmastime, what the hell." She was standing two steps below him. He felt her eyes running up and down his legs. "I'm on my way to the store, so tell me what you like." Her eyes climbed up to his ribs and made him feel ticklish. "I mean, I'm not buying steak if you're allergic to beef or you've lost your teeth or anything like that."

He laughed, exposing his teeth and opening the split in his lower lip. Intending to say no, he said, "Steak is fine." He'd truly love a steak dinner. When had he last eaten steak?

"Well, aren't you going to ask me in?" She came up the two steps, forcing him back into the porch.

"You said you were going downtown."

"I said I was on my *way* downtown. I can come in for a minute." She brushed past him into the kitchen and kicked off her boots. "God, some things never change. No dishwasher, no microwave, this is the same stove and fridge she's had all her life." Her tone was full of disdain. "Look, the same Infant of Prague." She picked a statuette off the shelf over the sink and held it out to French, who had followed her in without closing the doors. "This little fellow's been watching Nails McGee wash dishes ever since I was a little girl. And look at that single-slice toaster, would you. God, this house is prehistoric." She put down the statuette and opened and closed several cupboard doors. "This time of the afternoon I like a jolt. Where does she keep her booze, do you know?"

"No," chirped French, tight with apprehension, alarmed by her lack of respect for Agatha's property. He stood by the open door, shivering, hoping she'd get the hint.

"My mother keeps brandy and beer on hand, but I can't stand either one. Maybe I'll pick up a bottle downtown—what do you like?"

"Look, Imogene. I ate a big lunch. Maybe some other time."

"Would you close the door? It's cold."

"I mean, I don't know, I don't think I can handle a steak dinner. I ate this big lunch."

She turned to face him. Leaning back against the counter,

her hands thrust deep in the pockets of her coat, she said, "Close the door, would you?"

He closed the door.

She smiled one of her rare little smiles. "French, how you been?"

"Not too shabby."

"My mother said you were asking about me."

"Yeah."

"Well, I figure any man bothers to ask about me, I better follow up. Are you dating anybody these days?"

The question made him smile, which further opened his split lip.

"What's so funny?" she asked.

Wasn't it obvious? Couldn't she tell by looking at him that he was utterly undatable? He said, "How about you? Not dating anybody?"

She tried to look coy, but she wasn't very good at it. "Wouldn't you like to know."

Actually he wouldn't. He'd inquired only to fend off her inquiries. He cleared his throat and said, "I suppose in the city . . ." He let his voice trail off, allowing her to finish the sentence if she wished, for he had no idea where it was going.

"In the city . . ." she repeated softly, and he saw her eyes shift away from him, her attention turn inward. He touched his lip and examined his finger for blood. No blood. He drew his lip into his mouth and softened it with his tongue as he waited for her to come back from her thoughts.

"So what's it like living here all this time?" she asked.

"I don't live here. I live at the Morgan."

"I mean in Staggerford."

He shrugged. "It's a town."

She smiled. "I see you in the summer sometimes, on that bench at the tourist center."

He nodded. "It's a job."

"How long you been an Indian?"

"Eight years."

"It was ten years ago I moved away."

He nodded again, calling to mind her replacement at the public library, a short, wide woman named Lucy Kopka, who kept the library somewhat less organized and less quiet than

Imogene had, but whose agreeable nature (said Agatha, who served on the library board) made it a much more inviting place than before, a more comfortable place to browse.

"You went to Berrington," said French.

"Six years in Berrington, then this job in St. Paul opened up."

"How is it?"

"It's a good job."

"How do you like St. Paul?"

"It's a good town. You know, bigger. I guess I'm a city woman at heart."

In the living room, "Jeopardy!" had given way to another game show. They heard the cries of the ecstatic host. Imogene's smile turned sardonic. "Am I keeping you from something?"

"No," he said, feeling less jittery. He wondered if he should reveal Miss McGee's stash of bottles. Having earned two of Imogene's smiles in quick succession, and having proved he could talk to her without seizing up, he began to relax. He decided he liked her looks. Her face was not beautiful by magazine standards (he'd studied thousands of women in magazines), nor perhaps by standards lower than that, but by French's standards she was far from ugly. Something saved her. Certainly not her mouth, set in that cynical crimp. Probably not her eyes—they were cold. Maybe it was her brown hair, which stood out fluffily all around her face. Or maybe her voice. He liked her voice. It was sultry. "What do you drink?" he asked.

"Scotch."

He chuckled. "So does a nun I know."

"What's that supposed to mean?"

"Nothing." He led her into the dining room, where he lifted two bottles from the buffet. "Sister Judith likes scotch."

"Judy Juba, God, what a ditz."

"Weird all right."

"Mother tells me you and Judy were here for Thanksgiving."

"Seven of us," he replied, lest she think of them as a couple.

"Must have been a barrel of fun."

In the kitchen, Imogene popped ice cubes out of a freezer tray while French found glasses and poured brandy for himself, scotch for Imogene. He added a tiny splash of water to each glass. Imogene took off her coat and scarf and draped them over a chair.

"Cheers," she said, taking her glass from him.

"Cheers."

Standing in the kitchen, they sipped, savored, examined their drinks, and sipped again. He stole glances at her, sizing her up. She was wearing a green sweater with white, horizontal zigzags and a calf-length brown skirt. She'd filled out, but she still had a waist. He liked a woman to be fleshy like this where she ought to be fleshy, and trim where she ought to be trim. She had good ankles. The hands were awfully large.

"I got away from that sort of thing," said Imogene. "That's why I moved."

"What sort of thing?"

"Thanksgiving dinners with Agatha McGee. I mean I could see myself becoming an old lady along with her and my mother, and then replacing them when they die." She sat down at the table and splayed out her big hands, studying her short, uncolored nails. "Like Judy Juba. God, can you imagine living with that doddering old lump of a father of hers, and having nothing to liven up your days except a wake now and then to lead prayers at?" She turned her eyes on French. "Sit down, why don't you?"

Quickly and obediently, he hiked himself up and sat on the counter, in front of the toaster.

"Here, at the table," she said.

"This is okay." He needed distance between himself and those large, splayed-out hands. "Sister Judith's being transferred when her year's up."

"Where to?" she asked.

"Who knows?"

"Some other dump." She drank and smacked her lips the way her mother did. She said, "Thank God I saw the writing on the wall when there were still jobs out there. Think of it, I could still be rotting away as Staggerford's librarian."

Staggerford's Indian felt a twinge of resentment. "It's not a bad town."

She laughed a low bubbly laugh that changed her expression only enough to give him a glimpse of her teeth. They were much better formed than he remembered. She'd obviously had some work done.

"French, honestly, are you settled in here for life? I mean the Morgan, the tourist center—that's it?"

He hunched his shoulders, hung his head, gazed at his dangling feet. "Why? What would I want any different?"

She was silent for a long time then, examining him, evaluating him as a reclamation project. Should she go to work on him or forget him? He wouldn't be easy. His hangdog posture, for one thing. His ill-fitting clothes. His habit of tilting his head to the side, which gave him a slightly deformed look.

And what would be her reward for taking him on? There was no guarantee he'd warm up to her. Did a man like French even have a sex drive? That's what she was here to find out. And if he did, two hundred miles, one way, was a killing distance to drive on weekends, even for making love. And where would they do it? Not at the Morgan. She couldn't imagine taking off her clothes in that seedy dump.

French raised his eyes from his dangling moccasins and found Imogene studying him. This gave him the jitters. He turned his gaze out the kitchen window, afraid of being analyzed. What was she finding? Could she tell he liked her and didn't like her at the same time? Did she know that he liked having a woman in the house with him, but not one who stared at him as if he were a freak? Could she sense how much he wanted—and how scared he was—to touch her? Did she have sex in mind? Did a woman like Imogene even have a sex drive?

He downed his drink and without a word left the kitchen. He expected her to follow him into the living room, and was relieved when she didn't. He modified the sound on the TV and sat down on the couch. After a few minutes he began to wish she'd join him. What was she doing out there?

Sitting alone in the kitchen, Imogene was sipping her drink and absently going through Agatha's recipe box while she pondered her own unhappiness. Most of the cards were toasty brown with age, written in various hands. Tollhouse cookies. Shepherd's pie. Marble cake. She recognized her mother's penmanship on several of the cards. She imagined herself moving back home and exchanging recipes with Agatha and other old friends of her mother's. This caused her spirit to sink, her stomach to cramp with fear. Was this her only alternative to staying in St. Paul, this sterile life of the village crone?

For Imogene was extremely unhappy in St. Paul. Never mind her brave talk about being a city woman, she missed this town of two banks, one zip code, and no parking meters. For the first thirty years of her life Staggerford had been her course of study, its gossip her textbook. You couldn't just pull up stakes and put all this out of your mind. You had to somehow find out what the next chapter of gossip revealed—who went broke, who gave birth, who died of what. St. Paul was discouragingly full of people she had no knowledge of.

Jell-O salads. Chicken teriyaki. Peach delight. If only she could be Staggerford's librarian again—only this time married. Working here, she used to imagine the man of her dreams pulling up in front of the Staggerford library in an expensive car and coming in to research some local facts—say he was a realtor in need of a plat book from years gone by—and she would help him and win his love and marry him and have his baby. He was a tall, lean man with a certain amount of sophistication and a certain amount of money, he wore suits and fashionable neckties, and he was satisfied to move to Staggerford and live here for the rest of his life.

Breaded meatballs. Soufflé. Corned beef and cabbage. French was tall and lean like the man of her dreams, and he had no ambitions outside of Staggerford, but there the similarities ended. French had gone into decline. She pictured the French of fifteen years ago. She was watching *Bonnie and Clyde* with him at the Orpheum. Already, at twenty-nine, she was Staggerford's head librarian, a job she'd won through persistent prayer and argumentation, the prayers having been said by her mother and the nuns of St. Isidore's, and the argumentation having been carried on by Imogene herself at the meetings of the library board she sat in on. Agatha McGee, who chaired the board in those days, couldn't very well turn her down, Imogene's mother being her closest friend, and the board never had reason to regret the appointment. In time even Agatha, never her champion, had to admit to Imogene that she had most of the skills they'd been looking for; she was frugal, organized, and had a nose for primary sources.

Imogene had taken French on as her stop-gap boyfriend until the man of her dreams showed up. They went to a few movies, took a few walks, had a few drinks. French worked at the feed mill in those days and expected to be drafted. She remembered hoping that the blood and sex of *Bonnie and Clyde* would arouse French to make a few aggressive moves in her car after the movie, but it never happened. Indeed, he acted as though he disapproved of her own aggressive moves. So, over the years, did other men.

After half a dozen dates French disappeared into the armed forces. Imogene didn't miss him. What was there to miss? He was a slow starter in love, as in most other things, and the language of intimacy, like the physical aspects of intimacy, seemed far beyond him. A year passed before she wrote to him.

Her first letter, a duplication of several others she sent to Staggerford's servicemen, was prompted by an article she'd read on soldiering and the importance of support from the home front. Her second letter, not a duplication, was prompted by the frightening suspicion that the man of her dreams might have driven through town without stopping, might have missed his opportunity to save her from being an old maid. No man in a suit ever stepped out of a sleek new car and came into the library looking for a plat book. No man in any attire at all, for that matter, gave her the time of day. She made eyes at Miles Pruitt, the high school teacher who roomed at Agatha's, but he was even less responsive than French had been. Which was just as well. For one thing, Miles Pruitt didn't conform to her ideal. He was overweight, he often failed to pay attention when she explained things, and he was quicker of mind than she was. (She liked her men a little on the dumb side.) And for another thing, he was eventually shot to death by a deranged person. In retrospect, French seemed worth a second look.

When French didn't answer either letter, she'd felt vaguely injured. She wrote once more, at length, and once more received no reply. That was when an emotion entirely unfamiliar to Imogene began tugging at her heartstrings—desperation. To remain in Staggerford was to assign herself to certain spinsterhood. She began reading the employment notices in her library newsletter, and when the top job opened up in Berrington (six times the population of Staggerford, forty-eight percent of it male), she sent off her application, set her mother and the two or three nuns left at St. Isidore's to praying novenas, and made a nuisance of herself at meetings of the Berrington library board until she was hired.

Her career in Berrington was difficult because she was head librarian in name only, not in fact. The true boss was the chairwoman of the board, Mrs. Wilber Steegman, who came in every day and snooped and meddled and told Imogene what to do. Following orders had never been Imogene's strongest suit, and she fumed in silence, repressing her resentment while she weighed her alternatives. She concluded that the state department of education was her best bet. State jobs paid well, and the population of St. Paul was twelve times that of Berrington, fifty-two percent of it male. During her third year in Berrington, a state position opened up and she applied. By this time Sister Judith, not known for her piety, was the lone nun left at St. Isidore's, so Imogene's mother recruited Agatha and a few other friends to do the praying, and Imogene was hired.

In St. Paul, Imogene dated a lawyer named John Koozer, a descendant of the famous flour-milling Koozers, and for a time she entertained dreams of being his wife, but she soon came to understand what a full-time job that would be. John Koozer liked her to listen when he talked, and he talked all the time, even when sober, which wasn't all that often.

There was another man with whom, to this day, she regularly ate lunch in the cafeteria of her office building, an accountant named Malory. She liked Malory for his slow and turgid brain waves, and it was obvious that he liked her for the way she could open up a topic at 12:03 and worry it nonstop until 12:28, when they went back to work. He was one of those rare creatures who liked being lectured. Each noon she singled him out for instruction, and each noon he stayed the course. The partition of nations in the Middle East. The keyboard functions of her office computer. The life cycle of the gypsy moth.

Imogene closed the lid of Agatha's recipe box. She looked around the kitchen and sighed, wishing Accountant Malory had some sex appeal. He was short, pale, and paunchy. He had pudgy little fingers. His eyes held no mystery, promised no passion. Imogene was starved for passion.

She finished her drink. Standing up and putting on her coat and scarf, she regretted not taking the entire week off from work. Other years, two days of vacation at Christmas was about all she could handle, what with her mother having such an incurious mind, and Agatha McGee being in and out of the house all day, and Imogene's friends (what few she'd had) all wrapped up in their children. Today, however, with her mother and Agatha overseas and French back in her life, she regretted having to drive back to St. Paul tomorrow. It might take longer than one night to get French interested in passion.

"Hey, French," she called, "I'll see you at my place at six?" He mumbled something, and she went into the living room and asked, "How do you like your steak?"

"I'm not all that hungry, Imogene."

She sat down next to him on the couch. "Look, I'm cooking steak no matter what, so you might as well join me."

He was watching a cartoon with the sound off. She took his hand. He quickly withdrew it.

"We could eat here," she said, realizing he'd be hard to move across the alley. "How about if we eat here?"

He shrugged.

"We'll eat here."

She kissed him lightly on the cheek and hurried away.

15

IMOGENE GUNNED THE ENGINE of her black, almond-shaped car, let out the clutch, and fishtailed down the icy alley. She followed River Street toward the business district, driving slowly, enjoying the view. It was dusk now. On her right the Badbattle was dark and light in irregular masses like the hide of a Holstein—black in the swift places where it hadn't yet frozen, white with snow-covered ice. The tree line along the far bank was purplish-black against the dying pink light in the sky. On her left warm lamplight glowed in the windows of the houses belonging to the Wempners, the Koenigs, the Simpsons, and the Jacobsons. Blinking Christmas lights were draped in trees and strung along rooflines. In front of the hospital a spotlighted company of life-size figures in garish robes—Mary, Joseph, and the Wise Men—were gathered in the snow and gazing down into the snow-filled manger. Imogene was charmed. She turned up the radio and sang along with Karen Carpenter. She could not remember, ever in her life, being quite this happy. Never mind her government job, never mind St. Paul—Staggerford was home.

She came to the stoplight and stopped. Main Street, though brightly lit, was quiet and nearly deserted, the seasonal music and the shopping frenzy having been switched off when the last store closed on Christmas Eve. But plastic Santas still smiled cheerily down from the lampposts, and a light still burned in the window of Buckingham Furniture, where the annual Dickens display was featured. This year it was the Cratchit family and guests approaching the table for Christmas dinner. Bob Cratchit, despite his tall, crooked hat and his threadbare vest, couldn't help resembling the robust and handsome mannequin he was. Tiny Tim, too, had a hearty, well-to-do American look about him. The figures, Imogene knew, had been borrowed from Marsha's Ready-to-Wear next door. She'd last seen Mrs. Cratchit in Marsha's window in August, wearing a Spandex biking outfit. Scrooge was a six-foot cardboard cutout loaned by the Orpheum.

Imogene, pulling slowly away from the stoplight, moved her thoughts along the byways of Staggerford lore. She recognized the Dickens display as the work of the vocationally frustrated Mrs. Daniel Buckingham, Jr., who'd left behind a budding career as a set designer in Minneapolis when she moved to town to marry the furniture scion. One of her children, now a rather homely nine-year-old, had been born in Staggerford Hospital on the same New Year's morning that Agatha McGee's godson, Stephen Meers, was born. Randy Meers, Stephen's stepfather, was handling the sale of Marsha's Ready-to-Wear, Marsha having decided, due to gradually declining health, to close out her gradually declining business and move to Florida, where her daughter lived. Marsha's daughter was married to Lloyd Druppers, son of Theodore Druppers, the man who owned the grocery store which Imogene, having made a U-turn in the middle of the block, was now parking in front of.

This was typical of the way Imogene's mind worked when she applied her prodigious memory to what she heard from her mother and what she read in the *Weekly*. To Imogene, every piece of hometown news was a jigsaw piece to be studied, turned this way and that, and finally pressed into the puzzle of Staggerford history. These pieces came in all sizes—but none bigger than the one she was offered by Theodore Druppers.

"Lucky you caught me, I was about to lock up," said the storekeeper from behind his meat counter, rolling up a slab of round steak and wrapping it in paper. "Your mother get off all right?"

"Quarter to nine this morning," replied Imogene.

Sealing the paper with tape, he said, "Surprising about Agatha, wouldn't you say?"

"Good for her to get away."

"But good for her to get engaged?"

Imogene cried out: "What's that?"

"Sylvester Juba."

Louder: "Go on."

Druppers nodded sagely, handing her package across the meat counter. "I know of only one other case like it—Mavis Larson, remember? Fell in love in her old age and got herself in a hell of a mess."

"Mavis Larson was off her rocker. What are you saying about Agatha?"

"You haven't heard? Her and Sylvester?"

"Sylvester Juba asked her to marry him last June on the steps of the church, and she told him to buzz off. If that's what you're talking about, it's water over the dam."

"Yeah, well, he was in here the other day saying the offer's still open, and their trip to Europe is for the purpose of trying each other out." The butcher made a snorting sound.

Imogene's tone was fierce. "Good God, since when did you start believing Sylvester Juba? That broken-down masher's off his rocker."

Theodore Druppers smiled his unhurried smile, confident of his evidence. "Think about it, Imogene. Would she go to Italy with Sylvester if she was trying to put him off?"

"She's going to Italy with a group."

"A group, yes, but a group that includes Sylvester. Remember, this is Agatha McGee we're talking about. Would she go to Italy"—he said it slower this time—"with the man she was trying to put off?"

Imogene pursed her lips and thought about it.

"Agatha's always been one to analyze how things look," Druppers continued. "If Agatha was determined to put Sylvester off, wouldn't she make that clear by dropping out as soon as he signed on? And so isn't her staying with the trip a kind of statement? Doesn't it say she's allowing Sylvester some room to hope?"

She frowned.

"Now I'm not saying they'll ever get as far as the altar, mind you. I'm just saying she hasn't a hundred percent told him to go to hell."

Imogene wrinkled her nose at the butcher and carried her meat to the checkout counter. Druppers followed her, his checkout girl having checked out for the day, and rang up the sale.

"How long you home for, Imogene?"

"Go back tomorrow."

"Got yourself a boyfriend in the city, have you?"

"Wouldn't you like to know."

Same old Imogene, thought the storekeeper as she swished out the door. Same unfriendly cluck.

He watched her get into her low, black car, and after she'd driven away, he switched off the lights in his window and stood for a minute gazing absently across the street at the Bob Cratchit family, wondering who Imogene was feeding with all that meat.

They prepared the meal together in Agatha's kitchen. French peeled the potatoes, and Imogene fried them with onions. French tore apart lettuce for the salad while Imogene set the table in the dining room, using Agatha's best china. Both of them stood at the oven, peering hungrily at the broiling steak, and when it was ready to eat, Imogene carried their plates to the table and lit Agatha's candles while French poured out two glasses of Agatha's chokecherry wine. French, a quick eater, was already chewing his first bite when Imogene asked, "Don't you say grace?"

"Not usually."

"We'll say grace," she declared, blessing herself. He did not pray along with her, but stopped chewing, out of respect. Her "Amen" was followed by, "Put your napkin in your lap."

He did so and asked, with sarcasm, "Anything else?"

"Honestly, you men," she said.

"What men?"

"Men in general. If it wasn't for women, men would be totally uncivilized."

Eating diligently, French pictured the Morgan, which had no women in residence. True, Grover had bad breath and a few favorite curse words, and some of the traveling sales reps told dirty jokes, but you could hardly call the Morgan uncivilized. Would life in the lobby be more refined if women lived there? Less dusty, maybe—women were good at housekeeping. And certainly less quiet, women being the more fluent half of the human race. Maybe that's how you identified a civilized society, by its noise and clean surfaces.

Imogene, determined to teach by example, sat up straighter

and chewed more slowly than normal. "What did you do Christmas, French? I hope you enjoyed yourself more than I did."

"Why, what did you do?"

"I spent Christmas Eve with my mother and Agatha, and Christmas Day with my mother and Elsie Olson and the Curry sisters, and I don't know which was worse. Yes, I do. Christmas Day was worse. At least with Nails McGee you can have a conversation—you can have one, that is, if you're careful what you talk about—but Elsie Olson and the Curry sisters are all three of them deaf as posts and they keep fiddling with their hearing aids and don't pay the least bit of attention to what you're saying, and when they come out with something themselves, it's about their ailments or their pensions. Three hours of arthritis and social security over Christmas dinner—it was the pits. How did *you* spend Christmas?"

"I stayed home."

"Home? At the Morgan?"

He nodded.

"God," she said, picturing the narrow, three-story building of dark brick, the curtainless windows, the cavernous lobby. "Dismal."

"Not so bad. Grover was there."

She pictured the fusty desk clerk. "Grover's dismal."

"Grover's not so bad."

"What did you do?"

"There was a football game on."

"What about dinner?"

"Dinner?" It took him a moment to remember. "I had dinner in my room."

"With Grover?"

"No, Grover went out. He's got a brother out in the country."

Imogene looked awestruck. "You were all alone for Christmas dinner?"

He nodded.

"What did you have?"

"Sardines."

"God, sardines." She whooped with laughter.

Her glee made him smile. "And crackers," he added, hoping to add to her amusement.

"God, crackers," she said, her laughter subsiding. "What else?"

"Tea," he said happily. He considered telling her that the tea bag had been used before—his privations obviously delighted her so—but he withheld this fact lest he seem to be asking for sympathy.

"Tea and sardines? What else?

"That's it, I guess."

"You're kidding."

"No, I think that was all."

Leaning to her left, she frowned at him sternly around the candles. "French, what is it that makes you deprive yourself that way, stay in that firetrap, live like a mouse in a hole? It's Vietnam, isn't it? It's your post-trauma shock syndrome. Well, I've got news for you, French, it's treatable. It's an illness, and you have to see a doctor because it's treatable."

Her strident tone caused the bottom to drop out of his happiness. He stopped eating. With his fork he moved his food around on his plate. "No," he mumbled, "I'm okay."

"It's an illness," she insisted. "Nobody's okay who eats sardines in his room for Christmas dinner."

"That wasn't illness—that was being broke."

"Being broke means you're not working, and not working is one of your post-trauma symptoms."

He was slow to respond. When he did, he was sorry that his defense should sound so weak. "I work summers."

"Work year-round," she shot back. "That's what normal people do."

To be labeled abnormal by Imogene made him enormously sad. French put down his fork, turned his head away and sighed.

Sensing his unease, she felt very strong and useful—she was making headway. "It's nothing to be ashamed of, French. You just have to get back on track, and lead a normal life. Nobody can do it for you. You have to do it for yourself. You have to start by getting a job. I see jobs in the *Weekly* every week."

"Damn few," he said with energy, his resentment building.

"How many do you need? There were two last week."

"Yeah, the bakery and Simley's Jewelry."

"What's wrong with the bakery?" she asked. It was impossible, of course, to picture him behind a jewelry counter.

"The bakery's nights. I sleep nights."

"Sleep days for a change."

"Sleeping days isn't normal. 'Lead a normal life,' you said."

"All right, last week there were other jobs."

"Yeah, Kaylene's Boutique."

Imogene laughed. "Oh, French, you're a riot."

He turned toward her, looked at her darkly. "Let's just drop it." His tone was tense and ominous.

"There's always the grain elevator. They're always hiring."

"I worked there already. Grain dust—you can't breathe."

"There's other places."

"Let's drop it," he said with heat.

"Be sure to look at the ads this week, and next week, and on into spring. The economy improves in the spring, French. I'm sure you'll find yourself a year-round job that's more useful than the one you've got. Pretending to be an Ojibway doesn't do anybody any good. It's a cliché, it's lazy, and it only promotes misapprehensions about Indians. You've got all these productive years ahead of you, and you've got your good lean body to take care of, so get out and get exercise, get out and get a useful job, get out and live a useful, normal life for a change. You'll be surprised how your outlook will improve. Life will seem—"

Because she was cutting her meat as she spoke, she did not see that French, beyond the candlelight, was rising silently from his chair and lifting his plate off the table; she did not see him standing at his full height and pausing for a moment with the plate held out in front of him and then bringing it swiftly down on the edge of the table with a crash, scattering steak and potatoes and shards of china in all directions.

"Good Christ!" cried Imogene, jumping to her feet and feeling for a morsel of food that had shot into her fluffy hair.

French stalked into the dark living room and turned the television on.

"What the hell!" shouted Imogene, following him. "What the hell was that all about?"

He waited for the picture to materialize, adjusted the sound, and then he strode over to the couch, nimbly avoiding the hand she put out to him. He lay down with his arms and feet rigidly crossed.

"Just what the hell was that all about?" she repeated loudly, trying to sound angry and offended while feeling neither of these emotions. What she felt was excitement and fear. She was thrilled to have caused such a fine explosion in such an introverted man. She'd broken his shell, and she was very proud of herself. As for her fear, she was afraid she'd ruined her chances of getting him into bed. She softened her tone. "You couldn't help it, could you, French? You had to convey your frustration somehow, and you chose to do it by breaking a piece of Agatha's best china."

He kept his eyes trained on the television screen, his lips pressed tightly shut.

She stood over him, her knees pressed against the couch. "It's women, isn't it, French? You were never sure of yourself around women. You had stepsisters but you never had girlfriends. We had dates, you and I, but we never really got as far as boyfriend-girlfriend, if you know what I mean. You went off to war to prove to women that you were a man, and the war sent you home less of a man than you were to start with, and you've been living without a woman ever since, and your frustration level is sky high. You don't need to explain, French, I can read you like a book. You slink around looking as harmless as an old cat, but you're a walking volcano. Everybody thinks you're dormant, but you're far from dormant. You're ready to blow your cork at the drop of a hat."

She stepped over to the TV and silenced it, leaving the picture for him to watch. She went into the dining room, saying, "It's the beginning of better times for you, French. Blowing your cork is just the beginning." She extinguished the candles and switched on the hanging lamp. "You needn't apologize, French. I know where your anger is coming from, and I'm not taking it personally. I can imagine how it's been building up and building up, and I just happened to be the one you popped your cork in front of. Don't worry, don't apologize, it's perfectly all right."

She carried her plate to the kitchen and returned with a

dustpan. She got down on her knees and began picking food and china off the carpet. "In fact, it could be a very big step forward, blowing your cork like that. I mean sometimes it takes weeks of psychotherapy to get people to open up and let out their demons, and here I got you to do it inside of five minutes. I don't want to take all the credit—I'm no therapist, God knows—but I've done a lot of reading about therapy and I can pretty well tell what buttons to push."

She moved around under the table on her knees, and then crept across the room, following a trail of broken china as far as the doorway to the sun room. There she got to her feet, switched on the ceiling light and examined the rug and the polished oak floor for debris. There was none. She stepped over to Agatha's desk and looked at the two pieces of mail French had brought in earlier in the day. One was from the power company, obviously a bill. The other envelope was an odd, un-American size. This she picked up and studied.

> St. Brigid's
> Ballybegs
> County Kildare
> Eire

The envelope was wheat-colored. Much of the small stamp was hidden under the ink of the postmark, but Imogene turned it this way and that and made out the face of either a dragon or Samuel Beckett. She carried the letter into the living room and waved it in French's line of vision. "Hey, this might be important," she told him.

French, willing her gone, said nothing. But he was conscious of exerting only half his willpower. With his other half he was willing her to stay.

"Are you mad at me?" she asked, dropping to the floor beside the couch and tucking her skirt under her legs. "Let's have a little talk, French. What a person needs at a time like this is a good little talk."

What could he say? An apology, he'd read, was the best remedy for shame, but he was too ashamed of his outburst to talk about it.

"I'm wondering if we should call Agatha." She leaned so

close to his face that he felt the warm breath of her words. Her hair smelled of fried onions. "We could call her tomorrow in Rome and read her the letter over the phone."

At this he twitched with alarm. Opening Agatha's mail? Was there no limit to this woman's depravity?

She tickled his ear with the letter. "It might be urgent. Who does she know in Ireland, have you any idea?"

He shot out his hand, trying to snatch the letter from her, but she was too quick. She uttered a smug little chuckle and tucked the letter under her skirt.

Robert Taylor, on the silent TV screen, was involved in a gladiator contest.

"We wouldn't have to open it. We'd call and tell her who it's from and leave it up to her whether we should open it. But you'd have to do the talking. She'd be pissed if she knew I was in on it."

French was relieved to be handed the responsibility. He'd let sleeping dogs lie.

Imogene uttered a humorless little laugh. "She doesn't like me, and never has. Nails McGee has her favorites, as you know. You're one of them, and I'm not."

Wordlessly, French rose from the couch and went into the kitchen. He filled the sink with hot water and began washing dishes. He washed the greasy frying pan first, then the broiling pan, then the plates and bowls, including those from lunch.

Eventually Imogene came and stood beside him at the sink. She ran a finger up his spine. He jumped. She asked where Agatha kept her vacuum. He nodded toward the pantry, and there she found an old upright Hoover with a sagging, threadbare bag and a frayed cord. She wheeled it into the dining room and went to work on the carpet, while French washed the silver and glassware, drained the sink, and wiped off the counters and stove.

When their chores were finished, French made a beeline for the couch and lay down again, covering himself with the afghan. Robert Taylor was still on the screen, now silently addressing Deborah Kerr in what appeared to be terms of tenderness.

Imogene came in, turned the sound up to a barely audible

level, and sat down again on the carpet. Again her hair was
very close to his face, and again he smelled onions.

When it became clear that Robert Taylor and Deborah Kerr
were in loving agreement, another actress of their era came on
the screen extolling diapers for old people. This was followed
by an ad for soap, during which Imogene asked a question so
softly that he didn't understand it. It sounded something like
"What did you think of your mother?" He didn't respond.

Actually, that *was* her question. She was getting the silent
treatment—she knew that—and the question no doubt struck
him as impertinent, but she'd read in a book that a man's sexual relations might reflect the sort of mother he had. She repeated the question.

He sighed.

"I don't remember much about her," she said. "I have a
clearer picture of your father. He came to town in that old
truck and sold corn on the street corner. He was a nice-looking
man. Your mother must have died much earlier, because I can't
think what her face looked like."

Mrs. Lopat was stout, she remembered only that about her.
Mr. Lopat was tall and lean and worried-looking. His complexion was dark, like his son's. In August he sold corn by the ear
on the stoplight corner. He gave you a sad smile when you
bought some, and hung his head dejectedly when you passed
him by. The Lopat farm, less than a mile from town, was obviously too small to make a comfortable living on, and gradually, after the three Lopat children grew up and left home, it
became no farm at all. By the time Mrs. Lopat died and Mr.
Lopat moved into the Sunset Nursing Home, it was reduced to
a weather-beaten house and a caved-in barn surrounded by
rusted machinery and dilapidated sheds in a grove of diseased
elms. Now nothing was left. The farmstead had been leveled
and cleared and turned into the back nine holes of the municipal golf course. Who got the money for the farm? Imogene
wondered.

"Who got the money when your farm was sold?" she asked.

French sighed again, struggling to marshal the memories
crowding into his head. He had an urgent need to tell her about
his boyhood on the farm with his mother and father and stepsisters. Nobody, not even Grover, ever asked him about his

boyhood. Where would he begin? How could he find the words?

"I suppose the money, divided three ways, didn't amount to much," prompted Imogene. She remembered the two Lopat sisters, particularly Rae, who was only a year or two ahead of Imogene in school. They were tall, large-faced girls remarkable for nothing except their laughably unstylish clothes. You never saw them with friends. Rae, who was said to be stupid, dropped out when she was sixteen and moved to Duluth. The older girl, Lou Ann, who was said *not* to be stupid, got her diploma and moved out west and married somebody respectable. A dentist, Imogene seemed to recall.

"Where do your stepsisters live these days?"

French cleared his throat and said, "We had forty acres."

"They were your father's daughters, right? Your mother was his second wife?"

He nodded. His eyes were on the ceiling. He was a boy again, sitting at the supper table in the farmhouse, where his good-natured mother was doing her best to soothe his fretful father. Life was difficult for French's father; each day presented him with a hundred things to worry about—the weather, the crops, the cost of food and clothing, the cost of gas for the tractor. Witnessing his father's unrelenting struggle to make ends meet, French had grown up ignoring money. Surely anything causing that much anxiety in a household ought to be dismissed out of hand. French didn't despise money, nor scorn it, nor secretly covet it—he simply gave it as little thought as possible.

"What's it like to have both your parents dead, French? Is it liberating?"

Again he cleared his throat. "Liberating? No, I wouldn't say liberating." He took his eyes off the ceiling and directed them at Imogene. "I'd say sad, more than anything."

"You miss them?"

"Miss them? . . . Sure. . . . Miss the farm." His gaze returned to the ceiling as he tried to recall how much the municipal golf course commission had paid for the farm. It wasn't much. He let his stepsister Rae have the entire amount. She made scarcely a living wage clerking in a convenience store. Rae had abnormally high medical expenses together with abnormally bad luck. Two or three years ago she drove off the highway into Lake Superior and broke her leg and nearly drowned. A year or two before that she tripped on a grating in a sidewalk and broke her thumb, her nose, and her glasses. French assumed that all the money had been quickly spent—it wasn't much to begin with. Rae called him up every few years to say Happy Birthday. His other stepsister, Lou Ann, he never heard from. She was living in Wyoming, married to a man he had never met.

"What do you miss about the farm?"

He looked back at the farm, surveying its pleasures. The smell of freshly-turned earth in the spring and fall. The sparkling heavens on icy winter evenings. The cool breeze on summer evenings. Playing cribbage with his mother at the kitchen table. Climbing the windmill and seeing over the treetops. Swimming in the creek. Fishing. "Lots of stuff," he said.

"You know what I miss from my girlhood, French?"

"What?"

"My closet."

What a strange duck, thought French.

"I had this big closet, and there was room for everything." She spread her arms, indicating ample space. "It had hooks and rods and shelves, and my father even built a little cabinet at the back to keep my rock collection in. Where do you see closets like that anymore? Get an apartment these days and where do you keep your stuff? You have to buy boxes that fit under your bed."

Her hand came to rest on the hollow of his shoulder. He closed his eyes and steeled himself, trying not to flinch.

"In Berrington I had an apartment with a second bedroom, so I used that as a closet, but you should see how cramped I am in St. Paul. Can you believe an apartment without a coat closet? I bought a coat tree."

The hand actually felt good on his shoulder. It moved down his arm to his elbow, where it paused. He kept his eyes closed and tried to relax. The hand moved to his wrist, and he allowed her to uncross his arms, to lift his left arm off his chest and lace her fingers in his. His hand was sweaty and trembling a little. He tried to think of something to say to distract her from his nervousness. He'd read an article recently about gender roles in social situations, but he couldn't remember a thing it advised. "I don't have a closet," he told her urgently.

"Oh, I'll just bet the rooms at the Morgan are horrid. Where do you hang your clothes?"

"There's hooks behind the door."

She laid her head on his shoulder. This too felt good. So good, in fact, that he patted her forehead with his free hand. Her forehead was cool, her hair soft. He hoped she wouldn't make any more aggressive moves for a while. For now, this was about all he could handle.

"French," she said softly, "I'm sorry if I made you mad."

He weighed his response before coming out with "That's okay."

"It wasn't a bad thing, really. I mean, you've got to come out of your shell, and that's one way to do it. It's just that we shouldn't have used her best plates."

"I'll buy her a new one before she gets home."

"I don't think you'll find one. It's rare china."

"It is?"

"You'd have to get a dealer to do a search, and if he found one, he could charge you a hundred dollars."

"Jesus."

"I could take one to the city and show it—you know, on the chance somebody has it in stock—but I'm pretty sure it would require a search."

"Try it anyway, would you?"

He felt her head nod.

They watched more of the movie, and at the next commercial break, Imogene, with a crick in her neck, rose to her knees and said, "Sit up, would you?"

French obeyed, and she sat down next to him on the couch, nestling into his arms.

"A hundred dollars?" he said. "Are you serious?"

"At least. It's real old."

"Jesus."

Peter Ustinov, in a sheet, spoke madly and happily as Nero, while French and Imogene began a tentative exploration of one another's bodies.

"How many plates has she got left?" asked French.

"Eleven."

"Maybe she won't miss it."

"Agatha? Are you kidding?"

During the burning of Rome, they kissed and fondled and loosened their belts and buttons.

"Let's find a bed," purred Imogene.

"Let's," said French, inflamed.

Imogene stood up, stepped out of her skirt, and headed for Agatha's bedroom.

"Not there," said French.

He led her up to his old room at the head of the stairs.

At two in the morning they woke up and realized they were hungry. "I'll get us something," said Imogene, switching on the bedside lamp. "What'll it be?"

"More of the same," said French, laughing, reaching across her and switching it off.

At three they woke up famished. Again Imogene turned on the light and asked what he wanted.

"Steak," said French, shielding his eyes from the brightness. "Bring me my steak."

"Your steak's in the garbage."

"Garbage!" he shouted, horrified by the waste of it. "I only ate a few bites."

"It was on the floor, in case you don't remember." Imogene got out of bed and slipped into her sweater.

"You threw it away?"

"It was covered with fuzz."

"You could have rinsed it off."

"I saw a can of tuna in the cupboard. How about a tuna sandwich?"

"Anything," he said, watching her tie his flannel shirt around her waist, knotting the sleeves in front. "I'm starving."

"With mayo?"

"Yup."

"What to drink—milk?"

"There isn't any."

"Tea, then?"

"Tea's fine."

He watched her leave the room, his shirttails swinging below her broad hips, then, smiling blissfully, he lay back and covered his face with his pillow.

Dicing a little onion to add to the tuna spread, Imogene too felt blissful. Not only did French have a sex drive, he outperformed Delbert Vaughn and John Koozer, the other two men she'd gone to bed with. Delbert Vaughn was her classmate in college, a fellow library-science major who twice took her to his rumpled bed in his frat house on rainy afternoons and skillfully taught her how to go about it. After they graduated, he broke her heart by not answering her letters. John Koozer, the black sheep of the grain-milling Koozers, was more or less a sexual dud. The one time they'd gone to bed together, he tried various methods of enlivening himself, such as whispering obscenities in Imogene's ear, but to little effect.

When the teakettle began to sing, Imogene went into the living room and picked the letter from Ireland off the floor. She brought it into the kitchen and held it over the steam until the flap came free.

Dear Agatha,

I do not mean to press myself upon you, and of course you are free to decline, but I have arranged to be in Rome when you are there. May we meet at high noon of your first full day in the city—Thursday, December 28—under the obelisk in St. Peter's Square? Or inside, at Michelangelo's Pietà, *if it's raining? I have my reasons for needing to see you, and I pray you will wish to see me.*

Fondly,
James

Just as she'd suspected, a phone call to Rome was necessary. She carried the letter upstairs on the tray of sandwiches and tea and showed it to French. She insisted that he place the call.

"Not on your life," he said with his mouth full.

"Yes, yes, yes, call her now, this minute, because it's late morning in Rome. That will give her twenty-four hours to decide if she's going to meet this dude."

French grinned playfully. "I'll tell her you opened her mail."

"Like hell you will. You'll say there's this letter from Ireland and you're wondering if you should open it and read it to her."

He laughed. "And I'm calling her at four in the morning because the mailman just came."

"It's not four in the morning in Rome. It's ten or eleven."

"But it's four in the morning *here*. Don't you think she knows that?"

This gave Imogene pause. "When does the mailman come?"

"Around ten or eleven."

"All right, call her then. It'll be suppertime in Rome. That'll still give her overnight to decide about meeting him." Imogene looked at him coyly. "A woman likes to have choices."

Her look was lost on French. "Who's this James?" he asked.

"How should I know? Maybe she'll tell you. Now promise me you'll call her."

He slipped the letter into its envelope and studied the handwriting. Heavy and bold, yet shaky. "I might," he said, but with no intention of doing so. Miss McGee had left no instructions to phone her.

"You *will*."

"I might." He turned the envelope over and licked the flap. He pressed it down, but it wouldn't stick. "We'll have to find some glue."

"Not if she tells you to read it."

"Look, Imogene, don't be an idiot."

She shot him a scathing look that said no one dared call her an idiot.

His reaction to her fearsome scowl was profound amusement. He shook with mirth, as though he'd made a wonderful joke. "Look, if she tells me to read it, am I going to heat water and pry it open like this? Don't be an idiot," he said again, and again he laughed.

Later, downstairs to prepare more food and tea, Imogene searched Agatha's desk for glue, and that was when she found the other seventy-seven letters from James.

PART 2

16

T HE MINNESOTANS HAD SLEPT very little
over the Atlantic, the plane bumping along through unsettled
weather. At sunrise, passing over Ireland, Agatha had beheld
the island's entire width from six miles up, the land greenish-
brown, the water greenish-silver, the coastline etched with a
delicate line of froth. Passing beyond it, she craned her neck,
looking back at the indentations along the Irish Sea, guessing
which was the bay at Ballybegs. Then she watched the south
of England pass beneath her, the English Channel, the Conti-
nent. Feeling the sensation of descent in her ears, she imagined
herself landing in Dublin, and James at the airport to meet her.

What would his first words be? How well would she conceal her nervous excitement? *Agatha, you're a beautiful sight
to these sore old eyes of mine*, she imagined him saying, and
she too would indicate her pleasure, but in words more restrained. *We must never allow this to happen again*, he would
say, *this interruption in our companionship*, and she would
agree, admitting how much she missed their exchange of letters. *Agatha, I swear, not a day of these three years has passed
that I've not thought fondly of you and wished to know what
you were thinking.* She would admit to a similar longing, withholding the fact that with her it had been virtually every *hour*
of every day.

Lillian, who had been knitting through the night, let her needles and yarn fall to her lap and said, "Agatha, don't pilots
ever go to the bathroom?"

"What makes you ask?"

"I never see them come through."

"There's a toilet in first class."

"Oh."

149

How long would they be together before she admitted to James that she'd been writing him letters and tearing them up? And how long before James came out with the pressing matter referred to in his note to the bishop? *Utmost urgency*, was the phrase, yet there was nothing urgent in the letter that followed. Was it a trick? She'd have to pin him down on that, make it clear that she disapproved of tricks.

"Agatha, there's a three-month-old baby in Alabama weighs over fifty pounds."

"You've been reading those papers again."

"And there was a man died in North Dakota, and they started up his heart with jumper cables."

"Why?"

Air traffic was stacked up over Rome. While the plane circled, Agatha watched the flight attendants passing news to one another in hasty little conferences. The news, judging by their expressions, was grim. Waiting for the captain's voice on the intercom, all the passengers grew restless—all but Lillian, who sat placidly knitting.

"Are you making any New Year's resolutions this year, Agatha?"

"I never do."

"Fidel Castro is."

"He is?"

"It was in the paper. He's giving up cigars."

The plane landed at last, stopping a quarter mile from the terminal. The captain's voice, slow and without inflection, came over the intercom. "Please don't be alarmed, ladies and gentlemen—there is absolutely no danger to us—but we have been asked to remain parked out here for the time being, because a little over an hour ago there was gunfire in the departure area of the terminal. The police have everything under control, but arrival and departure services were interrupted for a time, and we'll just have to wait our turn at the gates. I repeat, no threat or danger exists at this time. It's just going to take a few minutes to get you where you're going."

It took over an hour. Rumors flowed among the passengers in waves. A terrorist attack. An outbreak of war. A traveler gone berserk. Five dead, ten wounded. Ten dead, fifteen wounded.

The plane never did taxi up to the terminal. Buses and trucks came out to pick up the passengers and their baggage. Agatha and Lillian, sitting near the front of the lead bus, watched an ambulance pull away from a doorway with its siren screaming and its lights flashing. The rumored numbers increased. Twelve dead, twenty wounded.

The bus moved around to the far side of the terminal, and there they saw three more ambulances parked under the wing of an enormous El Al jet, their lights pulsing, their doors standing open. They saw two medics emerge from the terminal carrying a blond, curly-haired child on a stretcher. A third medic followed close on their heels, holding a packet of plasma high in the air, its tube attached to the girl's right arm.

"Dear me," said Lillian, tears instantly welling up in her eyes, "that child can't be more than ten years old—what's the world coming to?"

Agatha, speechless, shook her head.

The bus moved on and they caught a glimpse of another stretcher emerging from another door, this one bearing a body entirely covered by a blood-soaked sheet. "What's the world coming to?" Lillian repeated, and again Agatha shook her head. Dozens dead, said the rumor on the bus. Dozens and dozens wounded.

The bus pulled up to a wide door guarded by two soldiers with submachine guns. Standing beside one of the soldiers was an attack dog on a leash. The passengers filed off the bus into the sunshine—it was now mid-morning of a beautiful Junelike day—and then into the shadowy baggage area, where they came under the impassive gaze of several more soldiers and several more dogs. An airline official directed them to a baggage carousel, where he said they must remain until their coach came for them. They must not wander into other parts of the terminal.

Father Finn came up behind the two women and laid a consoling arm across Lillian's shoulders. "Are you all right?" he asked, detecting her tears.

"I saw them carry out a child not more than ten, Father."

"Yes, I saw that."

"What's the world coming to?"

His answer was a pat on Lillian's back and a squeeze of her

arm. He turned to Agatha, who looked pinched and distraught. He wanted to comfort her with a touch as well, but Agatha was not someone you touched. She might allow herself to be comforted with words—if they were well-chosen and brief. He said, "What a shame to begin our tour this way. Things can only get better."

Agatha nodded grimly, fighting off a sensation like claustrophobia. She felt as though she were trapped underground, the horror upstairs pressing down on her.

Suddenly a series of clipped, hysterical shrieks echoed off the wall, and Father Finn hurried around the baggage conveyor to comfort the young woman who was making the deafening noises. She was the smallest and youngest-looking of the students. She must have been college-age, but she looked fourteen, looked, to Agatha, like a pixy. Two of her friends joined Father Finn at her side, consoling her and silencing her with soothing words.

When they had all collected their baggage, Professor Albert Finn gathered his Minnesotans around him and counted them. The professor's morning appearance was that of a tramp, thought Agatha, his cheeks bewhiskered and sallow, his jogging outfit wrinkled, his hair awry. His sunny nature, however, was undimmed. "Listen, everybody," he said, beaming his kindly smile at all of them, "this is an awful thing to run into right off the bat, but the weather is perfect, our very own private bus is here to take us into the city, and after a nap and a shower and a good meal, we're all going to feel a whole lot better."

Darrin, who stood a head taller than everyone else in the group, conveyed a piece of news he'd gleaned from travelers at the baggage carousel. "There was something like thirty people killed or wounded," he said, "and there's still dead bodies upstairs."

"I guess there's blood all over the place," added Trish. Her eyes danced and she had gone very pale.

"We better get out of here," urged Darrin, "before we're all dead meat."

Another student, a red-haired girl with an orange backpack hanging from her shoulder, broke down and wept silently into her hands.

"There's no danger to any of us, Darrin." A note of reprimand sounded in the professor's voice. "It happened nearly two hours ago, and it's all over and done with. Now if you'll all please follow me in orderly fashion, we'll go to our hotel."

Boarding the silver and burgundy coach, a shiny, new vehicle with plush seats, enormous windows, and an unfriendly, bushy-browed driver at the wheel, Agatha saw that the hysterical student had a sympathetic seatmate, but the sobbing redhead did not. Agatha dropped into the seat beside her and took her hand, patting it gently. "My name is Agatha McGee."

She was a small, snub-nosed young woman, wearing a bright green jacket and large ceramic earrings in the shape of saucers. Smiling and dabbing at her eyes with the heel of her hand, she said, "Hi, I'm Lisa Berglund. Isn't it awful?"

"Horrible."

"Did you see the bodies they carried out?"

"Simply horrible."

"It made me feel sick."

"Likewise," Agatha admitted. Looking about her, she saw that most of the exhausted travelers sat in tense, glassy-eyed silence, waiting for the bus to move. Father Finn, who instead of taking a seat had gone up and down the aisle saying reassuring things left and right, was now leaning over the pixyish girl whose hysteria had subsided into tears and shudders. Across the aisle Lillian's needles clipped speedily along. The professor, last aboard, took a seat two rows in front of Agatha.

Lisa Berglund, still clinging to Agatha's hand, said, "You're the one Dr. Finn said would help us with our papers."

"I am."

"Oh, I'm so glad. I'm a terrible writer."

"Do you have a topic?"

"Not a clue." The young woman unzipped the backpack in her lap and drew out a wad of folded papers. She read from one of them. " 'A six page paper in which you somehow relate Galileo to your firsthand impressions of Italy.' "

She showed it to Agatha, whose only comment was, "A hyphen missing. Six-page."

This set Lisa Berglund off on a prolonged, helpless fit of giggles.

When the bus began to move and the gears proved noisy

enough to keep the professor from overhearing, Agatha said, "Don't get me wrong, he's no doubt an excellent teacher, but I have the impression his standards have slipped—at least where papers are concerned." She felt like a traitor, speaking against one of her own profession, but any sign of shabby schooling aroused feelings of resentment she couldn't hold in.

"Yeah, that's the word on Dr. Finn all right—biggest burnout on campus," said Lisa in lowered tones. "But they say his tours are still good. This one especially." Her voice brightened, rose in volume. "I've been dying to come on this one ever since I started college. I'm a senior and I'm in over my head with student loans, but I just *had* to borrow another bundle and come over here and walk in Galileo's footsteps. I'm a general science major, see, and I want to teach high school, and I figure if I don't see Europe now, it'll be years and years before I'll get another chance. I mean I've got this boyfriend, and we'll probably get married before too long, and you know how it is—you get busy with your family and your job and all, and you put off Europe till you're old and retired. My boyfriend's name is Larry. Have you been to Europe before?"

"Once, three years ago. To Ireland only."

"Was it fun?"

"It was . . ." Agatha broke out in a vague, faraway smile. "Ireland is beautiful."

The bus was creeping along very slowly in a line of traffic.

"You're a teacher, Dr. Finn says."

"I was. I'm retired."

"Science?"

"Not really. Only a watered-down kind of science for sixth graders, along with language, math, geography, religion, and civics."

"But you're interested in Galileo."

"We'll see."

"I've been interested in Galileo ever since my dad bought us kids a telescope when we were little and he took us out in the pasture and taught us the stars." Lisa's speech was fast and fluent, energized by the emotion she'd carried from the airport. "We live on this dairy farm up near International Falls, and my dad has two main interests in life, cows and stars. Actually, his interest in stars came from my mother. She was a high school science teacher before she got married, and she knew all about stars and telescopes and stuff, and over the years he's gotten more and more into that, while she's gotten more and more into farming. I mean for somebody who never grew up on a farm, she took to farming in a big way. She does all the books and stuff."

"How many in your family?" inquired Agatha. The girl's life story, told in her confident voice, had the effect of relieving Agatha's stress as well.

"Five kids. I've got a sister and a brother near my age, and two brothers a lot younger. I don't think I want five kids myself. A woman has to have some interest other than her kids, don't you think?"

"I'm no expert."

The bus began to move faster. Lisa, with a last look at the terminal, said, "Fifteen dead, I heard. Doesn't it spook you?"

"I should have stayed home."

Lisa turned to her, studied her with concern. "Things can only get better."

"That's what Father Finn told me."

Glancing across the aisle, Lisa said, "Which one is Father Finn? The one with the gray sport coat?"

"Yes, he's the professor's brother. The woman he's sitting with is named Lillian Kite, an old friend of mine."

"I'm glad you older people came with us. I like older people."

"Thank you," said Agatha, whose heart was warmed by this bald, unexpected statement of goodwill. And yet, despite her fondness for her new young friend, she felt a wave of sadness creeping toward her. It was the old familiar tide of her depression. It had followed her across the sea.

"My grandpa and grandma lived with us on the farm, and I miss them. Especially my grandma. Besides, I don't really know any of these other students very well. I mean, I've been in classes with some of them, and I know some of their names—that's Paula who made such a scene in the airport, and that's Betty Lou sitting beside her—but none of my friends came along. They said they couldn't see wasting their Christmas vacation on Italy—can you believe it?"

The wave of gloom overtook Agatha. She tried to suppress

a sob, but couldn't. Lisa Berglund discreetly looked away and fell silent.

After a minute Agatha regained her composure and apologized. "I haven't been myself lately, and seeing those people on stretchers . . ."

"You've been ill?" asked Lisa.

Agatha hesitated, judging how much of herself to reveal. "Ill-tempered," she said.

"Why?"

Agatha shot her a look of disapproval—she disliked snoops—and then told her why. "If you've led a useful life, it's hard to get old and feel useless."

"I know, I saw it at home with my grandpa. He got so he couldn't do stuff around the farm, couldn't drive the tractor, couldn't help with haying, and he got real cranky."

"That's me—cranky."

"Now my grandma, on the other hand, she was okay with growing old. I mean she just sort of sat back and let my mother and us girls take over all the housework and cooking and stuff. She spent her last years watching TV and talking about the weather. She watched six weather reports every day, three at noon and three at night."

"And died before your grandfather."

"How did you know?"

"The relaxed ones go first."

Lisa nodded. "She slept away."

"God's got it backwards, you know. He leaves the cranky ones and takes the agreeable ones."

"Not backwards if you think of it from His viewpoint, I suppose."

Agatha smiled at this theological insight. Charmed by Lisa, and lulled by the soft rocking of the bus, she was suddenly sleepy. She lay her head back and applied her willpower to the loosening of her neck and shoulder muscles. Patting Lisa on the arm, she said, "I'm very glad you've come along, too."

Just before falling asleep, she heard Professor Finn calling to his brother, "Hey, Franny, see over there, that's one of the seven hills of Rome, the Aventine."

17

A T THAT MOMENT, NEAR the crest of the Aventine Hill, Father James O'Hannon, clad entirely in black except for the white scarf at his throat, stepped shakily out into the sunlight on the arm of his young friend, Denis Worthy. They left the ornate doorway set deep in a wall of red brick and walked slowly along a juniper-shaded pathway toward a garden wall. Denis Worthy wore the black, ankle-length habit of the Order of St. Benedict, and over that a brown zippered jacket. He asked, "Will it be a taxi this morning, Father?"

"No, the bus," said James O'Hannon resolutely.

"Good," replied the younger man, happy to know that his old mentor was feeling stronger today. Father O'Hannon had often claimed over the years to enjoy the jostle and mix of humanity on buses and trains, and yet yesterday, coming in from the airport, they'd paid dearly for a taxi because he was feeling poorly.

Denis Worthy drew open the door in the garden wall and they left the quiet, leafy grounds of the Collegio di Sant' Anselmo, where James O'Hannon had spent the night in one of the monks' spartan guest rooms, and where he would return for seven more nights (or possibly fewer, depending on Agatha McGee's state of mind) before his flight back to Ireland. They descended a stone stairway to the traffic-choked Via della Marmorata.

At street level James O'Hannon let go of his companion's arm and turned in a slow circle, taking in the noise and color of the Roman morning—the motor traffic, the foot traffic, a shopkeeper working his awning, the call of a news agent from his stand across the street, the call of a bird from a juniper overhanging the garden wall. Completing his circle, he faced into the sun and closed his eyes, warming himself in its glow. Here at last was the thick, nourishing Mediterranean sunlight he'd been dreaming of throughout his recuperation from surgery.

"You set the pace, Father. The bus will be stopping up ahead, near the fruit stand."

"Thank you, Dinny." James did not grasp Denis Worthy's arm, but touched it now and again for security as he walked. "You'll need patience."

"Not a bit of it."

They had covered only a very short distance when James began to chuckle, his eyes filled with mirth. "Do you know what this city does for me, Dinny? It makes me laugh. These Italians, they shout and gesture like madmen. Look at that man up ahead, making his point by talking at the top of his lungs and poking his friend in the chest with his finger. Where else in the world do you see that, I ask you?"

"In Cork," said Denis.

"Ah, no, Cork's like Dublin, a city of mutterers. Two men meeting on the street in Cork wouldn't be standing there carrying on like these two. For one thing, it would be raining, and if it wasn't raining, they'd be thirsty. They'd duck into a pub and mutter."

Denis, a sandy-haired, freckle-faced monk in his late twenties, laughed, aglow with the pleasure of being in the old man's company after all this time. As an Irish Benedictine transplanted to Rome for a year of seminary training, Denis had spent his first week abroad pining for home, and now, even with homesickness behind him, he was profoundly touched by the lilt of Father O'Hannon's brogue. This old priest from Ballybegs had been his boyhood inspiration, had shepherded him through the minor seminary, and had supported him in his decision to change course in mid-training, forsaking the secular priesthood in favor of the Benedictine monastery in the South of Ireland. Three years ago Father O'Hannon had traveled by train to see him taken into the novitiate, and he'd come again a year later to witness his profession of vows. Since then they'd kept in touch by mail, and when James recently wrote to inquire about a few days' lodging in Rome, it was Denis

Worthy's pleasure to arrange it with his superiors at Sant' Anselmo and, yesterday, to meet his plane from Dublin.

At the airport Denis had been shocked by his old friend's sickly appearance. His color was bad. There was a gray darkness around his eyes, and a lighter gray pastiness elsewhere, the man's customary ruddiness entirely lost from his cheeks. He'd lost some hair as well, and what remained had gone completely white. Gone, too, was his old agility. There was something of a wobble in his walk. The old man's mind had not weakened with his body, however, and that was a great relief to Denis. In the taxi from the airport James had spilled out the news from Ireland as only he could tell it, elaborately setting the scene and then cutting to the heart of matters with his edge of wry humor.

And now, waiting at the bus stop, the young monk fished for more of the same. "What about your retirement party, Father? Surely the parish did you justice after all these years."

"Indeed, St. Brigid's put on a farewell party the likes of which Ballybegs might never see again, the porter and the whiskey flowing like water, along with the tears of more than one sentimental old parishioner."

"I wish I could have been there. You must have been moved."

"My eyes were dry the whole time. For one thing the din of the music and talk was so loud I couldn't hear half of what anybody was saying, and for another thing, my mind was on my intestines, which were due to be cut into within the week. There's something very thought-provoking about serious surgery, my lad. Never schedule it back to back with festivities. The band will be playing 'The Wild Colonial Boy,' and the young ones will be kicking up their heels on the dance floor, and some farmer will be giving you an account of last week's pig market, and you'll be sitting there contemplating your bowels."

The bus to Vatican City arrived, and they boarded, finding seats near the front. James was due to have lunch with an old friend from Ireland, a priest named Andrew Corcoran, who for the past many years had been attached to the Irish delegation to the Vatican, and Denis was researching a paper in the Vatican library, which accounted for his attire. Away from Sant'

Anselmo, he wasn't required to wear his habit, but he'd found it useful in opening doors around the Vatican, particularly doors to the archives containing the manuscripts he needed to examine.

James continued as the bus moved downhill. "You see, while I was saying my farewells to the good people of St. Brigid's, I was rehearsing my farewell to life itself. It was my secret, of course. I'd told no one about my appointment with the scalpel, and I'm sure they all wondered why I was acting so low-spirited, why in spite of the pints they pressed on me I stayed sober as a tree. It wasn't my finest moment, Dinny; I'm not proud to think how I might have spoiled their fun. It was simply one of those times when a man can't help being a little distant and self-involved, and after the surgery was over and I was on my feet again, I wanted to go back to Ballybegs and apologize not only for being a wet blanket but also for leaving them with a browbeating sermon."

"At your final Mass, you mean?"

"No, no, at the party, no less. There were speeches, you see, the music interrupted by speeches and more speeches, and when it finally came time for me to get up and regale them with what they hoped, I'm sure, would be sweet and touching tales from my years in Ballybegs, I said nothing sweet or touching at all. It was neither the time nor the place to hector those good people, but hector them I did. I talked about the Troubles."

Denis shot him a surprised look. "Why?"

"I couldn't seem to help myself. I'd been brooding about the Troubles for some long time, but never aloud, mind, never in the pulpit on Sundays."

The bus picked up speed as it neared the bottom of the hill. James, catching a glimpse of the Tiber, fell silent.

"Brooding?" Denis prompted.

"Yes, brooding. Because the Troubles had finally been brought home to me, but that's another story." The bus careened around a corner, and James gripped the seat ahead. "I used to think the pulpit was a place for theology alone, not politics, and so I'd been strictly avoiding the Troubles year after year, while the corpses piled up in Ulster. Give the people a rest from all that—that was my thinking. The Troubles hang over them all week like a cloud, so give them a bit of God's hope inside the church on Sunday morning and leave the Troubles alone."

"Oh, but you touched on them now and then when I was a boy."

"The lightest of touches then, and less and less over the years. But it dawned on me recently that I'd been getting it backwards. The Troubles might have been hanging over *me* like a cloud, but they hadn't been hanging over my parishioners. You know it yourself, Dinny, the Irish are world-beaters at ignoring the unpleasant, are they not? God help us, we ignored Hitler. It was the same with the Famine, I'm told. My grandfather was a lad in the Famine—he lost his mother and father and two of his brothers to starvation—and he never spoke of it as long as he lived. I have my mother's testimony for that. He lived to be the sort of old fellow'd talk a leg off you, yet never a word of the suffering in the Great Hunger."

The bus turned left and crossed a bridge. The dome of St. Peter's came into view.

"And wasn't I cut of the same cloth as my old granddad? Wasn't I as much of an ostrich as everyone else in the South? Well, enough of that, I said to myself as I made my way to the podium, clearing my throat, the mob clapping and calling, 'Father, Father'—enough of that entirely, I'll take my leave speaking out against the violence. I waited for the hall to grow quiet, and I waited a few moments more for effect, and then I began by saying that every time a life was lost in the North, we should have held a vigil at St. Brigid's. A life on either side, I wasn't saying the Catholic dead alone."

"You'd have had a good many against you, doing that," said Denis Worthy. "Praying for Prods."

"Would I now? And wouldn't that be the proof of my failure? But I think you're mistaken, Dinny. I think my people know right from wrong in their hearts. I think if I had spoken out years ago, and kept it up, and pressed them to put aside their indifferences to the killing up North—who knows?—their outrage might have spread from Ballybegs across the length and breadth of the Republic. I should have been a voice for peace and forgiveness in the land"—James shook his head sadly—"instead of what I was."

"Simply the best parish priest in the land."

"Go on," said James, but he colored slightly at his admirer's praise, the flush of pride coming faintly into his cheeks. "So that was the gist of my farewell address, Dinny, my regret at not having done my duty by them, not having rubbed their noses in the killing in the North."

"How did they take it?"

"Politely until the end, what choice did they have? 'Let the old man carry on if he must, he'll soon be gone and out of the way.' But then, at the end, I made a great mistake. I wrapped it up with a tale I'd heard not long before from a Belfast man who swears it's true. The perfect tale, I thought, to illustrate how twisted and cruel we've become as a people. There was this priest in Belfast, I told them, who was hearing confessions, and a man came into the box and knelt down and said, 'Bless me, Father, for I have sinned, I have shot a British soldier,' and the priest said to him, 'Get on to the mortal sins.'" James turned to his young friend. "That's not a joke, Dinny."

Denis Worthy knew it wasn't. He could tell by James's dark look. "Your audience thought it was?"

"It brought down the house. They laughed till they cried. The band struck up 'Down by the Glenside,' the dancing resumed, and I went back to my place and endured the rest of the party, but barely."

Swaying with the movement of the bus, James and Denis sat silent for five minutes or more, their eyes straight ahead, watching St. Peter's dome grow larger over the driver's right shoulder.

"Do you ever get used to it, Dinny, being here day after day? I mean does it ever get to be old hat—St. Peter's and all?"

"Never. It always seems a privilege, being in Rome."

James emitted a long "Ah" of satisfaction. "A privilege it is surely. I'm feeling it now, a lift of the spirit. I should have come here more often over the years."

"I should have come here more often over the years, Andy."

"Why didn't you?" Monsignor Andrew Corcoran asked, looking up from his food.

"Well, it's not an easy thing to explain. I was taught to feel unworthy of Rome, you might say."

"Unworthy of Rome? If you only knew just how unworthy you'd have to be."

They were dining in the sun, their overcoats off, facing each other across a small table, which the proprietor of the restaurant, at the request of the two priests, had moved outdoors and set against the warm stucco wall. Now, in the early afternoon, there were very few pedestrians on the wide sidewalk, very little motor traffic along the Via della Conciliazione. Their conversation was interrupted occasionally by the waiter or by a bus or a lorry with a noisy engine.

"It was the bishop who ordained me that put me in that way of thinking," said James.

"That would be Billy the Kid," said Andrew Corcoran, eating hungrily from his bowl of pasta and casting his mind back to the year he and James had been ordained in the same week but in different parts of Ireland, himself in Galway, James in Maynooth.

"You remember him, then."

"William John Murphy, of less than happy memory," said Andrew Corcoran.

James, having eaten very little but as much as possible while avoiding intestinal pains, sipped his mineral water and studied his friend. Andrew Corcoran, a long-faced man with a prominent jaw, had grown a short white beard since James last saw him, scarcely a week's whiskers, really, so close-cropped it was. He had a wide, thin-lipped mouth that easily and often turned up in what would have been a smile if it didn't seem to contain more weariness than pleasure. It was this smile that James had to focus on today in order to gauge the man's reactions, for Corcoran's expressive gray eyes were hidden behind sunglasses.

"I wonder," said the monsignor, smirking, "did the man have any idea we called him Billy the Kid?"

"A little man with a little man's needs," said James. "He cultivated his loud voice and his officious manner to compensate for his littleness. You couldn't like him if you tried—he saw to that, his judgments so harsh and quick. But of course it was my own littleness, wasn't it, that kept me from coming here over the years."

"Was it?"

James looked past his friend and down the wide avenue leading straight into St. Peter's Square. From this angle the base of the obelisk, where today he had met Andrew and tomorrow he would meet (God willing) Agatha, was hidden from view by a construction of wood and straw representing the stable at Bethlehem. "A tacky innovation," Corcoran had called it as they strolled around it. "Some retrograde has obviously gained the ear of John Paul." Yet James found it quite tasteful and pleasing, and said so. Indeed he found it necessary. On a splendid summery day like this, how would you know it was Christmas without a crèche?

"Remember our holiday over here, Andy, the four of us? What were we, third-year seminarians?"

Corcoran nodded. "You and I and Pat McBride and Liam O'Donnell. A pleasant enough time, I seem to recall."

"Ah, we had ourselves a wonderful time. Don't tell me you've forgotten how fiercely the four of us were bitten by the Vatican bug, how we went home determined, one way or another, to get back over here as often as possible."

Up went the corners of Corcoran's mouth. "Quite the zealots we were."

"Pat McBride was the first to come back—the very next year. Took his moral theology over here, remember? And he's been shuttling back and forth for fifty years."

"He looks me up," said Corcoran sourly. "Tiresome man, if you want the truth."

"Don't I know it? He comes through Ballybegs every so often. You'll be seeing more of him than ever, now he's retiring."

"And Liam O'Donnell I haven't thought of for ages. He dropped out, am I right?"

"To marry his Moira, don't you remember? You went to his wedding."

"I did?"

"You did, and I didn't," said James. "William John Murphy forbade me to go."

"Bishops," said Corcoran, shaking his head. "Now, why would he do such a desperate thing?"

"Because Liam, like myself, was one of his own men. Marriage might be contagious, you see, and he'd lose me as well. But you went. Your bishop was altogether more human."

"Bishop Scanlon, a good man, I've always said it. But isn't it curious you should recall my seeing Liam married, while I haven't the slightest memory of it myself."

"Not curious at all. I recall it because I was dying to be there."

The monsignor paused in his eating. "What's become of your appetite, James?"

"The doctors removed it."

"Not for good, I hope."

"They say not. It's supposed to return little by little as my digestive tract knits itself back together."

"Well, I should think by this time . . ." Corcoran resumed eating, expertly twirling his spaghetti around his fork. "Get back to your being unworthy of Rome, James. I'm all ears."

James lifted his napkin off his lap, shook it out, folded it neatly and laid it beside his plate. "Andy, tell me, are you ordinarily overestimated, or underestimated?"

"By whom?"

"By people in general. Are you thought to be more capable or less capable than you really are?"

"That's intriguing. I'd have to give it some thought. What are you getting at?"

"I'm thinking that most of my life I've been overestimated—thought to be wiser, holier, more efficient than I am—don't ask me why."

"But we *know* why—you're a priest in Ireland." This was said with a mixture of disdain and mirth, a tone others might have found offensive, but which James chose to overlook. Monsignor Andrew Corcoran's strain of haughtiness went back to his student days, and his friends had long ago learned to expect and ignore it.

"But Bishop Murphy was the exception. I never knew what evidence he found for it, but from the day he met me until the day he died, he was convinced I was a dunce. When Pat told me he was off to Rome to study, I went to the bishop and asked if I might be granted the same privilege. No, he said, my type was better suited to staying home. 'My type?' I said to him. 'What *is* my type, Your Excellency?' His response was a windy discourse on how clearly he could see into the minds and souls of his men, how well he understood their talents and capabilities, how he had a great reputation among his fellow bishops for pointing his troops in directions they were meant, by their nature, to go. He said I wasn't to trouble myself about foreign study, wasn't to fill my head with fancy plans. I was to stay at Maynooth and keep my nose in my books and he'd ordain me as one of God's infantry."

"Fancied himself a military man, did he?"

"Loved talking like a general—ask any of his troops. God's infantry, my eye. God's dullards is what he meant. Long before any of us were ordained, he'd made up his mind which of us were fit to rise up in the Church, and which of us were to spend our lives in remote parishes where our stupidity wouldn't be an embarrassment to him."

"Not realizing," said Corcoran, wiping tomato sauce from his chin whiskers, "that it's the remote little parishes that *make* a man stupid."

Irritated by this remark, James allowed a second or two of silence to pass, giving his friend time to realize what he'd implied.

"Present company excluded, of course," added the monsignor, again looking up from his food.

"We aren't entirely a nation of morons, Andy."

The monsignor nodded, indicating he'd been properly chastened.

"You know how those early disappointments can have their effect, Andy. All these years I've gone around with the vague notion that Rome didn't want to see very much of me. Don't ask me to be logical about it."

"Where have you gone, then, for your holidays?"

"Lourdes, fairly often. And home to Kilrath, of course."

"But, James, you can't make me really believe that Billy the Kid actually forbade your coming to Rome on holiday."

"No, but he was a great one for Lourdes. Urged his troops, if they must go abroad, to spend their holidays there."

The weary smile again, turning sardonic. "Crutches and canes."

"You've been there yourself?"

Corcoran nodded. "A thick layer of fraud lies over the place."

"It's a holy place, Andy."

Corcoran's eyebrows rose above the dark glasses. "You witnessed a cure?"

"No, I didn't." James shook his head and cast his mind back to his several springtime visits to Lourdes, the aroma of sunshine on blossoms, the lustrous green hills, the babbling waters. He might leave Ireland with a frigid gale sweeping across its rough pastures and rattling the rectory doors, and overnight he'd be set down in the lovely park that was the south of France. Such tranquility. And it wasn't the peace of the landscape alone. It was the peace of being among all those pilgrims with their minds on higher things. That's what he meant by holiness. Holiness didn't come down on a beam of light from above. It rose up from the people. All that single-minded devotion, all those prayers directed heavenward, all that sheer *belief*. It produced a sacred aura you could almost see, almost smell, almost reach out and run your hand over, like silk.

But of course by the end of the second day, the spell, for James, began to evaporate, and he would set off for home. You couldn't keep your eye heavenward forever. Sooner or later you had to notice the cloying saintliness of certain clergymen playing to the adoration of the tour groups they were leading. You couldn't miss the merchants relieving the faithful of their cash. And, worst of all, your silent devotions were sure to be interrupted by the weeping breakdown of some poor soul in a wheelchair whose crippled limb, bathed in the waters, was still a crippled limb, or the despairing cry of some anguished wretch for whom faith and prayer and an airline ticket from the States did nothing to alleviate her migraine. Yes, reality broke in, and you quickly boarded the train for the ferry terminal on the coast. But a year or two later you'd be back again, mingling with the crowds and standing again where Bernadette knelt, in order to verify that the uplifting otherworldliness created by pilgrims gathered at a holy site had not been some kind of hallucination. Reality broke in? Indeed, the feeling of

holiness was so overpowering, so tangible, that it might have
been reality that was broken into.

James was brought back to his Roman lunch by Corcoran's
question. "Who's your replacement at St. Brigid's, James? Do
I know him?"

"Marty Walsh. Not a young man. You may have met him."

"Don't believe so."

"They're getting a good priest, but it will take them a while
to know it. He's quiet, not very outgoing. I can't see him mingling with the farmers on market day."

Corcoran shuddered. "You yourself were always a man for
the fair, as I recall."

"Right, I kept a few sheep of my own over the years. Now
and again a few pigs."

Corcoran, bending low over his bowl, spooning up the last
of the sauce, gave thanks for never being expected to mingle
with farmers on market day. "And where have you moved to?"
he asked.

"Nowhere yet. Marty Walsh and I are sharing the house for
the present. That way I'm close to my doctor in Dublin."

"You'll move home, then, when the time comes?"

"That's the plan." This was said with an abruptness that
caused Corcoran to raise his eyes from his bowl. James's expression had turned dark. "I was fourteen when I left Kilrath,
Andy. A strange thing, is it not, to call a place home when you
haven't lived in it for fifty-six years?"

Corcoran, patting his mouth with his napkin, pushed his
bowl aside, drew his wineglass near. "Well, your mother was
there all the while. Your brother and sister."

"So they were."

"How is your brother? Still the jolly publican?"

"He's gone downhill, and the pub along with him."

"Well, there you are. Your next career. The O'Hannon
brothers behind the bar." Monsignor Corcoran enjoyed this little invention to the point of laughing out loud.

James smiled in response, but weakly. "If you could see the
place, Andy."

The laugh died away. "Not in tiptop shape?"

"Hopeless."

"Well."

Both men, sensing this was a dead-end topic, pushed their chairs back from the table and turned them to face the broad street. They watched the passing buses and cars, which were growing more numerous now, the midday lull coming to an end.

"Isn't this miraculous, Andy, sitting outdoors in December?"

"A rare day, I have to say it, even for Rome."

James put his head back against the wall and closed his eyes. His friend lit a cigarette.

"What about yourself, Andy? They'll be putting you out to pasture sooner or later."

"My days are numbered, you're entirely right about that."

"Will you stay on here?"

"No, like yourself, I'll be going home."

They were silent for a minute.

"Galway is a grand city," said James.

"I don't look forward to it, all the same."

"Grander by far than Kilrath."

"Yes, no arguing that."

They fell silent again, until the waiter, clearing away, stirred them to life.

"Andy, would you ask him what time they open tomorrow?"

There was a brief exchange in Italian. "He says noon."

"Would you ask him to reserve his best table for half past one?"

Another exchange. "He wants to know how many."

"Two."

"Due," said Andrew Corcoran, and he offered to write the name O'Hannon on a piece of paper, but the waiter assured him it was unnecessary.

Left alone, they lapsed into silence once more.

After a time James said, "I'll need two tickets to the audience hall next week."

"Easily done."

"Seats close to the Holy Father."

"Not so easily done." Corcoran puffed on his cigarette. "Your best plan is to arrive early enough to get yourself seats on the middle aisle. After his homily he comes down the aisle greeting people. It's something of a mad crush, but if you're situated right, it's possible he'll take your hand. Surely you've been to a papal audience before."

"I have, but not since the new hall was built."

"Two tickets, you say?"

"Two. A friend and I."

"The young Benedictine?"

"No."

"Let me guess. Pat McBride is coming over again."

"No, this is a friend from America."

Corcoran's eyebrows shot up. "America? You should have brought him along. I like meeting Americans."

"It's a woman. And her plane only gets in today."

"Oh, that reminds me," said Corcoran, extinguishing his cigarette, "did you hear terrorists shot up the airport this morning?"

James gave a start. "Not da Vinci."

"Da Vinci right enough. Ten or twelve dead, a great many wounded."

James straightened up in his chair. "Not Americans surely."

"No word on nationalities, but it was at the Israeli departure gate. Three or four men with machine guns spraying bullets left and right."

"Lord God."

"Some Palestinian fringe group, they're saying. Two of them shot dead by police, one taken alive."

"Ireland all over again," said James, relaxing a little. Agatha would have no business on the departure level.

Andrew Corcoran's mouth turned down in disapproval. "Don't talk nonsense, James. Purposely killing the innocent? Not in Ireland."

"How can you say that?—the innocent of Ulster dead by the hundreds."

"But not on purpose, James. The innocent have never been targets."

"On purpose or not on purpose, tell me the difference. A child in a park in Derry, Andy, shot in the head by a stray plastic bullet—tell her the difference. A woman out shopping in Andersontown, blown off her bike by a homemade bomb." James's voice rose with the color in his cheeks as he brought his fist down on the table, attracting the notice of passersby. "Old men in front of a shop in Williamsport, Andy, three of them talking one minute about the races and the next minute two of them as dead as stones in the road, caught in a crossfire of rifles."

Monsignor Corcoran, a career diplomat, conceded the point. Dead was dead.

James fell silent, and then, after a minute, said, "Forgive me, Andy, it's my one great regret that I've done nothing to quell the Troubles."

"But how could you, James? It's in their blood."

James, rising from his chair, answered in a subdued voice, "I don't know how, Andy. I only know I could have tried."

And so it was in this minor key that they said their good-byes, donning their overcoats and shaking hands, the Roman diplomat striding off in the direction of the Tiber, and the village priest from Ireland slowly making his way up the street toward the obelisk, where he would meet Denis Worthy and return with him to Sant' Anselmo.

18

"W_{HERE} $_{YOU}$ $_{BEEN?}$" $_{ASKED}$ Grover, without needing to be told, and without taking his eyes off the suppertime news on TV.

French, blowing on his fingers, crossed the lobby and sank into the chair beside him. "Miss McGee's," he said, his voice quavering with cold.

"Since yesterday morning?"

"Why not?"

"She say you could sleep there?"

"More or less." French kicked off his right moccasin, brought his knee up to his chin and vigorously rubbed warmth into his foot. "Any business?"

"Sales rep from Duluth. I put him up on two." Grover shifted in his sunken chair and turned to French. "Bunch of freaks shot up the airport in Rome."

French looked startled. "That so?"

"Reports are sketchy," Grover quoted the newsman. "Thirteen believed dead."

"They say who?"

"Mostly Jews."

"Nobody from here?"

"Maybe they'll tell the names."

But the newsman had moved on to local items, and they sat watching a department store executive in Rookery comment on Christmas revenue, then a taxi driver in Berrington announce his retirement.

At a commercial break Grover turned to French once again and said, "I suppose if it's the right thirteen dead, you can stay there forever."

172

"What do you mean?" French was now working on his left foot.

"I mean, who will the house go to when she dies?"

"Not me."

"You sure?"

French uttered a small noise of dismissal, something between a chuckle and a hiss.

"Why not you, French? She hasn't got any family."

"Are you nuts?"

"Stranger things have happened. Remember that woman left her house to her cats?"

"What woman?"

"Woman on the news last summer left her house to her cats."

"Miss McGee hasn't got any cats."

Grover blinked four or five times and wrinkled his nose—a habit he had when he was tense. "Where you planning to go when the bulldozers start up, French?"

"Where *you* planning to go?"

"That's what I'm getting at."

French, looking into Grover's small, cold eyes, caught the drift of his scheme. He had to laugh. "You and me housemates on River Street? You *are* nuts."

"I got income. I could pay you rent."

"Jesus, Grover, wake up. Miss McGee's not leaving me her house."

"Stranger things have happened. It's well-known she's partial to you."

"And what if she did—where would we live till she died? She's not even sick."

"I figure we can live there *before* she dies if you work it right. You move back there to live, see, and after she's used to being a landlady again, you point out how she could double her income by renting out another bedroom."

"Forget it, Grover. She doesn't need the income."

"How many bedrooms she got? Five? Tell her you got this friend—clean habits, no pets."

French laughed. "No pets I'll grant you."

"Five bedrooms, or six? House like that, I bet there's six."

"There's four."

"All right, four. A shame, ain't it, all them empty rooms and us without a roof over our heads?"

French facetiously cast his eyes upward. "Roof blow off the hotel while I was gone?"

Grover made a leveling gesture with his hand. "Come summer, bulldozers."

"Come summer, something will turn up."

"Like what?"

"Come summer," said French, laughing, "we could both be dead."

Grover scowled at him reprovingly and asked, "What the hell's got into you?" French's levity seemed to Grover a kind of betrayal. He much preferred the other French, the gloomy one. "You been smoking dope?"

French shook his head. "Better than dope."

"You been sneaking Miss McGee's booze."

French shook his head again, smiling at the newsman, who was introducing the weatherman. "Better than booze."

"Well?"

French cast a sidelong glance at Grover, his smile turning sly, his eyes half closed. "Nookie," he said.

Grover blinked repeatedly and said, "I don't believe you."

"Who asked you to?" French put on his moccasins and stood up.

"Nookie? Who with?"

"Never mind," said French, heading for the stairway.

Grover whined, "Where you going?"

"Up."

"Come back here, we'll play some cribbage."

"Tomorrow," said French, climbing the stairs.

Although part of his pleasure with Imogene had been the thought of bragging to Grover about it, French now found himself without any such desire. The pleasure had proved much too satisfying, too precious, to talk about it in the lobby of the Morgan Hotel.

Near midnight Grover emerged from Room 2 in his socks, pajamas, and overcoat to answer the hotel's only phone.

"Yeah?" he grunted gruffly, hoping by his tone to discourage late-night calls, though his daytime response—"Morgan"—was scarcely more civil.

It was a woman wanting French.

"What do you want him for? I'll give him your message in the morning."

She snapped, "I want him now."

"He's in bed."

She giggled. "So am I."

Grover climbed to the second floor and called up to the third. French opened his door and said, "What do you want?"

"Telephone."

"Telephone?"

"Some dame," said Grover.

"Shut up!" shouted the sales rep on second.

Padding downstairs in his bare feet and underwear, his shag rug clutched about him like a cape, French assumed it was Miss McGee. She was the only person who ever called him up. It was no doubt daytime in Europe and she was fretting about her furnace.

"Hello," he said loudly, throwing his voice across the ocean.

"Honestly, that Grover."

"Yeah, I know." It was a moment before he realized it was Imogene. Her voice excited him a little.

"He's such a boor."

"He likes his sleep," French told her.

Her voice turned girlish. "French, I'm in bed."

"Yeah, I was too."

"Aren't we the bedbugs, though?" She giggled.

"Sure are."

After spending the night and most of the morning in bed with him, she'd left him at noon and gone home to bathe and pack her suitcase. Around three, when she came back across the alley to say good-bye, they'd gone back to bed, dozing and waking while day turned to evening. It was nearly six when she left for the city.

She giggled again. "I suppose the neighbors are talking."

"I doubt it."

"The Rathmanns. They must have seen me going in and out."

"They're gone."

"And the people on the other side, the Ericksons."

"They haven't got hardly any windows facing Miss McGee's."

"We'll make it my mother's house this weekend."

"Whatever."

"I can get away at four on Fridays. I'll be there by eight."

"Eight's fine."

"Look for my car and come in the back door."

"Okay."

"French, are we out of our minds?"

He said nothing. He'd let her decide.

"I mean where is this leading us?"

He wondered himself. Surely she'd tell him.

"I mean, this weekend, fine. Agatha's house, my mother's house, fine. But after this weekend, where?" Her tone shifted from romantic to matter-of-fact. "At this point you should be asking yourself where we go from here, French, because I'm sure you're just as repelled by the idea of sex without commitment as I am. Do you see what I mean?"

"I see what you mean," he said, though he did not find the idea all that repellent.

"Now, don't get me wrong, French, I'm not saying you have to move to the Twin Cities right away, but eventually you'll have to consider it."

"I will?"

"Of course. Don't you see why?"

"Why?"

"Because I can't be driving four hundred miles up there and back every weekend," she said sternly. "And when I do, where do we do it? Not at the Morgan, that's out. I refuse to do it at the Morgan."

French was relieved to hear it. Grover would no doubt stand outside his door and listen.

"I mean, I foresee the day when we can both move back to Staggerford, but for the time being we have all these things to think about. The four hundred miles, where we do it, sex without commitment—all that."

He said nothing. He felt suddenly sad. The playful woman he'd been in bed with had been replaced by this voice on the wire making impossible demands.

"What are you thinking?" she asked.

He was thinking, How do I get out of this? His response was a subdued, drawn-out "Well . . ."

Apparently she sensed from his reticence that she might be losing him, for her next words were girlish again. "Listen, I just called 'cause I was lying here thinking what bedbugs we were and what a lovely time we had—it was *real* lovely, French—and to say good night. Didn't you think it was lovely, too?"

"Sure." He was standing on the icy linoleum with one foot on top of the other.

"*Real* lovely?"

"Yup."

"Okay, French, I'll let you go. Sweet dreams."

"Thanks."

"Till Friday."

"Right."

"Good night, French."

"Good night."

"Can't you say my name?"

"Imogene."

"Can't you say, 'Good night, Imogene'?"

"Good night, Imogene."

"Good night, sweet prince."

He politely waited until he heard the circuit broken before he hung up.

Came a hollow voice from Room 2 as he climbed the stairs: "Good night, Imogene?"

"None of your business, Grover."

Hanging up her bedside phone, Imogene told herself she must go to sleep immediately—she had to get up at six-thirty for work—yet she couldn't resist reading one more letter. She'd read five or six at a coffee shop on the way south, and arriving home, she'd read a dozen or so before unpacking her bag, then another dozen after getting into bed. The letters were riveting. They afforded Imogene a many-sided examination of a certain man who signed himself "James," together with the people and landscapes he moved among.

The letter she studied now was more reflective than most of

the others. It was about friendship, and apparently written in
response to Agatha's observations on the subject. This was part
of the fascination for Imogene, this filling in of Agatha's side
of the correspondence from the evidence contained in the replies. It was a challenge to her investigative powers. She
learned in this letter, for example, that both James and Agatha
felt shortchanged where friends were concerned. James described a few men he'd befriended over the years who had
died or otherwise dropped out of his life, and then he went on
to commiserate with Agatha for what she'd evidently claimed
was a lifelong dearth of companions. He speculated that it was
probably a natural result of her having taught all her life in a
parochial school, which meant that her colleagues were nuns,
and nuns were women apart. When the dismissal bell rang and
the students went home, he wrote, the teaching nun washed her
blackboard and scurried back to the haven of her convent.
Whoever heard of making friends with a nun?

He continued, "If your neighbor Lillian is the best you've
known in the way of companionship, Agatha, I have to agree
that you've not been dealt a full hand. I'm all too familiar with
that sort of friend, that agreeable warm body incapable of any
sort of mental stimulation."

Imogene was outraged. Imogene, whose bond with her
mother, though enduring, was almost entirely without emotion,
felt a rare surge of compassion for the agreeable warm body
that had given birth to her, had nursed her and reared her and
provided her with a warm and comfortable home well into her
adult years. It was cruel of Agatha to portray her mother as
anything but gentle and kind. Agatha was egotistical and arro-
gant. Agatha, for half a century the moral exemplar brooding
over the Catholic half of Staggerford, was a whited sepulcher.
How dare she speak of her oldest, truest friend as though she
were some kind of furry animal with a mind to match. Agatha,
at heart, was heartless.

Imogene flung the letter to the floor, switched off her bedside lamp, and lay fuming in the dark.

19

*A*GATHA WENT DOWN TO breakfast feeling it was time for bed. Her mind was clouded, her eyelids were heavy. The previous noon, having settled into her private room on the second floor of the Hotel Bellarmino, she'd fallen into a fitful sleep while most of her companions went for exploratory walks, using maps of the city provided by Professor Finn. In the evening she'd gone down to the dining room for a group dinner that proved arduous and disturbing. Talk of the airport atrocity being unavoidable, everyone fell into a somber mood, and the pixyish young woman given to hysteria needed once again to be comforted by her friends and Father Finn. After dinner Agatha had slept four or five more hours, and then, waking for good at two this morning, had passed the rest of the night fussily unpacking her luggage and inattentively reading the paperback life of Galileo assigned to the students by the professor.

Standing now in the doorway of the small dining room, her coat over her arm, her eyes darting among the several tables, she saw that she was the last of the Minnesota group to show up. She threaded her way to the far corner and sat down with Lillian and the Finn brothers. She surveyed the meal set before her—a roll—and said, "Breakfast is too grand a name for it."

Professor Finn thought her remark vastly amusing. When he stopped laughing, he asked, "Are your accommodations satisfactory, Miss McGee?"

"Everything is very clean," she said, cleanliness being her foremost requirement. Her only complaint about the hotel, which she left unspoken, was its small dimensions. Her room, the lobby, the lounge, the very table at which they were breakfasting, seemed designed for Lilliputians.

"I'm afraid my brother and I have the best view," said Father Finn. "Front and center, over the street."

"Afraid?" asked Agatha. "Why do you say afraid?"

"Well," the priest cleared his throat, "I don't like being treated better than the rest of the group. I mean, I don't believe holy orders should give me—"

"Listen, holy orders doesn't mean squat at this hotel," said his brother jovially. "You're in that room because you're with me."

"What I can't get used to," said Lillian, "is hearing people talk and I don't have a clue what they're talking about. You wonder how *they* know."

"I'm sure they wonder the same about us," said Father Finn.

"When I came down this morning, the man at the desk asked me about the bone journey. I suppose he meant the catacombs."

Professor Finn bounced on his chair with amusement. "No, Mrs. Kite, he was probably saying good morning."

"He never said good morning. He said, 'Bone journey,' and I said, 'No, the Galileo tour.' "

"That set him straight, did it, Mrs. Kite?"

"Yes, he seemed satisfied with that."

Agatha saw the professor trying to catch her eye and share this little joke with her, but she looked away from him, refusing to join in any conspiracy against her friend.

"Agatha, you're always so dressed up," said Lillian, eyeing her green knit dress. "Didn't you bring slacks?"

"I don't own any, Lillian, except gardening slacks."

"Imogene bought me this outfit in the city." She was wearing gray slacks and a coral blouse with a big bow in front. Her traveling jacket, a gray poplin garment with large pockets at the breast, was draped over the back of her chair.

"Very nice," said Agatha, observing that her friend as a rule appeared more fashionable when her daughter left her alone.

A waiter came with coffee and tea. Another waiter brought a fresh basket of roles. Agatha, eating hungrily, regretted that her pastor had apparently brought along no priestly clothes. Staring into his coffee and looking as sleepy as Agatha felt, Father Finn wore his tweed sport coat over a shirt of small checks, which was open at the throat. His brother the professor, dressed this morning in a pink button-down shirt under a sky-blue windbreaker, opened a small notebook and consulted a list of names. "Everyone present and accounted for," he said, glancing around at the other tables.

Agatha asked, "Are your mental clocks out of kilter, the rest of you, or am I the only one?"

This prompted a lengthy discussion of sleep and wakefulness, which Lillian capped off by recounting a dream she'd had in the night. She and several strangers, carrying heavy suitcases, were trudging along a street in single file behind a slow-moving fire truck.

"A travel dream," said Father Finn. "I have dreams about suitcases whenever I fly to my sister's in San Diego."

"More likely it's about the terrorist shooting," countered his brother.

"Oh, the shooting," said Agatha, making fists of both hands and shaking her head. "I've been trying to put the shooting out of my mind. How many dead—have you heard officially?"

"I'll find us a *Herald Tribune*," said the professor, rising abruptly from his chair and hurrying out of the dining room.

The priest got to his feet as well, apologizing for abandoning the two women. "I have some office to say before the coach picks us up," he told them.

Alone with Agatha, Lillian spoke confidentially. "I know he's a professor, but couldn't he be wrong all the same? There wasn't any shooting in my dream. I never dream about bad things. We were just walking along behind the fire truck."

"I suppose he meant that the fire truck could stand for the ambulances we saw at the airport. The siren and flashing lights, you see."

"But it didn't have its siren going in my dream. The lights weren't flashing. It was just driving along like an ordinary truck."

"I see. Then maybe it's not about the shooting."

"But the professor said it was."

"He's not a professor of dreams, Lillian."

"That's what I was wondering."

"He's a professor of physics."

Lillian dabbed at her lips with her napkin. "Does that mean what I think it means?"

"Physics? Gravity and heat and energy and things like that."
Lillian gave her a skeptical look.

Agatha, famished, spreading marmalade on her second roll,
said, "Why, what did you think it meant?"

"Different kinds of laxatives."

"No, it's not that."

"I wondered."

Lisa Berglund hesitantly approached their table and asked,
"Miss McGee, could I introduce you to a couple of friends?
The three of us are hoping you'll help us with our papers."

"Of course. Bring them over. Pull up another chair."

Lisa turned and beckoned across the room, and Agatha
watched two young women rise from a table and come forward. One was the pixy whose emotional outbursts had twice
set everyone's ears to ringing. Lisa introduced her as Paula.
She had a short haircut, a nervous way of nodding her head
when she spoke or listened, and small eyes that squeezed shut
when she smiled. Her friend was a large, round-faced girl with
busy dark hair. Her name was Betty Lou.

Agatha introduced the three girls to Lillian. "We've been
friends and neighbors since we were younger than you," she
said. "Do sit down and tell us about yourselves."

Paula, who looked even younger up close than she had
seemed from a distance, was first to respond. Her voice was
high-pitched and cheerful. "I'm from the Twin Cities. My
dad's an engineer with a firm that designs conveyor belts. My
mom last year opened her own business, a movie-rental store
in Burnsville. She's always loved movies, and so renting movies has done a lot for her state of mind. Like, I mean her over-
all disposition is changed. She's just plain nicer around home
to my dad and my sisters and me." This being her complete
résumé, Paula beamed her most intense smile at Agatha and
Lillian, her eyes squeezing shut.

How curious, thought Agatha, to respond to an inquiry
about oneself by describing one's mother. She turned to the
other girl.

"I'm from St. Paul," said Betty Lou. "My dad's a lawyer,
my mom's a psychotherapist. I've got a sister and a brother.
They're both younger than I am."

Betty Lou's speech, in contrast to Paula's, was slow and

soft. Whereas Paula came at you with an aggressive kind of cheerfulness, Betty Lou regarded her listener with a passive and level gaze. Agatha guessed that anyone so imperturbable must come from a serene and stable family, and apparently she guessed right.

"We all get along good, my mom and dad included. The five of us go to a cabin up north for a month every summer. We go to Clearwater, Florida, at Christmastime—which I'm missing this year for the first time in my life. We've been three times to Europe, but never Italy. My dad and mom couldn't understand why I wanted to go to college in Rookery, it's so far from the city, but of course once I made up my mind, they were fine with it. I'm a senior. I thought this trip would be interesting because I like science. I've always liked science. In high school I won first place at a science fair for an electric scarf I knitted. I made it out of polyester yarn interwoven with heating tape. You carried two double-A batteries in your pocket, and it felt cozy around your neck on cold days. If it was windy, you wrapped your face in it. The judges said I ought to try for a patent, and my dad said he'd look into it. I guess he's still looking into it. He's sort of slow with stuff like that."

"I need to get the pattern from you," said Lillian.

"There isn't any. I made it up as I went."

"And why *did* you choose Rookery State?" Agatha asked.

"Some friends from high school were going there, including a boy I had a crush on. That, and I liked the north woods and lakes in the summertime and thought I'd probably like it there year-round. Which I do. It turned out that my friends dropped out after the first year, and the boy I liked didn't care all that much for me, but I can't leave the north. The lakes especially. I want to stay up there after I graduate and get a job in natural resources. I want to analyze lake water."

"And you?" asked Agatha, turning back to Paula. "What will you do with your degree?"

"Gee, I'm a senior, and I can't decide. My mom wants me to go in with her and rent movies. I don't know for sure if I want to rent movies. I might and I might not." She beamed her urgent smile at Betty Lou, at Lisa, at Lillian, at Agatha. "My dad says I can be anything I want to be, but renting movies is

out. He says it's work for idiots. I guess I wouldn't mind being
a teacher, but I'd have to go back after graduation and get my
teaching certificate. I mean that's like another whole year of
college, and I'm not sure I could stand that. I might do it, and
I might not. If I'd've planned my course of study better, I
could be getting my teaching certificate along with my B.A.,
but I didn't do very good at planning my course of study. I
took a lot of courses that don't count toward my major."

"Which is?"

"Humanities." Paula intensified her smile.

"What area of humanities?"

"Just humanities. It's a major for people like me who
haven't figured out where they're going. When I get home
from this trip I'll talk it over with my parents and see what I
ought to do next year."

Paula's smile, which at first had struck Agatha as cheery
and wholesome, now struck her as desperate. Stretched to its
painful limit, it was the pleading smile of someone deeply in
need of something. Of what? Guidance, Agatha speculated;
Paula was looking for guidance from her parents, who were
apparently at odds and mixing her up. And surely companionship; her smile said, Understand me, be my friend. And, above
all, love. By what flaw in God's plan (Agatha asked herself)
were most people in need of more love than they were getting?

At this point, Lillian addressed the three girls, describing at
length and with pride her daughter Imogene's career in librar-
ies. The girls listened politely. Meanwhile, Agatha, finishing
her tea, pondered the shortage of love in the world.

She called to mind her Thanksgiving dinner, and analyzed,
one by one, the lonely-hearts at her table for whom love, that
most natural of resources, seemed in alarmingly short supply.
Frederick Lopat was loveless, but he didn't seem to mind.
Sylvester Juba was loveless, and the lack of it was making a
randy old fool out of him. Sister Judith's religious vow had cut
her off from love and marriage, and didn't Sister Judith's smile
contain the same sort of urgent pleading that Paula the pixy
displayed in hers? And Lillian? Was it the lack of love in
Lillian's life that made her such a fan of the tabloids and soap
operas? Well, at least Myron Kleinschmidt was not deprived,
thought Agatha. And yet, if the congressman was secure in his

marriage to Elena, why had he turned up on her doorstep looking utterly bereft on the afternoon before Thanksgiving? What
was that all about?

And yourself, Agatha? Are you not feeling deprived? This
was James speaking, whose inquiries were becoming more au-
dacious by the day, but she could handle them. *I'm a lot like
Frederick Lopat, James, loveless but not suffering from it. God
loves us all, does he not? What more do I need than that?
Whatever the cause of my malaise, I assure you it isn't the
lack of love in my life. It's the lack of pencils and quizzes and
lesson plans. Perhaps you, James, are still feeling the pain of
our breakup, but I have recovered very nicely, thank you.*

"People!" Agatha was drawn out of her thoughts by the
voice of Professor Finn calling, "People, people!" He was
standing in the doorway of the dining room, waving a newspaper and summoning his travelers. "The coach is here, people,
please come along."

Agatha rose from her chair and put on her coat, the same
tan, all-weather traveling coat she had worn in Ireland. The
three girls slipped into their jackets; all variations of the same
jacket, it seemed to Agatha—bulky, many-pocketed garments
of colorful poplin equipped with more zippers, buttons, and
strings than one could possibly need.

"We'll have to meet to plan your papers, girls. I should
think this afternoon or this evening would be none too soon.
We mustn't let time get away from us."

"Oh, we can't this afternoon," said Lisa. "Dr. Finn is taking
us on a tour of Galileo places."

"This evening, then?"

"Tonight Betty Lou and I are going to a disco," said Paula.
"See, we met these boys, Miss McGee."

"At dinner, then," said Agatha. "Shall we sit together at dinner?"

The young women said yes, and so did Lillian.

"Everything you need there, Father?" asked the young
monk, a certain Brother Larry from America, whose assignment it was to see to the needs of visitors at mealtime, a simple job this week, James O'Hannon being the only guest.

"Everything, thank you," said James, the lone diner in Sant'

Anselmo's large refectory. He regarded his toast and scrambled eggs, and added, "My compliments to the chef."

"I'll leave you, then. I've got a class in patristics coming up in a few minutes."

"Ah, the Church Fathers. Interesting, is it?"

"It's boring me out of my skull, to tell you the truth." The hair on Brother Larry's perfectly round skull was cropped extremely close, the next thing to shaven. He was a large young man, a former athlete at the University of Wisconsin, he'd told James. An all-conference left fielder, whatever that meant.

"It seems an odd time to be having classes, Larry, between the holidays."

"Well, it's a tutorial, really. We meet when it's convenient for my prof. See you this noon?"

"No, not this noon. I'm going out again for lunch."

"Supper, then?"

"Yes, I'll see you at supper, Larry. Thank you."

The sound of the young man's footsteps on the stone floor echoed off the walls of the long room and then died away, leaving James at his solitary breakfast with a large book open beside his plate. He bent to his food, glad to be hungry this morning after weeks of diminished appetite, glad to be sure-handed again after a long and irritating period of shakes and tremors, glad to be feeling no twinges or cramps in his bowels. His gladness, however, stemmed from more than his recuperation from illness. This was his day for meeting Agatha McGee in St. Peter's Square.

The book beside his plate was an atlas from the library upstairs. Yesterday Brother Larry, telling James about his home in what he called the Middle West, had answered James's questions about a neighboring state called Minnesota. James told him that although he had a good friend living there, he had no idea where the friend's town was in relation to places he'd heard of, like Lake Superior and the Mayo Clinic, and so this morning, sitting down to breakfast, he found this atlas lying open to the Minnesota page. Brother Larry was wonderfully attentive.

He studied the map. He saw the blue expanse of Lake Superior dwindling to a point at the port of Duluth. Squinting at the small print, he found the Badbattle River and followed it through the black dot of Berrington (Bishop Baker's town) and on to the smaller dot of Staggerford, which was situated slightly west and north of the center of the state. It took him several minutes of tracing concentric circles with his finger before he found Rochester in the southeast corner. A priest in Dublin, Father John Rowland, had gone to Rochester years ago for intestinal difficulties of a serious nature, and to this day insisted that the Mayo Clinic had saved his life.

Professor Finn's covey of travelers followed him down the steps of the Hotel Bellarmino and out into the chilly sunshine. Overnight the weather had reverted from June to April. They boarded yesterday's plush, purple coach with yesterday's grumpy, heavy-browed driver at the wheel. Standing at the driver's shoulder this morning was a large, gray-haired woman wearing a colorful shawl over her dark green, long-skirted suit and hugging to her breast a large tattered notebook.

"Buon giorno," she said to each Minnesotan in turn, to which most of them responded with a "Hi" or "Hello." Agatha said, "How do you do," and Professor Finn, the last aboard, said *"Buon giorno,* Signora Razioni. *Come sta?"*

"Bene, grazie," she told him, smiling faintly, and then, turning to the passengers and planting her feet wide apart for stability as the coach began to move, she spoke into a microphone. *"Buon giorno,* my friends, I am named Anna Razioni, and this morning I am showing you places of ancient and Renaissance Rome. We stop first at the Trevi Fountain, and we end nearby noon at the Villa Borghese. Tomorrow morning I show you Vatican City."

"Bone journey, bone journey," said Lillian aloud to herself, trying out the native tongue.

Agatha, at her side, looked up the Trevi Fountain in Imogene's guidebook and read aloud, arousing in Lillian very little interest until the title of a movie came up.

"Why, I saw that movie, Agatha. I saw it at the Orpheum forty years ago, and I saw it on the movie channel last fall. You mean we're going where they actually made it?"

"That's what it says."

"It's a magic fountain. You throw money in backwards, over your shoulder, and you come back to Rome someday."

"A superstition."

"In the movie it was three women from America. They wished for men, I think."

"And got them, no doubt."

The bus floated on cushiony springs along narrow streams of traffic and came to a stop next to a small shop of trinkets and postcards. The shop's proprietor, a squat, unkempt woman with a broom in one hand and a carnation in the other, was chatting noisily and unintelligibly in her doorway with a woman selling flowers out of a bucket, while not twenty feet away a bearded derelict lay sleeping on the sidewalk, his head resting on a pillow of stone. These three might have been presenting a play or skit, so entranced and respectfully silent were the fourteen Minnesotans descending from the bus. Like yesterday's carnage at the airport, this scene, with its Roman actors floodlit by a sun too high for January, reminded them how far they'd ventured from home. In neither Rookery nor Staggerford did anyone ever lie down to sleep in the street or speak a language you didn't understand. At home, flowers exposed to the open air at this time of year quickly froze and turned dark as prunes.

Signora Razioni, directing what sounded like an insult at the derelict, stepped around him and led the group up a steep, walled street that twisted into a small open square, where the waters of the Trevi Fountain were gushing and splashing half in shadow, half in sun. Agatha, approaching respectfully, studied the sculptures. Neptune, like a commander surveying his troops, looked down on his chargers rearing up out of the water, each steed carrying a horseman on its back. Why weren't Neptune and the horsemen wearing any clothes, Agatha wondered, and why was the fountain so closely hemmed in on all sides by these rather unattractive four- and five-story buildings? And rather sooty buildings at that. She raised her eyes and saw, peering down at her from an open window to the left of the fountain, a man in an undershirt scratching his stomach.

Professor Finn gathered the group in a circle around Signora Razioni, who delivered a lecture less enlightening than the Trevi entry in Imogene's guidebook. When she finished, the students dispersed, tossing coins and wandering around the chilly square with their hands in their pockets, and peering into the windows of shops not yet open for business.

Lillian found two coins in her purse and handed one to Agatha. "Backwards, over your shoulder."

Agatha complied as Lillian watched.

"Did you make your wish?"

"I did."

"That you'd come back to Rome someday?"

"No, that I'd brought a heavier coat."

Lillian, closing her eyes in concentration, took her turn.

Lisa Berglund came and stood at Agatha's side, enraptured, it seemed, by the fountain. "Isn't it magnificent, Miss McGee?"

"Yes, but it seems to need a different setting. Wouldn't it be more magnificent with a long approach?"

Lisa cocked her head. "I guess you're right."

Lillian, still facing away from the water, said, "Look, here comes the bum."

The bearded derelict, having been roused from sleep by Signora Razioni and having trailed after the group, was now working his way around the square, his hand out for money. Most of the students, Agatha observed, came up with coins for him, but Darrin, standing with his back to the fountain, his earphones in place, taunted the man by holding out a coin, and when the man reached for it, he tossed it over his shoulder into the water. This caused the half-dressed man in the high window to shout and clap his hands in appreciation. Darrin, impressed by his own cleverness, grinned triumphantly. The panhandler, impassive and weary, turned from him and moved on.

"You creep!" squealed Trish, rushing at Darrin and swinging her shoulder bag, hitting him a glancing blow on the side of his head, disarranging his earphones. "You absolute creep!" It wasn't clear whether she was scolding him in earnest or in fun.

"He *is* a creep," murmured Lisa. "I can never understand why Trish hangs around with him."

Agatha, at the panhandler's approach, found herself of two minds. By giving him money, would she encourage him in his slothful ways? One heard of beggars being as secretly well-off as those they begged from. Moreover, was this man in collusion with Signora Razioni? Getting off the bus, had she alerted him to her entourage of innocent foreigners? On the other hand, he appeared authentically needy, and Agatha feared being uncharitable.

Her indecision was solved by Lillian, who again went into her purse for coins, and again handed one to Agatha.

He was a tall man, bent at the waist. The stains on his long coat were overlaid with newer stains, and his skin was the color of wet cement. Pressing the coin into his hand, Agatha looked for a long moment into his bleary brown eyes and saw a hopelessness so abject and mournful that her doubts were immediately dispelled. Here was poverty that went beyond indigence. Here was an empty spirit, a man deprived of his humanity. She thought of Frederick Lopat and thanked God that Frederick's decline had been halted short of this lowly, lifeless state. The dead look in this man's eyes might have been that of a lower form of life. Lower even than a dog, thought Agatha, for dogs show more vitality in their eyes. These eyes might have been a frog's. She finally had to look away.

And so she understood something of what Paula the pixy was feeling when, a few moments later, the man approached her and Paula screamed. All turned to see what the bloodcurdling noise was about. Paula appeared to be dancing. Her outcry ended in a loud sobbing noise, and her footwork reminded Agatha of a jitterbug step, a hopping or skipping motion that speeded up as the man came closer. Betty Lou, her impervious friend, linked arms with her and said consoling things softly and close to her ear, but to no effect. Betty Lou then put her hand out to stop the beggar's approach, and it was either this gesture or Paula's voice rising hysterically that broke through the man's haze and caused him to stop and turn and walk in a crooked line across the square and disappear down a shadowy lane. Paula fell sobbing into Betty Lou's arms.

"What ails the poor thing?" asked Agatha.

"Plumb nuts," was Lillian's diagnosis.

"All I know is, she's not very stable," Lisa Berglund confided. "Last year one time they put her in the hospital for acting that way. They say it's usually men. I guess certain men touch it off."

Betty Lou led Paula to the edge of the pool, where they sat down on the stone ledge. Father Finn joined them there. He and Betty Lou, from either side, leaned close to her, spoke to her, patted her hands. Paula, nodding, continued to sob. Behind them the spouting, falling water sparkled like diamonds, for the sun had climbed up over the rooftops and was spilling its warm sunlight into the square.

Denis Worthy, judging by the vigor in James O'Hannon's stride, assumed it would be the bus again this morning, but he asked anyway, to make sure. "Bus or taxi, Father?"

"No hurry. Lovely morning for a bus ride."

As they emerged from the walled garden and stepped out into the Via della Marmorata, gusts of wind played with wisps of James O'Hannon's white hair and whipped Denis Worthy's ankle-length scapular around his legs.

"Colder this morning," said Denis.

"Bracing," said James happily.

"Warmer by noon, they say."

"Perfect."

When they drew abreast of the news agent across the street, James took some currency from his pocket and handed it to Denis. "Could I ask you to go over there and see if they have a newspaper an Irishman can read?"

Denis, the hem of his habit flying, dashed across the street between cars and lorries and dashed back again. James scanned the front page of the *Herald Tribune* as they walked.

"Five terrorists," said James. "Thirteen dead, sixty injured. Hand grenades and submachine guns. Bullet-riddled luggage, and the floor covered with blood."

"Savagery," said Denis.

"Lord God!" James came to a halt. "Three Americans among the dead."

"Not your friend, surely."

James read aloud. " 'The victims were passengers boarding El Al jets to New York and Tel Aviv.' "

"Definitely not your friend then."

James nodded, conceding that Agatha would not have been

among them. Yet he was shaken. He felt for a few moments that he might vomit. He handed the paper to Denis and proceeded along more slowly than before.

"Here it comes," said Denis peering down the street.

"Run for it, if you want," said James. "I'll take the next one." They were a considerable distance from the bus stop.

"I'll get the driver to wait. Take your time."

"No, I'm perfectly able—"

But Denis was running ahead to the bus stop, and when the vehicle came to a halt, he stepped out in front of it. The driver, prevented from moving, laid on his horn and shouted angrily out the open door while James slowly made his way along the curb and climbed aboard.

20

*T*RY *AS* *SHE* *MIGHT,* and despite the urging of Signora Razioni, Agatha could not reconstruct the Roman Forum in her mind, not with so little to build on. Walking among the confusing mass of broken columns and leveled foundations that lay scattered throughout the grassy acreage, she wondered aloud, "How old does debris have to become before it's historical?"

Professor Finn, amused, asked, "Not much impressed with antiquities, Miss McGee?"

"A flaw of character, I'm sure, but my interest in history has never gone back to classical times."

"Picture here the *rostra*," Signora Razioni called out to her Americans, drawing their attention to a slab of marble at her feet. It was all but covered over with sod, and what showed through was pocked and grimy. "How you say? Podiums! Orators stand here and speak to the people!"

More impressive to Agatha than the slab of marble was the color of the grass. "Green grass in January, Lillian. Imagine."

"I know. You'd think it was spring."

"Picture here the Temple of Vespasian," said the Signora, walking on ahead. "And over there the Temple of Saturn."

Agatha fell into step with Paula, who seemed to have recovered her composure. The girl sensed Agatha's question before she asked it. "I'm fine, Miss McGee, I'm just fine. I know I shouldn't be affected by things like that. I'm a lot better than I used to be. A *lot* better."

"Don't apologize," said Agatha. "I understand what you were feeling. Seeing the man up close, I was unnerved myself."

"But you didn't see the look he gave me. He was raping me with his eyes."

"Heavens."

"And the awful things he said to me, it was just terrible."

This surprised Agatha. "He spoke to you?"

Paula shuddered. "I can't tell you what he said. It was too dirty and terrible."

Agatha had not seen the derelict speak to anyone. And if he had spoken, was it likely he knew English? Nor had his expression changed as he went from person to person. It was a look of defeat, not aggression.

"I know things like that happen in life, Miss McGee, and we should learn to ignore them, and I will someday, I know I will, but I guess I just have this oversensitive nature, and it's taking me longer than most people to get used to inappropriate behavior."

Agatha kept her counsel, suspecting that something grotesque was going on in Paula's imagination.

"You do believe me, don't you, Miss McGee, that the man said threatening things to me? I can tell you his exact words if you want, but they were very dirty."

"I sympathize, Paula. Please keep them to yourself."

"But you do believe me?"

"I sympathize. Hurry along now, the Signora is calling us."

Paula veered away from her, rejoining her friend Betty Lou.

Among the few other tourists strolling through the Forum this morning were two elderly American women who had attached themselves to the Minnesota group, their attention caught by the stentorian voice of Signora Razioni. They eventually fell into conversation with Lillian Kite, a conversation so engrossing that the three of them, without realizing it, wandered off and had gone quite a distance down a broad, sandy path before Agatha called to Lillian.

"That's all right, Miss McGee," said Professor Finn. "They're headed for the Colosseum, and so are we."

Turning and acknowledging Agatha with a wave, Lillian did not wait for the group, but kept moving along the path at a lazy saunter, talking to her new friends. One of these women, the smaller of the two, looked to Agatha to be about seventy-five years old. She had white hair, blue-tinted, and wore a short tan jacket over a purple skirt. She had an enormous patent-leather purse hanging from her shoulder. The other woman, larger and more demonstrative than her companion, was obviously younger, in her mid-sixties. She wore black slacks and a red sweater under a transparent plastic raincoat. She shot her arms out as she spoke. Her hair, dyed to a black sheen, reflected the sun like metal.

Whatever topic had brought them together in the Forum, it was laundry they were discussing when Agatha caught up with them outside the Colosseum.

"I wash every Monday," said the smaller woman with the blue hair. "I've been washing every Monday for fifty years."

"I wash when I need to," said Lillian.

"We've been rinsing out a few things in our room," said the larger woman in the see-through raincoat. "Our hotel has no laundry."

"I'll be doing that too," said Lillian, "but I don't know where I'll hang things. Our hotel has such little bitty rooms."

The larger woman continued, "Another thing our hotel doesn't have is variety on its menu—everything's so salty. Are you one to watch your sodium intake, Mrs. Kite?"

"I should, but I don't. When my daughter was living at home, she used to keep after me about sodium, but now that she's gone, I keep forgetting."

Agatha divided her attention between this discussion and the words of Signora Razioni, who was preparing the group for its entrance into the Colosseum. "You will see the excavations where the underground rooms are revealed. In these rooms the wild beasts and the gladiators wait until the time for their performance."

"Sodium is hell on blood pressure," the larger woman told Lillian. "Annabelle's husband died of a stroke."

"He had three strokes all in one weekend," stated the other, enumerating them on bent, arthritic fingers. "Friday, Saturday, Sunday, one, two, three. On Monday he was dead."

"My husband died of a heart attack," said Lillian. "Sudden as anything. Massive. Alive one minute and dead the next."

"My husband had heart trouble too," said the large woman, "but it was cancer that took him."

Signora Razioni lectured, "You will see—how you say?—

levels. You will see levels for seating fifty thousand people. Performances, man against man, man against beast, every afternoon, year after year, and the crowds never went smaller. How so many, you ask, day after day? Let me tell you something. Rome brings slaves from all over the empire, until the ratio of slaves to Roman citizens comes to thirty-five to one. Think of it. You have thirty-five slaves. Comes the serious problem of how to keep you occupied—no need for you to work. So the gladiator combat keeps you happy. Combat man to man, man to beast. On one day alone, the day the Colosseum is dedicated, in the year eighty A.D., five thousand beasts perish. How many human people, God knows."

"Hilda had her man longer than I did," the older woman explained to Lillian. "I'll be a widow nineteen years in August."

"Six years in March," said her partner blithely, as though bidding a hand of bridge.

The two of them waited for Lillian to declare.

"I'd have to think," she said.

"Sixteen," Agatha prompted from a short distance away.

"Think of it—sixteen years," sighed Lillian, as though amazed.

After gazing at the wonders inside St. Peter's Basilica for an hour or so, James stepped out into the sunlight flooding the piazza. He had been on his feet for two hours, and he was tired. It was a mistake to have left Sant' Anselmo so early, but his eagerness had not allowed him to catch a later bus.

He crossed St. Peters' porch and sat down on a step. Leaning back against a pillar of stone, he watched the movement of people across the piazza. Those that came his way, converging on the steps leading up to the bronze doors, regarded him with curiosity—a man in priestly black taking his ease on the stones—but he was too tired to feel self-conscious. He rested his head against the pillar and closed his eyes.

Bells woke him. He squinted across the piazza, and when he saw no one loitering at the base of the obelisk, he was half afraid to look at his watch. What if he'd slept beyond the time? What if she'd come and gone? He pushed back his shirt cuff and saw with relief that it was noon exactly. He got to his feet a little too hastily and had to wait for a moment of wooziness to pass before he descended the steps. Crossing the piazza, he assured himself that she was standing on the other side of the obelisk, admiring the crèche.

But she wasn't.

Perhaps she was delayed. Roman traffic. Or a bus with engine failure. Or she'd taken a wrong turn between the bus stop and St. Peter's. He quieted himself with this sort of speculation for a time, but by twelve-thirty he was pacing around and around the obelisk, darting his eyes here and there at approaching strangers and asking God to allow Agatha back into his life.

At one o'clock panic set in. How many times in his life had he advised the distraught, the depressed, and the angry not to let all their hopes be one hope, not to invest their passions in one person, not to be so single-minded as to become myopic and narrow. How useless, he realized now, to try talking sense to the passionate. How foolish to dictate the way emotions ought to go.

By two o'clock he'd made three trips across the stones and up the steps and into the basilica to see if she was waiting for him at the *Pietà*.

At three o'clock Denis Worthy found him standing at the base of the obelisk, looking ashen and ill.

Agatha wrote at the table of teakwood marquetry in the narrow lounge of the Hotel Bellarmino.

Dear James,

Whether due to a simple case of jet lag or the fact that we were greeted by thirteen murders at the airport, I'm traveling slightly off balance, stupidly tired at noon and wide awake at midnight; but I'm determined by tomorrow to recover my normal self by force of will, for tomorrow is our day at the Vatican.

This noon I was sitting on a low wall at the edge of the Villa Borghese when you imposed yourself so forcefully on my thinking that I actually murmured your name aloud, and the girls sitting at my side, one a tiny bundle of nerves named Paula, and the other a stolid presence named Betty Lou, accused me of daydreaming and wanted to know who James was. So that's why I write to you now instead of waiting, as I'd in-

tended, until I'd seen St. Peter's. I write, in part out of whimsy, to ask what you may have been doing or thinking this noon in Ballybegs that I should be so vividly conscious of your presence here in Rome. I write, too, out of concern, because this apparition or intuition or whatever it was has left me with an anxious feeling. Not totally good vibes, as these students would say.

They're off with their professor on a tour of Galileo sites this afternoon. In addition to Paula and Betty Lou, there's a dimpled blonde named Trish who appears fatally attracted to a dolt named Darrin, who plays rock music in his shirt pocket and pipes it into his ears. There's a girl named Lisa who keeps returning to my side to convey her observations of Rome, whether as a kind of reality check for herself or as a favor to an old lady, I can't say, but she is sweet and earnest and pretty and I've already become quite attached to her. That leaves five others I'm not yet acquainted with. Some I may get to know at dinner tonight, for that's when I hold my first seminar for those desiring help with their papers. Yes, James, once a teacher . . .

As for my adult companions, Lillian at this moment is asleep in a chair facing me across the room, a hairy rock star eyeing me from the front page of an Italian tabloid crumpled on her lap. Dr. Finn, as I said, is out with his brood of scholars. He's a peripatetic man of good humor and clipped speech, clipped thoughts. If only he'd clip his mustache. His brother the priest is up in his room doing whatever priests do in their rooms after lunch.

Proofreading, Agatha saw an improved image of herself reflected in the letter. Here, it seemed, was a woman of lighter heart than the one who left home two days ago, a woman actually capable of an amusing turn of phrase or two. Nothing hilarious, mind you, but the remark about the professor's mustache wasn't half bad. Perhaps she'd left her low spirits at home after all. She felt happy enough at this moment, daring enough, to throw caution to the wind and end the letter with "Wish you were here," and she wrote a trial draft of these four words on a scrap of paper before recovering her discretion. She wrote *Fondly, Agatha* instead.

"But isn't it possible she left home before your letter arrived?" asked Denis Worthy on the bus crossing the Tiber. The bus was crowded, James sitting, Denis standing over him, speaking to the crown of his head.

The head wagged no. The tired eyes raised themselves to Denis's. "I mailed it on the sixteenth. No letter has ever taken ten days." The eyes fell.

"But maybe this once." The bus leaned left and Denis steadied himself with a hand on the back of James's seat. "I'm saying it's just possible."

James, saying nothing, thought not. For James it came down to two possibilities, one worse than the other, and neither involving late mail delivery. The likelier possibility was that she didn't want to see him. He couldn't blame her, he having played so false with her, and she being so deeply wounded. Time, he knew, did not heal *all* wounds. And if it was to be a friendship of letters only, well, all right, he could live with that—letters were immensely better than nothing—but it left him feeling very foolish, this wild goose chase to Rome.

The bus leaned right. Denis said, "Count the days, Father. Remember Christmas is in there, along with a weekend."

James again wagged his head, again murmured, "No letter ever took ten days," and tried to keep his mind from straying into the second possibility—that she was one of the three Americans gunned down in the terrorist cross fire. This horrible thought, no less haunting for its being unlikely, made him very agitated. From the moment he'd conceived it in front of St. Peter's, it gave him no rest. He couldn't stop imagining Agatha lying in a pool of blood beside her bullet-riddled suitcase.

Later, in his spartan room on the third floor of Sant' Anselmo, lying on his bed with his shoes off, but too restless for the nap he'd been looking forward to, James counted backward on his fingers. Say she left home on the twenty-sixth before her mail was delivered. No delivery on the twenty-fifth, Christmas, nor on the twenty-fourth, Sunday. That still left seven days for the letter to make its way to Staggerford. Hadn't six been the upper limit? He tried to think back three years. Well, perhaps once or twice, seven.

This caused his imagination to shift, blessedly, away from the gunned-down travelers and take up Denis's supposition:

she didn't know he was in Rome. She was moving about the city, seeing the sights, perhaps even writing him postcards, without any reason to believe he was looking for her. This possibility lifted his heart and made it ache at the same time. He'd have to locate her. But before that, he'd have to ask Bishop Baker of Berrington for help. And for that he'd have to locate Brother Larry and ask him how to phone America. He sat up quickly, pausing on the edge of the bed to allow his customary few seconds of dizziness to pass, then he slipped into his shoes. Pulling on his black cardigan and patting down his hair, he hurried along the hallway, his untied shoelaces ticking on the tiles, in search of Brother Larry.

Bishop Dick Baker, breakfasting in his office on milk and orange juice, the former to settle his chronically uneasy stomach, the latter to ward off a theatening head cold, dialed the rectory in Staggerford and heard the voice of Sister Judith on tape. "Hi, I hope your day is happy. You've reached St. Isidore's. Father Finn's in Italy and Sister Judith's God knows where, but you might reach her at home."

Next he dialed the number she recommended and got Sylvester Juba.

"Mr. Juba, this is Dick Baker calling."

"Who?"

"Your bishop."

"Then tell me one thing," the old man said without pause, as if he'd been expecting the call, "how can you let our pastor run off on vacation with a Sunday and a holy day back to back and nobody to say the Masses?"

The bishop laughed. No one he knew took this man seriously anymore. Sylvester Juba had once been a pillar of St. Isidore's, contributing generously his money and expertise to its various building projects, but age, it was pretty well agreed, had made a fool of him. "It's Father Finn's reward for Christmas, Mr. Juba. Christmas is hard on priests."

"I'm not talking about Christmas, I'm talking about New Year's. Or have you done away with New Year's as a holy day?"

The bishop swung around in his swivel chair and looked out at the falling snow, a dry, small snow swept along on the wind like dust. "You'll be nicely taken care of by one of the monks from St. Andrew's. Father Virgil, I believe. He's been at St. Isidore's many times."

"Those monks don't come cheap. How much does the abbey charge for a monk this year, a hundred bucks?"

"Sixty, as always."

"That's a hundred and twenty for two days, out of St. Isidore's treasury."

"Think of it as a Christmas gift to your pastor."

"I'd like to see a rule keeping our priests home where they belong."

"I'm calling for your daughter, Mr. Juba. Is she there?"

The old man shouted her name, then continued. "I'd like to see a rule keeping our cash in the bank and not skimmed off by that monastery."

"I understand that."

The nun's voice came on the line. "Bishop, what's wrong?"

"Nothing's wrong, Sister."

"You can't operate without rules," said her father. The Jubas were evidently speaking into two phones. "Rules make the world go 'round."

"Whenever my bishop calls, I think, What did I do wrong?" She delivered this with a shrieking laugh that hurt the bishop's ear.

"Don't be such a pessimist," he advised. "Be positive, like me. Whenever I hear from Rome, I assume they want to make me a cardinal."

"Richard Cardinal Baker," she gushed. "It has a wonderful ring to it."

"Dick," he reminded her.

"Without rules you're everybody's sucker," said the old man. "I learned that in the lumber business. At first I had a policy, if one of my men needed a board or a handful of nails for something he was building at home, I'd say, 'Go ahead, help yourself,' but those crooks taught me a lesson in a hurry. One of them carried off an entire door frame, door and all, and Herman Hauser took home enough shingles to shingle his goddamn barn."

"Sister, I'm calling to ask where Father Finn's group is staying in Rome."

"The hotel's called the Bellarmino." She spelled it for him. "I've got the number at the rectory. I can call you back."

"No, the name's all I need. Someone's trying to reach Agatha McGee."

"Not an emergency, I hope."

"No, nothing like that. He's an old friend who happens to be in Italy and wants to look her up." Was this too much to reveal? It was out before he thought.

"I didn't know the dear thing *had* friends," said Sister Judith.

"Now, now," said her bishop.

"I don't mean anything disrespectful, Dick. I just mean Agatha's had loads and loads of respect from everybody all her life, but that's different from friendship, if you see what I mean."

He knew she was fishing to know the friend's identity, so he asked evasively, "How's the parish running? All the gears meshing, cogs turning?"

"I can tell you more next week. The parish council's meeting on the sixth to evaluate my first half year."

"Flying colors, I'm sure."

"I canned them both," said Sylvester. "The one with the door frame brought it back, but I canned him anyway."

"I don't know, Dick. A couple members are soreheads. I'm too modern for them."

"Flying colors, no doubt about it. Now I'll have to let you go, I'm wanted on the other phone."

"Okay, Dick, hang tough."

"Good-bye, Sister. Nice talking to you, Mr. Juba."

"After that I had rules."

"The best policy, I'm sure."

"They paid for every goddamn nail."

21

*N*EXT MORNING, LEAVING THE dining room after breakfast and crossing the lobby with Lillian, Agatha glimpsed out of the corner of her eye an elderly priest rising from the leather couch in the lounge and starting toward her. He had an umbrella over his arm and a look of absolute terror in his eyes. Ignoring him, she turned to Lillian to ask if she had thought to pack an umbrella, and that was when the priest spoke her name, and she knew, by his voice, that it was James.

By his voice, not by his face. His face had undergone an alarming change, a transformation such as time alone could not have caused. Time in conjunction with illness perhaps, or with grief, or with privation of some kind, but time by itself—a mere three years—could not have left his face so pallid and sunken, his hair so thin and white, his eyes so vulnerable. His mouth was an old man's mouth.

"James, what's happened to you?" she blurted, laying her hand on his wrist.

At this, he smiled his handsome, great-hearted smile, and instantly she saw the James she had loved. The smile firmed up his mouth, dismissing fear from his eyes and raising a trace of blushlike color in his cheeks. It made him younger by years, and more robust; it made him taller somehow.

"James, you're so far from home," she said foolishly, as if she were not farther.

He took her hand in both of his own. "You didn't know I was here, then?"

She looked perplexed. "Here? At this hotel?"

"No, I mean in Rome."

She said, "How was I to know?" and wondered why this reply should strike him as so agreeable. Half closing his eyes, he uttered a long, satisfied "Aaaaah."

"Well, how *was* I to know, James?"

"I wrote you."

"Oh, the mail," she lamented. "It's a scandal."

"Shocking," he concurred, and behind his beaming smile a trace of his apprehension reappeared. "I proposed meeting you at the Vatican. Yesterday. I was afraid when you didn't show up—"

"Maybe he wrote the wrong zip code," suggested Lillian, who was waiting to be introduced. "I've heard wrong zip codes can take up to three extra days."

"This is Lillian Kite, James. My friend and neighbor."

"Of course. How do you do. I'm very pleased to meet you."

"This is Father O'Hannon, Lillian. We met through the mail."

"From Ireland," said Lillian, shrewdly narrowing her eyes. "I can tell by his brogue."

"How did you find us, James?" *Us*—as though Lillian were half his reason for searching.

"By telephone," he said. "Bishop Baker."

The students, waiting for the bus, were quietly clustered at the glass double doors leading outside, their spirits subdued by the sunless, drizzly morning. Standing a little apart from them were the Finn brothers, quietly conversing and glancing curiously across the lobby at James.

Agatha couldn't hold back the question. "Have you been sick, James?"

When he nodded, his eyes shifting away and his smile weakening, Agatha's feelings for him, long submerged, rose to the surface and threatened to engulf her. Joy. Sorrow. Resentment. Love. Longing. They were all mixed up together. Confused and suddenly short of breath, she lowered her eyes as she concentrated on suppressing them.

Lillian said, "We were in Ireland a few years ago." At this, Agatha raised her eyes and exchanged with James a sad, meaningful smile, which escaped Lillian's notice. "The salmon and the ham were the best we ever ate, but the Irish can keep their sausage. We said so, didn't we, Agatha?"

"We did."

"Mealy."

"Lillian, please give me a few minutes with Father O'Hannon alone. I'll see you on the bus."

Lillian nodded agreeably. "I'll scoot upstairs and get my umbrella."

Agatha led James back into the narrow lounge he'd stepped out of. She pulled a second straight-backed chair up to the writing table, and they sat facing each other across its surface of cracked marquetry.

"What is it, James?"

He smiled shyly. "Intestinal cancer."

"Dear God. Have they operated?"

"They did." His smile, though dimmed, did not entirely leave his face.

"They got it all?"

"They'll know more after my next examination."

"You're on medication?"

"I was. And may be again."

She found the look on his face disconcerting. What did a man with cancer have to smile about? Again she felt her emotions rising up in rebellion against her polite reserve. She wanted to shame him for hurting her. She wanted to embrace him. "You're in Rome on church business?" she asked, carefully modulating her voice.

"Like yourself, I'm a pilgrim." He judged it too soon to tell her she was the object of his pilgrimage. She might bolt.

"Isn't it awfully soon to be traveling?"

"I'm getting my strength back, a bit more of it every day."

They fell silent. His smile continued to puzzle her. It was now quite placid, untroubled. Did he share none of her chaotic emotion? She returned his smile, but briefly, tensely. "A bus is coming any minute to take us to Vatican City."

As though on cue, the coach pulled up, and the group at the door began filing out. James waited expectantly for her to invite him along, and when she fell silent again, sitting there with her eyes slightly averted, his smile disappeared. He frowned and sat forward. "I had hoped to show you St. Peter's myself, Agatha. Would you allow me?"

For the first time in her life she was feeling the urge to be coy. It was no contest, James O'Hannon over Signora Razioni, but was it wise to act eager? She lowered her eyes for a moment, recalling the pain she'd carried home from Ireland. And then, looking up and sensing the pain her hesitation was causing James, she said, "Well, of course."

At the bus, waiting their turn to board, Agatha said, "Dr. Finn, this is Father O'Hannon, a friend from Ireland. Since he's going to the Vatican, I told him he could ride with us—was I being presumptuous?"

"More the merrier, Father O'Hannon, welcome aboard. Here on vacation, are you?"

"That's right." James shook the man's hand.

"You could have left the rain in Ireland, you know. Wouldn't have hurt our feelings any."

"You'll have to forgive me, Dr. Finn."

"Here, meet my brother, he's in the priest business too. Franny, this is Father O'Hannon. And these two clowns are my assistants. This is Trish, and this is Darrin."

Handshakes. Greetings. All aboard.

Sitting with Agatha near the back of the bus, James chuckled and said it was like meeting characters out of a well-loved novel, the flesh-and-blood Lillian Kite and Father Finn, whom he knew so well through her letters, being precisely the people he'd pictured. "But with your priest, there's a twist to it, Agatha. I sense that the character somehow knows me better than I know the character."

"I can't say what he knows about you, James. He knows whatever Bishop Baker told him."

"Oh, Bishop Baker." James laughed. "Now there's a rare churchman for you."

"Deviant, I'd say."

"That evening we spent together in Ballybegs, 'Dick,' he was saying by the end of it, 'Call me Dick, and I'll call you Jim.' I've never been called Jim in my life."

"Somewhere in his training he got the idea that chumminess was next to godliness."

"As a lad, I was called Jamie or Shamie, but nobody's ever called me Jim except the bishop of Berrington. It's so downright American."

"And so tiresome."

"But isn't the simplicity of it endearing, Agatha? I never

meet one of those pally types that I don't have to admire their innocence. Trusting as five-year-olds, they are, and just as well-meaning—out to form an immediate bond with everyone they meet. My sister was like that. Perfect for the pub trade. It was like sitting down before your own hearth, having a pint in O'Hannon's, she was that warm and chatty across the bar."

"But by nature, I'm sure."

James gave her a quizzical look.

"What I mean is, your sister was no doubt sincere."

"And your Bishop Baker is not?"

Draw your own conclusions, said Agatha's raised eyebrows, I'd rather not give voice to my suspicion that Bishop Baker rehearses the way he presents himself.

But she *was* perfectly willing to give voice to her outrage over the closing—by episcopal edict—of St. Isidore's Elementary, and their discussion of the bishop continued, Agatha recounting the steps leading to its demise, James making sympathetic remarks, and both of them all the while perfectly aware that Bishop Dick Baker, as a topic, was the small talk by which they were finding their voices. He was merely a bridge to more interesting things, a bridge across their nervousness and excitement and wonder at being together again.

When, a bit later, they were interrupted by Signora Razioni's amplified voice pointing out something on their right, something on their left, and something up ahead, James and Agatha obediently cast their unseeing eyes right, left, and ahead, while looking into themselves and sorting through the hundred things they wanted to talk about.

"On the other hand, your friend Lillian seemed not to know me," said James after Signora Razioni switched off her mike.

"She has no idea who you are, James. Apart from Janet Meers, and now maybe Father Finn, nobody in Minnesota knows a thing about you."

Imogene Kite knew hundreds of things about a man reared by a widowed mother over a pub, a man with one sister (deceased) and one brother (alive but ineffectual in the family business), a man whose entire life had been spent in two or three counties of Ireland. She knew these things because his letters were lying around her apartment on the arms of chairs, on radiators, on the kitchen counter, wherever she happened to be when she finished reading them.

Though he made only scant references to God or religion, this James fellow must have been a devout man, for his only trips abroad had been to Rome and Lourdes, and he inquired, in an early letter, about the liturgy at St. Isidore's. Whereas he was not in the least reluctant to set forth his opinions (he liked art museums and plays, he abhorred television and movies) and reveal his eccentricities (having never learned to drive a car, he got around by bus and bicycle), Imogene thought it odd that he wasn't more forthcoming about his work. From certain bits and pieces in the early letters, she'd concluded he was a teacher of some kind, and so it was with a good bit of surprise that now, lying sleepily in bed near midnight, she came to the final letter about his retirement from the priesthood. Having read it through, she let it float to the floor and reflected that this was the last piece in the puzzle, the one fact she'd been needing in order to see the man whole. Why had it been withheld? Had Agatha known? What had Agatha withheld on her side?

It was typical of Imogene's narrow habits of mind that she gave no thought to the broader question of what this exchange might have meant to Agatha and James, what emotional bond it might have formed between them, what difficulties it might have caused. Imogene, always careful to mark off the boundaries of her interests, was intrigued by only two aspects of the correspondence. One was the fresh, though twice-filtered, view of her hometown as it came to her in James's responses to Agatha's letters. There were many people of Agatha's acquaintance—the young realtor Randy Meers and his wife Janet were only two—to whom Imogene obviously hadn't been devoting enough of her curiosity. They came more fully alive in these replies from Ireland than they ever had in Imogene's estimation of them. Was Randy Meers really the cad Agatha made him out to be? Was Janet really that far superior to him? Sister Judith Juba was another example. Anyone causing Agatha to seethe and froth so vehemently must be more of an entity than Imogene had ever guessed. Judy Juba was evidently that odd contradiction in terms—a nun worth knowing better. On the other hand, it was reassuring to find that certain people in Staggerford were exactly as bloodless and boring to

Agatha as they had always seemed to Imogene. Theodore Druppers. Congressman Kleinschmidt.

But interesting or boring, they were Imogene's people. Oh, to be back in Staggerford, she pined as she switched off her bedside lamp. Oh, to be once again in charge of the quaint old Carnegie library on Lincoln Street, and to know all that Agatha knew.

Entering through the sculpted bronze door, Agatha was at first disoriented by the enormity of St. Peter's. Gazing up at its dome, she was overcome by a kind of vertigo. While James furled his umbrella, and Signora Razioni recited numbers having to do with the basilica's dimensions, Agatha looked desperately about for something familiar to focus on, something small enough to restore her bearings. Her eyes falling to the restored *Pietà* of Michelangelo, which had been defaced by a maniac with a hammer fifteen years earlier, she stepped up to its protective shield of glass and examined the marble for hairline cracks.

"Yes, this is the one I keep returning to," said James, coming up behind her. "Have you ever laid eyes on anything more stirring?"

Satisfied that the restorers had left no visible damage, she stood back to take in the artistry of it, and was immediately drawn to the Virgin's face, so pure and innocent, so young, so beautiful. Meanwhile, James, standing beside her, was transfixed by the Savior's inert face, drained of life.

"She's so young," breathed Agatha.

"He's so dead," sighed James.

They shifted their gaze then, each to look through the other's eyes.

"Yes, that's death," said Agatha.

"She *is* young," James agreed. "I never really noticed before. She has to be in her late forties at the Crucifixion— he's thirty-three—but she looks fifteen. How fanciful."

"There's no fancy involved, James. It's the effect of the Immaculate Conception."

She saw perplexity cross his face, and her heart fell. Was the man losing his grip on the faith?

"Free of original sin," she prompted. "Free of corruption."

"Ah, yes, so that's it." He smiled at her. "Forgive me for being so slow."

"I thought for a minute you'd gone the way of Sister Judith and the heretics."

"Sister Judith and the heretics," he echoed, chuckling. "Sounds like a rock group."

They proceeded slowly up the right-hand aisle, James pointing out the august figures in marble and bronze and calling them by name, Agatha marveling in particular at the exquisite grillwork adorning the Chapel of the Holy Sacrament. At one of the four piers facing the papal altar, they came upon St. Peter in bronze, sitting with his toes protruding from under his cloak. James stepped up and kissed them, and as Agatha unhesitatingly followed his example, she heard a man's voice echoing from behind the pier: "Now just around this corner you'll see a statue of St. Peter, and if you wait around long enough I guarantee you'll see some poor dope kissing its foot."

Backing away from the apostle, Agatha took James's arm and asked if he'd heard the remark.

"A skeptic among us," said James.

The voice continued in the same vein—"The riches, the pomp, the hypocrisy of it all"—and Agatha was shocked to find it belonged to Dr. Finn, who stepped around the corner of the pier with four of his students trailing behind him, Darrin—sans earphones for a change—bringing up the rear.

"Look at what Galileo was up against," the professor continued evangelically, throwing his arms out left and right, and not realizing that the number of his listeners had grown by two. "The Church had this unimaginable wealth and power, and all poor Galileo had on his side was the truth—he didn't stand a chance."

Agatha saw wonder in the eyes of three of the students—including Darrin—as they gawked at the magnificence surrounding them, and she saw the same wonder, together with admiration, in the fourth student, Paula the pixy, as she gazed at her professor. The group came to a halt near the bronze St. Peter and waited for the promised spectacle to unfold itself, but no one else—no foot kissers—happened to be in the vicinity.

"I think I'd better speak up," said Agatha, rehearsing to herself a brief defense of the papacy.

"No, allow me," said James, leaving her side. He stepped between Professor Finn and his followers, saying, "Excuse me, please," and after he had kissed the toe, he turned to the group with a little flourish and sidestep shuffle (reminiscent, thought Agatha, of Jimmy Durante in the early days of television) and he said, "That's how poor dopes do it."

The students looked dumbfounded. The professor looked chagrined. James bowed from the waist and rejoined Agatha, escorting her quickly away.

"My, you're light on your feet." She was trying to be solemn, for they were approaching the papal altar, but James, taking her elbow, could feel her quaking with suppressed laughter.

"Not as light as I seemed, Agatha. It's all in the timing."

"Yes, timing is important, isn't it?"

"Timing is everything!" he declared with a fond little squeeze of her arm.

James knew from previous visits that too much of St. Peter's could shut down your senses, and when, after an hour and a half, he judged that Agatha was nearing the point of overload, he suggested they leave by way of the crypt. She nodded, rather glassy-eyed, and he led her down a stairway of stone to a marble hallway of chapels and tombs.

Popes lay buried here. Agatha, speechless with awe, more deeply affected than she'd been upstairs, first paid her respects to Peter himself, ensconced in a chapel of gilded pillars, mosaic walls, sculpted angels, and crouching lions. Then she moved on to Popes of more recent history, pausing before the tombs of the three who had dominated her last fifty years. There was Pius XII, the ascetic taskmaster who had lent his stern and unforgiving personality to the Church at mid-century. Next was the fat and avuncular John, who'd made a great fuss about throwing open the Church's windows to blow away the stuffy air, and then conveniently died before the dust rose and got in everyone's eyes. And then there was Paul, the fretful inheritor of John's inspired carelessness, who probably died of agony over the mess dumped in his lap. Before each polished sarcophagus was a bouquet of fresh red roses in a brass vase. In contrast to the grandeur upstairs, there was a timeless simplicity about these tombs. They appealed to Agatha's sense of how death should be presented to the world—straightforward and unadorned. She said so to James.

He nodded absently, his mind obviously engaged by last things.

"But I wouldn't want to be buried in a cellar," she added. She was thinking of the hilltop cemetery outside Staggerford, and the plain, gray McGee stone tastefully chosen by her parents when her brother died in a flu epidemic. More and more often in recent years she drove out there to stand over the graves of her father and mother and brother and the rectangle of earth awaiting herself. She loved the view from there, the wooded river valley below her, the sweep of fields beyond. Not that your resting place mattered when your time came, but you liked to think of it beforehand. She was consoled by the thought of open, airy distance. She didn't envy the current Pope this basement in his future.

Following arrows, they turned left and right, climbed a few stairs and found themselves outdoors at ground level. The rain had stopped. A chilly, fresh wind was blowing. They came to a gift shop and went in. The shop was staffed by nuns wearing garments Agatha hadn't seen since 1968, when the sisters of St. Isidore's Convent gave up their medieval widows' weeds. Among the shoppers were Lillian Kite, selecting a rosary, and Father Finn, poring over an illustrated book of psalms with a cover of embossed velvet. Three or four Rookery State students were looking at statuettes.

For friends back home—Frederick, Sylvester, the Meerses— Agatha was selecting several pewter medals depicting various saints when Lillian edged over and asked her, "Agatha, which of these for Imogene, the reddish one or the brownish one?" She was holding two rosaries up to the light. Each bead was a tiny egg of bright stone, marbled and polished.

"My, they're exquisite, but are you sure it's something she'd want, Lillian? Doesn't she brag she hasn't prayed the rosary since she was thirteen?"

"She'll go back to it, give her time. We quit ourselves at that age, remember?"

"Who did?"

"You and me."

"We didn't," said Agatha sharply. James chuckled. Father

Finn, looking up from his velvet-covered book, smiled benignly over his glasses.

Lillian pressed her point. "You said the rosary was boring and we should read prayers out of books instead."

"I said no such thing. You dreamed it."

Lillian addressed James. "So we chanted Latin prayers on Agatha's front porch all one summer. We were twelve or thirteen."

James, highly amused, said, "More boring than the rosary, I imagine."

"Scads more boring," said Lillian, pleased to have an ally. "My stars, we went on and on. Litanies, the works. We had to say things over and over and over."

"*Ora pro nobis*, for example?"

"*Ora pro nobis*—you got it." Turning back to Agatha, she said, "I was thinking she might like the brownish one."

Agatha had taken the red rosary from her. "I was going to say this one. Doesn't it seem richer? And look, the crucifix is pewter."

"I know, but Imogene's partial to brown."

"If I didn't have a dozen rosaries already, I'd buy this for myself," said Agatha.

Suddenly Lisa Berglund was at Agatha's side, saying, "Oh, that's beautiful, that's exactly the rosary my mother would want. Are you buying it, Miss McGee? Are there any more like it? It's the one thing I've seen in Rome that she'd just love."

Agatha turned it over to her.

"Are you sure, Miss McGee? Because if you want it yourself, I'll find something else."

"No, please take it, and I won't be tempted."

"*Scusi,*" said the wimpled nun behind the counter, offering another red rosary identical to the first.

"Hey, this is so *cute*," said Trish, rushing up and taking it from the nun. "Hey, Darrin, how do I look in this?"

"Cool," said Darrin, shambling over and watching her slip the rosary over her head.

"Would you buy it for me? Please?"

Darrin lifted the crucifix off her breast and read the price. "Yipes, that's way too much for a necklace."

* * *

James and Agatha, leaving the shop, strolled toward the front of the basilica, where the group had been asked to reassemble. The sun was blinking between swift-moving clouds. Besides being very tired, James was feeling ill at ease. He'd not yet invited her to have lunch with him. For one thing, he'd been feeling inhibited all morning by the group she was traveling with, and for another, he was waiting for her to express a bit of joy at seeing him. As things stood, he was afraid she might decline. He wondered if her reserve was a reflection of his own. He felt blocked, awkward, fearful he would lose her.

"What was it he called us, James? Poor saps? Imagine, the gall."

"Poor dopes, I think he said."

"Poor dopes, poor saps—what's wrong with him? I can't imagine why, if he feels that way, he comes here at all."

"He's here on a mission, apparently, fighting Galileo's case for him."

"He's about three hundred years too late."

"So he is, but it's safer now. Three hundred years ago he might have been burned at the stake."

Agatha threw him a skeptical glance. "Surely not for arguing that the earth moves around the sun."

"For less than that, in some cases. Putting people to death in God's name—it's a matter of record."

Ill-equipped to disagree, she fell silent. Church history, to Agatha, was largely the lives of the saints. She avoided looking into its darker corners.

"I've seen this sort of thing before, Agatha, certain malcontents returning again and again to the source of their displeasure. There was an old woman in Ballybegs used to stand at the door of St. Brigid's every Sunday, rain or shine, and curse the faithful coming out after Mass. Poor soul, she was balmy."

"But Dr. Finn's an educated man, not some nitwit. Think of the damage he's doing."

"But just look at this," said James, pointing, "Isn't this the lovable side of the Church?" They had come out onto the piazza, now more populated than earlier, currents of people flowing in many directions, the main tide washing up the steps and in through the bronze portals. There was a little old lady with the shakes, followed by a pair of bejeweled women in furs and leather skirts and patterned hose, escorted by men in thick, rich overcoats. There were teenagers in jeans, and two old men with hearing aids, clutching identical canes. There were nuns and priests and a scar-faced woman with worn shoes and a tattered tote bag. Some were presumably arriving for the midday Mass—today was the Feast of the Holy Innocents—while others were sightseers, identifiable by their cameras, maps, and gaping faces.

But Agatha wasn't looking at these people. She was scarcely aware of his words. Her eyes were aimed far off, scanning the city where it rose on the far side of the Tiber. She, too, was ill at ease, waiting for James to suggest their next move. Surely he had no desire to ride the tour bus for the rest of the day. Why hadn't he expressed more joy at their reunion? Was it his ill health? Or was it her own reticence that was dampening his spirit? And why *was* she so reticent? She felt obtuse, almost lethargic.

"I've always said, Agatha, and these people prove it, that more glorious than the monuments erected in his honor is God's talent for drawing his faithful from all walks of life."

"That's true," she said vaguely, noticing that from a distance the thousand colors of Roman buildings blended into one color. The shade was that of a ripe apricot.

The sight of Agatha's companions approaching from three directions spurred James to action. He stepped around to face her, looked desperately into her eyes and said, "Agatha, I couldn't bear it if you got back on that bus and left me here."

There was no hesitation in her reply. "And I couldn't bear to do it, James."

"Then I have to ask how you are planning to spend the afternoon."

"Lillian is meeting two friends here at twelve o'clock, two women from Indiana, whom she came across in the Forum yesterday. She asked me to join them."

"Must you?"

"No. And I'd rather not."

"Then I have a place in mind for lunch."

"I thought you'd never ask."

22

M IXING LATIN WITH HIS meager Italian, James apologized to the waiter for not showing up the day before. The waiter, taking their coats, said, *"No, no, non si preoccupi, non importa,"* and by means of gestures and one or two words of English, he asked if the father would like a table moved outdoors again. *Grazie,* said James, the wind was a bit brisk for that, but a table next to the window would be grand. Take your pick, said the waiter's gesture, a sweep of the arm indicating the absence of other diners.

The table next to the window was small, and their knees bumped as they sat down. Between them stood a pink gardenia in a slender vase. The waiter laid menus before them and pointed to his wristwatch, indicating that their food would take a while, this being very early for lunch. James, nodding and patting the air with both hands, conveyed his contentment. The waiter suggested wine, but it was declined. Agatha ordered fish, because although the Church had long ago relaxed the meatless Friday law, Agatha had not. James ordered fish because he liked it. The waiter brought them mineral water and bread and then left them alone.

"Well, Agatha," James said, and then sighed and smiled and sipped his water, as though this were his statement in full. He was relieved to be sitting. He was confident that his vitality would return, but for now he was wooden with fatigue.

"James, what does it mean—your tracking me down like this?" She regretted sounding abrupt, but she was impatient to talk things out. They'd been together three hours with scarcely any private moments.

"It means I wanted to see you."

"Yes?" she inquired, needing more explanation than that.

216

"Look, Agatha, if only my letter had found you before you left home, then I'd know whether you were sitting here of your own volition. Had you received my invitation, you would have accepted it or rejected it. The way it is—my walking in on you this morning—you didn't have much of a choice, did you?"

She evaded this question by asking another. "When I didn't appear in St. Peter's Square yesterday, why didn't you take it as a rejection?"

He smiled ruefully. "A foolish reason, maybe—the terrorist attack at the airport. The paper said three Americans had died, and the names were withheld. I had to confirm for my peace of mind that you were not among them. It was most unlikely, of course, but you understand how a fact like that won't let you rest."

"It was terrible, James. We saw the dead carried out."

He nodded, scowling. "Seventeen innocent dead, according to the paper."

"And the terrorists shot dead as well, they say."

"All but one. He was wounded and tried to hide under the bodies, but the police pulled him out. Then they had to protect him from the survivors, who sought to tear him to pieces."

"Has he revealed who put him up to it?"

"Kadhafi of Libya is calling it a holy act, but he's not taking the credit. The man they captured was trained in Iran and came to Italy by way of Syria."

"A holy act, imagine!"

"You see, we're still putting people to death in the name of God. The killers in Ulster talk that way."

"It's all so horribly depressing."

Chewing bread and sipping bubbly water, both of them stared silently out the window for a time.

"Agatha, I have to ask this." His voice was strained and tight. He was sitting earnestly forward now, leaning on his forearms. "If my letter had arrived in time, would you have met me, or not met me?"

"Met you, of course."

At this, he relaxed, sat back, nodded, folded his large hands across his front and smiled.

"My curiosity wouldn't have allowed me to ignore you."

"Curiosity alone?" He'd hoped for more than curiosity.

"No, not only curiosity. Duty as well."

"Duty?" Was it unreasonable to hope for a motive beyond duty?

"Who wouldn't feel compelled by a friend's urgent pleading?" she said. "I suspected illness. At our age, what else?"

Well, duty was vastly better than curiosity. In duty there was commitment, allegiance—if not love. "That clears the air for me, then. You're not sitting here against your will."

"I do very little against my will, James." This was not delivered as sharply as it might have been. It was softened with a demure smile.

Gathering up what vitality he could muster, he inhaled very deeply and said, "I have to tell you straight-out that I have never stopped thinking about you, Agatha, and I have never stopped wondering if you were thinking of me. Three years ago you discovered my deceit, and my reason for deceiving you. A foolish reason, I grant you, but compelling all the same. I was afraid my priesthood would stand in the way of the closeness we'd come to. I apologized. You accepted my apology, but not my request that we stay in touch."

She made as if to reply to this, but he frowned and raised his hand to silence her. "That's all well and good, I said to myself at the time, I've seen my way through all these years without any sort of heart-to-heart companionship, and I'm well able to carry on from here." He smiled in a self-deprecating way, as if to say, Such a fool. "I was still a young man of sixty-seven, with a young man's confidence and a young man's health, and I was too busy about my parish to brood. Well, now I'm an idle old man of seventy, and while my thinking grows clearer, my body's in decline. When the doctors suggested I might be brought down by cells misbehaving in my large intestine, when they implied that I might be mortal like everybody else, I felt suddenly desperate. I felt lost. I felt I had to get through to you, Agatha, and see if you'd had a change of heart. Your return letter was the change of heart I was hoping for." He paused, raising his eyebrows, inviting her to respond.

"Yes, I had a change of heart," she admitted softly.

"Ah." Again the deep breath, the sip of water, the relieved smile.

"James, what do you mean, your thinking grows clearer? It's always seemed coherent enough to me."

It took him a few moments of searching to answer this, his eyes turning inward—the look of someone who'd opened a drawer and found it messier than he expected. "By that I mean . . ." He stalled.

She coaxed him along. "Your letters have been clear from the start, James. Never murky."

After a little more rummaging, he said, "Look, Agatha, try to imagine somebody living in harness all his life, his days laid out for him, his opinions prescribed, his habits handed down to him like shirts and shoes. There are people who actually spend their entire lives like that, can you imagine it?"

"I can," she said, thinking the description, in a way, fit herself.

"I'm talking about priests the world over, not excluding present company. Priests are like puppets, Agatha, and bishops have control of the strings."

"I thought it was God."

"No, it's bishops."

"But in God's name surely."

He nodded. "So bishops would have you believe. And in some cases it's true. Some are godly men indeed." He paused, as if calling to mind those who weren't, and then hurried on, as though they didn't deserve mention. "I'm not saying any of this is wrong, Agatha. It's the way things work in the Church—step out of line and you get your string jerked. I went into the priesthood knowing all this. No deception. No surprises. My point is simply that a man of my training and way of life is not inclined to be very inventive in his thinking. The creative spark gets snuffed out. He's at his best following orders."

"*Giving* orders—that's been my experience of priests."

"All right, but giving orders handed down from above, don't you see? Not orders the priest has invented."

"Years ago we had a priest at St. Isidore's who ordered the parish to cancel their subscriptions to *Look* and *Collier's* and all secular magazines. Surely that didn't come from above."

"No, you're right, and there you've hit upon the one great flaw in the system. Only the nutcases get to be creative."

"He said all advertising was the devil's work."

"And did you cancel?"

"My parents came down on opposite sides. My mother insisted we cancel. My father said no."

"And you?"

"I wasn't old enough to have an opinion."

"Who carried the day, do you recall?"

"We canceled. In household matters, my mother had the last word." She paused to smile at the memory—a fond and faraway smile—and it was several seconds before she returned to the present. "But you were saying?"

"I was about to say now that I've retired from the active priesthood, my strings are cut."

"No, James. Once a priest, always a priest."

"Yes, I believe that, but not always a priest with strings." She looked skeptical, quizzical.

"I'm now free to re-create myself," he said rather proudly.

"Oh, dear." A shiver of fear climbed her spine. "Will I like the new James?"

He laughed. "Will I *myself* like the new James might be more to the point."

While James examined his bread plate for bread crumbs, lifting a few to his lips, Agatha's attention was drawn to a family of three entering the restaurant and being shown to a table. The husband's dark suit and the wife's red dress were of a fashionable, expensive cut. Their son—Agatha judged him to be nine—wore a dark suit as well. The boy studied the menu seriously while his parents chatted with the waiter. Agatha, listening, wished she understood Italian, wished she spoke it. Compared to English, it sounded so full and round and nourishing. The party laughed—all but the boy—and Agatha smiled.

With her eyes on the family, James was free to study Agatha. Her hair and brow and mouth were not as he remembered them. The curls in the short white hair were more tightly made than three years ago, and no glints of red remained. In her brow she had developed more and deeper worry lines. The mouth was pinched. Nothing had changed in the eyes, however. They were the same guileless, all-revealing eyes he remembered from their meeting in Dublin. Small and blue, they were, alert and utterly honest. People with eyes like that couldn't dissemble if they tried. No secrets, no cunning—the eyes gave everything away. He watched the smile spread across her face, and though it was directed at the family of three and not at him, it gladdened his heart. It was reassuring to glimpse her softer, warmer side.

She turned back to him, the smile lingering on her lips. "And so you're about to start giving your own orders, is that it?"

"No, no, Agatha, you miss my point. What I meant, concerning orders from above, was the effect they have on a man over a lifetime. With others making the decisions for you, your power of judgment withers away. Now I'm free to give myself orders, to try out ideas of my own—that's all I'm saying."

"What are they? Will you tell me?"

"It's why I've come to Rome—to tell you."

"Good." Watching him take another sip of water and wipe his lips with his napkin, and then cock his head and squint into the light falling through the window, she realized she was holding her breath.

"Two ideas, then, Agatha, for your approval. One has to do with my health, the second with my place in heaven." Still facing the window, he spoke in a lower and less animated tone than normal, as though downplaying his message. "First my health. Cancer of the large intestine. Diagnosed in late November by an old doctor I've known for some years. Surgery soon after, in Dublin, at the hands of a balding young surgeon I keep trying to have confidence in. He's a surly, inarticulate lad you can tell hates being spoken to as much as he hates speaking. His interest in humanity is limited to the internal organs only, particularly the *diseased* internal organs, and he talks, when he talks, in numbers alone. So many centimeters of tissue removed. So many days of liquid nourishment. So many weeks of convalescence. The odds of a full recovery at such and such a percentage."

"What percentage?" Agatha put in, and again she held her breath.

"Sixty."

"That's not enough!"

James drew his eyes from the window and looked at her apologetically. "He says sixty."

"He's wrong," she announced.

James was amused by her certainty. "I suspect you're right. I've never been one to trust muses and ghosts and messages in dreams, Agatha, but there's a voice I can't identify telling me that with the bald boy doctor in Dublin, I'm not in the best of hands. He reads my innards and talks about diverticulitis and nodules and the possibility of another operation." He was looking her square in the face now, gauging her concern by the furrows in her brow. "Had I ever felt this way in the past, I would have consulted my bishop about it, and my bishop would have recommended another surgeon or told me how good mine was. He's that kind of bishop, minding every aspect of the lives of his men, never hesitating to tell us who should pull our teeth or cut our hair or where we should bank our money. But now that I've retired and the Church is leaving me alone to think my own thoughts, I am free to follow this strange voice I keep hearing."

"And it's telling you ... ?"

"Consult the Mayo doctors."

Because he stressed the second syllable—"May-*oh*"—it was an instant before Agatha realized he meant Rochester, Minnesota, instead of County Mayo. Her reaction—he could read it in her eyes—was surprise and agreement, with perhaps a trace of apprehension.

"It's the last word in medical care, is it not?"

"My father went to the Mayo Clinic for his asthma," she said. "They gave him a green and yellow pill that he took for the rest of his life."

"You believe they're reliable, then."

She nodded. "My mother went there for arthritis, and they gave her aspirin—but what can you do for arthritis? Yes, if the Mayo Clinic isn't the last word, at least they make you think it is."

"You've not been, yourself?"

"No, I've been blessed with amazing health. Rashes and corns and a head cold every few years."

"Well, what would you say to my flying to the States, seeing the doctors, and then taking the train to Staggerford and putting up at a hotel for three or four days?" He sat forward as before, leaning his weight on his elbows, but this time with more energy in his voice, renewed vitality in his eyes. "Is it a pipe dream, Agatha, or would you show me your town and have me in to dinner?"

Overcome, she uttered, to her surprise, a little chortle.

"In other words—and you must tell me the truth because I'll read it in your face if you don't—would I be welcome?"

He saw the answer in her eyes before she found her voice. "Yes, come by all means," she said, "and for every statue you've shown me this morning, I'll introduce you to a flesh-and-blood Staggerfordian." But the eyes, in fact, said more than this. Together with her flushed cheeks and the rearranged lines of her brow, her eyes said that his idea excited her and worried her. They said that while her assent was spontaneous, she distrusted spontaneity. "Yes, come by all means," she repeated, chuckling and trying to look amused while trying to stifle her misgivings. He was invading her life again.

"That's grand, then," he said.

"There is no train," she said, "and the hotel is a fleabag. We'll provide the transportation, and we'll put you up at the rectory."

We? Who was we? he wondered, but didn't ask. Herself and Father Finn, he supposed, and maybe Lillian for good measure. But "we" was more than that. By we, Agatha meant all of Staggerford, everyone in town, the cohesive whole of the place. Gone was the alienation she'd been feeling for the past six months. Jolted out of her malaise by her transatlantic flight—or was it by the sight of James?—she was finding it possible to think of Staggerford once again with pride and affection. Staggerford was Ernie Shaw the postmaster, Theodore Druppers the grocer, and Doris Bertram the seamstress stitching away in the front room of her house on Parker Street. Staggerford was Lillian across the alley, the Rathmanns next door, Frederick Lopat in the Morgan Hotel, and Janet Meers and her family in the Morning Star Apartments. It was Sylvester Juba sadly bereft of his common sense and wallowing in his indignities, while his daughter, the misguided nun, rose in the ranks of the Church. It was St. Isidore's entering a dark time, and the public library short of funding, and the city hall needing a new heating system and its bricks pointed. Staggerford was clergymen, clerks, secretaries, garage mechanics, nurses, and street-repair crews. Staggerford was the community of souls whose values Agatha, more than anyone of her generation, had helped to sustain. Staggerford was her entire life, and James was coming to see it.

"When?" she asked.

"I would come in March. The airlines will be discounting tickets in March, I'm told, and chemotherapy will be behind me."

"Easter's in March this year. Come for Easter."

"I will indeed."

She flushed and lowered her eyes, asking herself if she'd live to regret urging him to come. The answer, of course, was in the alternative. She'd never outlive the regret of *not* urging him.

It was later, after their food was served, that James revealed his second new idea, the one he claimed would determine his place in heaven. He approached it indirectly, which, as Agatha was rediscovering, was typical of his conversational style. He seemed to enjoy the preamble as much as the main idea. He put her in mind of a painstaking set director, preparing the stage.

He began by telling the story of his cousin's son, who had recently died in the Troubles. Con Stitch was his name, and he died a week short of his twenty-eighth birthday. "Executed," said James in a chilling tone.

"Heavens," said Agatha. "What was his crime?"

"Informing."

"Informing whom? Of what?"

"Let me back up," said James, putting down his fork and folding his hands in his lap. "Let me start with his forebears." Though only a short way into the meal, he was already losing his appetite. The scampi did not agree with him.

"Years ago my cousin Margaret O'Hannon, a tall, good-looking woman now in her fifties, married a man from the North, an Ulsterman but a Catholic nevertheless. A good-enough man he is, but a man with no trade of any kind, and so out of work a good deal, and on the dole. His name is William Stitch, and his days of idleness have far outnumbered his days of gainful employment over the years. They live in Newry, a border town on the Ulster side."

"I remember seeing it on the map," said Agatha. "South of Belfast."

"Right you are. Near the coast. It's Margaret and William in Newry who are the parents of Con."

"Con for Conrad?"

"Con for Cornelius, but nobody ever called him that. Con he was known as, from a wee lad. And like a good many lads in Northern Ireland, when Con Stitch reached a certain age, he drifted to Belfast for work. He found the odd job here and there, but nothing permanent. What he did find, worse luck, were friends like himself, young men idling in pubs and putting their hopes on the horses. Margaret and his dad saw precious little of him. Once in a great while, down and out in Belfast, he'd come slouching back to Newry for his mother's cooking and the odd pound his dad might have in his pocket, but he was a city lad now, he liked to say. And if that's how city lads looked, said his mother, then the city must be very Hell. Seedy, he was, Agatha. Holes in his clothes. Tinkers looked better than Con."

Agatha, eating vigorously, paused long enough to say, "There's not going to be a ray of sunshine in this story, I can tell."

"Ah, but there is, Agatha, and I'm coming to it now, a bit of sunshine and hope in the form of love. A young woman from Derry stepped into Con's life. Suzanne was her name. She'd come to Belfast like Con, to find work, and found it, thank God. An office of creamery inspectors took her on for computing work. She'd taken the training in Derry, and was said to be greased lightning on the computer. She met Con in a pub and in no time at all they were married in Suzanne's home parish. I did not attend. I had a wedding of my own that day in Ballybegs. According to my cousin Margaret, Suzanne's parents were a bit on the stiff side, the father being something important in the town government and the mother not hiding her alarm over her new son-in-law. Oh, Con was a handsome enough lad, and very tall and well-spoken, but he happened, at the moment, to be lacking a job."

James paused, turned his gaze out the window again and said, "Well, back in Belfast he got a job, right enough, or I should say a series of jobs—as a terrorist."

Agatha gave a little start. "James."

"Yes, it seems more than one of those boys in the pub were pledged to the IRA, and Con had just the qualifications they were looking for—nerves of steel, foolhardy daring, and the need to be important." James's eyes remained fixed on the street. "In other words, he fit that profile we're always seeing in the Sunday supplements—young men drawn into the revolutionary cause not so much because they believe in it, but because it makes up for certain deficiencies in their nature. Con had no standing, the IRA gave him standing. He'd been aimless, the IRA gave him goals. He'd been ashamed of living off his wife's income, the IRA gave him money. He had no job skills, the IRA taught him how to make time bombs."

Agatha had stopped eating. "I know what's coming, James."

James brought his gaze indoors and nodded, not grimly, but pleasantly, as though to lessen the dire impact of the events he was about to relate. "Because whatever he did for the IRA at the start—and I'm sure he was the merest flunky—he ended up making the clocks that set off the bombs. It was his nerves, you see, and his finger dexterity—he'd taken piano as a boy— that made him perfect for working with the tiny circuits of timing devices."

Agatha looked horrified. "He killed people."

"Indirectly. He was one or two steps removed from the deed. He made the devices in his kitchen and turned them over to the boys who hooked them up to the dynamite."

"In his kitchen? His wife at his side, cooking dinner?"

"Made a tempestuous wreck of Suzanne, it did. At Con's funeral, I wouldn't have known her. I'd met her soon after they married, she and Con having stopped in Ballybegs on their way to Dublin a time or two." James's pleasant smile faded into a frown. "Three years later, there at the gravesite, I wouldn't have known her. Her looks gone. Thin as a stick. Complexion all splotchy. Cords standing out in her neck. And, the worst thing, she kept opening and closing her mouth in the most distracted way. At the wake, at the church, and then at the grave, weeping and moaning, and chomping her mouth open and shut. I thought she might be insane."

"This is a terrible story, James. I can't bear it."

"I'll stop, if you like."

"No, I couldn't bear not knowing."

"Well, Con's career as a bomb expert didn't last long. The Brits found out what he was up to—who knows how?—and invaded his house one fine summer night and carried him off. After midnight it was, Con and Suzanne in bed, and the brutes breaking in and carrying him off in his nightclothes. Except one man stayed behind, making sure Suzanne didn't alert the IRA. Sat in the front room with a gun, he did, promising that if she stopped fussing and behaved herself, Con would be back before sunrise. He asked for tea, and she made it, at the point of his gun. This scoundrel had another function as well, and that was to shoot Suzanne if Con didn't agree to become a turncoat. It would only have taken a phone call—'the man's not coming 'round to our view'—and he'd have shot her dead in her nightdress and robe. But that didn't happen. With Suzanne held hostage, Con agreed to inform, of course, with very little torture involved. He was dropped off in less than three hours with only a couple of burn marks on his arms, and the man with the gun said good-bye and thanks for the tea."

"And Con went straight to the police."

"Agatha," said James impatiently, as though she were a student lagging behind in her lessons. "He'd just *come* from the police."

"Good Lord, James. Police don't do that to people."

James considered this for a few moments. "No, you may be right. There's no way to prove that a policeman laid a hand on Con that night, but you can be sure the police were alerted to the operation and were looking the other direction. Don't you see, Agatha, by going to the police, Con, a bomber for the IRA, would get no help at all? He'd get solitary confinement for the rest of his life—if he was lucky."

"It makes me sick," said Agatha, turning her attention back to her plate and digging in.

"But three hours' training is hardly sufficient for an informer, as Con was shortly to prove by his abbreviated career and violent death. He went on as before, supplying his mates with the deadly devices he wired together—but now things had changed. One change was the hysterical wife he had on his hands. She never went back to work with the creamery inspectors after that night. She was all nerves and weeping. And another change was that each time a device left his house, he rang up a number on the phone that got him a woman's voice saying, "Betty Jane's Bible and Bookshop," and he reported what he knew about the impending explosion. Which was precious little, you see, because Con never rose high enough in the brotherhood to be privy to the where and the when of explosions, or who the victim was to be. Con was nothing more than a device himself, you might say, to be activated when needed and ignored when not."

"He might have saved lives by informing," said Agatha shrewdly, hopefully.

"He *did* save lives by informing, and that's how he lost his own." James scowled fiercely, explaining. "He thwarted at least one bombing, Con did, his little piece of knowledge being just enough, apparently, to put the Brits on their guard at the right place and time, and one of the IRA boys was captured with the bomb in his coat. And so a bit of flesh and blood and brick and mortar was given a reprieve for that day or week or—who knows?—forever. All of which made the IRA suspect they had a stool pigeon in their midst. And *that* may have been the Brits' intention in the first place—the night they rolled him out of bed."

She looked at him inquiringly. "To make the IRA suspicious of him?"

"Precisely, saving the Brits the trouble of putting poor Con out of commission."

"Heavens, it's all so complex and sordid."

"A nightmare, Agatha. As complex and sordid and frightening as a nightmare, and nobody's dreaming it. It's daily life in Ulster, and that brings me 'round to my new idea." He fixed her with his eyes. "I'm going to work for peace."

Agatha studied him intently.

"If I survive this cancer, I'm going to work for peace."

"How?"

"I'll speak out."

"What could you say that hasn't been said, James? It seems to me there's no solution—the little I know about it."

"Solution or no, I'll speak out."

"But it's a nation of hard, grudging hearts, James. You've said so yourself. Hearts set against each other for life. You once wrote that in a letter."

With a raised finger and a tight mouth, James spoke through his teeth. "I will speak out."

"To whom?"

"I will tell the story I'm telling you, Agatha, the life and death of Con Stitch. And I will add what followed the funeral, the chaotic effect of it all on the family. With the first shovelful of dirt sounding on the coffin lid, Con's young widow crossed the line into raving dementia, and William Stitch in his drunkenness began weaving among the gravestones and shouting curses to high heaven, and my poor cousin Margaret somehow got it into her head that Suzanne should stay in Newry with her and William, and Suzanne's parents had to pry the poor girl out of her grip. And that's only the one day. I can go into the long-term effects on Margaret as well, the fishwife she's turning into and the ugly way she and William are treating each other day after day."

Agatha let out a long breath and shook her head woefully.

"So I'll tell the Con Stitch story in all its dark detail, and then I might tell one or two others I've heard. Three stories, no more. Stories can move people, Agatha. I learned that in the pulpit. You can preach till the cows come home and not awaken a single soul, but the right story, well told, goes straight to the heart. Isn't that so?"

"It's true." Particularly if it's told by James O'Hannon, she would have added if she weren't reluctant to encourage him. His plan struck her as futile as well as perilous.

"Changing minds by appealing to hearts, Agatha, that will be my mission."

"And to whom will you speak?"

"Rotary Clubs, garden clubs, sodalities—any group that will let me in the door. I'll climb into a pulpit now and again—I have friends with parishes on both sides of the border who will welcome a Sunday off. And when I run out of clubs and pulpits, I'll take my stories into shops and pubs, and if the shops and pubs are closed, I'll tell my stories on the street. In Ireland there's no shortage of listeners if you have the knack of telling."

Agatha chose her words carefully. "James, I don't like to be a spoilsport, but you're no spring chicken."

He looked delighted. "Thank the Lord."

"You're seventy. You'll wear yourself out in no time."

"But I'll be of *use*, don't you see. Better being of use than bemoaning my idleness."

A defensive look came into her eye. "As *I* do—is that what you mean?"

"May I be frank, Agatha? Your letter does not paint an attractive picture of retirement."

Her lowered eyes acknowledged the truth of this.

"I need employment, Agatha, and dear old Ireland needs peace."

"But as a soapbox preacher?" Her tone was edgy, and her eyes revealed great agitation. "It's your health I'm worried about."

By which she meant his death. For she was suddenly panic-stricken at the thought of living out her life without him.

Leaving the restaurant, James drew a booklet of bus routes from the pocket of his overcoat and determined that a number 17 would carry Agatha to within a block of her hotel.

"There are alternatives," said James, detecting a daunted look in her eye. "I'd be pleased to accompany you. Or if you need a rest from my constant jabber, I can find you a taxi."

"Would it be too much to ask you to come with me?"

"Say no more," he told her happily, and he stepped into a tobacconist's shop for a pair of bus tickets.

They boarded a bus and settled into a seat near the back. "Agatha, let there be no misapprehension, I'm in Rome because you're in Rome. If you were in Paris, I'd be in Paris. London, I'd be in London."

She shot him a look. "So your claim to being a pilgrim was less than frank."

"Not at all. There are various kinds of pilgrims."

"Heavens." She laughed. "That makes me a shrine."

He did not respond to her mirth, but pressed on with his

frankness. "I'm here until next Thursday, same as you. If it were up to me, we would spend each day together—we'd visit the Pantheon, the Vatican museums, we could even go to the ocean—but of course it isn't up to me. I'm intruding on your tour and taking you away from your friends. I leave it to you, then, how much you wish to see of me." He drew a pen from an inner pocket of his overcoat and jotted a number on a corner of a page of his bus booklet. He tore it out and gave it to her. "I don't have a phone within easy reach, but this is the porter's office at the college where I'm staying. He's on duty from early morning until early evening. Leave your name and number with him, and I'll ring you back as soon as I can."

A disconsolate look suddenly appeared in her eyes. "We're leaving in the morning for Assisi and Florence."

"Tomorrow?" he said with dismay. "Already tomorrow?"

"Assisi tomorrow and on to Florence Sunday afternoon. Back to Rome Tuesday evening."

"What's Galileo's connection with Assisi?"

"There is none, as far as I know. It's Father Francis Finn's connection with his patron saint. He prevailed upon his brother to stop there on our way to Florence."

James looked wistful. "I have never been to Assisi."

"What about Florence?"

He shook his head. "Only Rome."

She squeezed her eyes tightly shut while she consulted briefly first with her heart and then with her better judgment. She found them in accord.

"James, let me ask you . . . why don't you join our tour?"

23

DELAYED BY THE HEAVY Friday-night traffic leaving St. Paul, and further delayed by a series of snow squalls in the north, Imogene Kite did not reach home until after ten o'clock. She parked in the alley behind her mother's house, but instead of going in, she carried her suitcase along the carefully cleared path leading to Agatha's back porch. Pounding on the door and waiting for French to open it, she eagerly imagined the two of them returning to the guest room upstairs.

For she had changed her mind about entertaining French in her mother's house. There was both anger and envy in her decision. She was furious that Agatha should be sending out letters describing her mother as a warm body with a dull mind. All the way north she'd been relishing the sweet revenge of sleeping with French on Agatha's bleached and virginal sheets.

And Imogene's envy, though less clear in her mind, was even more intense than her anger. Reviewing her night in bed with French (which she'd spent every spare moment doing for the past two days), Imogene had sensed that part of the ecstasy was in the location. By going in and acting as mistress of Agatha's venerable ark on River Street, she'd been invested with something of Agatha's omnipotence. By preparing a meal in the old lady's kitchen, by dining at her table, by sleeping in one of her bedrooms, she had stolen something of Agatha's soul. She was now back to steal more.

For Imogene aspired to everything Agatha had achieved in life, except spinsterhood. Of all the world's curiosities that Imogene had made a study of, it was Agatha's place in Staggerford that most fascinated her. She wanted someday to assume the mantle of Agatha's eminence. She had already gone far in developing Agatha's style of self-reliance and Agatha's strict habits of mind, but she was still a long way from achieving Agatha's ascendency over her fellow citizens. This would take time, and of course it couldn't be done in St. Paul. She had put her mother on alert, instructing her to call her on the phone the minute her successor in the Staggerford library—the fat and hypertensive Lucy Kopka, wife of the natural-gas man—quit or was fired or died of a stroke. It would mean giving up her civil service seniority and earning less money, but perhaps French by that time would be working year-round at something more respectable than his Indian act. She would try to steer him back into the post office.

A mean little wind blowing across Agatha's backyard picked a swirl of snow off the porch roof and dropped it down the inside of Imogene's coat collar, sending a chill down her spine. She carried her suitcase around to the front door and rang the bell. She crossed the porch and looked in the front window. All was dark. French had been here to take in the mail (she checked the mailbox) and shovel the walk, but the dark TV meant he was gone. Like the aimless, the homeless, and the jobless she'd been reading about in the news, French had lost all sense of time. He'd obviously forgotten this was the night of his sweetheart's return.

Driving downtown to pick him up, she had an unsettling thought. Anyone who would sleep at the Morgan when he had a warm and spacious house to stay in might be more unbalanced than she'd suspected. This weekend she must carefully gauge his potential as a husband. What if he was too twisted to rehabilitate?

She parked in front of the dilapidated Morgan and peered in through the smudged glass of the door. The dimmest of lights burned at the far end of the lobby, which appeared to be empty. She put her head in at the door. "Anybody here?" she called.

"Yeah, what you want?"

She recognized the croaking voice of Grover before she spotted him deep in his sunken chair, his ghostly gray face canted up at the TV screen.

"French here?" she asked.

"Close the door. You born in a barn?"

She stepped in and pulled the door shut with difficulty. It didn't fit its frame. "French here?" she repeated.

"Third floor." Grover was staring gravely at Johnny Carson. "Thirty-two."

She climbed two long, creaking flights and found French's room, not by number—the hallway was pitch-dark—but by its being the only room with a slit of light under the door. She stepped close and heard his voice. A droning monotone. She couldn't make out the words. She waited for another voice to respond, but the drone continued. After a minute she rapped and called his name.

She heard something drop, perhaps a shoe or a book, and the droning stopped.

"French, it's me."

Silence.

"French, did you hear me?"

"Yup."

"Well?"

"You want to come in?"

She opened the door and beheld French's home. High ceiling. Scuffed furniture. Clothes piled high on the bureau. A dim lamp burning beside the bed. The bed, too, piled with clothes, as well as blankets and a shag rug. There was one tall window with its worn-out shade pulled down, and through the cracks in the shade came the lemony gleam from the streetlight below.

It wasn't until he said "Hi" that she realized the pile of things on the bed included French. He lay flat, sandwiched between layers, a magazine standing up on his chest. A thick magazine slid off the bed and landed beside the thicker one that had already fallen. One, she saw, was an anthology of *Esquire* articles. She had catalogued that very same issue some eight years ago.

"I thought you'd be at Agatha's," she said quietly, trying not to be stern.

"I was."

Of course. That was it. He'd been waiting, and gave up. "Sorry I was late," she said. "I should have called."

"That's okay," he said. He didn't tell her that after shoveling the walk, taking in the mail, and watching "Jeopardy!," he'd hurried away to avoid her. She'd frightened him by declaring herself opposed to sex without commitment; also by her startling suggestion that he move to St. Paul. Sex without commitment, here in their hometown, was the best he could offer.

Stepping closer to the bed, Imogene was further encouraged by the fact that he had his overcoat on. "My car's downstairs, if you're ready."

He smiled weakly. He made no move to get up. Yesterday and today he'd had long talks with Grover about Imogene. Grover advised passive resistance. Don't show a woman you're scared of her, Grover instructed, or she'll get overbearing. And don't argue, or she'll get hysterical.

She sat down on the backless chair and asked, "Who were you talking to?"

"Nobody."

"I heard a voice."

"I was reading."

"Out loud?"

He nodded.

"You shouldn't do that."

"I shouldn't?"

"It slows you down."

"That's why I do it."

She looked perplexed.

"We don't get that many magazines here at the Morgan," he explained. "You got to make them last through the month."

She drew her coat collar tight around her neck. "Is it always this cold in here?"

"Only in the winter," he said, and then laughed heartily, pleasantly surprised by his own wit. He laughed until the bed quivered and squeaked.

She got to her feet. "French, let's go."

He stopped laughing. He licked his thumb and turned a page of his magazine. "I think I'll just stay here and read, Imogene."

"French!" This was a strident reprimand.

He turned another page. Don't show a woman you got emotions, Grover advised. She'll outemotion you every time.

"French, look at me!"

He looked.

"We had a date!"

"I think I'll just stay here and read."

"French, we had a date!" Her tone was frenzied, her look scorching.

"If it's all the same to you," he added, turning another page.

"If it's all the same to *me*!" Now she was hysterical. "I've just driven two hundred miles to see you, bumper-to-bumper coming out of the city, ice on the road, blinding snow! If it's all the same to *me*! It *isn't* all the same to me, French! We had a date!"

He shrank down in his bed, peering up at her with alarm and fascination, wondering how anyone could be so furious and articulate at the same time.

"All you had to do was pick up the phone and tell me the date was off!" Her hysteria carried her voice up into a screeching falsetto. "What were you thinking, French? Do you think a woman enjoys driving two hundred miles to be stood up?" She paused, waiting for him to answer. "Do you?" she asked, her voice dying out in a breathless squeak.

"I think I'll stay here and read, Imogene." Just stick to your story and be consistent, Grover had told him. Never get into a pissing contest with a skunk.

She stood over him with her fists on her hips. "Why?"

"Because."

"That's no answer!"

He turned another page.

"Why?" she asked again. "Tell me why."

It was the way she pressed herself against the side of his bed and leaned over him that suddenly enraged him. "Get out," he ordered, swatting her heavy coat with the magazine.

She stepped back, smiling malevolently, looking pleased in a dark, ferocious way. Having failed to rouse him to love, she'd at least roused him to anger. "You know what you are, French? You're an emotional cripple."

"Get out," he ordered. "Get the hell out of my room."

"All right, French." She strode to the door, where she turned and spoke in a steady, controlled voice. "If I go out this door, you've lost me. I'm counting to three. One . . . I was going to take you out to dinner in Berrington on New Year's Eve, but not now. I was going to get a plate to replace the one you broke—I was even going to pay for it—but not now. Two . . ."

Suddenly she was weeping. She stood at the door wiping her eyes with the gloves she clutched in her hand, realizing that her dream of a fulfilling life in Staggerford was the airiest of fantasies. Her voice came out in a whisper. "Three." Opening the door and stepping into dark hallway, she saw through her tears a figure scurrying away and turning a corner. It was Grover; she could tell by the glint of his metal suspender clips. She left the door ajar for light and went heavily down the stairs.

Crossing the lobby, she looked for Grover, prepared to call him a nosy rat, but he'd gone to his room. She marched out to her car and marched in again, carrying a brown mailing envelope containing the letters from Ireland. She climbed to French's room and entered without knocking.

"Listen, these belong to Agatha. They're letters." She stood over the bed, holding the envelope open and tipping it to show him. "They belong in the bottom right-hand drawer of her desk."

"You took her letters?" he asked incredulously.

"The bottom right-hand drawer, remember, and if you don't put them back exactly the way they were, you'll be in plenty of hot water."

"I'm already in hot water over that plate."

"This'll be hotter. Now listen, they go facedown, with the earliest letter on the bottom and the latest on top."

"You mean you stole her letters and read them?" He appeared truly awed.

"You got that? The whole stack facedown."

He reached up and took the envelope. "Jesus."

"Which drawer?" she asked, testing him.

"I heard you."

"Tell me."

"Bottom."

"Left or right?"

"Left."

"No, you idiot!" She shouted this before noticing that he was laughing. His bed, moved by his mirth, was jiggling and squeaking.

"Oh, you!" she growled angrily and throatily, foreseeing the competent Mrs. Kopka holding down her job for years to come, no vacancy occurring until she herself had a higher salary and more seniority with the state than she could possibly abandon, foresaw herself living out her career in St. Paul, probably with her mother for company.

She charged out of the room screaming, "You emotionally crippled idiot!" and slammed the door.

24

"*LOOK AT THE VINEYARD*," shouted Professor Finn, springing out of his seat at the front of the bus and facing his travelers with the microphone to his lips. "Look at that old stone farmhouse." He kept this up all the way to Assisi, pointing out the obvious and disturbing the serenity of the sun-drenched morning in the Umbrian hills. Agatha assumed he was trying to compensate for the absence of Signora Razioni, whose expertise did not extend outside the city of Rome. "Look at that village up there on that hill," he exclaimed. "Isn't it marvelous?"

"What's it called?" asked John Schrupp from his seat in front of Agatha. John Schrupp enjoyed testing his professor. He and his seatmate, Stuart Camp, had joined Agatha's writers at last night's dinner, bringing the total to five. This left three students, besides Darrin and Trish, who elected to forgo her help.

Dr. Finn shrugged happily. "No doubt it's called Saint Something."

"He doesn't seem embarrassed by his ignorance, does he?" John asked his friend Stuart, a wrestler with freakishly muscular shoulders and chest and biceps. *A radical hunk* had been Trish's description of Stuart Camp's upper body. James had called it gargantuan; Agatha, grotesque.

"Geography isn't his field," Stuart said.

"Obviously," said John prissily.

Trish and Darrin were sitting across the aisle from John and Stuart this morning, Darrin with his music plugged into his ears and his knees protruding from ragged holes in his jeans. Trish was scanning a tabloid borrowed from Lillian. On the front page, under the headline LOVE NEST? was a life-size head shot of Princess Di. Trish, too, had a question for her professor. "Have they got Diet Coke in Assisi?"

Dr. Finn, amused beyond reason, laughed heartily and said he'd check it out.

"I never found one can of Diet Coke in all of Rome," she lamented.

Agatha had spent several miles of this trip conferring, one by one, with her five students. This being Day Five, they were required to describe the subject and structure of the papers they would write. On Day Nine, in Rome, they were to present her with their first drafts. On Day Ten, flying home, she would confer with them again.

Lisa Berglund had been first. Her primary interest (oddly unfeminine, thought Agatha) was scientific calculation. She was eager to visit the History of Science Museum in Florence and its display of measuring devices. By noting the dates of these various mechanical inventions, such as the astrolabe and the compass, she intended to determine the state of scientific inquiry before Galileo came upon the scene, and then show how it expanded during his lifetime. Not all of this sixteenth-century flowering was Galileo's work, said Lisa. There were other giants among his contemporaries, such as Kepler and Descartes, and she would include their discoveries and inventions as well.

"And your theme?" Agatha had inquired.

"My theme?"

"Your main idea. What do you mean to convince your reader of?"

"Just that these few people gave science a big push."

"But can't you take it a bit further? Isn't there a principle that we might apply in our own day?"

Lisa strained to conceive a principle but gave up. "Not that I know of, Miss McGee."

"Do think about it," Agatha advised. "The reader likes to take something useful away from a paper."

"Between you and me, I don't think Dr. Finn reads these papers."

"I read them," countered Agatha in the tone that for nearly fifty years had stilled her classroom and sent young minds back to work on flawed projects. Developed early in her career, it was a tone by which one or two syllables became a decree, and it was accompanied by a facial expression that brooked no compromise. She felt very good, putting this tone to use after all these months. "I weigh every word," she added, and Lisa agreed to think about it.

Lisa's place was taken by the wide-bodied wrestler. While everyone else on the bus wore a sweater or jacket, Stuart was dressed this morning in a plain white T-shirt, for the purpose of displaying his barrel chest and oversized biceps. Professor Finn's guided walking tour of Galileo's Rome had had a strangely melancholy effect on this young man. He couldn't get it out of his head, he told Agatha, that Galileo had been wrenched away from his life's work and made to reside in Rome for all those weeks while awaiting his hearing at the Holy Office. It must have been like wrestling, he said. For several hours before a match, Stuart needed to psych himself up, needed to empty his brain of everything but wrestling, and if his concentration was interrupted, he was thrown off track and felt disoriented. Thus, he would write his paper in the first person, using the Great Man's voice and imagining the Great Man's thoughts as he struggled to concentrate on his scientific writing while at the same time contemplating the damage the Church was likely to bring to his life's work. "It must have driven him almost crazy, Miss McGee. He must have felt terrible."

Agatha was amazed that such a sophisticated idea should be articulated by an athlete. With her limited experience of sports, her image of athletes as dolts was drawn largely from the mumbling and stammering ball players who appeared on her TV screen if she didn't switch off the news immediately following the weather. True, some of her bright sixth graders had gone on to become football and basketball stars in high school, but none of them had seemed to take their sport as seriously as Stuart did. They did not, as far as she knew, flex their biceps, massage their thighs, and fondle their sinewy forearms, as Stuart was doing now at Agatha's side. They never spoke to her of psyching themselves up.

"That's quite original," she told him. "Will a physics professor approve a creative paper?"

The question amused the wrestler. "I can't say from personal experience, but I've heard you could copy six pages out of the phone book and get your grade from Dr. Finn."

Stuart's place was taken by John. Since their itinerary called for a day trip from Florence to Pisa, it was John's intention to climb the Leaning Tower and describe it as a piece of architecture. "I mean, all you ever hear about the tower is that it leans and that it was part of Galileo's experiment with falling objects. Well, I'd like to consider it from an aesthetic viewpoint, Miss McGee. What it looks like in its setting. What you see from the top of the stairs."

Agatha was skeptical. "Can you get six pages out of that?"

"I can pad it. I've been padding papers ever since grade school."

Assuming that the young man was testing her tolerance for unethical scholarship, she ignored this remark and said, "You'll need a theme, a conclusion. It can't be merely description."

John Schrupp, looking defensive, said, "I think it can."

"But what's the point?" she asked, suppressing her irritation at his defiance, at his prissy manner of speaking.

He pondered this, then lifted his hands and formed a rectangle in the air. "My paper will be a photograph, Miss McGee. Exact description. The lights and shadows. The texture of the place."

"What's the point of a photograph?"

He shot her an impatient look. "A photograph doesn't need a point. It just *is*."

Her teacherish tone: "That's why most photographs don't hold the eye very long, Mr. Schrupp. A paper needs a point. Please think about it."

"All right," he said abruptly, meaning to indicate that she'd injured him. "I'll think about it."

Next was Betty Lou, the ponderous, inscrutable friend of Paula the pixy. Betty Lou's was the most comprehensive idea of the five. She planned to write about the Medici family, Galileo's patrons during his years in Florence. She admitted that her paper would say more about the Medicis and their way of life than about Galileo, but it seemed worthwhile to Betty Lou to flesh out the lifestyle of the family who sponsored him. Agatha listened with approval to Betty Lou's list of sites to be visited—the Pitti Palace; the Uffizi Gallery; the Medici Palace;

the Church of San Lorenzo, with its Medici chapel. She listened with admiration to the theme Betty Lou would incorporate into her paper—present-day scientists seeming so antiseptic, so divorced from the arts and humanities when compared with their predecessors of long ago. Agatha wondered how anyone as wise as Betty Lou could be satisfied to spend her life analyzing lake water.

Paula the pixy was last. Her topic excited her. Indeed it threatened to unhinge her, for there was a spastic quality in her head movements as she told how she would visit Arcetri, a village outside Florence, and write about Galileo's living there in his old age, under house arrest, cared for by his daughter. "My theme will be the total wickedness of the Church," seethed Paula, quivering with eagerness and anger. "Dr. Finn says the Pope reduced his sentence from imprisonment to house arrest because he knew Galileo was old and sick. Wasn't that kind and caring of him, though?" She asked this with scathing sarcasm. "Wasn't that typically Christian, Miss McGee? Wasn't that hypocritical to the max? And to think the poor man's crime was only saying how the planets move."

While Agatha tried to formulate a defense of the Church she'd loved for a lifetime, Paula went on in her headlong manner. "Actually, this was my mom's idea. There's a movie out on Galileo that my mom saw. She said it shows how the male-dominated Church treats people in this cruddy way all the time, and of course it's the same outside the Church, too. She says the world will never be at peace until its male power structure is destroyed."

"What does your father say to that? Does he agree?"

She turned to Agatha with her biggest, tightest smile. "My dad never agrees or disagrees with my mom. Not to her face. What he does is snicker. Like when she told him about that Galileo movie, he just snickered and said, 'You sure get a lot out of movies.' But then when Mom's not around he lets me know what he really thinks of her." Paula looked suddenly serious. "Do you think she's an idiot?"

"Your mother?"

"For saying that about the male power structure. My dad thinks she's an idiot."

"Heavens, there's nothing idiotic about expressing an opinion."

"Do you agree with her about male domination, Miss McGee? You're a woman."

"Our experiences have obviously been dissimilar, your mother's and mine. I've never felt oppressed by men."

"But all women have, Miss McGee. You have, I have, we all have."

Agatha, startled to be told what she felt and wishing to end the discussion, considered putting the girl in her place with a word of reprimand, but Paula seemed too fragile for that. She said evasively, "Maybe I've been too dense to realize it."

"See, that's exactly the attitude men have forced upon us. We think we're too dumb to know any better."

Agatha blinked and swallowed and started over. "Paula, I take back what I said. I don't really believe I'm dense, and I shouldn't have said so."

"My mom and Dr. Finn would get along super. He says everything my mom says about the Church. He is *so* brilliant, *so* sensitive. Don't you just love him?"

She was spared responding to this by the doctor himself, who popped out of his seat as though on cue, announcing, "People, people, there's Assisi up there on the hill. Isn't it a picture?"

Against the snow-covered, cloud-shaded peak behind it they saw a sunlit city resting on the shoulder of a mountain, a city built, it seemed, all of one stone, and that stone was the color of ripening wheat.

"I've never taken a group to Assisi before, but I like to adapt my tours to the needs of my people, and my brother the priest needs a dose of St. Francis." At this he laughed uproariously, and Paula the pixy followed his example, her shrill laugh turning heads and hurting Agatha's ears. No one else thought it particularly funny.

"We have no tour guide lined up in Assisi," the professor continued, "so you'll be on your own to explore as you wish. I'm hoping that a day and a night here will give you a feel for the Italian small town, and then tomorrow morning it's on to Florence."

"Don't you just love him?" asked Paula again, smiling her squeezy smile.

"Good luck with your paper, Paula."

With Paula gone back to her place beside Betty Lou, James moved ahead two rows to sit beside Agatha. Having made arrangements with the professor last night, James and his luggage had arrived at the Bellarmino Hotel in a taxi this morning, just as the bus was loading.

"Your man is a capital fellow, Agatha." He'd been riding with Father Finn, talking shop.

"Yes, he's steady—just what we've needed at St. Isidore's in troubled times."

"Amazing, the similarities between his parish and mine."

"That's encouraging. The Church isn't in fragments quite yet."

"I asked him why his brother seems hell-bent to destroy whatever religious faith these youngsters might have. Did you know the man had once been in the seminary himself?"

She shook her head. "He's never talked to me about his brother."

"One of those cases of sudden conversion, only the reverse of St. Paul's. Christian one minute, agnostic the next."

"How dreadful."

"A voice from nowhere saying the Creed's a fraud," said James. "God's a myth, and the spirit of man is no more immortal than dogs and cats."

"The devil's voice," she replied.

"No doubt about that."

The bus climbed a loaflike spur of Monte Subasio and eased itself into a parking lot outside Assisi's encircling wall. Their luggage was loaded into a small van, which the travelers followed on foot through a gate in the wall and uphill along a narrow cobblestone street.

"Hey, this ain't no small town," said Darrin.

"Compared to Rome," answered Dr. Finn.

"They better have Diet Coke," said Trish.

From the moment Agatha set foot inside the gate, she had the sensation of floating, an odd buoyancy of body and mind not unlike inebriation. She loved whatever her eye fell upon in

Assisi. The domed and towered churches so numerous, the narrow streets of stone so austere and clean, the medieval fortress at a higher elevation brooding watchfully over the rooftops, the floor of the valley spread out below the town in a crazy-quilt pattern of greens and ambers and winter browns—all of this appealed at once to Agatha's eye for beauty, and fed, somehow, her hunger for spiritual transcendence. She felt nourished and consoled. She didn't see how she could possibly board the bus tomorrow morning and leave it behind.

She revealed this to James shortly after noon in the Basilica of St. Francis. The pair of them had been exploring this building of holy treasures for an hour or more. They had started in the crypt, kneeling to say a prayer before the stone coffin of the saint, after which they had moved around the lower church in a kind of trance, taking in the candlelit chapels and the countless frescoes depicting the Holy Childhood and the Passion and myriad other scenes from the lives of Christ and his saints. They had stood a long time studying Cimabue's portrait of Francis—his tonsure and fringe of red hair, his little mouth and long nose and big ears, his eyes looking worn-out by the privations of the abstemious life he'd chosen to live—and they'd agreed that a handsome Francis would not have been nearly so inspiring. Then, climbing the stairs and coming out into the tall and airy upper church, filled as it was with a hazy noonday light that lent the frescoes a kind of soft, ethereal beauty, Agatha had blurted, "I can't stand to think of leaving here, James."

"Exquisite, isn't it?"

By following Giotto's two dozen illustrations from the life of the saint—Francis gives away his mantle, Francis preaches to the birds—they found themselves at the arched doorway leading outside.

"Are you tired, James?"

"I'll soon be wanting an hour in my room, Agatha. Then we can take up where we left off."

Strolling back to the hotel in the chill sunlight, she said again, "I can't stand to think of leaving here."

"Why do you fret about leaving at all? We've just nicely arrived."

"Because I've never felt so suddenly attached to a place. I

need to walk every street of this town, James. I need to look into every church. I need to see how it looks from up there." She stopped and pointed to the fortress—"I need to find the main piazza and watch the people. Don't ask me why, James, I can't explain it, but if I can't stay here for the rest of my life, I must stay at least until Tuesday."

"And why shouldn't we? I'm sure we can catch up to the others."

His "we" was a gift. "Oh, James," she said, taking his arm and feeling doubly blessed. Assisi and James. What more could she ask?

A half hour later she was standing alone on a height over-looking Assisi. At her back were the massive stone walls of the fortress, and above the fortress stood Monte Subasio with snow in its creases and a halo of haze at its peak. Above the mountain the windy blue sky was crisscrossed with mare's tails, and the chilly sun was beaming its light down in patches on the vast floor of the valley below the town.

Feeling the urgent need to make the most of her time in this blessed place, she had left James at the door of their hotel and hastily climbed the switchback streets upward and out of town. Now, referring to the map of Assisi in Imogene's tour guide, she was able to pick out the Basilica of St. Francis, the Church of St. Clare, and the Cathedral of St. Rufino. Turning to a map of Umbria, she studied the valley and picked out hamlets with names she couldn't pronounce. She moved closer to the brow of the hill, and, with the wintry grasses rustling at her feet and a few small birds chirping in a conifer nearby, she held her coat tight to her throat and studied the streets below her, retracing her route, picking out the roof of the building where James lay napping.

She looked at her watch and saw that she must start her descent if she was to be waiting in the lobby when he awoke. But before leaving the height, she took several deep breaths of the bracing mountain air and brushed a tear from her eye—a tear caused by the wind, she told herself—and asked aloud, "Dear Lord, if it's wrong for me to be the female companion to a priest, then why does it feel so right?"

25

"*A BIT OF REST* makes a new man of me entirely," said James, crossing the lobby to Agatha's chair and looking as though his bit of rest had aged him. His back was bent, his step unsteady. She saw traces of sleep in his eyes.

"Wouldn't you do better with a cane?" she asked, getting to her feet with her coat over her arm, prepared to go outside again.

"No, no, it's just that I hurried too quickly, getting up from bed." He sank into the chair next to hers. "My strength ebbs and flows like the tide, Agatha." He smiled up at her imploringly. "Will we have a cup of tea while we wait for the tide to come in?"

"A good idea," she said eagerly. For the past five days, without quite realizing it, she'd been missing her afternoon tea.

"They'll serve us in there," he said, pointing to a doorway. "I already asked at the desk."

Lifting his coat off his lap, she carried it with hers, and he followed her into a large, bright room overlooking the valley and facing the afternoon sun. Except for a waiter reading a newspaper at a far table, they had the room to themselves. They chose a table next to wide French windows giving out onto a narrow balcony. Beyond the balcony, wisps of haze were threading themselves over the floor of the valley.

"Where did you go, Agatha? What did I miss?"

"I went up to the fortress and looked down on Assisi from above. I've never known a town to be so intriguing from all angles. Below, above, inside and out."

"Yes, the place has been charming people for seven centuries."

"It's more than charm, James, and it's more than views.

There's a spirit here I can't define, and it seems to be in the stones. It's not in the people—I've spoken to hardly anyone—it's in the streets and the buildings, it's in the air. Do you have any idea what I'm talking about?"

He nodded agreeably. "I felt it in the crypt. The ghost of Francis."

"Yes, that's no doubt the source, but for me the spirit is spread all over town. I'm walking through it wherever I go."

"Similar to St. Peter's, would you say?"

"Similar, but more so. I was thinking, up there at the fortress, what a small-town creature I am at heart. What I'm feeling here I could never allow myself to feel at the Vatican, because the Vatican is Rome, and Rome is a city, and cities make me tense. I'm at home here because it's closer to Staggerford's size. I can take it all in." Looking out over the vast tableland of the valley, she added, "My soul contracts in the cities. It expands in the country."

"Well, now, myself, I've never felt differently about cities as opposed to towns, maybe because Dublin, for me, has always been at the other end of a very short ride on the bus."

"This may strike you as crazy, James, but on my way up to the fortress I saw a woman leaning out her second-story window hanging clothes on a line, and I knew exactly what was going through her head. Yesterday in Rome, I saw a woman looking down at me from an upper-story window, and nothing came into my head about her, except that she was an absolute stranger living a strange life in a strange land. I could no more understand her than I could understand an alien from outer space. And all because she was a city woman, and I am not."

The waiter served them bread and cheese with their tea. Eating, they watched the sunlight glimmer and die as rain clouds advanced across the valley.

"And what was the woman thinking, Agatha, as she hung out her clothes?"

"She was planning her afternoon, which included a nap and a trip to the grocer's and ironing a dress for Sunday."

"And our friend here?" James asked quietly, indicating the worried-looking waiter who had returned to his table and his newspaper at the far end of the room. "What's on his mind would you say?"

She studied the man. He was dark and muscular. He had spread the paper on the table and was reading with his finger. "You say, James. I'm better with women."

James quickened, pleased to be a partner in her game. "Well, he looks married to me. He looks like the father of more little ones than he'd counted on. He's thinking he doesn't mind working Saturday afternoons in the least. It gets him out of the house."

"He looks too husky to be a waiter."

"All Italian waiters look that way."

"Has he no ambitions beyond this job? Something more challenging?"

"Yes, it's to read every last word of that paper."

Agatha uttered a quiet little laugh, and James was pleased to have caused it. But her amusement was quickly dispelled. She was once again at the height overlooking Assisi, and asking God to explain the paradox of a woman like herself, churchly and honorable, feeling as if she were married to a priest. Watching the smile fade and her expression darken, he wondered what unwelcome idea had suddenly come into her head. Her eyes, unseeing, were fixed on the wrought ironwork of the balcony. Something told him not to attempt following her to the private place she had gone.

Raindrops appeared on the window, and soon the lobby filled with voices as the students came in from their explorations. Lillian, too, came in, and found Agatha and James in the dining room.

"Did you see St. Clare?" she asked breathlessly, sitting down at their table and unzipping her jacket.

"Not yet," said Agatha. "She's on our agenda."

"Then I won't go into it."

"Into what?"

"Into how she looks. The professor took us. You can see her teeth through her cheek."

"You mean she's on display?"

"I won't go into it. And her complexion, my stars. Her skin is like horsehide."

"Not surprising, considering she's been dead seven hundred years," said James.

"You have to see for yourself, I won't go into it. And her hands. Don't miss her hands."

"I might not go," said Agatha. "It sounds gruesome."

"Her hands are all wrinkled."

"That's enough, Lillian, more than enough. I'm not going."

"Oh, you have to go. You have to see her. You've never seen anything like it."

"No, I won't be party to anything so outrageous—leaving the poor woman's body on display."

"Italians like their relics," said James.

"Saint or no saint, I say it's outrageous."

"The professor says we'll see more of that kind of thing in Florence," said Lillian happily. "He says we'll see Galileo's finger under glass. I'd like to try a bite of that cheese, Agatha—it looks like Wisconsin Colby."

They were soon joined by Father Finn, just back from the Cathedral of St. Rufino, and five minutes later by his brother, just back from the Temple of Minerva. More bread and cheese. More tea. A bottle of wine. Talk of vineyards and weather and raincoats. The clouds thickened and darkened. The rain increased.

Another bottle of wine. Lillian spoke of sacred relics, and Dr. Finn gingerly moved the conversation to Florence and the public burning of Savonarola. James O'Hannon brought it back to Assisi, remarking on the beauty of the Basilica of St. Francis, and the professor tugged it back to Florence and the pulpit from which Galileo was first denounced as a heretic. Father Finn brought it back once more to Assisi, telling the story of how the body of St. Francis had been hidden by his disciples in order to thwart his devoted followers from other towns, primarily Perugia, from stealing it away. He said that in 1818 the body was discovered under the floor of the lower church in the very same stone coffin displayed today in the crypt.

Dr. Finn smiled derisively and said, "Prove it."

His brother was momentarily at a loss for words.

"Prove it's really Francis," Dr. Finn insisted.

"Albert, Albert," said his brother quietly but reprovingly, and this was followed by an awkward few moments of silence around the table, the professor lowering his eyes to his wine and James O'Hannon casting his gaze out the window.

The waiter returned to ask, in English, if anything more was needed; he was going off duty.

They shook their heads solemnly. "My, that's funny-tasting cheese," Lillian told him.

When the waiter left, the professor raised his eyes and put on a cheery smile, which he aimed at no one in particular. "My apologies, friends. I'm clearly outnumbered in this group of believers. I promise to hold my tongue for the rest of the tour." He left the table and returned to the lobby, where a number of students sat visiting and comparing postcards.

When the wine and cheese were gone, Lillian went up to her room, leaving the three at the table silently uneasy.

"The rain is ending," said James.

"A blessing," said Agatha, unfolding her pamphlet with its map of Assisi. "Will you feel like going out?"

"I'm feeling tip-top," he said, his eyes more animated than before, the tide of his energy obviously rising. "Shall we pay our respects to St. Clare?"

"Oh, James," she chortled, dismissing the idea with a little wave of her hand, yet hoping he'd insist.

Father Finn, brushing crumbs from his lap, made a moaning, guttural sound which Agatha recognized from St. Isidore's. It was his nervous throat-clearing preamble to any unpleasant announcement from the pulpit—the diminishing requirements for receiving Holy Communion, the rising interest rate on the parish debt.

"I feel I should apologize for Albert," he said, removing his glasses and addressing Agatha. "He promised me he'd be discreet on this tour, but he can't seem to control himself."

She asked, "What's his problem?"

Her mild-mannered pastor looked mildly bewildered. "A long-standing grudge. He was following me into the priesthood when he did a complete about-face."

"But that was years and years ago. What's keeping him so resentful?"

He squeezed the bridge of his nose. "Albert's pretty unhappy. Two marriages went bust. He's not very effective in the classroom. He used to be involved in research—some aspect of aerodynamics, I never understood it exactly—and a team of professors from the University of Michigan got ahead of him and stole his thunder. That was ten, fifteen years ago. He's been taking people on tours ever since, twice a year, summers and Christmas." The priest replaced his glasses, settling them firmly onto the bridge of his nose. "He's a man driven by his frustrations."

"Ah, the poor soul," said James, shaking his head sadly.

"I'd say he's a man doing a good deal of harm in the world," said Agatha.

Father Finn grimaced at this, fearing it to be true. James shot her a quick look, surprised by her unforgiving tone.

Lisa Berglund entered the room, inquiring of Agatha and James whether they would care to accompany her to the Basilica of St. Clare. "Paula and Betty Lou and Trish and Darrin have been there. They saw St. Clare in a glass coffin, and I'm wondering if you want to see her. I'm a little spooked by the idea, but I guess I have to see her. I mean, if I didn't, I'd always wonder."

"So would I," said Agatha.

"May I come along?" asked Father Finn.

The four of them followed their shadows across town on wet stones, the clouds sweeping off to the north, the sun hanging low in the west. James and Agatha were slowed by the upward-sloping streets. Lisa and Father Finn walked on ahead, discussing their cameras.

The church was dark and austere and smelled of melting wax and old damp wood. The flickering candles near the main altar gave too little light for a proper study of the frescoes high on the walls. Kneeling at prayer before the altar were three hooded, faceless nuns.

The church tugged mightily at Agatha's spirit. The odors, the chill, the nuns, the stark lines of the place—all of this spoke to her of faith in its elemental form. Consulting her pamphlet, she led the way across the nave to a side chapel, where they beheld the painted cross that spoke to Francis, urging him to repair the neglected churches of Umbria, and, in effect, to renew the Church of Rome. At the back of this chapel was a wide, floor-to-ceiling iron grate, behind which an old nun wearing a black mask popped out of her chair when Agatha and her friends approached. She darted about like a canary in a cage, pointing to the treasures in her keeping, naming them in a staccato voice, clear and high-pitched. She'd evidently seen enough tourists in her time to pin down their origins, for her message was uttered in English. "The hair of the saint!" she exclaimed, pointing to Clare's curly brown locks in a glass reliquary the size of a lunch pail. "The tunic of St. Francis," she said, indicating a garment resembling sewn-together gunnysacks with holes.

Agatha supposed that the nun's black mask, about the size and shape of the Lone Ranger's, signified the resolve of her order (the Poor Clares) to live out their lives apart from the secular world. But not too far apart—the last thing the nun pointed to was the money box bolted to the outside of the grill, and when each of them had dropped in a coin, she nodded approvingly and returned to her perch.

There was a sign posted in the stairwell to the crypt warning visitors that the remains of St. Clare had discolored with time. Such understatement! Lying under glass, dressed in her habit, her hands on her breast, the saint was every bit as ghastly as Lillian had claimed. Her face had indeed turned to black leather, and her sunken cheeks were ridged in the shape of her teeth.

"Not the least bit edifying," said Agatha, turning away and hurrying up the stairwell.

In the long shadows outside the church, the four of them stood conferring, each needing to know what the others made of the spectacle.

"Why do they show her?" asked Lisa.

"They believe it's a sign of her holiness that she hasn't decomposed," James explained.

"But she's a mummy."

"Yes, she's gone down a good deal," James agreed.

"I don't know," said Father Finn thoughtfully. "I'm glad to have seen her."

"Me too," said Lisa. "It's like *Nightmare on Elm Street*."

"It's all so Italian," said Agatha, "and not edifying in the least."

"I'm afraid I can't agree with you," said Father Finn. "I'm glad to have seen a great saint in the flesh. Seeing her dead makes it easier to imagine her living. Easier than just reading about her, I mean."

This unexpected view gave the others pause, particularly Agatha, who had seldom known this man to express an original notion.

At length James said, "It's true, is it not? The body, the actual body, reminds us she was more than a pious story. A mortal woman she was, of her place and time."

"And it's not the Italians' fault that seven hundred years have gone by since she looked more presentable," added Father Finn.

"I see what you're saying," said Lisa.

"I see I'm outnumbered," said Agatha.

At the end of dinner, in the hotel dining room, Dr. Finn rose to make announcements. Tomorrow, Sunday, the bus would leave at ten o'clock sharp. Tomorrow and Tuesday they would see the sights of Florence. On Monday, New Year's, museums being closed, they would travel to Pisa for the day. He went on to say that a notebook had been found in the lobby and a purse had been lost in the street. Large postcards cost more to mail than small ones. The hotel had only one phone for overseas calls, so those calling home would please be brief about it. He finished with a word about James.

"I want to formally welcome Father James O'Hannon of Ireland to our group. He replaces a man from Staggerford who had to cancel at the last minute. Most of you have met him. If you haven't, you'll want to introduce yourselves, so you can hear his brogue. Would you like to say a few words, Father?"

"Only my thanks to all you good people," said James from his chair, not rising to his feet because doing so would cause him a few moments of dizziness. "I came to Italy expecting to meet this dear friend of mine," he acknowledged Agatha with a nod, "and perhaps to give the Vatican a quick visit. I had no idea I'd fall in with you wayfarers. It's a grand thing to be carried through Italy by a dozen Galileo fanatics."

The students applauded politely.

"When you're next in Kilrath, Ireland," he added, "stop in at O'Hannon's public house for your stout or porter or whatever your poison might be. Tell the man you're one of the Galileo mob, and you won't pay a penny for your refreshment."

The students applauded wildly.

Leaving the dining room, James and Agatha invited Father Finn into a comfortable corner of the lobby, where they proposed their change of plan. Did he like Assisi well enough to stay on with them? "Yes, indeed," he responded, and went off in search of his brother to see if they might rejoin the group on Tuesday.

Next they proposed it to Lillian, but she was eager to get to Florence, where she was to meet her newfound friends from Indiana. They were going to an open-air market that offered (they'd heard) dressmaking fabric dirt cheap.

James soon excused himself for the long night's sleep he required. Taking Agatha's hand, he said, "Good night, and thank you."

"Good night, James—thank you for what?"

He smiled sleepily. "Well, for one thing, for extending our stay here. The group's next three days sound terribly frenetic for a convalescent."

Sensing that he was about to thank her for other things, perhaps of a sentimental nature, she said good night again and sent him off to his room.

She crossed the lobby to a good reading lamp and opened her Galileo paperback, a difficult book, but didn't read. Instead, she entertained a series of impressions from the past four days. The colors and the sounds. The heights and the crypts. The horror of terrorism and the peace of Assisi. The vistas, the people, the food, the weather.

And James.

A few more days in his company, then three months without him. Then, God willing and his health restored, she would see him in Minnesota for a part of Holy Week. Then after Easter . . .

After Easter, she dared not speculate. After Easter was the rest of her life.

26

EVENING IN ASSISI WAS morning in Minnesota. Lying late in her girlhood bed, filling her head with bitter thoughts about the craven French Lopat and the traitorous Agatha McGee, Imogene was surprised by the doorbell. She rose and peered down from her frost-edged window, expecting to see French, jittery and contrite, standing on the back step, but no one was there.

She turned and looked with distaste into the mirror over her dresser. She devoted a few moments to teasing her hair out from the matted side of her head, attempting to make it symmetrical with the fluffier side. When the doorbell sounded a second time, she put on her chenille robe and went downstairs to the front door, where she found Sister Judith Juba smiling at her through the glass.

"Judy, what's up?" she said, presuming that the nun had news, presumably bad, concerning the tour group.

"I saw your car, Imogene. I was on my way downtown. I didn't think you'd be here this weekend with your mother gone to Rome." Sister Judith stepped into the entryway, where her long sheepskin coat gave off the sharp chill of winter and caused Imogene to shiver. "The Lord is working behind the scenes—I've been wanting to see you."

Imogene looked puzzled and a little fearful, both halves of this last statement striking her as ominous.

Sister Judith, inveterate toucher, clutched the shoulder of Imogene's robe, gushing, "You're impossible to get ahold of, do you know that? You've risen so high in state government that you're never home when I call. Your mother gave me your St. Paul number and I called and called."

"When?"

257

"Earlier this week. Tuesday. Wednesday."

A wistful look crossed Imogene's face. She'd been across the alley, in bed with French. "What did you want?"

"I want to interview you for the *Weekly*."

Imogene nodded complacently, not surprised that the reading public should need to tap into her prodigious knowledge.

"Not now, not this minute," said the nun, running her hand down Imogene's forearm and flexing Imogene's wrist. "It's Saturday morning and you've got things to do, and I've got things to do, and you'll want time to gather your thoughts, but I'd like to do it this afternoon if possible."

"Why not?" agreed Imogene, her eyes narrowing. She was hatching a scheme of vengeance.

"You've seen my column. It's called 'Women of Staggerford,' and it runs whenever Editor Fremling has room for it, and whenever I can find a proper subject."

"I'm not *of* Staggerford," said Imogene staunchly. "I'm of St. Paul."

"But Staggerford formed you. It's about women from here making a name for themselves in careers. I did one on Agatha McGee in teaching, and Louise Meers on the city council, and Marsha Skoog in the dress shop. You'll be the first of my subjects who went out and made your mark in the larger world. We'll run your picture."

"How's two o'clock, then? If you're taking a picture, I'll need to fix my hair."

"Two is perfect. The Lord is at work."

It was nearly two-thirty when Sister Judith returned, carrying a tape recorder, a notepad, a camera, and three back issues of the *Weekly*.

"Here, in case you haven't seen them—some of my columns on women." She spread the papers and equipment across the coffee table and dropped her sheepskin coat across a chair next to the Christmas tree. She was wearing a yellow sweat suit. "I think I did best on Louise Meers, and it was because she had so much to say. Agatha wasn't all that forthcoming about herself. You know how she can be—very private. You wonder what she has to be private about, don't you? Her interview was last spring, and mostly what she talked about was the closing of the school, and of course the Church came in for some pretty heavy criticism, which I couldn't print for obvious reasons. I mean, I *am* the Church, am I not? And so I ended up with a pretty thin column. The closing of the school really knocked her for a loop. My, your tree is nice."

Imogene wanted to tell her not to be patronizing—the tree, after three waterless days in her absence, was turning rusty—but she held her tongue.

"My, I like your outfit," said the nun, sitting down on the sofa.

"Thank you." Imogene was quite fond of it herself—a dress of purple plaid, with buttons of pearl.

While Sister Judith spoke into her recorder, testing it, Imogene went to the kitchen for coffee and a plate of Christmas pastry she'd found in the freezer. Returning, she pulled a chair up on the other side of the coffee table, out of the nun's reach.

"Speaking of Agatha," said Imogene, pouring weak, tea-colored coffee into Sister Judith's cup, "she's not the woman you think she is."

"Oh? Who is she then?" cried Sister Judith, laughing excitedly. She aimed the recorder at Imogene and took up her notebook and pen. "The older I get, the more interesting she becomes to me. I used to think—"

"She's a whited sepulcher!" Imogene's voice was harsh, her expression ferocious. "Just wait till you hear this." She unfolded a piece of paper from the pocket of her dress.

"Should this be in the article?" asked the nun deliciously. "I mean, I can see how Agatha's career might have influenced your own."

"Use it as you see fit." Imogene pursed her lips, scanning the list she'd jotted down from memory while drying her hair. Where to begin? At the beginning, she decided. "Did you know there's a man named James in Agatha's life?"

"James who?"

"A priest from Ireland."

"What do you mean, in her life?"

"He's in Rome right now, to meet her."

The nun nodded shrewdly. "So that's who called the bishop.

Somebody called the bishop from Rome, trying to reach her. I gave him the name of her hotel."

"So, you see?" said Imogene, smiling smugly, as though this fact validated everything else she was about to reveal. "I have here a list of people Agatha has defamed and slandered, and the bishop is one of them. She calls him intransigent."

Sister Judith, after a moment's consideration, agreed. "He *is* intransigent, and what's wrong with that? He sees his way and follows it."

"And she says he's a fool besides."

"Well, Dick Baker's nobody's fool, but I'm not surprised she thinks so. I mean, it really knocked her for a loop when he urged the parish council to close the school. I actually felt sorry for her."

Angrily disappointed by the nun's tolerance, Imogene moved on. "Agatha says my mother is a warm body with a dead mind."

Sister Judith suppressed a giggle. "Who did she say that to?"

"This James guy. Think of it!—her friend of a lifetime—my mother—a warm body with a dead mind."

Though she could easily imagine Agatha making this amusing statement about Lillian, Sister Judith discreetly feigned dismay. "Agatha is so candid sometimes."

"You know very well my mother's been at her beck and call for seventy years. She's over there in her kitchen practically every day seeing to it that she eats right."

"Let me see that list," said the nun, laughing nervously. "What does she say about me?"

Imogene withheld the list. "She says you're a magpie."

Sister Judith didn't get it.

"That means you're a sucker for anything bright and shiny. I looked it up in a dictionary of slang."

Sister Judith, relieved, said, "That's me all right, but how does she know about magpies?"

"The Irish priest would know about magpies. They have magpies in Ireland. I looked it up in *Birds of the World*."

"Where did you get that list, Imogene?"

"And Janet's husband, Randy Meers? She used the words 'lazy' and 'arrested development.' "

Sister Judith nodded. "She had her misgivings about that marriage. She thought they were mismatched."

"Randy Meers is not a case of arrested development, Judy. He's making tons of money."

"He's matured a lot," Sister Judith agreed. "Janet has been really good for him."

"And the sons of Theodore Druppers. Here's what she evidently said about the Druppers boys." She consulted her list.

"What do you mean evidently?"

"I mean it's obvious she wrote these things to James."

"How do you know? Did she tell you?"

"Never mind how I know."

"Did she show you the letters?"

"Let me finish. She thinks both the Druppers boys are dishonest."

"Well, she should know. She had them in school."

Imogene uttered a furious, hissing sigh. "For God's sake, Judy, don't you see what I'm saying? She's been trashing the whole town. She's been holding herself up as the model of virtue around here for most of the twentieth century, and all the while she's been running us into the ground. There's more. There's scads more." She glanced again at her list. "There's Myron Kleinschmidt, and Father Finn, and some people in the rest home. There's Daniel Buckingham, there's Marsha Skoog, there's Addie Phelps's son and daughter, there's others. She calls your father a ruined soul. She says he's controlled by demons. She hasn't a good word for anybody."

Sister Judith sat forward, letting the notebook slip from her lap. "Imogene," she said, trying to infuse her voice with an authority she didn't command, "tell me how you know these things."

Imogene studied the woman, gauging her trustworthiness. She was a mental lightweight, but not treacherous. Quite honest, actually. Quite dependable, in the way such innocent souls often were. "I read the priest's responses to her letters. A whole stack of them. Three years' worth. He stated his opinions about the people she had described to him. He named them by name. Sometimes he quoted her and sometimes he paraphrased. So where I don't have her exact words, I have his reaction to her exact words. I'm not making any of this up."

The nun's eyes grew wide. "You read her mail?"

"I won't say how I came by the letters. I'm only telling you I read them, and Agatha's not the immaculate conception everybody makes her out to be."

Sister Judith picked up a sugar cookie, studied it, nibbled it. "Surely you don't expect me to print this stuff."

"Print it, don't print it, I don't care. One way or another it'll get around. I can get on the phone." Imogene made a portentous face—large, insinuating eyes—allowing the nun to surmise the effect of phone calls.

"What does she say about Myron?"

"She thinks he's all façade. Nothing to him. I'll call Janet Meers first. She's always been such a disciple of Agatha's—this'll wake her up."

"Janet and Randy are gone to Las Vagas."

"I'll call them from St. Paul when they get home. There's no hurry."

The nun carefully laid her nibbled cookie on a napkin, laid the napkin on her knees. With her eyes closed in meditation, she licked sugar from her fingers. Her father controlled by demons? A ruined soul? Would Agatha actually use language that pernicious?

"And wait till I tell my mother," said Imogene.

The ramifications, for Sister Judith, seemed mostly ethical. With her eyes still closed she said, "You still believe in the Lord, Imogene—your mother told me you attend a prayer group in St. Paul." Her eyes opened and her smile reappeared, but now it was a troubled smile. "I hope you've prayed about this."

"Lay off, Judy."

"I'm just saying you should take this to the Lord."

"I did. The Lord said, 'Get Agatha.' "

The nun's smile froze. "The Lord doesn't talk that way, Imogene."

"Not to you maybe."

"Not to anybody."

"Listen!" boomed Imogene. "We all know what the Lord thinks of whited sepulchers. It's in the Bible."

Sister Judith, daunted now, indeed a bit frightened by the ruthlessness of Imogene's rancor, sought to change the subject.

Putting on a cheery face, she said, "But now we have to talk about you, Imogene. After all, that's what I'm here for, to write about your career."

On their second cup of coffee the nun was gradually able to shift Imogene's attention away from her list of wronged Staggerfordians, and the rest of the interview was a recitation of the stages Imogene had passed through on her way to becoming a media specialist for the state of Minnesota at a salary of $31,000, with health benefits, a reserved parking space, and three weeks paid vacation.

27

*T*HE NEXT MORNING, RETURNING to the hotel after Mass, Agatha and James found their friends setting out on foot for the parking lot outside the city wall. Agatha, at Lillian's request, accompanied them, listening to Paula the pixy's last-minute writing ideas on the way. Standing at the city gate, she saw the coach off, saw their faces beaming down at her from the expansive windows, hands waving vigorously, Lisa throwing a kiss, Lillian raising a knitting needle in a kind of blessing, Darrin signaling "Peace" with two fingers, Paula the pixy gritting her teeth in pain or happiness, you could never tell which.

The coach curved downhill and out of sight, leaving a smudge of exhaust in the air. When the sound of the engine died away, it was replaced by a silence so absolute that Agatha thought she'd gone deaf. She took a roundabout way back to the hotel, giving James the hour he'd requested for reading his breviary. A winter Sunday in Assisi. The last day of the year. The entire citizenry might have died in the night, the streets were that empty. Bold lines of sun and shadow fell across the cobblestones. A cat looked down at her from a high window-sill.

The hotel was all but empty as well, the lobby chilly and dark, the dining room closed, the desk clerk yawning and rustling the Sunday paper in the little office behind the registration counter.

At length, James came down from his room. "Will we go off in search of lunch, Agatha?"

"Yes, I'm ready."

"Shall we ask your Father Finn?"

"He's already gone out. He confesses to being something of a loner, and liking it."

"Being alone has its merits, as we know well enough, Agatha. And its drawbacks as well, wouldn't you say?"

"At times." She smiled and added, "Sundays can be lonely."

Having walked a considerable distance and finding no restaurant open, they came to a bench facing the sun, and James suggested they sit. The bench was small, forcing them close together. They lifted their faces to the warmth.

"I've never been so affected by a place, James."

"For me, it's similar to one or two places in Ireland. Kesh, for one. It's a mountain pilgrims climb in the west. Cashel is another—a great heap of holy ruins in the Midlands."

While the sun warmed their faces, a breath of December air crept down the mountain and chilled the backs of their necks.

"I'll be honest with you, James. I left home feeling very dull and useless."

"You said as much in your letter."

"And now I feel . . ." She didn't know how to phrase it. Was there a word to indicate how light her step had been since she arrived in Assisi, how tireless her curiosity, how sublime this morning's Mass in the Basilica of St. Francis? "I feel I'm on the road to recovery."

"That's grand. Certain places are graced with the power to lift our spirits, there's no denying it."

"But I'm worried I'll have a relapse."

"Not likely, I'd say."

"But it is, James. It *is* likely—once I'm home."

"Ah, leave off with your fretting, Agatha." He waved his hand—a dismissive gesture. "If it's dull and useless you are, I'll write you lots of letters, and that will take care of the dullness. As for the uselessness, I'd say find yourself a job of work to use up your time."

"A job of work?"

"Anything to keep the hands and the mind occupied. What they call volunteering. Hospital work."

"I'm no good with the sick, James, and never have been. Why, a sliver can make me nauseated."

"I'm sick," he said softly, patting her hand. "You're doing wonders for me."

She flushed with pleasure at the touch. "You're not sick anymore, James. You're weak. Weak I can handle."

"Aaaah," he purred with satisfaction.

They were silent for several minutes, basking in the sunlight, both of them going over in their minds this morning's Mass. Sitting beside Agatha during the lengthy homily delivered in Italian, James had been carried back to his young boyhood and those happy Sunday mornings when the Mass was sheer mystery, when liturgy of any sort seemed created simply as an occasion for him to crowd into the same pew with his beloved family. How secure he'd felt as a lad, pressed between his mother and sister. He'd felt that same secure and happy attachment this morning with Agatha, as though Agatha were his next of kin.

For her, this Mass with James at her side had worked the sort of miracle that pilgrims pray for. It had finally put to rest the horror of the Mass in Ballybegs when she'd discovered the truth about James. For nearly three years the memory of that awful Sunday morning had possessed her like a spell. Not a day went by that she didn't see again, striding out onto St. Brigid's altar in his vestments, the man she'd expected to sit beside in a pew. But now that shocking sight, while still etched in her memory, had lost its power. Again and again, leaving the church and then walking back to the hotel from the parking lot, and now sitting in the sun with her eyes closed, she purposely called the memory to mind, testing her reaction, and not once did she shudder. The hex was dispelled.

And thus, with her thoughts no longer enmeshed in the past, she felt free to consider the future. "James," she said rather tentatively, "I've told you about Myron Kleinschmidt, our representative in Congress."

"The little man with the public face."

"He wants me to manage his campaign office."

"Ah," he said, not entirely comprehending. "And what does that entail?"

"Some six months before election day, which is in November, he sets up campaign offices in various towns. He wants me to manage the Staggerford office."

"There you are, then. Your job of work."

"But it's not that simple. The McGees have always been Democrats."

"And he's ... ?"

"Republican."

"And you feel a strong allegiance for his opponent?"

"Actually, no. I'm an independent. I've been voting a mixed ticket for most of my life."

"Then that's why he wants you, I'd wager—to show the world he's convinced an independent thinker of his views. What *are* his views?"

"Wishy-washy."

"Change with the direction of the wind, do they?"

She nodded. "He's consistent on only one issue, pay raises for congressmen."

"Do it anyway, Agatha. Manage his office and send him off for another term. It will give you satisfaction."

"But my father was a staunch Democrat."

"Aaah," said James sympathetically. No need to remind an Irishman about the importance of family tradition. "So it would feel like a betrayal."

"Exactly."

James pondered this. "I'm wondering, would it be like going over to the British side after a lifetime as a Home Ruler? Would it be that bold?"

"No, nothing so extreme as that. In American politics, it's not a difference in goals so much as methods."

"Well then, where's the harm? Wouldn't old Peter McGee want his daughter to be her own woman?"

"But I wouldn't be my own woman, you see—I'd be working with no conviction. Myron's reelection is immaterial to me. I'd be doing it simply to feel useful."

"All the more reason. Peter McGee would not want his daughter feeling useless."

She spoke in a subdued voice. "I suppose he wouldn't."

He patted her hand again. "Take on the job, Agatha."

She clutched his hand momentarily, squeezing it with both of her own. When she relaxed her grip, he did not withdraw his hand.

* * *

A half hour later they emerged from a narrow street into the town's main piazza, having found it with the help of Agatha's pamphlet. A fountain dribbled a little water into a pool. Beyond the fountain a man stood at a car window, visiting with the driver while the driver's wife hurried into a little shop selling fruit and newspapers. Two boys wearing suits sat on the pavement, their bikes beside them, poring over a soccer article in the Sunday paper. Across the way a woman in a red dress put her head out the door of her house and called to her child or her dog (neither appeared), using a name that sounded like "Pasta."

The street they'd followed had been steeply uphill, so they sat on the lip of the fountain to catch their breath. Agatha watched a woman in furs cross the piazza holding the hand of her little daughter, who wore a serge coat and leggings and beautiful black boots with purple laces.

"James, I'm struck by how well everyone dresses in Italy."

"I've thought so myself. Here as well as in Rome. Weekdays as well as Sundays."

"Yes, they all seem to have a style about them. In Rome I saw men studying clothes in the shop windows. You seldom see that in America."

"The Irishman is no fashion plate either."

"American men never seem quite comfortable in their suits. In fact, some don't seem to own one. The professor is off to Florence in his jogging outfit."

"I have to confess to a meager wardrobe myself, Agatha, and all of it the same color." He chuckled quietly, and she gave his hand two or three reassuring pats.

They watched the driver's wife cross from the shop to the car. She was a golden-haired woman wearing a straight gray coat with a brilliant blue scarf tied loosely at the collar. Her cuffs were black fur, her shoes were taupe. The car drove away, and the man who'd spoken to the driver straightened his tie and stepped into a house. The two boys returned the paper to the newsagent and sped downhill on their bikes. The woman in the red dress gave up calling "Pasta" and shut her door.

Alone in the piazza, the water bubbling softly at their backs, James looked at Agatha and said, "Will I tell you a story?"

"Oh, please." No one told stories like James.

"About a man named James Stephens, Agatha. He's been on my mind of late."

"The poet," she said, calling to mind an anthology of Irish verse belonging to her father. It stood to this day on the third shelf of the bookcase in her living room.

"No, not that one. This James Stephens was older, and nothing so tame as a poet. He made his name as a rebel over a hundred years ago. Imprisoned more than once by the British, he was. Jailed both in Dublin and London, and after escaping his guards one time in the 1850s, he set out to incite a rebellion."

"Another rebellion."

He nodded in agreement. "One of the many. And this one a unified, coordinated affair, an uprising all over Ireland. He did his job well, and he did it on foot, taking his time, walking from city to town to hamlet throughout the land, meeting secretly with the oppressed and the malcontents wherever he went, sowing the seeds of armed revolution. The seeds required a decade to germinate and grow, but bear fruit they did, in the rising of 'sixty-seven."

"A failure," said Agatha.

James smiled at her. "You know your Irish history."

"I'm only guessing," she said.

He nodded, his eyes turning serious. "The safest of guesses, of course, the history of Ireland being one failed rebellion after another. Indeed, the rising of 'sixty-seven was put down in a matter of hours. It was wonderfully planned and coordinated, but insufficient to overcome the occupation forces of the Queen. Ill-trained farmers and laborers going up against the militia with sticks and pikes and butcher knives and getting themselves slaughtered in the bargain." His expression darkened. "Nothing's changed, Agatha, except the weapons. Now it's bombs and rifles."

He fell silent, and she waited, certain the tale would come around to James Stephens again.

"I don't know how many years he spent on the road, James Stephens. Two years? More? I only know by the time the rising came about, he was deposed as its godfather. Some controversy, some dissension at the upper level of the Fenian brotherhood, and they put him out to pasture, forgetting, apparently, that he'd been the missionary who started it all. And isn't that what he was, after all? A missionary inciting war?"

She waited through another long silence, sensing that he was about to liken himself to James Stephens.

"I see myself in his shoes, Agatha, but inciting peace instead of war. If one man, traveling hither and yon and ministering to a people's fighting spirit, could bring about a nationwide uprising like that, well I ask you, why couldn't a man put in a year or two, hither and yon, ministering to the poor creatures wounded by that fighting, and perhaps bring about some lasting change?"

It was some time before she spoke. Her voice sounded weak and far away. "Why not indeed?" She intended to add a word of caution—his age, his failing health—but she withheld it.

He'd hoped for a stronger reaction from her. "You're not entirely convinced?" he asked.

On the contrary, he had stirred something deep in her soul, some urge to be of use to him. To Ireland. To the cause of peace in the world, no less. This deep-seated urge was what held her speechless. This, and the vivid fantasy that flashed through her mind, a vision of herself and James entering an assembly hall at dusk, a hall full of people who had gathered to hear James speak about the atrocities in Ulster. The two of them had come in out of the rain and the hall was bright. So bright, in fact, that Agatha—here on the lip of Assisi's central fountain—blinked and feared for a moment that she was having a stroke. She put her hand to her forehead, closed her eyes and said, again in a faraway voice, "I'm convinced. And afraid."

He sensed the change that had come over her. "Agatha?"

She nodded, her hand still held to her brow, her eyes still closed. She was trying not to lose her vision of the assembly hall, though it frightened her.

"Agatha, am I putting you to sleep?" he asked humorously.

"It must be the altitude." She opened her eyes and smiled faintly. "I felt sort of carried away there for a moment." She took a deep breath and patted her breast. "Or maybe it's hunger. The restaurants must be open by now."

"Of course." He got to his feet, apologizing for delaying

their meal. They angled across the piazza, then changed direction, choosing a street with a downward slope.

"You haven't heard the last of my mission, Agatha. You're free to listen or not, as you please, but I'll no doubt be running on about it for days."

Still she seemed distant, subdued. Which made him self-conscious, embarrassed, apologetic.

"Maybe by running on about it, I'll talk myself out of it, and wouldn't that be a relief?"

"Would it?" she asked seriously.

"I'd be free then to spend my retirement like ordinary men, with my feet up and the telly tuned in to the soccer."

"No, James, you must never do that." She uttered this with vigor. Having caught the spirit of his mission, she longed somehow to lend him her strength.

After lunch they passed the rest of Sunday as any couple might—reading, napping, writing postcards, and planning their week. Father Finn was a ghostly presence, slipping in and out of the hotel and spending a great deal of time reading in his room. When they went out again in the late afternoon for a brief walk, they caught sight of him turning a corner at the far end of the street. They hurried to catch up with him, but they caught only a trace of his cigar smoke.

Later, joining them for dinner in the hotel dining room, Father Finn spoke at length about a biography of St. Francis he'd just finished. It was a book that James too had read, some years before, and since they both admired it so much, Agatha asked to borrow it.

She took the book to her room and read, engrossed, until nearly midnight, paying particular attention to the bond between Francis and Clare. It put to rest for good her misgivings as the woman in James's life. Francis and Clare were saintly, chaste, and intensely in love.

28

AFTER MASS AND LUNCH the next day—New Year's—they returned to the hotel, James to nap and Agatha to sit in the deserted lobby with a teapot at her elbow and her *Life of Francis* in her lap. She did very little reading, however, distracted as she was by the snoring of the clerk in his little office behind the registration desk, and by unsettling questions proliferating in her head.

Wasn't any year that began at this happy height destined to lead downhill?

What were the true ingredients of her present contentment? How much of it was caused by James? By Assisi? By the mere fact that an ocean lay between herself and her discontent at home?

She'd never before left Staggerford for more than a night and day without longing to be back in her familiar neighborhood, living her familiar routine. What had become of her homing instinct? Where was that longing now? Since boarding the plane in Rookery, she'd given no thought to her furnace, her mail, her plants, her snowy sidewalks.

She must not return home to her idle ways, that was a given. Was Congressman Kleinschmidt's offer a blessing in disguise? Was it too much to hope that managing his campaign office would prove rewarding as well as diverting?

Who would she invite to Easter dinner with James?

She stood up and crossed the lobby and stood at a window facing the empty street. Thank the Lord, she thought, there was no question about James's cancer, no doubt whether the poor man would live or die. He would live. She knew this for certain. She knew it the way she knew, upon waking each morning, what day of the week it was, what month of the year.

Some things you know without being told. His cancer was cured.

James's sleep was long and profound, like the sleep of the drugged, and he came down with sheet creases running along the left side of his face. "Forgive me, Agatha. I know what you're thinking: how did you get mixed up with a lout this lazy? But I give you my word, before my surgery I was never one to take naps."

"It's your system knitting itself back together, James. You mustn't apologize."

He chose a soft chair, facing her across a table of magazines. "It's you that's putting me back together, Agatha. It's like a miracle, waking up to the knowledge that we're under the same roof."

Though she flushed with pleasure at this remark, she wished he'd refrain from talking this way. She was already steeling herself for their parting in Rome, and sentiments such as this would only make it more difficult. She moved the talk to firmer ground. "Where will you be living, James? Will you be staying on in Ballybegs?"

"I won't. The new man has very kindly invited me to remain in the rectory for as long as I need doctoring in Dublin, and I've taken him up on that. As you know, it's an easy ride on the bus from Ballybegs to O'Connell Street. But sooner or later I'll be drifting home to Kilrath." He lowered his eyes and set his mouth in a joyless crimp. "I'll move in with my brother."

"Matt," she said, recalling the photograph taken outside the O'Hannon pub, the tall, smiling man with rolled-up sleeves standing on James's right.

"Matt's a dear man, no mistake about that, but he hasn't the head for business. Nor the ambition. You'd think, would you not, that by operating a pub in Ireland you'd have a guaranteed income for life, we Irish being so fond of our spirits and porter. But the pub took a steep downward turn after my mother and sister died."

"There's a competing pub in Kilrath?"

He nodded. "Three of them. At first I thought it was his own drinking that made him so neglectful—Matt likes his jar near at hand—but I've come to realize it's simply not in his nature to be in charge of things. I'll take the bus down to Kilrath of a Sunday afternoon and see the cold, dingy place my boyhood home has become, and I'll take a broom to the floor and I'll dust off the bottles and I'll build up a fire in the hearth, and Matt will work alongside me right enough—busy as ants we'll be for a couple of hours—and then we'll tend to the bookkeeping and take care of the bills he's forgotten to pay, and he'll be full of promises about changing his ways."

"But he doesn't have the will to follow through?"

"Two or three weeks later I'll go back and find he hasn't lifted a finger. Everything's dusty and dirty again, including the glasses he's drawing the beer into, and there'll be a threatening letter from the Guinness people and the Smithwicks people, and the people that supply the little packets of potato crisps."

"Your mother and sister were the managers, I take it."

"Especially my sister. Marion was the heart and soul of the place, after my mother got old. I never knew how much Matt depended on her until after she was gone. Working alongside Marion all those years, he never stinted or slowed down, but the minute she was out of the picture, he turned out to have no more direction than a gnat on the evening breeze. It's more than a little worried I am, let me tell you."

"And is he worried as well?"

"Full of false hope he is. 'Matt, we'll be having to close the place down,' I'll say to him, sitting amongst the empty stools, and he'll laugh and tell me, 'Wait till you come home for good, James, it's a powerful team we'll be.' The poor man thinks I'm going from priest to publican."

"Surely you've told him you're not."

"Many times over, and I could just as well be speaking to the coatrack. He's always been one to ignore what he'd rather not hear."

James fell silent. He watched Agatha lift a finger and thoughtfully tap her lower lip. It was a gesture he'd seen more than once these last three days. It meant she was forming a fresh idea.

"Maybe you *should* be a publican, James."

"Agatha!"

"I'm serious."

"Grueling work it is. On your feet far into the night."

"More grueling than preaching peace to Ulster?"

He sighed. "You don't think much of my plan."

"I don't think it's safe."

"Safe enough. No worry there."

"A man of peace moving among those who love war? Aren't you afraid of becoming a target?"

"No worry there," he repeated, smiling in a vague, distracted way. She was right, of course—there *was* risk involved—but his safety did not concern him. The prospect of bodily harm was overridden by the sacredness of his mission.

Sensing this, she took another tack. There were practical considerations. "If you close down the business, what will you live on? Do priests get pensions in Ireland?"

"A laughably tiny amount, scarcely enough to keep a church mouse in cheese. But I've been putting by a nest egg. I've owned sheep wherever I've lived, keeping them with farmers of my parish. I've bought and sold a good many pigs in my day. What I have will doubtless be adequate." He looked grim again. "I hadn't planned to carry Matt as well as myself, but I think we can manage it. The pub is ours free and clear, of course. It's been in the family since 1911. Solid as a fortress it is, with rooms at the back and upstairs. More rooms than a couple of old men could ever need. We'll take in a lodger if we have to."

Agatha recalled her two lodgers, Miles Pruitt and Frederick Lopat, as well as the several short-term roomers she'd taken in over the years—new teachers in town searching for permanent quarters—and she thought of the work involved. She had to laugh to herself, imagining James and his brother running a rooming house.

"What are you smiling at, Agatha?"

"You don't know what you're getting into with lodgers. If Matt's the lackadaisical type and you're out making speeches around the country, who's dusting and sweeping and washing the linens?"

He was a little put out by this. "We're not exactly helpless Agatha. After all, I've been my own housekeeper for forty years."

"But you're out on the road making speeches."

"Out and back, you see. Haven't I told you Kilrath's location?"

"A town in the Midlands is all you've said."

"Ah, well then. It's right where it belongs for my purpose. In the Midlands, yes, but north of center, scarcely nineteen miles from the Ulster border, making it easy crossing over and back. Say I'm out on my mission two or three days of the week—the next morning I'm home and sleeping late in my own bed. Two or three days of the week, at my age, will be my limit, Agatha. I'm no Mother Teresa. I know my limitations. I've seen enough horse races to know the importance of pacing, I assure you of that."

She was not reassured. "That's all very well, James, but how many times can you cross the border without getting shot or blown up?"

"Ah, there's not a zealot in Ireland who'd dare kill a priest."

Her face was compressed in dark disapproval.

"It's not a war zone," he went on. "It's not an embattled border, despite what you read. It's mountains and rivers and farmsteads. It's little towns and a few troubled big ones. You've been across Ireland, Agatha. You'd have a hard time telling Ulster from Galway."

"Except for the gunfire and dynamite craters." Did he think she never read the papers?

"That's in Belfast," he said. "I'm talking about the countryside, and that's where I'll be doing my work."

This did nothing to soften her stony, frightened look, so he went on. "You must come back again, Agatha, and see for yourself. The Free State has no monopoly on Ireland's beauty."

She looked away. She looked at her *Life of Francis*, opening it for a moment, then closing it. She looked very nervous. She straightened the cuffs of her white blouse, protruding from the sleeves of her navy-blue suit, and then rose abruptly from her chair and asked, "Shall we go in and sit by the window? It's our last Umbrian sunset."

"Right you are." He rose eagerly to his feet.

They crossed into the empty dining room, took their places at the table by the central window and gazed wordlessly across the plain below them. This afternoon's sky was less dramatic than yesterday's, but the colors of the land were richer. As the sun sank from view, the distant hills became deeply purple and the fields turned darkly russet. Here and there stood thin groves of gray timber. Headlights moved along the thin roads connecting farms and hamlets. Tiny spots of light came on in faraway houses.

Silent they sat, James aware of her agitation but puzzled as to the cause, Agatha aware of his puzzlement but not trusting her voice to put him at ease. She was trying to control a strange commotion in her breast, a kind of flutter or tremor caused by his invitation to Ireland.

They watched dusk come on, flattening the domes and towers of distant churches and blending them into the earth. She would never return to Ireland—that had been her assumption three years ago, that had been her vow. James, by living there, had put Ireland off limits. So why, now, did everything seem suddenly reversed, her assumptions overthrown, her desires upside down? By what trick of fate or hellish magic had James, by *not* living there, made Staggerford now seem off limits? For his invitation to Ireland had made her not want to go home.

Presently, when dusk became darkness and moving headlights were all that remained of the valley, James watched Agatha turn her head slowly toward him, preparing to speak. She was climbing, it seemed, out of a deep river of thought. She said finally, and with her eyes slightly averted, that she had to retire for the night.

He was dismayed. "But I thought we might go out and look for dinner, Agatha. It's clear nobody's in the kitchen here."

"I have to retire," she repeated, rising from her chair and gathering up her book and her purse.

He stood and took her hand. "As you wish. I trust you're feeling all right."

She did not reply, nor did her eyes meet his. They were focused intently on his chest. They appeared unnaturally moist.

"Good night, then," he said.

She withdrew her hand and threw it up and around his neck, bending his cheek to hers in a grip like a vice. It lasted only a moment, this embrace charged with a current so electric it jolted him, and then she was gone.

29

A BRISK NORTH WIND was holding the temperature below zero despite the sunshine as the morning Greyhound, beeping its horn, pulled up in front of the Hub Cafe. Daniel Buckingham, Jr., proprietor of Buckingham Furniture, helped two old men up the steps and into adjoining seats, and then hurried indoors to join his fellow merchants gathered around the central table of the Hub for their ten o'clock coffee.

"The wife's uncles," he explained, filling his cup from the merchants' insulated pot, which the waitress had already filled three times. "They came on Friday, and I thought they'd never go home. The one is up all night going to the bathroom, and the other one coughs all day." Daniel Buckingham, Jr., a youngish man partial to plaid flannel shirts and string ties, was already developing the face of a heavy drinker, his nose pink and veined like a shrimp.

"Yeah, we had both my stepsons and their families," said Harrington, manager of the Orpheum Theatre. "Grandkids underfoot all the damn weekend." Harrington, though nearly sixty, was the newest of the Main Street merchants. He was also the most dapper-looking, turned out this morning in a copper-colored suit, a paisley tie, and a sky-blue shirt with a white collar.

Theodore Druppers, who'd spent New Year's in bed with the flu, raised his rheumy eyes to the door, coughed and said, "Well, look who's here. If it isn't the timber baron himself."

Carrying a brown paper sack and growling asthmatically, Sylvester Juba moved his great bulk between the little tables of the Hub and dragged a chair up to the merchants' table. They shifted sideways, making room. He lowered himself stiffly into the chair without removing his coat, groaning and wheezing

278

and dabbing at his runny nose with his dirty silk scarf. It wasn't often these days that the old lumberman joined them. Having lost interest, after retirement, in Staggerford's business climate, he'd lost interest as well in the merchants. He'd also lost, after three accidents, his driver's license, and was dependent upon his daughter for rides downtown.

"Hi, Syl," said Daniel Buckingham, Jr.

"Hello, Mr. Juba," said Harrington, who did not yet feel qualified to address the dour old man by his first name.

"Take a load off your feet, Syl," croaked the fleshy woman on Harrington's right. This was Marsha Skoog of Marsha's Ready-to-Wear, noted as the first woman to go into business for herself in this town, a business that had slowly grown through the sixties, thrived in the seventies, leveled off in the early eighties, and was now dying a fairly rapid death, a victim of new trends in catalogue shopping and new discount stores in Berrington. Marsha's voice had been brought very low by cigarettes and whiskey, and her dwindling trade seemed to be taking its toll on her figure and face. She'd always been rather heavy, but never so fat and frumpy as lately. She'd grown careless with her makeup and her merchandise. She wore clothes off the expensive rack in her store, and then tried to sell them with her face powder on the collars and wrinkles across the front.

"Hi, Mr. Juba," said Randy Meers respectfully. Randy, the junior half of Meers Realty, was the youngest person at the table. He was a handsome, blond, dark-eyed man in his late twenties. Before Buckingham's entrance, he'd been describing Las Vegas to the merchants of Main Street.

"Hi, Sylvester," said Carl Meers, Randy's father and partner in real estate. This beefy, self-important man with the intense black eyes of a hunting hare had a repertoire of nervous habits, such as rolling and unrolling his necktie, which he was doing now.

"How you been, Syl?" asked Grocer Druppers, clearing his raspy throat.

"Rotten," barked Sylvester with such vehemence that his jowls quivered. "The market's down."

"Don't worry about the market," pronounced Carl Meers. "The market always comes back."

"It damn well better," growled Sylvester, peering into his paper sack. "It was down all last week."

"It's always a little sluggish after Christmas," Daniel Buckingham assured him.

"I never pay any attention," said Harrington. "My money's in CDs."

"Me neither," said Druppers. "Municipal bonds are good enough for me."

"I lost my shirt in the market one time," croaked Marsha Skoog, smiling bitterly. "Never again."

"Coffee," called the senior Meers. "We need more coffee over here."

French Lopat, sitting at the counter, looked up from the Ann Landers column and saw that both waitresses were occupied, so he rose from his stool, picked the Silex coffeepot off its hot plate and carried it over to the merchants' table. Filling the insulated pot, he put a question to the more approachable Meers, Randy.

"You guys got any rentals?"

"Sure we got rentals, French," the handsome young man replied. "What do you need?"

"Just a room. Come spring, they're tearing down the Morgan."

Randy's father took over. "We don't rent rooms, French. We rent apartments, houses, condos, you name it, but we aren't into single rooms. Randy can show you a nice, small apartment on Fifth Street, partly furnished, three ten a month, heat and cable TV included."

"I can't afford three ten a month. I just need a room."

"Get the government to subsidize your rent," advised Carl Meers. "Get HUD approval, and it won't cost you any more than what you're paying at the Morgan."

"Naw," said French backing away, sorry he'd brought it up, chagrined to be the center of attention. "I just need a room."

"Listen, it's simple," insisted the overbearing Mr. Meers. "Just go to the HUD office in Berrington—it's in the courthouse—and apply for help with your rent. What are you paying at the Morgan?"

"Naw, that's okay."

"Tell me what you're paying at the Morgan, French. I'll bet you're paying way too much for that rathole."

"Hundred and twenty."

Mr. Meers laughed heartily. "For that flophouse? Really? Hundred and twenty? You've got to be kidding." He nudged his son with his elbow.

French returned to his stool and hunched his shoulders up around his ears, trying not to listen to the conversation he'd started.

"Did you hear that? Hundred and twenty for a room at the Morgan?"

"Highway robbery," said Marsha.

"Highway robbery?" exclaimed Druppers. "I'll tell you highway robbery. The wife and I paid a hundred and twenty a *night* last time we were in the Cities."

"It'll do a lot for downtown when the Morgan's out of there," said Harrington.

"Yeah, Christ, what an eyesore," Daniel Buckingham agreed.

"More parking," said Theodore Druppers.

"Yeah, blacktop, with yellow lines," piped Randy Meers.

"Who owns the Morgan?" asked Harrington, the newcomer.

"My wife," said the elder Meers, laughing uproariously. "That's what's so funny. She bought that dump on speculation five years ago, and the city's paying her a fortune for it."

Randy lowered his face to his coffee and steeled himself against what he feared was coming. Someone at the table was certain to make a cutting remark about his mother, whose shady transactions were legendary. Until recently she'd served on the city council, and the hotel transaction was doubtless one of her many insider deals.

"Shut up, everybody, and listen to this," said Sylvester, relieving Randy of his fears. Sylvester, who resented being ignored for more than a minute at a time, produced from his paper sack a small battery-powered cassette player with PROPERTY OF ST. ISIDORE's stenciled on its leather case. He shoved it to the center of the table, saying, "Who knows how to run this goddamn thing?"

The group stared silently at the machine for a moment, then

Randy punched the ON button. They heard a woman's metallic voice:

"She says you're a magpie."

There was a pause and everyone looked at Sylvester.

"That's Imogene Kite," he explained.

The voice continued, "That means you're a sucker for anything bright and shiny. I looked it up in a dictionary of slang."

Another female voice, this one fainter, asked, "Where did you get that list, Imogene?"

"That's Judy," said Sylvester over their voices. "Turn it up."

Randy increased the volume in time to hear Imogene say, very loud, "And Janet's husband, Randy Meers. She used the words 'lazy' and 'arrested development.' "

Randy Meers punched the OFF button and asked, "What's going on?" Bewilderment and injury were written on his face.

His father angrily echoed his words. "What's going on here, Sylvester?"

"Turn it on and listen," Sylvester ordered. "Imogene's talking to Judy. It's things Agatha McGee said."

Carl Meers restarted it.

Imogene's voice: "Randy Meers is not a case of arrested development, Judy. He's making tons of money."

Sister Judith's voice: "He's matured a lot. Janet has been really good for him."

Imogene: "And the sons of Theodore Druppers. Here's what she evidently said about the Druppers boys."

"Hey, Sylvester," said Theodore Druppers, over the sound of the tape, "where did you get this?"

"Shut up and listen," commanded Sylvester. "We're all on there."

Imogene: "She thinks the Druppers boys are dishonest."

Sister Judith: "Well, she should know. She had them in school."

Imogene: "For God's sake, Judy, don't you see what I'm saying? She's been trashing the whole town. She's been holding herself up as the model of virtue around here for most of the twentieth century, and all the while she's been running us into the ground. There's more. There's scads more. There's Myron Kleinschmidt, and Father Finn, and some people in the rest home. There's Daniel Buckingham, there's—"

"Hey, wait a minute," shouted Daniel Buckingham, flinging out his arm and punching the OFF button. "What the hell is this?"

"Am I on there?" asked Harrington with trepidation.

"Am I?" asked Marsha eagerly.

Sylvester's baggy face assumed its look of superiority, the corners of his mouth clamping sourly down, his eyelids hanging at half-mast. Half his mission was already accomplished— arousing their curiosity. The other half—arousing their resentment—was soon to follow. He felt it already emanating from Buckingham on his right, whose finger remained on the OFF button. Buckingham was known for his short fuse, and Sylvester was growing excited, anticipating a citywide backlash against Agatha McGee. A ruined soul, she'd called him. Controlled by demons. Well, to hell with Agatha McGee. He'd fix her wagon.

"Where did you get this?" demanded Buckingham. "What's she talking about? Why is it on tape? What the hell's going on?"

Marsha asked, "How does Imogene know what Agatha says about everybody? They're not exactly friends, you know."

"She could be learning it through Lillian," Theodore Druppers speculated sadly. He was profoundly disturbed to know that Agatha distrusted his sons. Did she know something he didn't? His son Lloyd was in Florida, married to Marsha's daughter and making what Theodore thought was an honest living cleaning swimming pools. Gerald was in Atlanta working for Delta.

"It's all written down," Sylvester explained. "Agatha wrote it all down."

"And showed it to Imogene?" Marsha sounded skeptical.

"I couldn't be on there," said Harrington fretfully. "She doesn't know me from Adam."

"It's all explained on there how Imogene happened to read it," said Sylvester. "Just listen."

But Buckingham, emitting seething sounds from between his tightly clenched teeth, was removing the tape from the player.

"Leave it be!" demanded Sylvester.

"I'm making a copy for myself." Buckingham rose from his

chair. "I'll bring it back in a minute—I want a copy to take home to the wife."

"Make a couple," said the elder Meers. "If my boy's on that tape, he ought to have a copy of his own." He turned to his son and said crossly, "Play it for Janet, Randy. She's always been so high on Miss McGee."

Randy sat with his chin in both hands, the picture of discouragement.

"Play it for your own wife," Sylvester told Carl Meers. "She's on there with the rest of us."

"Make one for me, too," said Marsha. "Am I on there, Sylvester?"

"I don't think you're on there."

"Make me one anyway," she called happily. "It's quite a tape."

French, who'd been eavesdropping, watched Buckingham stride out the door and angle across the street to his furniture store, a section of which was devoted to electronics for the home, dual-well tape decks included. Imogene's voice on the tape had called up no particular longings in French's heart, nor any regrets. Her imperious tone, on the contrary, confirmed his belief that he'd been wise to back off. And as for the Agatha bashing, well, that just proved how vicious she could be. A complete bitch was what Grover called her.

"You know, she can be pretty hard on people," he heard Druppers say in a somber, resigned tone.

"She can be damn wicked," said Carl Meers with heat. "Wicked and mean."

"A scary woman," Harrington agreed. "Though I know her only to say hello to on the street."

"She's never liked me," whined Randy.

"Oh, you men, don't be such babies," scoffed Marsha. "Agatha's harmless and you know it."

Agatha? French was shocked. He'd thought they were talking about Imogene. Agatha wicked? He pictured himself saving Agatha's reputation by rushing across the street and snatching the tape from Daniel Buckingham before it was copied. He'd take it to the public library and listen to it on the library's player, with earphones, to see if he himself was mentioned. He wouldn't mind if he was. He'd prefer Agatha's criticism to her constant doting solicitude. Why didn't she baby someone else for a change? Say Randy Meers. Randy sounded like he needed it.

Sylvester Juba said, "She's been ruling the roost around here long enough. It's time somebody took her down a peg or two."

"She's always got her nose in our business," said Randy. "Janet tells her everything."

"Where does a woman like that get her authority?" asked Harrington. "I mean, teaching third grade? Come on."

"Sixth grade," Marsha corrected him.

"Her father was a prince of a fellow," declared Sylvester dramatically. "And so was her mother."

"You can get plenty fed up with a dame like that," said Carl Meers, rolling and unrolling his tie. "A little of that pushy stuff goes a long way."

"You can, that's true," said Theodore Druppers in a tone of wonder, as though he'd been fed up for a long time without realizing it. "You can get mighty tired of standing at attention whenever she comes in your store."

"Did you know she came out against Randy marrying Janet?" asked the elder Meers. "You know what Janet comes from—trash—and Miss McGee thought Randy wasn't good enough for her."

"She's been pretty outspoken, I understand, against the movies we show," said Harrington rather timidly.

"She never liked me, even as a sixth-grader," claimed Randy.

"Let's face it, she's had her day," Sylvester put in, calling to mind the words on the tape concerning himself and feeling refreshed by the waves of resentment washing back and forth across the table. All weekend he'd been in a boozy funk, loathing himself and feeling helpless, but listening to Carl Meers and Theodore Druppers dare to speak out against the old dame, and counting on the volatile Daniel Buckingham to spread the word, he foresaw her downfall and felt supremely powerful and satisfied.

"You know what a woman like that needs," said Carl Meers suggestively.

Marsha laughed. "She needed that years ago. It's too late now."

"She needs to be brought down a few pegs," Sylvester reiterated.

Presently, Daniel Buckingham returned, handed the original tape to Sylvester and dropped two others onto the table. "Fight over them," he said as he left again. Marsha snatched up one of them, promising to pass it on to Carl Meers when she was finished, and Druppers took the other. Harrington said he didn't need one.

French, turning on his stool, watched the group rise to their feet, zip and button their coats, and file out the door, Sylvester Juba asking Carl Meers for a ride home. He imagined once again how he might have preserved the purity of Miss McGee's name by snatching the master tape away from Daniel Buckingham, Jr. It made him sick to think of it copied and spreading through town, irretrievable as gossip.

30

T HEY SPENT THE DAY in transit, Agatha and her two clergymen descending by taxi to a main-traveled road five miles below the hotel, where they boarded a crowded coach. Through a grimy window, Agatha kept Assisi in view as long as she could, watching the town grow smaller as the bus moved westward across the valley, watching it lose its sunny luster as an indigo rain cloud crept down the mountain behind it and cast a shroud of mist over its domes and towers. Finally, with Assisi nothing more than a scattering of small wet stones in the distance, she resettled herself in her seat and murmured to James that no other place in the world had ever seemed to her so otherworldly. James was asleep.

He slept all the way to the Autostrada del Sol, where they descended from one coach and boarded another—this one silver and burgundy and containing the Minnesota tour group. They were greeted with effusive high spirits and were given a loud and chaotic description—by everyone and all at once—of everything they had missed in Florence and Pisa. Baptistries and *duomos*. Statues and bridges. Outdoor markets and indoor tombs. Meals and paintings and walks beside the River Arno.

It appeared to Agatha that everyone had been bitten by the shopping bug. Lillian showed her a lovely blue scarf she'd bought for Imogene and a skein of purple yarn for Father Finn's next sweater. Darrin had five new tapes for his pocket cassette player. Agatha had to avert her eyes from the sweatshirt Trish was wearing, on the front of which was stenciled the genitalia of Michelangelo's David. John Schrupp and Stuart Campbell wore matching blue berets. The professor, Agatha saw with satisfaction, had availed himself of a Florentine barber, his hair short and clean, his mustache trimmed.

This smooth-riding bus, floating south between fields and rivers and misty hills, soon lulled Agatha to sleep, as it did a number of students who'd been out past midnight. James, now rested and alert, watched Father Finn, across the aisle, open his breviary and begin to read. Beside Father Finn sat Lillian, knitting. James saw, in the seat ahead, Lisa Berglund writing in her notebook. He heard Trish in the seat behind him ask a question.

"Should we go see the Pope tomorrow, Darrin?"

"What for?"

"The old folks are going. Dr. Finn says his brother can get us tickets if we want to go along."

"Who'd want to?"

"I don't know—I thought it might be cool. I guess he wears this neat white outfit."

"I seen enough Popes."

"You have not, you haven't seen any."

"I seen their statues."

"I guess this one talks ten languages."

"You mean he's alive?"

"Of course he's alive—what did you think?"

"I thought you couldn't be a Pope until you were dead and a miracle happened."

"That's a saint, you dumb shit. Come on, Darrin, go with me. He'll bless us."

Was there a teenager anywhere in Ireland, James wondered, who didn't know the difference between Popes and saints? How foreign America must be. How pagan. How mysterious.

Darkness, together with a fine, slanting mist, was falling on Rome as their coach let them off in front of the Hotel Bellarmino. Agatha accompanied James down the street and waved good night to the crowded city bus that carried him off to his lodging at Sant' Anselmo; then she turned and walked pensively back to the hotel, carefully picking her way among puddles. Tomorrow, their final day together, they would meet at the Vatican.

Shaking out and furling Lillian's umbrella, she went directly into the lounge, where three of her writing students awaited her, needing, they claimed, a last-minute session of editorial advice.

But more pressing than that, as it turned out, they needed to know about James. Where was he staying in Rome? asked Lisa. Where was his home and how long had she known him? asked Betty Lou. How had they first met, asked Paula the pixy, and wasn't it sort of boring talking to a priest all day?

Agatha, reluctant to let James slip from her mind, responded to their inquiries with seriousness and at some length. Gone, for the moment, were her inhibitions and habits of secrecy. She told of their discovering one another on the "Letters" page of *The Fortress*, an international Catholic newspaper, both of them having written in to express their objection to liturgical reform, and their correspondence had grown out of that. Yes, she had been to Ireland to see him. She described Ballybegs in some detail, as though she had spent more time there than she actually had, as though her one and only view of it had not been colored by shock and grief.

Before she quite knew it, she was instructing them in the fractured nature of life in Ulster, illustrating it with the story of Con Stitch. And then, her voice ringing with pride, she told of James's plan to devote his retirement to a kind of one-man peace movement, which struck the young women as wonderfully idealistic and probably hopeless. "What can one person do against the IRA?" asked Lisa. "Against all that dark history?" added the precocious Betty Lou.

"Oh my," replied Agatha, her hand pressed to her heart as though wounded, "one can't quit working to better the world just because the world is old and set in its ways. The enormity of a job is no reason not to *do* the job. James will start by winning hearts for peace, one by one, and then, from that, he hopes a grass-roots movement will spring up, and ever so slowly violence will be choked out." She realized, speaking for James in this vein, that she was speaking *like* James as well, the tone of her voice taking on his curious mixture of softness and firmness, her pauses his pauses, her words his words. His cause was her cause now.

This lesson in political science was brought to a conclusion by Trish and Darrin, who wandered into the lounge and sank sprawling into low, soft chairs. "What you guys doing?" asked Trish.

Lisa said, "We're working on our papers."

"When do we eat?" asked Darrin.

Agatha replied, "I believe we're on our own for dinner tonight."

"What's your paper on?" Trish asked Lisa.

"Scientific measuring devices."

"Interesting," said Trish, without interest.

"Mine's on male-dominated systems," said Paula.

Trish yawned.

"What are you guys doing tomorrow?" asked Darrin.

"We're going shopping," said Paula, speaking for herself and Betty Lou.

"I'm going to the Vatican Museums," said Lisa.

Trish said, "We might be going to the Vatican, too. Right, Darrin?"

"Yeah, we might go scope out the Pope."

31

"*THERE, I SEE HIM* coming," said Father Finn, who had secured tickets to the audience hall for himself and Lillian and six of the students. He'd been standing for several minutes with Agatha at the base of the obelisk, waiting to make sure James turned up.

"Where?" asked Agatha, shading her eyes.

Her pastor pointed across the piazza to James emerging into the sunshine from the shadows of the colonnade. He was accompanied by a young man in a monk's habit.

"Go ahead," said Agatha, sensing that her pastor was eager to find good seats in the audience hall. "Your group is waiting for you."

"Where *is* my group?" He turned in a circle, scanning the piazza and the throngs of people streaming across it. "Where did they drift off to?"

"There." Agatha indicated the cluster of Minnesotans gazing at the crèche.

He called to them. Lillian and the six young people, dull-eyed and stooped by fatigue, broke away from the cluster and followed him like sheep toward the audience hall. Well, it's no wonder they look beaten down, thought Agatha, who was feeling rather dull herself this morning. Isn't this Day Nine, and aren't we all overloaded with foreign impressions? Aren't we all tired of trying to understand foreign words, tired of sleeping in foreign beds? Anything less than the Pope and I would not be throwing myself into these droves of people this morning.

James, however, appeared refreshed, energetic. "Agatha, I want you to meet my guardian angel, Brother Denis Worthy."

Agatha offered her hand. "James has told me all you've done for him."

"Shown him which bus to board—that's about the extent of my help." The young man smiled with his whole face. There was gentle good humor in his dark, glinting eyes. "So you're the miracle worker."

Agatha shot James a quizzical look.

"Denis was remarking on the bus how my strength has come back in these last few days. Miraculous, he called it. I told him it was the company I'd been keeping."

Agatha waved her hand in a dismissive gesture. "Blarney's not my favorite form of speech."

"It's the truth," said Denis. "He was a shocking sight at the airport last week. I had to lift the poor man into a taxi."

Agatha, uncomfortable with sustained praise, changed the subject. "Will you come with us to see the Holy Father?"

"Thank you, I'm up to my neck in research, so it's off to the library with me."

"He's taking his master's in liturgy," James explained.

"Oh, how impressive," said Agatha, who, because she didn't have one, harbored an inordinate respect for advanced degrees. "What are you researching?"

The young man drew himself up straight and threw out his chest in mock arrogance. "You're looking at one of the world's foremost authorities on Armenian funeral rites of the third century, A.D."

"I suppose there's a good reason to know things like that."

He laughed. "If you discover the reason, Miss McGee, I hope you'll tell me what it is." He turned to his mentor. "Will we meet here at one, then, Father?"

One? Agatha was given to understand that the audience might not end before twelve or twelve-thirty. One o'clock would give them scarcely time to say farewell.

"Right you are, Dinny, one will be grand." He turned to Agatha. "The abbot primate has asked me to speak to the monks before I go home, and this afternoon is the only time we can all get together." He saw her expression change, saw the disappointment in her eyes. "They've been grand to me at Sant' Anselmo, Agatha. It's the least I can do in return."

"He's promised to give us his views on the Ulster question," said Denis.

"A chance to try out my talk on a captive audience, you see."

She felt tears pressing behind her eyes. Losing half a day with James felt like losing years off her life. The emotion was much like the betrayal she'd felt that Sunday morning in Ballybegs. A steely look came into her eyes, a steely tone into her voice: "I wish I could attend."

At this, Denis Worthy looked at her with a little grimace of regret. She knew the expression well, had seen it often enough over the years on the faces of nuns and priests, and had always been slightly offended by it. Off limits to the opposite sex, the expression said. That much of it she could understand. Mother Church, in what Agatha assumed was her wisdom, believed strongly in the segregation of genders. Indeed, she could remember the days when boys and girls were seated in opposite halves of classrooms, in separate pews at worship. No, it wasn't the segregation she resented, it was simply the facial expression, for mixed with the regret was usually a trace of smugness. And wasn't this true now, of Brother Denis? Didn't she sense in him the pride that comes with exclusiveness? She didn't have time to determine this for certain, because his expression shifted quickly to a farewell mode.

"Good-bye, Miss McGee, and thank you a thousand times for helping my man here back to health."

"Don't be excessive," she warned. "Your man simply needed a change of scene."

"No, I'm not being excessive. Another week in your company and he'd be running footraces." He gave her fingers a fond little squeeze. "Will you come and see us in Ireland?"

Immediately James answered for her. "Of course she will."

Agatha and James found their way to the audience hall, and by dint of his Roman collar they were allowed to enter without being frisked. (Or was it, Agatha wondered, by dint of her own appearance of abject weariness, the authentic touristy look no assassin would ever wear?) The hall, designed like a sports arena with a tilted floor and a deep stage, was filling fast, and James hurried her along, passing up seats Agatha would have chosen near the front, and finding, about halfway back, two seats near the center aisle.

They were early. They sat listening to a jazzy brass band playing show tunes. "Hernando's Hideaway" rose above the din of four thousand people in heightened conversation. Agatha was astonished. She'd expected silence, or the solemn tones of an organ. At the center of the stage stood a white thronelike chair, and serving as a backdrop to this chair was a mammoth sculpture Agatha thought remarkable for its ugliness—a human figure appeared to be struggling to rise out of a tangle of caramel-colored seaweed. Moving busily about the stage were cardinals in capes and skullcaps, lesser clergy in black soutanes, and bodyguards in business suits.

Halfway through "Lullaby of Broadway" the band stopped playing and an expectant hush fell over the crowd. Then John Paul II stepped onto the stage, setting off cheers and shouts and the flash of a thousand flashbulbs. He had an athlete's stocky build, an athlete's way of rolling his broad shoulders as he walked to his throne, where he stood acknowledging the thunderous ovation by extending his arms to the audience. He made beckoning motions with his hands, as if to say, I take you into my heart.

Agatha was thrilled. She had not expected to be so profoundly moved by the sight of this Polish prelate, playwright, and downhill skier who was serving as the present-day link in the line extending back to Peter, and ahead, no doubt, to the end of the world. The cheering increased, setting up a ringing in Agatha's ears and releasing a tear of joy that she quickly wiped away.

James bent to her ear. "A vigorous-looking man, wouldn't you say?"

She nodded, agreeing.

"Well-recovered from his gunshot wound."

She shuddered at the memory. Three years ago? Four? If not even the Pope was safe from assassins in his front yard, what made James think he himself could travel unscathed through Ulster?

The Pope sat. The crowd went suddenly silent, and sat as well. The Pope was handed a sheaf of papers, from which he delivered his weekly homily in Italian. Then he repeated it in French, German, English (it was a fairly predictable treatise on the sacredness of marriage), Spanish, and Polish.

This was followed, to Agatha's surprise, by a kind of one-ring circus. Out from the wings came a series of performers—clowns, acrobats, unicyclists, vocalists, and two men in a loose-fitting horse outfit who galloped and cavorted around the stage and made the Pope laugh. Each performance was directed not at the audience but at the man on the throne, the reigning monarch. He must have been nearly deafened, Agatha thought, by the trumpeter who played a screeching rendition of "O Mein Papa" very close to his ear.

Next, a long and tedious time was devoted to various cardinals and bishops stepping up to the microphone and acknowledging delegations of visitors from their home countries. Cries and shouts arose from each delegation in turn, while the vast sea of unacknowledged visitors grew glassy-eyed. Even the Pope looked a bit bored.

When this was done, the Holy Father made short work of blessing everyone, together with their rosaries, medals, and other sacramentals. Then, at last, he rose to his feet, gathered his plainclothesmen around him, and started down the central aisle to greet his pilgrims. There was a sudden swarming, crushing movement toward the waist-high barricades, everyone straining to touch his hand, his finger, his sleeve. Several large Americans, advancing on Agatha's left and jabbering in an accent she associated with cowboys and Lady Bird Johnson, spun her around and shouldered her out of position.

James, seeing that she had been forced back, gave up his place at the barricade and joined her. He helped her to stand on a chair, then climbed up and stood on the chair beside it. Linking arms for balance, they watched the Pope advance through the parted sea of bobbing heads, moving slowly, taking the hands thrust at him and clasping them, patting them. Here and there, coming upon an elderly man or woman, he took the aged face in both his hands and caressed it.

Witnessing this high-powered current of love moving back and forth between the Pope and his admirers, Agatha felt herself succumb to it, felt the primordial tingling in her spine that signaled deep emotion, felt that if it had been her face this vicar of Jesus held in his hands, she would never again be quite the same woman. If only he would lay those hands on her cheeks—those hands consecrated (through two-hundred-odd intermediaries) by the Apostles to offer the Sacrament of peace—she would then carry home with her the peace that passes understanding. Dear Lord, she said aloud, her words lost in the tumult, if not a touch of his hand, grant me at least a glance of his eye.

Then an amazing thing happened. The Pope, drawing abreast of them, stopped, lifted his eyes and gazed directly at James for a full five seconds. He then lifted his right hand and beckoned to him. James's response was a shy and respectful bow of his head, which appeared to cause impatience in the Pope, for he frowned and beckoned more vigorously. James turned to Agatha with an incredulous, uncertain look.

"Go," she told him.

James lowered himself carefully to the floor, and the crowd made room for him at the barrier. John Paul stepped forward, took James's face in his hands, turned it to the left and spoke briefly into his ear. Then he bent forward and touched his forehead to James's forehead, his hands still cupping James's face like a precious vessel. Then he moved on.

James, turning away, looked disoriented. Agatha got down from her chair and guided James away from the jostling and clamoring, guided him as far as the exit door, where a Swiss guard stood aside to let them pass into the hallway, at the end of which a pair of policemen parted to allow them outside. They walked, unspeaking, back to the piazza, which was unpopulated now, birds outnumbering the people, flocks of gray and white pigeons moving in slow circles over the sun-warmed stones and exchanging utterances made up of long vowels. "Due to doom" the birds seemed to be saying.

Steering James toward the steps of the basilica, away from the obelisk, where Lillian and the others might expect to find them, she asked, "What did he say to you?"

He looked at her uncertainly, a little dazed. "It was the strangest thing. How could the man possibly know about my mission?"

"He spoke of your mission? Ulster?"

"He said, 'Your mission . . .' " James stopped walking and closed his eyes. "Now just a minute, Agatha, I want to get this right."

She waited expectantly.

"He said, 'Your mission is sacred. You will never outlive it. Do not forget you have God's grace on your side.' "

She repeated the message silently to herself, committing it to memory.

"Well?" he said, studying her face intently, as though waiting for her to pass judgment.

She wanted to believe that by some miracle the Pope saw into James's heart, but she couldn't overlook the logical explanation. "He might simply have meant you're a priest forever, James. Priests never outlive their priesthood."

"Yes, that may be it." James looked down at a white pigeon which had walked stumpily over to him and stood now, unmoving, beside his right foot. "But why of the hundred or two hundred priests in that room was I the one he said it to? Did you see the look he gave me, Agatha?"

"I did."

"And didn't the sight of me seem to stop the man in his tracks?"

"It's true, he seemed suddenly struck by something."

"He told me, 'Do not forget you have God's grace on your side.' How does he know what side I'm on? Or even that I'm *taking* a side? Most clergymen my age are long past taking sides. I tell you, he saw into me, Agatha. He saw straight into my soul."

Agatha, squinting up at his face, pondered the evidence, and once she did this, once she seriously considered the possibility of something mystical or extrasensory having taken place, she became convinced of it. Yes, the Pope had seen into the soul of the man she loved. The Pope had commissioned— consecrated—his mission of peace.

"We've just witnessed a miracle."

"So we have." He lifted his hand to his brow. "I'm a little dazed by it."

They fell silent, looking nearly, but not precisely, into one another's eyes. The white pigeon at James's feet cleared its throat and cooed.

Then: "Good-bye, dear James. I'll be praying for you."

This appeared to jolt him. It was a moment before he spoke. "Ah, I see. It's time for farewells."

"You will let me know what arrangements you make in Rochester."

"I will."

"We'll want to know when to expect you in Staggerford."

"We?"

"Father Finn and I. He'll have to reserve the rectory guest quarters."

"How long shall I plan to be in Staggerford, Agatha? Will four days be too many?"

"Four days—out of a lifetime?" She laughed, concealing her sadness.

Again they fell silent. On other days it had been James who initiated their heartfelt conversations, but now he was oddly reticent. He shifted his weight from one foot to the other. So did the pigeon.

"Yoo-hoo, Agatha!" cried Lillian, crossing the piazza, braying in all directions. Her two friends from Valparaiso having flown home, she was dependent upon Agatha once again. "Yoo-hoo, yoo-hoo."

"James, I wonder," Agatha said tentatively.

"Yes?"

"The Holy Father held your face in his hands." She demonstrated, cupping air.

"He did that, yes."

"I wonder—it's silly—if you would—" She broke off.

"Yes?" he inquired. "If I would what?"

"This." She took hold of his hands. She gazed at the knuckles, the nails. She turned them over and studied the lines of the palms. Then, closing her eyes, she pressed them against her cheeks.

"Agatha," sighed James, his voice breaking.

PART 3

32

O*N THE MORNING OF* her first day home,
Agatha was neither surprised nor dismayed to discover the extensive use Frederick Lopat had made of her house. Her
kitchen cupboards were disorganized, her pantry stock depleted. The flattened pillows on the couch, together with the
popcorn between the cushions, indicated the hours he'd spent
lying there watching TV. Upstairs in his old room, finding the
sheets wrinkled and the bed carelessly made, she understood
what an irresistible temptation it must have been to leave the
Morgan and sleep in comfort for a few nights.

Maybe enough time had passed since his departure so that
he was ready to move back to her house. Maybe he'd outlived
the impulse that had abruptly caused him to leave. She hoped
so. Changing the sheets on his bed, she recalled what a comforting, affable presence he'd been as a lodger—not the intellectual companion Miles Pruitt had been, but fully as dear to
her as Miles. He was easier to please than Miles, and handier
at yard work and fixing things.

Returning home from the cramped quarters of the Hotel
Bellarmino, and haunted by the homeless men and women
she'd seen on the streets of Rome (there were many others besides the Trevi Fountain derelict), Agatha thought it sinfully
selfish of an old lady to be living alone in this spacious, four-bedroom house. Moreover, it was bad for her mental health.
Getting out of Father Finn's car last night and unlocking this
empty ark, she realized how completely James O'Hannon and
the tour group had lifted her out of solitary self-involvement,
and how directly her depression had been related to her six
months of living like a recluse.

Yes, I need to be a landlady again, she told herself as she

applied spot remover to the food stains on the dining room carpet. Dear Lord, help me bring Frederick back to this house of too many echoes.

On her second day home she discovered that her privacy had been violated. Emptying the side pockets of her suitcase and stashing her Italian maps and pamphlets and extra postcards into various parts of her desk, she opened the bottom right-hand drawer and was startled to see a padded manila envelope. She lifted it out and saw that it was a book mailer from a publisher she'd never heard of, addressed to Imogene Kite at the State Department of Education. She opened the flap and saw what it contained.

She sat there in shock, trying to imagine what had transpired in her absence. She guessed immediately that Frederick had let Imogene in and she'd burrowed like a ferret. Imogene was capable of reading other people's mail, she was that unscrupulous. She'd taken the letters home and then, returning them, had failed to conceal the theft—or disdained to conceal it, she was that brazen. Really, the only surprising thing was that French had let her in in the first place.

Minutes passed, her eyes resting on the snowy yard outside her sun room window, her mind going back over the many tender sentiments of friendship James had expressed in these letters, and which—dear Lord!— Imogene was now aware of. To say nothing of the many Staggerfordians named on these pages and discussed—in less than flattering terms. Imogene would have read every page in the worst possible light, attributing to her the worst possible motives. How could anyone as obtuse as Imogene understand that her correspondence with James had been her much-needed release from the strict propriety of small-town living? How could Imogene possibly know that by discussing people with James in sharply candid and fault-finding language, she had actually become more tolerant of them and—a paradox—had come to like them better? She recalled the first time she wrote to James about her impatience with Lillian, and how her feeling for Lillian immediately grew deeper after that, grew into something kinder than tolerance, something as complex as love. Surely it would take a person with more sensitivity than Imogene to understand this paradox.

She sat staring out at the snow for several minutes while her shock gradually diminished and was replaced by fury. She decided she'd better tell Lillian. Pulling on her coat, she stalked through the kitchen and was letting herself out the back porch before realizing that it would be useless to involve Lillian in this scandal. What could poor Lillian do, except make excuses for her villainous daughter? She returned to the kitchen, threw off her coat, and phoned the Morgan Hotel.

Grover put French on the line.

"Hi, Miss McGee. How was the trip?"

"Educational. Now, Frederick, I don't mind that you slept here, and I don't mind that you ate the last of my sauerkraut and seven or eight cans of soup and drank nearly all of my chokecherry wine. The food stains on the carpet I was able to get out with K2R, and the plants look healthy and thank you for bringing in my mail and keeping the walks clear."

At this point she paused.

"Frederick, why are my personal letters in an envelope with Imogene Kite's name on it?"

"You mean that tan envelope?"

"This book mailer from New York."

"Well, that's what she gave me. She came to the hotel the other night and gave me that package and told me where to put it. Bottom drawer on the right, she said."

Two or three quick breaths on the line. Then her voice, in a higher register. "It's a package of my *letters*, Frederick. My most personal *letters*."

"I wondered what was in there."

"You didn't know?"

"Nope," he replied. "She just said put it in the bottom drawer, facedown."

A short pause. Her voice returned to its normal pitch. "Now tell me, Frederick, honestly, how did she get her hands on my letters?"

"I don't know. I never saw her take them."

"But she was in my house. You had to know that."

"Well, see . . . she cooked me a steak."

"Here in my house!"

"Yup, she came to the door and asked did I mind if she came in and cooked me a steak."

"Why?"

"Why? I guess she was lonesome or something. You know, her mother gone and everything."

"She could have cooked it in her own house."

"Yup, that's true."

Silence on the line. Leaning on the registration desk with his eyes closed and his forehead cupped in his hand, French braced himself for what had to be next. The plate.

But the plate wasn't next. "Frederick, you probably know this, but I'll tell you anyway. Imogene Kite did not come over here just to cook you a steak."

Wow! How did Agatha know? The sheets, he supposed. Ashamed, he almost hung up.

"She came over here to snoop, Frederick. Imogene Kite has the instincts of a ferret."

"Yup, yup," he was quick to agree.

"I'm going to call her in St. Paul right now."

"I would." He sensed that she hadn't found the plate, that this would be as far as she'd push him. Experience had taught him that right in here somewhere she'd shift to her patronizing tone.

He was right. "Now I can see how a man in your position could be taken in by the wiles of an unscrupulous woman, Frederick, and the Lord knows a steak must have sounded very appetizing . . ."

As she went on in this vein, he tried not to listen, tried to remain the man he was and not revert to the sixth grader he'd been, tried not to fit himself into the third desk in the first row by the windows, tried not to see the neglected spaces staring up at him from his toothbrushing chart. But in spite of himself he lifted his elbows off the registration desk and straightened up, half expecting her to comment on his poor posture.

". . . but letting Imogene into my house was a lapse of your good judgment, you have to understand that, and you have to promise that when I next put you in charge of my house, you'll not let anyone in but yourself."

Not *if*, he observed, but *when*.

"Is that clear, Frederick?"

"Yup, it's clear, Miss McGee."

A pause. Two or three of her quick, nervous breaths again. The plate after all?

"Frederick, would you consider giving up that posing you do in the summertime?"

"Posing? You mean being an Indian? Naw, it's a job."

"You see, when the Morgan is razed next summer and you need a place to live, I was thinking you might wish to have your old room back. Is that possible?"

No, he didn't think so, not anymore. He was too firmly set in the ways of indigence and indolence and independence. He could never go back to being alert every minute to this strict old woman's wishes. He said, evasively, "I'd have to think about it."

"But I couldn't have you living here in that awful Indian getup and those dirty old feathers."

His Ojibway outfit was kept at the tourist center, where he changed his clothes every day, but he didn't tell her that. He repeated that he'd think about it.

His reluctance hurt her, but she didn't press him. "Come over early next week, Frederick. We'll clean the basement, and I've got a frayed extension cord I want you to look at."

"How's Monday?"

"Monday's ideal. I'll expect you early, around eight."

"Not eight, Miss McGee. I'm never up by eight."

"Well, you should be. You should practice healthy habits."

"I'll try to get there around nine."

"All right, no later. We have a lot to do."

Agatha replaced the receiver and let a few minutes pass before making her next call. Talking to French had partially dissipated her outrage, and she had to build it up again. Finally, with her anger fanned to a flame, she picked up the receiver and called information in St. Paul.

Imogene, who devoted a part of every Saturday to improving her mind, was reading up on Irish history when the phone rang. From the letters of James O'Hannon, filled as they were with words such as Free-Staters, Black and Tans, and the Royal Ulster Constabulary, she'd made a list of terms and historical figures for research, and it was Patrick Sarsfield's heroic defense of Limerick in 1690 that Agatha interrupted this morning with the words, "God help you, Imogene, you've done a very great wrong."

Nearly as astounding as the message was the fact that it came from Agatha McGee, who had never before phoned her in St. Paul.

"You came into my house and read my personal letters."

"What are you talking about?" she shot back. "I did no such thing."

"Don't compound your iniquity by lying, Imogene. I am holding in my hand a parcel-post envelope addressed to you at the Department of Education. How did my letters get inside this envelope if you didn't put them there?"

Imogene feigned the sound of a yawn. "I have no idea what you're talking about, Agatha."

"You were in my house. I've just been talking to Frederick Lopat."

"Oh, him." Imogene produced a frivolous little laugh. "He was in your house day and night."

"And you came over for dinner, he tells me."

"I did. He asked me over, and I had that envelope with me because it contained a book I thought he should read on post-trauma stress. It's what he's got, you know, from Vietnam. I've always been concerned about French, ever since the days when we used to date. Do you remember that, Agatha? French and I were an item one time?"

"Are you saying Frederick put my letters in this envelope? Be careful whom you accuse of your sins."

"I'm only saying I left the envelope with him, with a book in it. I really don't know why your letters should be in it. I suppose he was bringing in your mail and thought that would be a good way to keep it all together." Imogene impressed herself with her quickness of mind and her steady, assured tone. The old biddy was no match for her.

"This is not current mail I'm talking about, Imogene. These are letters from years ago, which were taken out of my desk."

"Well, whatever they are, it had to be French, because he had the envelope and he had the run of your house. Unless, of course, there were others he let in. I think you just better talk to him again."

The peremptory tone of this last statement caused Agatha to

boil over. "From the time you were seven years old, Imogene, I wondered how two people as honest and well-intentioned as Lyle and Lillian Kite could have produced an offspring like you."

This was an insult so outrageous that Imogene chose not to hear it. "Poor French," she said. "He lacks discretion."

"Remember the time in Sister Roberta's room, you took her stack of report cards off her desk and read every one of them before she discovered they were missing? Remember that, Imogene? You were in the fourth grade, and you had the instincts of a ferret even then. Sneaky and dishonest, you sat there looking Sister Roberta in the eye and said you had no idea how the report cards got into your lap."

"I asked him to see a doctor about his problems. I think you should urge him to do the same. He can be helped, but for some reason he doesn't want to be."

"Sister Roberta actually defended you, remember? She said you were experimenting with morality and you'd grow ethically stronger for making mistakes like that. I held my tongue. I didn't want to prejudice the faculty against you, but I saw in the girl you were, the woman you've become, Imogene. Sister Roberta was always too soft on her students. That's why she left the convent and went into interior design."

"What he needs is counseling, and of course there's nobody in Staggerford to counsel him. He'll have to take the bus to Berrington or Rookery."

"You stole those report cards about the time *The Bad Seed* came out, remember, Imogene? I went to *The Bad Seed* and sat there thinking of you."

"Berrington and Rookery both have mental health clinics."

"Overweening ambition, that's what Sister Mary Sebastian called your trouble in grade five, Imogene, and I had to agree. It was apparent by grade five that you couldn't stand anyone outscoring you on tests, and that's when you started copying and cheating. You never got away with it in my room, as far as I know, but in grades five and seven and eight you were a holy terror when it came to copying and cheating."

"I guess we'll have to continue this some other time, Agatha. I'm pretty busy today."

"And now, having read seventy or eighty of my letters, what are you going to do with all that information?"

"I did *not* read your letters."

"That's what I've often wondered about you, Imogene—what you do with all the information you have no business knowing."

"Listen, I have to run, Agatha. I hope you get this all straightened out. I think French is going through some difficult times right now, but there's help out there, if he'll ask for it. Good-bye, Agatha, I did *not* read your letters."

They hung up simultaneously.

On her third day home, Sunday, Agatha dined after Mass with Father Finn. Dinner was beef stew from the rectory freezer, and the topic of conversation was James O'Hannon's visit in March. He would occupy the large room behind the kitchen, which had been originally designed for a woman in the days of live-in housekeepers, a space Father Finn now used for storage. Addie Phelps, a talented cook who made house calls—she'd concocted and frozen today's stew—would be brought in to prepare breakfasts and whatever other meals would not be taken at Agatha's house. The solemnity of Holy Week precluded parties or receptions for their Irish visitor, but on Easter Sunday, Agatha would be having friends in to dinner, and she made sure Father Finn wrote this in his appointment book. Then they took up the matter of James's transportation.

"If he's flying out of Rookery after Easter, I can deliver him to his plane," said Father Finn, "but I can't get away during Holy Week to pick him up."

"And I don't trust my Plymouth to go that far. Are you sure you can't go? It may be as early as Wednesday."

"I won't have a free minute during all of Holy Week." This wasn't precisely true, Wednesday being the midweek breather in the annual marathon of confessions and liturgy, but he wanted no share of James and Agatha's first day together. He'd observed in Assisi that they loved one another, though he wasn't sure that Agatha knew it. Was she aware of the powerful effect James had on her, how much of her old self James had helped her find in Italy? The color was back in her face, energy back in her voice.

"Maybe I'll ask Janet to drive. Let me think about it. This is all predicated on James's condition, you understand. I mean, who knows what March will bring? He could be too ill to travel. He could be detained in Rochester." Separated from James, she'd lost her certainty about his recovery. She woke each morning, went to bed each night, praying for his good health.

"Yes, but we have to plan as though for the best." This priestly platitude dropped involuntarily from his lips—the habit of a lifetime.

"That's so true," said Agatha.

Encouraged, he expanded on it. "And be ready for the worst."

"Precisely." She liked this in a priest, this readiness to sum up her pronouncements—though it wasn't what she expected from James, for some reason. James wasn't quite the broken record this man was. James had more spine.

After dessert—molded Jell-O containing pineapple chunks— they carried their coffee into the living room, where Agatha told him about Imogene's invasion of her privacy. The priest said it was unbelievable.

Agatha disagreed. "It's entirely believable if you know Imogene. What it is is unforgivable."

Father Finn, whose powers included absolution, refrained from seconding this statement. "Such a morally abhorrent thing to do," he said, shaking his head.

"What will she do with all she learned from those letters, Father? What will become of all the secrets passed between James and myself?"

"You're not thinking blackmail, are you?"

She hadn't been, but she considered it now. At length she said, "No, I don't think she's imaginative enough for blackmail. Or brave enough," she added, rising from her chair and crossing the room to her coat and purse.

"Well, then, if it's not in her nature, I don't see much harm."

"But I'll tell you what there *is* in her nature. Hardness of heart. I do believe she's entirely without charity. Isn't that the ultimate offense against God and man, Father? Isn't that unforgivable?"

The priest, though he liked to concur with her, demurred. Helping her on with her coat, he mumbled, "Morally abhorrent behavior, certainly."

33

E ARLY THE NEXT MORNING, after delivering her son Stephen to school, Janet Meers showed up at Agatha's front door carrying the baby's blanket-covered car seat and inquiring about Italy.

"Janet, what a pleasant surprise. Come in. How was your trip to . . . your trip west?" Las Vegas, standing for depravity in Agatha's mind, was a name she never uttered.

"The trip was fine. Anywhere warm is fine this time of year." The young woman came in, kicking off her white sneakers in the entryway, and set the car seat on the couch. "Now, Agatha, I have something pretty awful to tell you, so promise me one thing. Promise me you'll let me finish before you pass judgment on Randy."

A marital spat, Agatha assumed. She watched Janet pluck away the blanket and reveal the baby Sara scowling and blinking and sucking her fist. With the birth of this one, thought Agatha, Janet had come into her own. Nine years ago her first baby, whose father fled, had deepened Janet, but it was a depth of anxiety. With this second child came stability, confidence, and something close to wisdom.

"There's a tape going around town, have you heard? Randy just played it for me last night. He got it from his dad, who got it from Marsha Skoog. It's a tape of an interview Sister Judith did with Imogene for her 'Women of Staggerford' column, but the first part is mostly about you."

Slipping out of her bright orange ski jacket, Janet sat on the couch and lifted the baby onto her lap. Agatha remained standing, a statue.

"It's awful to listen to. It's so whiny and stupid—you know how Imogene talks. It's all about the letters James wrote to

311

you. Or rather what you wrote to James. She explains on the
tape how the things that appear in his letters give away what
you wrote to him, and you wrote about lots of people, including Randy. It's just awful, Agatha, when you think how many
people are going to be hurt by this."

Agatha drew in a quick breath and put a hand to her breast.

"*I'm* hurt, to tell you the truth. I mean you've never had a
high opinion of Randy, and I've known it and I've lived with
it, but hearing it spoken on tape makes it hurt worse." Janet's
smile was disappearing. Her eyes were growing moist. "Did
you know anything about this, Agatha? Did you know she read
your letters?"

Agatha turned her stony face to the window.

"I called Sister Judith as soon as I heard the tape, and we
had a long talk. We decided I should be the one to tell you.
Sister's just sick about it. She played it at home while she was
working on the article, and the next day Sylvester stole it from
her and played it in the Hub Cafe. Randy was there, along with
that whole bunch of morning regulars, and I guess Daniel
Buckingham made copies and handed them out to whoever
wanted them." Janet drew the cassette from the pocket of her
jacket. "I didn't know about it till Randy brought it home yesterday. Here it is."

Agatha did not turn from the window, so Janet set the tape
on the end table. "Sister Judith's coming over later to talk to
you. She said about ten o'clock, if that's okay. She wants to
explain how it happened and see if there's anything she can do.
She'll bring along her tape player in case you want to listen to
it. I probably wouldn't, if I were you. I mean it's got to be
even more upsetting for you than for the people you wrote
about. But on the other hand, you might want to check it out
and see if Imogene was making any of it up. I mean it's possible, isn't it, that Imogene might have made a lot of it up?
What's she got against you anyway?"

Agatha turned from the window, her eyes on the cassette,
her hand still at her breast, fidgeting with a button of her
blouse. She said nothing.

"Sister Judith thinks it's jealousy. She has this theory that
Imogene wants to be like you but she hasn't got what it takes.
She says it was probably the interview that set her off. You

see, by appearing in the same column you'd already appeared in, she was comparing herself to you, and falling short, and so she decided to bring you down—that's Sister's theory. She's just sick about the whole thing. She says she should never have recorded that part of the interview, but she didn't know what Imogene was going to come out with, and she didn't think to switch off the recorder. And she should never have played it at home where her father could hear it. She told me to ask you if ten o'clock was okay."

Agatha bent over the tape and studied it for a moment before nudging it delicately with her forefinger. It might have been a large crustacean that had crawled up on her end table and died.

"It turns out Sister Judith is a big admirer of yours, Agatha. I guess I always suspected that, but lately she's been coming out and saying so. She's not upset in the least by what you said about her on the tape. Or about anybody else for that matter. She says you've never made a secret of your opinions, so what's the big deal? That's more or less my attitude too—except the part about Randy still hurts. And of course it irks Randy."

Janet, wiping her eyes, studied her old teacher for signs of emotion, but she seemed amazingly composed. No fire in her eye. No quiver in her hand as she picked up the tape.

"Could I ask a favor of you, Agatha? Could I ask you to just not say anything about Randy for a while—say six months—till you get to know him as he is, rather than as he was? I mean, he's different now. Everybody says so. He's not a bit lazy anymore. Once he started selling property, he turned out to be good at it." Janet uttered a little laugh that made Agatha turn and look at her. "If there's anything wrong with Randy these days, it's that he's *too* good at it. I mean he's high on real estate, and he talks about it day and night, and it gets a little boring."

Agatha stepped over to the cold fireplace and tossed the tape over the fire screen. It rattled down through the empty grating and onto the stone floor. She turned to Janet. "How many exist?"

"I don't know—a few, anyway. Daniel Buckingham copied them in his store."

"Who else has them?"

"Well, it's hard to say—he handed them out at the Hub. I guess Marsha Skoog was there, and that man at the Orpheum—what's his name, Harrington? Randy and his dad were there, and Theodore Druppers. There might have been others. I want you to know Randy did nothing to spread it around. He got the tape from his father and brought it directly home."

Agatha nodded thoughtfully, then sat down on the couch and took the baby from Janet, awkwardly tipping her and turning her until she was cradled in her arms. "Is she thinner?" she asked.

"Maybe a little. She's lengthening out."

The baby, still scowling, puckered her lips and blew bubbles.

"Doesn't she ever smile?"

"Fairly often, actually. Mostly at her dad."

Agatha kissed the baby and said, in a level voice, "Tell me about your trip."

Janet described the acres of slot machines in the hotel lobby, the vocalist in. the lounge, the Jacuzzi in their room. "Las Vegas is unreal, Agatha. The show playing at the hotel down the street was called *Nudes on Ice*. Some of the realtors went to it, but Randy didn't. He went with me to Wayne Newton instead."

"Did you gamble?"

"I lost quite a bit playing blackjack."

Agatha shook her head in disgust. "Remember when you didn't have a dollar to your name, Janet?"

"I was thinking of that all the while, but Randy was urging me on. We budgeted what we could afford to lose, and we never went over that. Randy actually came out a little ahead."

Agatha pressed to know more, and Janet continued on at some. length, describing the views from the airplane, their tour of Hoover dam, the colors of a desert sunset. She could tell that Agatha's mind was partly elsewhere, but she continued, as requested, until the baby fell asleep and Agatha suggested they move into the dining room for breakfast.

Over coffee and grapefruit and toast with Lillian's home-

made jam, Agatha opened up on the subject of Rome and Assisi and James.

"You mean he came to Italy to see you?" Janet squealed.
And a minute later she groaned, "Oh, no, not cancer." Then after another minute she shrieked, "You mean he's actually coming to Staggerford?" In her voice were all the emotions Agatha
felt but was too discreet to display.

Gratified to have such a receptive listener, she kept Janet at
the table for the better part of an hour, recounting her impressions of Italy and telling the story of Con Stitch and his life
and death in Ulster. She told her of James's plan to become a
missionary of peace. Then she moved on to a description of
her traveling companions from Rookery State and the scholarly
papers she'd read on the flight home. "Do you ever consider
going to college, Janet?"

The young woman smiled and rolled her eyes toward the
living room where the baby slept. "Maybe when Sara's in
school."

"You're college material, you know."

Janet laughed. "You've been saying that for the last ten
years."

"Scarcely any of the students on this tour had your brains
and character and resourcefulness. You'd breeze through."

"It would be hard. Rookery's two hours from home."

"You could start at the community college in Berrington.
That's one hour."

"And Randy would have to be convinced."

"And you wonder why I'm down on Randy."

Janet sighed.

"Be more than Randy's wife," ordered Agatha sternly.

"I am—I'm Stephen and Sara's mother." There was an edge
of irritation in Janet's voice.

"Be even more than that," Agatha persisted. "Be something
on your own. Since the school closed, I've worried you won't
put all your talents to use."

"What talents are those?"

"Your talents with people. After three months as my secretary, you could have been principal."

"It takes all the talent I've got to bring up my kids." The

young woman forced herself to speak patiently, Agatha apparently having no idea what children required of their mother.

"But they'll grow up and leave home," said Agatha, and she caught Janet casting an amused glance into the living room. "Yes, believe it or not," she continued, "your baby will fly the nest before you know it. I've seen generations born and grow up, Janet. I've seen babies turn into grandparents in the wink of an eye. Prepare yourself to be more than a has-been—that's all I'm saying."

It was a conversation they'd had before. Janet politely let her finish, and then she excused herself and got up from the table. She was turning to leave the room when Agatha gripped her arm and said, "Just a second."

She waited while Agatha stepped into the sun room and came back with the large, heavy envelope—Imogene's envelope, she explained, with James's letters inside. In her absence, Frederick had let Imogene into the house.

Silence fell between them then, Agatha examining Janet's face for signs of anger or at least indignation, and Janet showing only sorrow for the anguish she knew the old lady must be concealing.

"She denies it," said Agatha. "I called her up and she denied reading them, but here's the evidence." She plopped the letters onto the table, scattering crumbs.

"How could she deny it? She says on the tape that she read them."

"Evidently she doesn't know she was being recorded." A spot of cherry-colored fury now appeared high on each of Agatha's cheekbones. Her voice became thin and taut. "What could drive a woman to be so evil?"

"I don't know, I've never understood Imogene. Maybe she's mentally unbalanced."

"Worse than that, is my guess." She gripped Janet's arm again. "There are some people who do evil things for the sheer pleasure of it. Imogene had nothing to gain from this ruinous act, except the satisfaction of seeing an old lady's world come falling down around her ears. People like that are evil in their very nature, Janet. People like that . . ." She inhaled, drawing herself up to her full, short height, then pronounced, "People like that are possessed of the devil."

Almost simultaneously the doorbell sounded and the phone rang. Agatha, snatching up the packet of letters from the table, asked Janet to see who was at the door. The baby woke up crying. As Agatha stepped into the kitchen to answer the phone, Lillian came in through the back porch door, saying, "Agatha, there's a tape out, did you hear? It's a tape of Sister Judith interviewing Imogene. I was just on the phone with Dora Druppers, and she asked me over to hear it. Why don't you come along?"

It was James, calling from Ireland. He said he had secured his appointment in Rochester.

Janet, carrying Sara, led French into the kitchen. Lillian, drawn naturally to babies, patted the little one's head and wiped spit from its lips. She told Janet that she was three days getting over jet lag. She turned to French and said merrily, "I hear you're dating my daughter again." French, looking pained, opened the broom closet and stared at the brooms.

James said he had medical appointments in Rochester on Monday and Tuesday of Holy Week, so he'd be free on Wednesday, as they'd hoped, to travel north to Staggerford. Agatha said Wednesday would be fine, which was less than she wanted to say. She wanted to tell him—indeed, she was dying to tell him—that never had she needed his companionship so desperately, for she'd come home to disaster.

Lillian whooped with pleasure upon hearing that Janet Meers had seen Wayne Newton in person and that he'd looked straight at Janet while singing "Danke Shoen." The baby began crying again. French drew out a push broom and shut the closet door.

Agatha turned from the phone and addressed her visitors. "This is long distance."

"Who is it?" asked Lillian as Janet steered her out of the kitchen. French opened the door to the basement and slunk down the stairs.

James said he would see about plane tickets without delay. Agatha promised to arrange for his travel within Minnesota; the parish would pay for his airfare from Rochester to Rookery, since he'd be aiding Father Finn with the liturgy. "No," she insisted when James protested, "Rochester to Staggerford to Minneapolis is our gift to you. We'll be sending you instructions."

He stopped protesting and thanked her.

"Where are you?" she asked. "You sound like you're next door."

"I'm home. Came down yesterday for the week. We've had ourselves a long talk, Matt and I, and he's convinced me there's hope for the pub after all. Turns out it's been loneliness accounting for his behavior, and I can see it entirely, can't you? After a lifetime with Mother and Marion, the poor man is bereft and grieving still."

Agatha said yes, of course, bereavement was debilitating.

"We Irish, we're desperately attached to our women, we are."

Here James left an opening, apparently for a fond response, but Agatha passed.

"Well, Matt thinks my coming home is the answer, and I have to believe him, because arriving this time, I see he's been making himself busier around the place. He's been sweeping up, emptying the ashtrays, keeping the books, chatting up the patrons the way he used to. If he keeps it up, I do believe the pub can be saved."

"Not that you'll be a bartender yourself."

"No, no, not a chance of that, as I've said. It's only my living here he's counting on. And how did you find things at home, Agatha? Everything as you left it?"

"Nothing as I left it."

"Oh?"

"Everything's changed. What's the phrase from Yeats? 'Changed, changed utterly.'"

"How so?"

"I'll be writing it in a letter. This call is costing you a fortune."

"But tell me the nature of it, Agatha—I'll be worrying. Is it your health?"

"No, not that. My house was invaded by Lillian's daughter. She came in and snooped and made public what was meant to be private. With far-reaching results, I'm afraid."

"Why?"

"That's what I'm asking—why?"

There was a moment of silence; then he said, "I miss you, Agatha. It's really quite alarming how much I miss you. My actual reason for calling is to ask if you're feeling ..." A longer moment of silence. "If you're feeling anything similar to that."

It struck her as rash to admit it, but since he was making it so easy to answer, like a true-and-false test, she replied, in a subdued tone, "Yes."

"Ah, then, there you are, I'm not out of line in asking. I only had to know that, Agatha, and now I'll let you go."

After they had said their good-byes and James had hung up, she kept the receiver pressed to her ear, reluctant to break the dial tone, for it had what she imagined was an overseas buzz.

At ten o'clock sharp Sister Judith arrived with declarations of love and sympathy, throwing her arms around Agatha and pressing the little woman helplessly against her stiff, frigid coat. Janet and the baby had gone home by this time, and Lillian was on her way down the street to the Druppers' house. From the basement came the watery sounds of French hosing down the concrete floor in the laundry room.

"Agatha, you've heard the whole story from Janet, and there's nothing left for me to tell you except how sorry I am." The nun dropped her coat on the couch, where it assumed a sitting position. Sitting down beside it, she extracted from one of its enormous patch pockets her cassette player with ST. ISIDORE's stenciled on its case. "The Lord works in mysterious ways, Agatha. Someday, looking back, we'll see how it all fits into His scheme of things. We'd see it now if our minds weren't so finite."

"Apparently some are more finite than others," Agatha coolly observed. She remained standing, next to the piano, a fair distance from her guest.

The nun laughed. "I deserved that. Yes, go ahead, my friend, get it off your chest, you'll feel a lot better. Sit down here next to me and we'll talk it out."

"I'll stand, if you don't mind. I'll be needed downstairs in a minute. Frederick is here and we're cleaning the basement."

"I meant you no harm, surely you know that—I had no idea Imogene was harboring all that unresolved crud in her heart—

but I *am* guilty of carelessness. First of all, I should have kept
the tape recorder off until we got around to the interview
proper, and secondly, I never should have let the tape out of
my sight. I'm here to admit all that, and to apologize, and to
help you talk out your feelings." She placed the machine on
the end table and sat with her finger poised over its keys.
"Shall I start the tape, or would you rather we said a little
prayer first?"

"I'd rather say a few words of my own, and then get to
work. You've caught me at a busy time." Absently teasing out
the fringe of the runner hanging off the edge of the piano,
Agatha held the nun in her steady gaze, advising herself not to
be harsh with this simple creature. Though her innocence made
her dangerous, she meant well.

"I could come later if you're busy, like tomorrow. Not later
today because I'm up for review tonight at the parish council
meeting, and I've got lots to do to get ready. Can you believe
it's already six months since I took this job?"

Agatha said she could believe it.

"Another six months and I'll be moving on. I have an idea
Bishop Baker would like me at the cathedral. It's nothing he's
said outright, but it's clear the bishop and I are on the same
wavelength, and I know he's shorthanded. It's all a huge, huge
problem, of course, because what happens to Dad when I
move?"

Agatha looked suddenly apprehensive. "Surely you won't
leave him behind."

"That's the thing—he swears there's no way he'll leave
Staggerford. Well, if that's the case—and you know how stubborn he is—it means finding a live-in companion for him,
which won't be easy."

"Impossible, I should think."

The nun laughed again, a deep-throated laugh that struck
Agatha as inappropriate for the occasion, and she wondered if
the woman was following her father into dementia. "Nothing's
impossible with prayer, Agatha. You insisted on that in grade
six, and I'm sure you still believe it." The laugh died away, but
the woman's broad smile remained. "I'm sure somebody will
turn up needing a home, probably somebody right under our
noses. That's how the Lord likes to work, haven't you noticed?

The answer to a prayer is often close at hand—it's only a matter of seeing it with a fresh viewpoint."

"Which leads me to say this." Clearing her throat, Agatha clasped her hands at her waist and allowed a moment of silence to pass (she'd once coached declamation) before she began her address. "Our parents grow older and need more and more care, Sister Judith. I'm not telling you anything new, of course—you know this as well as I do—but I worry that you aren't aware of just how much your father has declined from the man he used to be. I worry that you haven't come to terms with his need to be watched over very closely, maybe even kept under lock and key, so that he doesn't go around causing any more damage and embarrassment than he already has."

She stepped away from the piano and positioned herself at the center of the room, speaking a little faster and a little louder—an orator at full throttle. "You're right, Sister Judith, I do not hold you responsible for anything but carelessness. Neither you nor I could have known what malignancy was festering in the heart of Imogene Kite, and we still don't know its cause."

"I'm sure it's jealousy. She tries to emulate you."

Agatha raised a silencing finger, brooking no interruption. "I'm assuming Janet's account was the true one. You simply turned on your wretched machine to record Imogene's account of her career, and out tumbled an account of the correspondence I carry on with a friend in Ireland. I haven't listened to the tape, nor do I intend to do so, but I understand it's a pernicious account, and it makes my position indefensible."

She strode to the fireplace and back, her eyes fixed on the nun, her hands cupping her elbows. Except for the white hair and the bent spine, it seemed to Sister Judith that the year might be 1959 again, the year of her confirmation, and this room might have been the classroom in which this same woman held forth on various aspects of adolescent morality. There was a kind of thrill in hearing the old lecturing timbre once again, in seeing the old forefinger raised and shaken as a point was made. So strong and sweet was Sister Judith's sense of nostalgia at this moment that she was sure it must be love. Yes, she decided, she definitely loved her old teacher.

Agatha continued, "What this will do to my friendship with

Lillian I dare not think, for I'm sure Lillian was mentioned in the letters and I'm sure Imogene said so. Am I right?"

Sister Judith nodded, smiling sadly.

"Poor Lillian, she's at Dora Druppers's house this very moment, listening to your tape. Well, if I know Lillian, it may very well wash over her and be forgotten—she's the least vengeful person I've ever known—but what happens when Imogene comes home to visit her mother? How do I avoid seeing her? When I'm invited across the alley for a meal with the two of them, do I come right out and say to Lillian that her daughter is a throwback to some primitive and ferocious form of humanity, or do I keep my mouth shut and pretend I have a headache?"

Sister Judith, unaware that the question was rhetorical, began to answer it. "The Lord will show you—"

"Now the tapes themselves," Agatha demanded, cutting her off in mid-sentence. "How many copies are there, and who has them?"

The nun's response—a shrug and weak smile—was meant to convey helplessness, but it looked to Agatha like apathy, which made her furious. "You mean you've made no attempt to retrieve them?"

Sister Judith extended her hands in a gesture of pleading. "How could I retrieve them? I only found out yesterday when Janet called and told me. You know yourself, when it comes to gossip, the ones involved are always the last to find out. I got on the phone with Daniel Buckingham right away and demanded he trace the copies he'd made and destroy them. He said that was impossible because they'd been circulating five days and people were making copies of their own. People can do that nowadays, did you know that, Agatha? They have what are called dual-well tape decks, and they can copy them at home. Well, when I heard that, I gave up. I mean how could I possibly retrieve a hundred tapes?"

A look of shock crossed Agatha's face. "Surely you exaggerate."

"Well, of course, I don't really mean a hundred, but I mean a whole lot." The nun sat forward on the couch. "Now look, my friend, I've gone over this from your angle, and I've prayed about it, and I've come to the conclusion that your best course is to ignore the whole thing."

"Ignore it!" Agatha was incensed.

"Be above it."

"Be above it?" Agatha was not quite so incensed.

"Look, your position is indefensible, you've admitted that. You probably *did* say those things in your letters. I mean they sounded to me like your opinions, and you've never been one to hide what you think, and everybody accepts that about you. And personally I didn't think what you said was all that damaging. For instance, Imogene says you called me a fool. So what? You've said that to my face at faculty meetings." Sister Judith laughed. "Remember the time you got up at that meeting and said the convent was a house of fools? That was when we were getting rid of our old habits and trying to look like the women we were instead of the medieval widows we weren't. I think what really fried you was our having Mr. Rick come in on Thursday evenings to do our hair. 'A house of primping fools,' you called us."

"That was over twenty years ago." Agatha remembered the occasion clearly, and with a twinge of nostalgia. She hadn't known at the time that casting away their habits would be followed by more startling changes, such as rescinding their vows and marrying priests. "Your memory is too long," she said.

The nun laughed. "But it was *true*. Weren't we the sorriest-looking bunch of women those first few years? What did we know about fashion? We'd been dressing like hags all our adult lives."

Agatha smiled, recalling the seven identical hairdos emerging from the convent on Friday mornings. "What in the world made you choose Mr. Rick? He made you all look like Brillo pads."

The nun shook with mirth. "Why do you think? He was a Catholic, and he was a *man*."

Who did Sister's hair now? Agatha wondered. It wasn't much improved.

"Look, here's the thing, Agatha. If I go around trying to get the tapes back from people, I only call more attention to them. If you go around trying to justify what Imogene says you said, you raise Imogene to the level of your adversary and your equal. Forget the tapes, forget Imogene, forget me if you need to, and it will all just naturally go away."

Agatha, standing at the piano once again, tracing with a finger the pattern in the blue wool runner, weighed her alternatives—engaging or not engaging in a struggle to clear her name. At length she murmured, "Perhaps you're right."

"Oh, I think so," said Sister Judith, springing off the couch and advancing upon Agatha with her arms out. "We'll just hunker down and let it blow over."

There was no eluding her hug.

34

D*EAR JAMES,*

I write again today to say my fears have become facts. Lord help me, the potential damage to my reputation, which I described in yesterday's letter, is no longer potential. By Easter I may not have a single friend left who will sit down to dinner with us.

I cannot recall one single day of my entire life when Lillian did not come calling or at least engage me on the telephone. Now there have been two in a row. I cannot recall Dora Druppers ever calling on me when she wasn't collecting for the Heart Fund or selling Avon products. Now she has come calling with a vengeance. Picture her sitting on my couch with her coat on—she's a rather heavy woman with rhinestones embedded in the frames and bows of her spectacles—and picture me in and out of chairs, nervous as a cat.

"What you said about our boys is a horrible lie," she said to me, "and how can they defend themselves? They're a thousand miles away."

"What did I say about your boys?" I asked in true innocence.

"You must know what you said. It's on the tape making the rounds. It quotes you as saying our boys are dishonest."

Well, at that, it came back to me. I explained to her that I was referring to the time Lloyd was home from the South for Christmas, and I inquired if he had married again after his divorce, and he told me he had not. I later learned that he had indeed married again, had married Marsha Skoog's daughter in a clandestine ceremony in Tallahassee. As for Gerald, I added, he used to take candy and cigarettes from his father's grocery store. Theodore told me one time how he tried and tried to break Gerald of his pilfering habits.

Gerald was in junior high—that was his mother's defense. "Do you think he'd be in his seventh year in the home office of the airline if he'd grown up to be dishonest?" she asked. "And I know what Lloyd was thinking when he told you he hadn't married again. He was thinking you'd light into him if you knew. He was well-aware that divorce and remarriage were anathema to you. He was always afraid of you, Agatha, and weren't we all! I said to Theodore at your retirement party when everybody was getting up and giving their testimonials, I said, 'Theodore, this is all poppycock—her favorite methods of teaching were threatening and scolding, and if any of these former students were honest, they'd admit that the main thing she taught them was fear.' Lloyd was afraid you'd read him the riot act if he admitted he'd taken Joannie Skoog as his second wife."

Well, you get the idea, James. I apologized to her for what I'd evidently said about Gerald. I admitted that it was unwise of me to assume that he'd carried his eighth-grade habits into adulthood—though I had no evidence to the contrary—and as I was seeing her out the door, I had the almost irresistible temptation to return to my pre-Christmas state of seclusion. It just seemed easier to pull down my shades and order my groceries by phone than to brave the negative ions emanating from practically everyone I meet on the street. What terrible damage have I done to these poor timid souls? I ask myself. And to my poor helpless self? It would be better for one and all if I simply stayed home.

But I did that already, from June till Christmas. I'm not really so bereft as I was before Christmas. Now I have a soulmate to tell my troubles to. . . .

                                                                January 25

Dear James,

Ignore it, and the tape will be forgotten, Sister Judith advised. And now I have your vote of support. But if, as you say, "anger dies with its provocation," why does resentment seem to follow me along the street when I go shopping, and why do the people coming out of church on Sunday morning hasten

*away with the briefest of greetings? Sylvester I can understand.
He can't look me in the eye because of the trouble he's
wrought, and I wouldn't speak to him if he knelt down in front
of me, but why should old acquaintances like Addie Phelps
bear me ill will? Addie Phelps was baking pies at the rectory
when I stopped in there the other day, and she made some
inane remark about the weather and turned her back on me.*

*And what's got into Marsha Skoog? I went in to inquire
about a dress in her window the other afternoon, and she del-
egated a sixteen-year-old to wait on me while she ducked into
the back room. Affronted, I decided to track her down and ask
her why I should be snubbed like that, after years of paying
high prices for the mediocre clothes she brings to town, so I
hastened through the curtained doorway and found myself
standing alone among empty clothes racks and hairless
mannequins with amputated limbs. I called her name once,
twice, three times, before she answered me from behind a door.
It was the door to the toilet and she said she wasn't feeling
well. Forgive me, but I sensed she was lying.*

*As for Lillian, she's gone, without telling me, to visit
Imogene in St. Paul. I got that from Father Finn, who, thank
the Lord, has not deserted me in my travail. Nor have the students from Rookery State. In yesterday's mail came a draft of
a social studies term paper from John Schrupp, along with a
kind note asking for my editorial help. Lisa Berglund has also
written to thank me for helping her get an A on her Galileo
paper. She says Paula has not returned to class since the trip.
Hopitalized for stress, she says. . . .*

February 2

Dear James,

*An encouraging word this morning from an unexpected
source, and on congressional stationery, no less, Myron
Kleinschmidt reminding me that I promised him an answer by
the middle of February, and he's earnestly hoping it will be
yes. He wants his office opened and his functionaries functioning around the first of April. He includes a paragraph of
praise, saying I am perfect for the job because I am noble, inspiring, and known far and wide. You'd think he was describing our National Anthem.*

I seem to be losing control. Reading that paragraph of blarney, I wept like a baby. (I wasn't going to admit this to you, James, but I can't seem to withhold anything from these letters.) A month of steeling myself against dark looks whenever I step out my door has apparently done great damage to my self-esteem, for I drank in these words of praise like a woman dying of thirst, and I couldn't stop crying.

Well, those tears were my signal. I saw more clearly than ever that I must go to work for this politician of dubious credentials, and I must do so because my need for that six-month job is even more urgent than his need to employ me. I'm without a base of operation in this town. I'm a has-been. I'm the old crone who carries her string bag uptown once a day for her yogurt and chop. Lillian can pass her days in her house knitting and watching TV and be the woman she always was, while I, without a public position, have become a queer old maid who has outlived her day and time. I'm telling the congressman by return mail that I want the job. . . .

February 15

Dear James,

Reading of your improving health and strength, I am overcome with joy, and I feel my own strength improving. I pray each day that Rochester will confirm your own optimistic prognosis.

Your manner of moving home—piecemeal—sounds very sensible. Now that you're half the week in Ballybegs and the other half in Kilrath, you're no doubt getting a better sense of Matt's condition and whether the pub will succeed or fail, whether your presence means as much to him as he promised it would.

My own life has changed so drastically in the past year that I scarcely recognize the woman living it. I used to have a wide view of things around here. I had connections with everyone in town. Did I ever tell you, for example, that when Theodore Druppers, after sixteen years as mayor, decided not to run again, a delegation from the city council came and asked me to be their candidate? This was fifteen years ago. I was flattered, but fortunately knew my limits. How could I prepare the next day's lessons while sitting through council meetings discussing sewers and road graders?

*Now, but for Myron Kleinschmidt, I am sought out for noth-
ing. My life is narrow and so is my vision. I have conversations with precisely five adults and two children: Father Finn
phones occasionally to see if I'm still living. Sister Judith
comes by to tell me the Lord is working in ways I can't see.
Lillian, I rejoice to say, is home from St. Paul and breathing
life back into a friendship I feared was dead. Frederick Lopat
is a silent presence at the edge of my days (this morning he's
down in the basement installing a light fixture over the ironing
board). Janet Meers and her children drop in quite regularly
and take me out of myself.*

*Come spring, incidentally, it is possible that Janet and
Randy will move out of the Morning Star Apartments and (I'm
selfishly sorry to say) out of easy access for me. It seems
there's a house coming up for sale on the river, seven miles
from town, and they are much taken with its design and location. . . .*

February 28

Dear James,

*Yes, I can understand your eagerness to line up more speak-
ing dates, particularly now that your first engagement, in Ar-
magh, went so well, but I can't get over my fear for your
safety. Every time I think of you crossing the border, I'm overcome by an apprehensiveness so strong that prayer is barely
able to alleviate it.*

*And yes, I can understand your frustration, seeing your
brother's car sit there idle and you unable to drive it, but you
must be thankful at least for the bus routes fanning out to
places you want to go. I agree with you that seventy is probably too great an age to begin driving. Were you an American,
you no doubt would have learned to drive as a teenager, as I
did. Isn't there an idler around Kilrath who will act as your
chauffeur? I read about Irish unemployment.*

*And speaking of unemployment, my own will blessedly come
to an end on April Fool's day. My congressman, perhaps foolishly, writes to declare me "crucially instrumental" in his run
for an eighth term. I am to be his "campaign director for the
city of Staggerford and the southern half of Berrington
County"—an auspicious title for sitting in a former barber*

shop handing out bumper stickers. He claims there's more to it than that—that I'll be asked to introduce him at luncheons, map out the routes of his door-to-door volunteers, and coordinate his telephone campaign. He says he wants me to host his victory party. He says if President Reagan comes to the Twin Cities in aid of congressmen, he'll see that I meet him. What makes him think I'd want to shake the hand of yet another politician?. . .

March 13

Dear James,

Ten days and you'll be on your way to Minnesota. Dress warmly, March can be ugly. Enclosed are your plane tickets— Rochester to Rookery on Wednesday of Holy Week, Rookery to Minneapolis the following Monday. I will be in Rookery to meet you. I have arranged for Janet Meers to meet Lisa Berglund, a student I'm sure you recall from our Galileo tour, the one who accompanied us that evening in Assisi to view the remains of St. Clare. While I'm at the airport awaiting your plane, Lisa will show Janet around the Rookery State campus and introduce her to an academic counselor. Moving Janet along in life has been one of my perennial ambitions. If she decides to go for her degree, she's likely to take up library science. Wouldn't I, as chair of the library board, love to see her take over our Carnegie library! Our present librarian, by the way, is resigning effective September 1, when her husband the natural gas man will be reassigned to a gas office in Iowa.

Having lost my hold on the Staggerford grapevine, I'm apparently the last to learn the shocking news that Congressman Kleinschmidt has separated from his wife. Much speculation locally (Janet tells me) on what this will do to his chances. I should have suspected marital strife when he came home alone at Thanksgiving and Christmas. He'll be home again at Easter to set up his campaign office, and since he's my new employer, I'd better ask him to join us for dinner.

Until we meet in Rookery, my prayers for a safe flight and a diagnosis of good health at the Mayo Clinic. If I lost you, dear James, I would die.

35

F RENCH RAISED HIS SHADE and saw steam rising from wet rooftops where yesterday there had been snow. Warm sunlight filled his room, lighting up the dust motes swirling around him as he shook out the clothes he'd picked out for Easter. The white dress shirt had been hanging, unworn, on a hanger behind his door for some years. The dark V-neck sweater, the blue corduroy pants, and the maroon socks with green starbursts at the anklebones had come to eight dollars yesterday at Goodwill, more than he'd paid for an outfit since before Vietnam, but the occasion (judging by Miss McGee's nervous preparations) seemed to call for a splurge. He'd even bought a box of candy to give her—a gesture recommended in an article he'd come across in an antique copy of *Argosy* on how to be a gentleman even if you hadn't been to college.

Dressed, shaved, and wishing his moccasins looked spiffier, he carried his black coat down to the lobby, bracing himself for Grover's irony.

"Jesus," said Grover, looking up from the Sunday funnies. "Where you preaching today?"

"It's Easter, Grover. Get with it."

Grover, who was wearing his robe over his underwear, seemed particularly intrigued by the button-down collar. "Where'd you get that shirt?"

"Had it."

"I never seen it."

"Got it from Miss McGee when I lived there."

"How come you never wear it?"

"Little too dressy. It belonged to Miles Pruitt. See this belt?" French lifted the sweater. "This belt was his too."

"Goes around you once and a half."

"I know, Pruitt was sort of fat. I had to punch new holes."

Slipping into his black coat, French went to the door. Grover, glancing at the clock, said, "Little early for dinner, ain't it?"

"Going to church on my way," said French.

"Church? Who you trying to kid?"

"It's Easter," French chuckled. "Get with it."

He set off down the wet street, facing into the sun and hoping to hear a robin. Last week, in the Hub, he'd overheard the merchants talking about songbird migrations (Daniel Buckingham and Marsha Skoog had already seen robins, the others had not), and the discussion had put French in a springtime frame of mind, had teased him out of hibernation and freshened his spirit, had made him more alert in daylight and able to read longer at night. He was also capable of more hours of work each day, which was fortunate because Miss McGee had a hundred things for him to do in preparation for her guest. More than once he'd stayed on through lunch and worked through the afternoon and taken supper with her as well.

Turning the corner at Main and Sixth, he glanced in the window of Glen's Barber Shop, which had gone out of business last year, and noticed a rearrangement of furniture. He stopped and pressed his forehead to the glass, shielding his eyes with both hands. He pictured Miss McGee sitting at the large metal desk which had replaced the barber chair at the center of the room. A couple of soft chairs had been added to the barber's straight-backs, and a coffee table had been brought in. On the long sideboard, where bottles of hair tonic once stood, were a number of telephones. Across the back of the room, above a filing cabinet, hung a faded banner French recalled from elections past: VOTE KLEINSCHMIDT.

Easter till November was a mighty long time for a campaign. Miss McGee explained that the Kleinschmidt forces were starting early because the Democrats were likely to nominate Dr. Harry Boyd, a brilliant and much-loved professor of social science at Rookery State College. According to polls in the *Rookery Morning Call*, Dr. Boyd was the first candidate in a long time with a strong chance of unseating the congressman.

Crossing Sixth Street and approaching St. Isidore's, where he hadn't attended a Mass for several years, French wondered if his renewed bond with Miss McGee represented a kind of regression. She'd admitted he'd become very important to her over the last couple of months, pointing out to him (as though it weren't apparent) that she was on the outs with a lot of people these days. One of her few stalwarts, she called him, and he was flattered every time she said it, but he wondered if by taking over his life for six and sometimes eight hours a day she might be carrying him backward ten years to his less independent self. Not that she'd pressed him into attending Mass this morning. No, he was here on his own, expecting it would please her, and expecting that Easter dinner would be easier to get through if he could say he'd heard her friend preach.

He climbed the steps to the vestibule and surveyed the congregation, looking for a place to sit near the back. Late Mass, he recalled from his days as a churchgoer, was always well-attended, and this being the day it was, the place was packed. An usher motioned to him from far up the middle aisle, and though he dreaded making a conspicuous entrance, he didn't have the nerve to defy the man.

The sanctuary was a splash of lilies. Father Finn was the celebrant, Theodore Druppers the reader. The taller of the two servers he recognized as one of the Rathmann boys. Sister Judith led the singing. At homily time Father Finn introduced the visiting priest, who climbed into the pulpit and spoke with an accent that reminded French of Barry Fitzgerald.

French had met the man at Miss McGee's late Wednesday afternoon when Janet delivered her home from the Rookery airport. French was sweeping a dusting of snow from the sidewalk when Janet's Jeep Cherokee pulled up. "Ah, Frederick, my man," the priest had said warmly, stepping out of the car and taking his hand, "Agatha's told me all about you," and French was honored to imagine his name passing between them. The man then stood for a minute with Agatha in the thinly falling snow, exchanging a few words with her, before getting back in the car to be delivered to the rectory.

French met him again the next day. Miss McGee had taken the man out for a tour of the town in her car, and when they returned to her house at noon for tea and tuna sandwiches, she'd invited French up from the laundry room, where he'd been reaming the floor drain. (Water seeping in from the spring runoff had caused a little flood.) French, joining them at the dining room table, found the man likeable, for a priest. He could talk about practical things. He described a sewer problem he and his brother were having in the family pub in Ireland. It appeared that digging up the line and laying new tile was the only remedy. The cost would be dear, he said, and the sewer wasn't the only thing that needed tending to. He said he wished he had a man of French's caliber working for him. "My brother and I are past it, Frederick. Grand it would be, a man of your talents around the place."

The compliment came to mind now, in church, as he sat listening to the Irishman tell a spy story—something about a maker of bombs who turned informer and was put to death by the IRA, a young man with a wife who later went insane. Ireland was a strange place, thought French, recalling magazines he'd read. Apparently a kind of low-grade version of Vietnam—beautifully green and peaceful-looking, with bombs going off in the streets. Was it a serious invitation, or was it all hot air? He pictured himself flying to Ireland to be the priest's handyman. He smiled, imagining the pleasure of telling Grover he was moving to Ireland. "Where you off to?" Grover would ask as he crossed the lobby with his shoulder bag and suitcase. "Ireland," French would tell him as he went out the door. Grover would be thunderstruck. A giggle escaped French, and a number of people in the surrounding pews turned to look at him.

Agatha was one of them. She was sitting in her accustomed place in the second pew from the front, her heart warmed and excited by James's mellifluous voice in the pulpit, when she turned to see French behind her. This warmed her heart further, and it wasn't only his presence that made her happy; it was the care he'd taken with his appearance. The cable-knit sweater was a pretty forest-green. She didn't recall giving the shirt to him, but it made her think tenderly of Miles Pruitt, because Miles had been partial to button-downs. Miles, of course, would have worn a tie.

Turning her attention back to the pulpit, she wondered how many of her fellow parishioners were catching the drift of what

James was saying. He'd left the story of Con Stitch and the IRA and moved on to the Resurrection. It was possible to rise up out of all that, he was saying; it was possible to put wrongs and hard feelings behind you. Detesting your neighbor was a kind of death in itself, he insisted, whether you went after him with a rifle or a sharp, unforgiving tongue. Your spirit suffered a little death of its own every time you failed in a kindness. Sometimes, he said pointedly, whole parishes and towns built up antagonisms; hatred got out of hand; people deserving of respect were shown no respect; people were made to suffer, due to a lack of understanding and love. "We must rise up out of all that," he urged, changing his voice into a lower, confidential register. "If you're guilty of calumny and backbiting, if you're adding your voice to small, ungenerous opinions of your fellows, then it is yourselves Easter is meant for especially. Easter exists to remind us we can rise up out of all that." He allowed a hushed moment to pass before adding, "Amen," and making the sign of the cross.

No, she was quite sure they hadn't got the drift. He'd been too oblique for them, and she was thankful for that. He'd told her of his intention beforehand, feeling obliged, he'd said, to purge himself of guilt—they were his letters, after all, that got Agatha in hot water. She'd urged him not to bring it up. "I'd be mortified to have it spoken of at Mass," she told him, and so he promised to be indirect. "Though at home I never had much luck using the indirect approach, Agatha. But maybe your American is a more subtle creature, maybe he likes dealing in symbols. In Ballybegs I always had to lay everything out in literal form." It's no different here, she might have said, but didn't. She allowed him to go ahead with his belief that Americans understood symbols; otherwise he might have compounded her embarrassment.

Her initial embarrassment had been in showing James around a town full of people averting their eyes, though her chagrin had not actually been very intense. Later, looking back, she would feel the tragedy of it, but on Thursday morning with James at her side—James fresh from the Mayo Clinic with a clean bill of health, James looking hale and ruddy and ten years younger than he'd looked in Italy—she was incapable of scarcely any emotion but joy. "This is Father O'Hannon from

Ireland, Theodore," she'd said in the grocery store, and Theodore Druppers said hello and shook hands with a pained look on his face and immediately busied himself with another customer. "Marsha Skoog, I'd like you to meet Father O'Hannon from Ireland," she'd said in the Hub Cafe. "Father is visiting at the rectory, helping Father Finn during Holy Week." Marsha smiled sadly at both of them. "Won't you join us?" Agatha invited, but Marsha said thanks, she'd only come in for coffee-to-go—a spur-of-the-moment change of plan, Agatha knew, for Marsha habitually spent hours and hours in the Hub.

It was there, sipping tea at the window table in the Hub and feeling a bit let down by Marsha, that she leveled with James, admitting that she wasn't able to present her town to him as she'd promised. Her townsmen were holding her at arm's length, she told him, and the best she could do was point them out, not engage them in conversation. They might as well do the rest of their touring by car.

She was glad that he hadn't minimized her problem, hadn't responded with false encouragement. "It's not a pleasant position you're in, Agatha, and showing me around should be the least of your worries. I know your town well enough as it is. I've lived here myself, don't forget, through your letters, and I've lived in towns like it for most of my life."

"Will I ever get back what I had?" she asked.

"I'd say yes to that. I'd say you're certain to get back the respect you deserve. They'll need a while longer to get over their resentment, these friends of yours, then another while longer to get over their shame, but the letters and Imogene's tape will be forgotten in time."

She looked at him inquiringly. "Shame?"

"I mean they'll come to be ashamed of their resentment, don't you see. They'll come to be ashamed of making you suffer like this, and that shame will be another reason for keeping you at arm's length. First their resentment, and then their shame—you won't be able to tell where the one ends and the other begins, there won't be an iota of difference in their behavior. It may be that they've moved into the second phase already, you can't tell. They may be already ashamed. But it will all pass in time."

"If I live long enough."

"And you will, of course. Your grocer will again have the spare minute to chat with you. Your woman there by the name of Skoog will again join you for tea."

"When?" she asked impetuously, teasingly.

He chuckled. "You can't pin me down as to the hour and day, Agatha, but you'll be pleasantly surprised. Your job with the congressman will help your cause greatly."

Entering church this morning for the earlier Mass (she was attending both Masses, since James was preaching), Agatha had caught sight of Myron Kleinschmidt sitting near the back, on the aisle. She'd tapped him on the shoulder on her way by, and he'd given her his beaming public smile and a vigorous nod of the head, which she took to mean that he'd gotten her invitation to Easter dinner. She'd been trying to reach him by phone since Thursday, when, according to the *Weekly*, he'd flown home from Washington, but she kept getting his answering machine. With his campaign about to be kicked off, she thought it odd that he hadn't called to discuss her schedule and duties, but he was no doubt occupied elsewhere. His district was vast and economic troubles were mounting. Farms and small businesses were going bankrupt. So were banks.

And it was odd as well, she thought, that he hadn't waited to have a word with her after Mass. She'd hurried out, expecting to find him on the steps, but he was nowhere in sight. Well, he was saving it all for dinner no doubt. And he probably knew that she had James on her mind for the present—the congressman had an uncanny ability to plug immediately into the local grapevine. Tomorrow, with James gone, she could give the congressman more of her attention. The *Weekly* said he'd be home a full week.

Not everyone missed the message in James's homily. Father Finn understood. Seated in the celebrant's high-backed chair between his two servers and looking out over his congregation, Father Finn studied those who had been stridently condemning Agatha for the past two months. He saw no signs of recognition in the faces of Carl and Louise Meers. He detected no uncomfortable squirming in the pew containing Addie Phelps and Dora Druppers. Theodore Druppers, in the lector's chair on the other side of the sanctuary, did not lower his eyes in shame.

Not that Father Finn believed in shame as a teaching device, but a hint of remorse would have been gratifying to see. It would have signaled, perhaps, a change of course in the vilification that had been going on much too long. The only face registering remorse was Sister Judith's, but that was no surprise. Sister Judith had already wept tears of contrition in the rectory office and begged Father Finn to intercede for her with Agatha.

He'd done so. He'd gone to Agatha's house and pleaded the nun's case. "Tell her I don't blame her," Agatha had told him. "She came and explained how it happened and she apologized, and I don't blame her at all. She showed very poor judgment taping the spoken words of Imogene Kite, but I know she didn't set out to hurt me."

"But Sister thinks you're still angry with her," Father Finn explained. "She says you act chilly toward her."

"Well, of course I act chilly toward her, I don't like her. But that's nothing new, I never did."

Oh my, she's grown hard, Father Finn told himself on his way back to the rectory to assure Sister Judith that all was forgiven. Agatha had always been capable of harshness, he knew, but never what he'd call hardness. Inflexible yes, for her own good reasons, but never mindlessly rigid. Imogene's tape seemed to have dehumanized the dear old woman, turning her to stone.

But then, lo, along came the hale and handsome James O'Hannon. He was no longer the tired and fragile old man Father Finn had met in Italy. Three days in Prince Charming's company and Agatha softened into the woman she'd been in Assisi. More smiles. Fewer frowns. Not so quick to criticize. She paused in her opinions to consider how they'd strike James. She paused in her eating (they'd taken most of their meals at the rectory) to cast admiring glances his way. And now there she sat with a rare look of contentment on her face, her smile beaming up at James in the pulpit. Never in his life had Father Finn witnessed so clearly the transforming power of love.

36

"*WHAT'LL YOU DRINK, FRENCH?*"

"Shot of brandy."

"Ice?"

"Nope."

Father Finn stepped over to the sideboard and poured two fingers into a highball glass. Handing it to French, he raised his own to eye level and said, "Here's to you."

"Likewise," French replied. He drank, grimaced, and exhaled noisily.

"Quite a story Father O'Hannon told."

French lowered his head and shook it. "Quite a story."

"Hard to believe things like that go on in the world."

"Hard to believe," French echoed, although, to be honest, he didn't find the story of Con Stitch all that incredible. Ever since Vietnam, French believed things like that. Atrocities came to mind at odd moments of the day. They recurred in his dreams.

Father Finn gazed at the table set for five. Had Lillian Kite been involved in the preparations, the side dishes would have been more plentiful, he observed, and the aroma from the kitchen perhaps more appetizing. Not that he didn't like ham well enough, but something smelled a bit singed.

He heard James's voice in the kitchen, volunteering his help. "Are the potatoes ready to come out?"

"You'll have to decide for yourself," said Agatha. "Here, poke them with this fork."

Father Finn thought it a shame but inevitable that Lillian should be preparing her own holiday dinner across the alley. Her unrepentant daughter, home for Easter, was understandably unwelcome at Agatha's table.

"What's wrong with that Lillian?" Addie Phelps had asked Father Finn with disgust. This was in the rectory kitchen on Good Friday, Addie standing at the counter kneading bread dough, and Father Finn sitting at the table eating a slice of her fresh banana cream pie. "Lillian keeps up with Agatha like nothing happened," continued Addie. " 'Didn't you play her the whole tape, Dora?' I asked Dora Druppers, thinking maybe she only heard the part where Imogene talks about her career, but Dora said, 'She heard the whole thing, Addie, beginning to end, and never seemed fazed in the least.' Can you believe it, Father? Not even where Agatha calls her stupid. Dora says she just went on sipping her coffee like it was a story on the radio. Sometimes you have to wonder about Lillian, don't you, Father? I mean you have to wonder if that pneumonia she had a few years ago kept the oxygen from feeding into her brain."

Fond of Lillian, and knowing more about it than Addie Phelps, Father Finn had not allowed himself to be drawn into speculation about Lillian's brain. It was Dora Druppers who intrigued him. The delight Dora took in playing the tape for one and all struck him as monstrously perverse. Looking up from his pie, he said, "What I wondered was why Dora played it for her."

"Well, it had to be somebody played it for her, Father, and Dora thought it should be a friend. She hung fire on it for almost a week, and then she came and seen me about it. 'Addie,' she said, 'Lillian's about the only person in town that hasn't heard this tape, and I hate to think what it will do to her, but she's going to hear it sooner or later and I think she ought to be among friends when she does.' She wanted me to be with her, see, but I bowed out. 'Don't get me involved in nothing like that with Lillian,' I said to Dora. 'Lillian's way too weepy for me to be in the same room with when she hears what Agatha said about her.' That's why you could have knocked me down with a feather when Dora said she never batted an eye, and that's why you have to wonder if she isn't a brick or two shy of a full load. And Agatha . . ." Addie Phelps made a sour face. "Agatha and me, we're not speaking."

He could tell by her delicious tone of voice that Addie Phelps cherished this excuse to be bitter. Addie, too, had been mentioned on the tape. Imogene, quoting James, who had quoted Agatha, mentioned Addie's daughter's child, born out of wedlock, and Addie's son's problems with alcohol. Nothing judgmental—Father Finn had listened to this part—but of course it was disconcerting to hear a recorded review of your children's problems from years ago. Addie had been letting off little geysers of anger ever since.

As for Lillian, bless her heart, she *had* been deeply wounded, but had saved her tears for him. She'd rushed directly from the Druppers' house to the rectory, scurrying up the front steps and flying past Sister Judith in the foyer and straight into his office at the back of the house. She was distraught and befuddled. She talked incoherently about herself as a rather ungifted student in school and about Imogene and Agatha as brilliant women of the world. She was humiliated, but resentment didn't seem to enter into it. Agatha had shamed her, yet she loved Agatha no less. You had to make allowances for Agatha, she said. Agatha was simply that way.

It seemed to Father Finn that whatever sorting out she had to do regarding Agatha might better be done at a distance, and thus it was on his recommendation that Lillian left the next day for St. Paul, where presumably her daughter made her feel welcome, for she stayed nearly three weeks and came home looking happy and talking about the things she'd seen on Imogene's twenty-one channels. Moreover, she came home determined to pretend that nothing had changed between herself and Agatha. And, thanks to Lillian's forgiving nature, nothing *had* changed—not even Agatha's simplistic view of Lillian as too slow or insensitive to have caught the injurious comments on the tape.

The priest was brought out of this reflection by the clink of glass upon glass—French helping himself to another dribble of brandy. Father Finn lifted a pickle out of the pickle dish, bit into it and chewed thoughtfully. At length, he said, "I wonder if they had children, Con Stitch and his wife."

"I wonder," said French.

"I don't think he mentioned children."

"I don't think he did."

"The cranberries," said James O'Hannon in the kitchen. "Will I turn down the fire under the cranberries? They seem to be boiling."

"Heavens, yes. They shouldn't be boiling."

Father Finn, contemplating the fifth place setting, recalled seeing the congressman at early Mass. He'd left before Communion, in a hurry, like someone taken sick. Or perhaps he was overcome with grief at losing his wife. Perhaps he'd better phone the poor man. He stepped over to the kitchen door and asked, "Agatha, shall I call and see what's holding Myron up?"

"Please," she said, pouring a steaming kettle of boiled corn into a sieve. "Tell him we're about to start without him."

He entered the humid kitchen and squeezed past James O'Hannon, who was wearing a flowered hot mitten on one hand and spearing baked potatoes out of the oven with the other. He dialed the Kleinschmidt number.

"Happy Easter," said the recorded voice of the congressman. "Tell me what I can help you with, and I'll get back to you as soon as possible. I'm in town till Wednesday, then it's back to Capitol Hill."

"Not home," he said, replacing the receiver.

"Dear me, it makes me wonder if he knows he's invited. I had to leave word on his answering machine."

"He could be on his way."

"We'll have to sit down and start," she said, anxiously watching James peel back the foil from the ham. "If I had half of Lillian's cleverness in the kitchen, we could wait, but everything's ready and there's no turning back."

James, assigned the chair at the head of the table, led them in grace. Although the ham was delicious, thought Agatha, the corn and potatoes were less so, and the brown-and-serve rolls hadn't come out like Lillian's. But her three guests, eating hungrily, seemed not to be disappointed. As for the empty chair, she was not greatly upset to think that Myron had missed her invitation, nor hurt, even, to think he forgot. Of the four men she'd invited, he was the least interesting, the least authentic, the least important for James to meet. Though he might possibly be the most needy, losing his helpmeet.

It was Lillian who'd first told her the Kleinschmidts were divorcing. Lillian had heard it from Dora Druppers, and then Janet, who was connected to the Republican Party through her parents-in-law, confirmed it. Promoting a *divorced* politician had not been part of her job description, but Agatha was determined to see it through. Had the breakup been caused by Myron's infidelity, she would have had to reconsider, but she was given to understand, by both Lillian and Janet, that it was Elena's fault, never mind the no-fault procedures in divorce court these days. A soybean lobbyist, they said, from Ohio.

"A savory dinner, Agatha," said Father Finn.

"Thank you. It's no trick to bake a ham."

"Real good," said French.

"Powerfully good," said James.

"Too bad we boiled away so much of the moisture from the cranberries," she said.

"Could I have more meat?" asked French.

Agatha, high on wine, ate very little. She couldn't keep her eyes off James at the opposite end of the table. She watched his hands manipulate his knife and fork, watched him lift his food in that odd, left-handed way of eating she'd seen overseas. She stole glances at his face, watching him chew. To think, at Thanksgiving, Sylvester had occupied that chair. Who wouldn't be depressed!

Table talk ran through the lovely weather, St. Isidore's imminent spring bazaar, and moved on to comparative prices of food in Ireland and the States. Then it petered out. There ensued a rather long, awkward silence, which Father Finn considered breaking with a comment on James's homily, but then he reconsidered, since the homily had been a veiled comment on Agatha's beleaguered state, a topic only Agatha had the right to introduce.

Agatha held her tongue because she didn't trust it. She'd been drinking wine at a great rate while preparing the meal, and now another glass at the table was making her hot and dizzy.

James, for his part, was full of inquiries but gave voice to none of them, unsure which might prove too personal in present company. His three days at the rectory had taught him that Agatha and her pastor held very little back from one another, but he wondered how much Frederick Lopat was privy to. That, in fact, was one of his questions. How did this strange, damaged man fit into this company? How far back in history would you have to go before you discovered the reason for Agatha's untypical, undemanding, mother-hen attitude toward Frederick? Why in years past, for example, had she come down so hard on Randy Meers for his lack of ambition while overlooking the same quality in this poor specimen?

Another of James's concerns was Agatha's state of mind. It was the opinion of Father Finn—as well as that of the amusing and irrepressible Sister Judith, who kept popping in and out of the rectory at odd moments of each day and evening—that the hullabaloo over Imogene's tape was diminishing and would soon be forgotten. James wanted to know just how seriously Agatha was injured, but he hadn't had a moment alone with her since their tour of the town on Thursday morning. She'd spoken then of her ostracism in a cool and candid tone and seemed not deeply wounded. He wanted to know if that was truly her reaction, or a brave front for his benefit.

And foremost, of course, were his questions about his place in her life. Was this to be the last time they'd see one another? Would she perhaps come to Ireland again? Could he afford a second trip to the States? It gave him an intolerably heavy feeling in his breast to think of leaving town tomorrow morning, to think that in the years ahead it might be letters only.

It was French who breathed, or rather sighed, new life into the conversation. "Northern Ireland," he mumbled, shaking his head ruefully. "It sounds like 'Nam."

"Like what?" asked James.

"Vietnam."

"Ah, yes, you served in Vietnam, did you not?"

He nodded. "All that green. All that death."

"Well, not death on the same scale as Vietnam, but you're basically correct. It's a green and perilous land, a new tale of woe every day, each more shocking than the last."

"That Con Stitch fellow. Did he have any kids?"

"He left no children, and that's a blessing, his widow growing steadily more disturbed. She's in hospital more than she's out."

"A blessing," echoed Father Finn.

Fixing his eyes on the molding high over Agatha's head, James grimaced and added, "But there's no lack of children suffering." He sipped his wine and brought his napkin to his lips, patting them absently as he frowned at something in his mind's eye. The others, sensing a story, sharpened their attention and waited.

He lowered his gaze from the ceiling and said, "I'm thinking now of a boy named Bobby O'Malley and his grandmother Mary O'Malley. They've been living together like mother and son in Belfast, a seven-year-old and his granny, since Bobby's mother died two or more years ago, died in a bus accident coming home from work one snowy evening. She was in women's and children's attire at Marks and Spencer, had been working there since before her marriage to Liam O'Malley, and was standing on the step of the crowded bus, ready to hop off at the next stop, when a car came sliding out of a frosty side street and caved the door in on her. She was the only one to die of it, may she rest in peace, though the man next to her was crippled for life. I'm related to the O'Malleys on my mother's side. My mother's mother was an O'Malley."

James looked at his listeners, one by one, with a small, apologetic smile playing across his lips. "This is no story for a day this fine, my friends, no story for Easter Sunday. I don't know what got me started."

"The boy has no father?" inquired Agatha, few things being quite so intolerable as an unfinished story.

"Oh, indeed he has a father, and a very good father, I'm sure, but the man works in Glasgow. Liam O'Malley. His line is cement. He's foreman of a crew that forms concrete to order. Culverts and stairways and the like. Liam O'Malley's an enormous, good-hearted man—I've got to know him quite well since the death of his wife. He'll bring the boy Bobby to visit me and my brother Matt now and again. He's home from Glasgow weekends, you see, and will drop down to Kilrath of a Sunday. He brought his old mother a time or two as well, before the IRA boys made a distracted wreck out of her."

"No," said Agatha sharply. "Not another terrorist tale." Her voice came out louder than she'd intended.

Again the apologetic smile. "Forgive me, I don't know what got me started."

"It was me," French confessed. "I asked if Con Stitch had kids."

James nodded and resumed eating.

"Well, what *about* Bobby O'Malley?" Agatha prompted sternly.

"All right, the story begs telling, so I'd better see it through. Bobby stayed living with his granny, as I've said, in their flat near city center. Not the best residential street, the motor traffic is constant, but the flat itself is quite comfortable. Second floor. Three bedrooms. A dishwashing machine. I don't think money's a worry to the O'Malleys."

"Why didn't the boy's father move home from Glasgow," Agatha wanted to know, "instead of making an orphan of the poor child?"

Both French and Father Finn stole glances at her, amazed to hear her speech slurred by alcohol.

James explained, "He'd not find work so easily in Belfast, being a Catholic. And he'd never equal his Scotland income. Liam's quite far advanced in the Glasgow cement works."

"Then why . . ." She lost the thread of her thought for a moment, then found it. "Then why didn't he move the child to Glasgow with him?"

James raised his eyebrows, surprised to be pressed on this topic. "I can't tell you the family's thinking, Agatha, but I'm guessing it was easier on the boy not to change houses, change cities, change countries. In Belfast, don't you see, he had a granny to act as his mother. I'm guessing Liam O'Malley couldn't arrange that sort of care in Glasgow."

"But the grandmother's a wreck, you said."

"Now, yes, but she wasn't at first."

James took another bite of food and sipped a little wine as he traced the events backward in his mind, beginning with Tommy Feehan's automatic weapon spouting murder from Mary O'Malley's second-floor window overlooking the street of traffic, traced the story back more than thirty years to his first and only meeting with Tommy Feehan, Tommy being an amusing, impudent boy of seven at the time, tagging along with the Belfast O'Malleys on one of their visits to Kilrath. It was a summer Sunday in the mid-1950s, an era of family reunions initiated by James's mother. Oh, the roistering, joyous good fellowship on that annual August afternoon when fifty to seventy O'Malleys descended on O'Hannon's pub from all over Ireland and filled themselves with baked chicken and

cake and put down pints and quarts of porter, slaking the thirst
caused by their incessant talk. James recalled, Tommy Feehan
and Liam O'Malley underfoot all day, inventing all sorts of
mischief.

"Liam O'Malley, as a very young lad, had a Protestant
friend named Tommy Feehan."

Agatha, overtaken by a surge of alcoholic vertigo, put down
her fork and closed her eyes.

"I didn't know ecumenical friendships were possible in Ulster," said Father Finn.

"It didn't last, naturally. Liam O'Malley being Church of
Rome and Tommy Feehan being Church of Ireland, they attended different schools, and by the time they were twelve
they'd acquired opposing political views, Tommy espousing
loyalty to the Queen of England, and Liam, as expected, de-
spising everything British including the very coins in his
pocket. But there was a time, as lads in neighboring flats, that
they were as close as mules at the same manger. As close, in
other words, as only boys of seven and eight and nine years
old can be."

James went on to describe the two excited, vociferous
young spirits as he remembered them at the O'Malley reunion,
tormenting the neighborhood cats and snitching pennies from
the purses of aunts and grandmothers. Liam O'Malley was the
red-haired one, and tall for his eight or nine years. Tommy
Feehan was dark of hair and broad-shouldered even then, built
stocky and close to the ground. Even then he was shifty-eyed.
"Time and again that afternoon my brother Matt chased the
two lads out from behind the bar, where they were sneaking
swallows of beer."

As James strung out his story, Agatha tried blinking away
her vertigo. She tried to right the spinning room by gripping her
chair seat with both hands. She tried to quell the echo in her
head by clearing her throat. Preparing dinner, she and James
had polished off one entire bottle and opened a second one,
which was now mostly drained. James seemed unaffected.

"It was last November that Tommy Feehan rang Mary
O'Malley's doorbell and gained admittance to her flat. She let
him in, of course, because he'd been a dear friend of the family and she hadn't seen him since he was a boy. He was wear-

ing a gray mustache, she reported later, and carrying a suitcase.
He said he was between trains and stopping by to renew his
old bond with the family and could she give him Liam's address? She said indeed she could, and asked if he had time for
a cup of tea. 'No,' he said, 'don't trouble yourself, it's really
only the address I came for. I understand he's working in Glasgow.'

"Mary O'Malley then crossed the room to fetch her address
book, and when she turned around, there was another man
standing at Tommy Feehan's side, a great hulk of a man wearing a beard and looking at her, she later said, as though he
meant to do her harm. And the door was closed behind them.
And Tommy Feehan had set his suitcase on her sofa and was
opening it and drawing out a long-barreled instrument she mis-
took at first for a piece of plumbing. She thought for a moment
that Tommy might be in the plumbing business and was about
to demonstrate some new device for conserving water in her
toilet. So it wasn't the gun that first caused her to be frightened, but the presence of the sinister second man in her flat,
and the door shut behind them. She told me later that she was
preparing a message of dismissal in her mind, intending to
send Tommy Feehan on his way with his toilet pipe and his
fearsome companion, when Tommy said, 'Keep quiet about
this, Mrs. O'Malley, and your grandson will live to be an old
man.' "

"How old is the woman?" asked French, trying to picture
Grandmother O'Malley in his mind. Entranced, he'd put down
his knife and fork and was intently leaning forward on both elbows.

"Middle sixties," said James. "A vigorous woman, before
this happened. Now she's a basket of nerves."

Father Finn, too, was entranced, but not so much by the
story itself, which he'd already been told at the rectory, but by
James's style of telling it. If only I had a fraction of this man's
gift for narrative, he thought, I'd be the effective priest I always wanted to be. If only I had his energy and sense of mission, as well.

Meanwhile Agatha had stopped listening. A darkening cloud
was moving over her inner landscape, demanding her attention.
It was the cloud of loss and loneliness. Tomorrow James

would be gone. She'd be alone again. She desperately needed *not* to be alone, day after day, yearning again for letters in the mail. Letters were no longer enough. She needed James. Or, if not James, at least a substitute for James, someone in the house to talk to. Frederick. Lord God, why won't Frederick come and live with me again?

"He said he was sorry," James continued. " 'Sorry, Mrs. O'Malley,' he said, 'but a great wrong needs righting and we can't do the job without your help. Just remember to keep it under your hat, and your little Bobby will live out his normal life span.' Well, with that, she knew the worst. She watched them throw open a window overlooking the street, and she knew without being told that the man with the beard was a marksman, not a plumber, and in a short time someone on the pavement below would be dead."

"A sniper," French said.

"A sniper indeed, Mrs. O'Malley was right about that, but wrong about the short time. They waited and waited and waited, the marksman sitting on a chair behind the curtain, Tommy Feehan pacing around in the shadows, and poor Mary O'Malley plunked down where she was told to sit, on the couch beside the suitcase, and shedding tears of desperate worry for her grandson and praying to high heaven that the victim, whoever it was, be spared. A half hour passed, she said it seemed like days, before the gun she'd mistaken for plumbing was fired and then hastily stashed in the suitcase and the two hellish creatures made for the door, Tommy Feehan stopping only long enough on his way out to say, 'Your Bobby will be delayed coming home from school, but home he will be nonetheless if you keep your mouth shut, Mrs. O'Malley. Instead of three o'clock, look for him at four—unless of course you speak a word of this before that time. If you can't find it in your heart to give us that hour's head start on the police, Mrs. O'Malley, then it's hard to say when he'll be home, or what shape he'll be in when he gets here."

Agatha sobbed. Father Finn, turning his head away from her, gingerly patted her hand. French, studying her face in furtive glances, saw her tears and was reminded of her Thanksgiving breakdown. Holidays were the pits for lots of people.

" 'And another thing,' said Tommy Feehan on his way out

the door. 'From this day forward, if you ever connect my name with what's happened here today, then eternity won't be enough time to see your wee lad home from school.' "

Here ended the story. Aware of Agatha's tears and assuming he'd caused them, James regretfully lowered his eyes and resumed eating. When French asked who had been shot, James merely shook his head, then Father Finn introduced Assisi as a topic. Had they heard that the Pope was inviting the world's religious leaders to Assisi to pray for peace?

No, James hadn't heard, but the site was ideal for the purpose.

French, helping to sustain the conversation, asked what Assisi was like, and the two priests were glad to describe it, and so Assisi carried them through to the end of the meal.

And what a miserable meal, thought Agatha. The ham overcooked, the potatoes underdone, the corn tasteless, and the cranberries lacking juice. An empty chair, a stilted conversation, and the hostess in tears. Easter, and what a stupendous failure.

"It's situated halfway up a mountain," said James.

"It's a town of perhaps four or five thousand people," said Father Finn.

"I've heard a larger figure than that," said James. "I've heard seven or eight thousand."

"Is that so? I'd have guessed smaller than that."

"Indeed, I can see why. Deceptively compact the houses are from a distance."

"Yes, it sits up there looking like any other little hill town."

The two priests went on in this tedious vein until they were all finished eating. Whereupon Agatha wiped her eyes, blew her nose and blurted, "I have a story to tell."

It had been a family secret shared early in the century by only six people, five of whom, including Governor and Mrs. Mortenson, were long dead. Only Agatha knew. She'd known since she was twelve. Her mother had told her, exacting a promise that she'd never tell anyone, a promise kept for fifty-eight years and now about to be broken.

"Many years ago I had a brother," she said, averting her eyes from her guests. "Because he was eight years older than

I, and because he was so nice to people generally, and so nice
to me in particular, I worshiped him." She fiddled with her
napkin, folding it and unfolding it. "He was the apple of my
parents' eye. He was accomplished on the piano. He played
the lead in his high school play. He was the swiftest runner in
the annual Fourth of July footraces. He was destined for
greatness—you could see it in the way he walked, you could
hear it in his voice. Here, can't you see in his face the sort of
person he was?" She got up out of her chair and went into the
living room, where she picked a small walnut picture frame off
the piano. She brought it to the table and passed it around.

This wasn't the first time Father Finn had been asked to
study the face of the man standing against the porch pillar
wearing a high collar and smiling handsomely. Once a year he
offered a memorial Mass for the repose of the soul of this dear
departed brother of Agatha's, this Timothy Joseph McGee forever nineteen in her memory, each February 16 (his birthday).

"He died of influenza at the University of Minnesota. He
wasn't yet twenty. He was planning to study law and join my
father in his firm. 'McGee and McGee,' my father used to sing
in happy anticipation." She raised her voice in imitation of her
father. " 'My firstborn and me, McGee and McGee.' " She was
overcome by a fresh flow of tears.

Father Finn passed the photo to James, who, despite the
fuzziness of its sepia tones, saw immediately the young man's
resemblance to his sister. The small, narrow face. The small,
wide-set eyes peering intently forward. The smile was
Agatha's too, but it appeared more natural on his face than on
hers, Timothy McGee obviously having inherited his father's
easygoing nature. James, handing the photo to French, wondered if Agatha's unremitting seriousness was traceable to her
mother. She seldom spoke, or wrote, of her mother.

"My mother was the first to learn of it," she said, recovering her composure. "You see, it was she who went through my
brother's effects after they were sent home from the university.
I don't believe she ever outlived her shame. You have to understand what a scandal it was to sire a child out of wedlock
in those days. You have to imagine the blot on the family
name."

"Isn't it the same in our own day?" asked James, but Agatha seemed not to hear the question.

"It was all spelled out in a note she found among his things. A note in a sealed envelope addressed to my mother and father. It gave the girl's name and said when the baby was due to be born." Agatha, tipping her head as though listening to a far-off voice, fastened her eyes on French, who was gazing at the photo. "They knew the girl, of course. She was a Staggerford girl, the daughter of my parents' cleaning woman. She cleaned here at the house twice a week, and once a week at my father's office. Her daughter was four and a half months pregnant when my brother died."

French didn't think this the best likeness of Timothy McGee. Countless times over the years he'd been made to study the other photos of the young man in Miss McGee's album, and he preferred the shot of him taken in his high school cap and gown. There his smile was impish, happy-go-lucky. Here his smile was somehow too perfect, like a fashion model's. Attractive to the girls, though, you could see that. Amazing to imagine any brother of Miss McGee's a ladies' man.

"Keeping it a secret became my mother's obsession. I don't mean she wasn't concerned about the girl—my parents did everything possible for the girl—but immediately that afternoon I was directed to make a vow in the name of the Sacred Heart of Jesus that I would never breathe a word of who the father was. Doubtless I wouldn't know to this day who the father was if I hadn't been with her in Timothy's room as she went through his things. She collapsed on the bed with the note in her hand. If I hadn't been there at that moment, I'm sure she'd never have told me. Nor would my father have told me. He was made to take the same vow."

"The girl herself told no one?" asked James.

"The girl herself was taken immediately to St. Paul, where she lived with a couple my father had known in his political life. They were wealthy. Their name was Mortenson, and they lived on Summit Avenue. Mr. Mortenson later served a term as governor."

"My grandma . . ." mused French. "She used to talk about Summit Avenue. I guess she lived there for a while as a kid."

"She lived with the Mortensons, Frederick, for the better part of a year, before and after your mother was born."

Silence around the table.

That this made him Agatha's great-nephew did not immediately dawn on French. What intrigued him at first was the fact that his mother, who'd spent her life on a hardscrabble farm, had been born on Summit Avenue in St. Paul. He'd seen Summit Avenue. The houses were mansions. And what intrigued him next was the fact that this dear mother of his, who'd withheld nothing from her children in the way of love, had withheld the knowledge of the upper-crust half of her origins. French wondered if his father even knew that his second wife was the daughter of a McGee?

Father Finn was visibly stunned. French and Agatha blood relatives! A secret kept for sixty years! Wasn't a priest expected to understand every last connection and intersection, licit and otherwise, among his parishioners? Really, what did a priest know?

To James, this secret explained a lot more than why French was present at Easter dinner. It explained why, when he came home from military service in need of care, Agatha had taken him in. Perhaps it even explained why he'd moved out, maiden aunts being notorious for doting on their favorites, sometimes to the point of suffocation.

"There you have it," Agatha concluded. "I'm going to start the coffee." She disappeared into the kitchen.

My God, my aunt, thought French, finally astonished by the fact. And the young ladies' man in the photo my grandfather.

James O'Hannon, musing further, made the connection between this secret and Agatha's behavior toward Janet Meers when she was Janet Raft and giving birth to Stephen out of wedlock. Just last night Father Finn had confided to him that many people were surprised by Agatha's wholehearted and nonjudgmental solicitude for Janet. They wondered why she suspended her customary rectitude. It was really no surprise, however, when you realized that by helping a fatherless child into the world, she might somehow be acting, sixty years after the fact, in her brother's behalf.

"Well, well," murmured Father Finn, weighing the morality of what he'd just heard. Agatha McGee breaking a vow of secrecy—now why in heaven's name would she do a thing like that? Surely for no frivolous or selfish motive. Perhaps she did it for Frederick's sake, believing that he deserved to know who he was.

Meanwhile, Agatha stood at the kitchen counter with a can of coffee in one hand and a spoon in the other, squinting out the window at the brilliant play of sunshine on the puddles in her yard. She was amazed at how relieved and clear-headed she suddenly felt, having finally awarded Frederick what she'd unjustly withheld from him all these years: his identity. Surely now he'd see fit to return to live in the house he would inherit.

Her composure restored by the shedding of this weighty old secret, she said nothing but correct, unemotional things when, later, James departed with her other two guests. After watching the car disappear down the street, she studied the small envelope James had left with her. "A little something to remember me by," he'd said, stepping back from their embrace and slipping it into her hand. It was heavy for its size, and lumpy, as though filled with small stones. She carefully lifted the flap and was thrilled to find the beautiful red rosary she'd admired in the Vatican gift shop.

37

*H*AVING HEARD NOTHING FROM her congressman by nine-thirty the next morning, Agatha began tracking him down. First she phoned his house and listened to the Easter greeting on his answering machine. Next she tried to reach his campaign office in the barber shop, and learned that the phones there had not yet been put into service. She called the bank, the city hall, Meers Realty, and Druppers' Grocery, but spoke to no one who had seen him downtown. She waited until ten o'clock before phoning the Hub, and was told by a waitress that yes, the congressman had just come in to join the merchants at coffee. Agatha donned her coat and hat, wrapped her scarf twice around her chin and throat—the wind was chilly and brisk—and walked downtown.

Entering the Hub, she was not aware of the cessation she caused in the conversation at the merchants' table, nor did she see Myron Kleinschmidt's expression darken when she sat down in the front window, blocking his way out.

He rose from his place and made his way to her table, stopping to shake the hands of three or four constituents as he went.

Looking up from her tea, she said, "Good morning, Myron, will you join me?"

"Thank you very much." He pulled out a chair and sat. He adjusted his cuffs, straightened his tie and smoothed his hair. "What's become of our springlike weather?" he asked.

"It's still March, remember."

"So it is."

They were interrupted by a bent, weathered old man who entered the restaurant and shook Myron's hand, instructing him to vote for higher tariffs on agricultural imports.

"We're in committee on that," said Myron importantly and evasively. Myron disapproved of tariffs.

"Farming's a rotten way to make a living these days," the old man said.

"I know all about it, my friend, and that's why I'm working so hard in your behalf."

"Prices going down, banks getting stingy."

Myron smiled indulgently. "You farmers are the backbone of our nation."

"I'm not a farmer."

"You're not?" Myron looked confused.

"My son-in-law's the farmer. I've got the gas station out by Pike Park. Pflepsen's the name."

Myron shook the man's hand again. "I'm happy to meet you, Mr. Pflepsen."

"Yeah, that's what you say every two years when you stop in the station."

Myron turned instantly humble, calling his apologies across the room as the old man withdrew to the coffee counter.

"Millard Pflepsen," Agatha told him.

"You see the impossible job this is, Agatha. Six hundred thousand people in my district and I'm expected to remember every one I meet."

"Brother of Leonard and Manfred Pflepsen," she added, demonstrating her suitability as his campaign aide. There was no question about her qualifications, she knew that, but once committed to a job she liked to prove her usefulness.

"And they expect me to make laws to satisfy every last one of them."

"Son of Jacob Pflepsen, who used to have the Pure Oil distributorship."

"I can't please everybody, Agatha, but I have to please fifty-one percent or my goose is cooked."

"There was a fourth Pflepsen brother who died in the war," she continued. "I believe his name was Nelson. He was the eldest of the four."

"You see, if my approval rating falls below fifty-one percent, I'm turned out of office."

She peered into his eyes and read the anxiety there. "What

are you fretting about, Myron? Your share of the vote has never been less than fifty-five percent."

"Agatha, it pains me to have to tell you this—Elena and I are divorcing."

She nodded.

"You've heard?"

She nodded again, hoping her face registered disapproval. It was no longer easy to call up that old robust mixture of outrage and sorrow that bearers of bad marital news had come to expect from her. Divorce being so common these days, her capacity to disapprove had been deflated through overuse.

"Then you've probably heard the reason," he said. "Another man."

"I have a hard time picturing it. Elena always seemed so sensible."

"Elena calls it sensible, what she's doing."

Her eyes were still fastened on his. She saw his anxiety increasing. "Is it hurting you terribly, Myron?"

"Terribly," he replied, somberly and truthfully. The pain of being abandoned, a new one for Myron, was not diminishing with time. "And you see what it does to my image. I mean it comes at the worst possible moment in my career."

"I'm not so sure, Myron. A few years ago, yes, but nowadays divorce probably isn't so damaging. Look at your president. He and Nancy swept the nation."

"But my district, remember, is a bit more traditional than the nation at large."

"Yes." She nodded, turning her gaze out the window. "At least there's that to be thankful for. I blame Hollywood for teaching the nation how to divorce."

After a few moments Myron said, "Agatha," and she turned to him. He was bracing himself by gripping a leg of the table with each hand, and he was leaning forward alarmingly close to her face.

"All I ask is that you try to see my side of things, Agatha. I'm sorry to do this. Hurting you is the last thing in the world I'd choose to do, but I haven't made up my mind about who should run my office."

She didn't immediately understand. "Which office?"

"My Staggerford campaign office."

She sat back in her chair, her expression a quizzical squint, her voice weak and quavering. "You're going back on your word?"

"It's really Elena's fault. Ordinarily, I'd have the incumbent's margin to rely on, but because of the divorce I'll have to reduce my risks in all other areas."

Her voice was a whisper. "I'm a risk?"

"All I ask is that you see my side of things, Agatha."

"Is it my age? Didn't you know I was seventy when you beseeched me to take the job?"

"Seventy's a fine age, it's not that."

"What is it, then? Why was I good enough for the job a month ago but not today?"

"Well, I hate to say this, but it's all the talk against you." Her heart fell.

"I know it's only temporary," he assured her. "I know you'll come out of this with your reputation intact. More than intact, probably enhanced. But right now I can't afford to have you represent me. There are simply too many people angry with you. Please try to see my side of it, Agatha."

"Think of the example Hollywood set," she said. "Wasn't Mickey Rooney married seven times?"

"I was sent a tape of your voice in the mail. I listened to it in the car, driving home from the airport in Rookery. You're very hard on people, Agatha, and a lot of them are upset."

"Who sent it?"

"I don't know. There was no return address."

"Was the postmark St. Paul?"

"I don't recall."

She scowled menacingly. "Myron."

"That's God's truth. I didn't save the envelope and I don't recall even looking at the postmark."

She cast her eyes outdoors again. A car backed out of a parking slot, and a pickup took its place. An old woman carrying a shopping bag stopped to visit with a young woman carrying a baby. A thin veil of cloud had turned the sunshine milky and pale. She said, "I believe Ava Gardner had at least three husbands."

"I'm sorry, Agatha. I'll be glad to have your help two years down the road. It's just this election I'm talking about."

"Think of Elizabeth Taylor's love life—what a travesty. Think of Zsa Zsa Gabor's. Think of what people like that have done to desecrate marriage nationwide."

For all her courage and fortitude, there were certain shocks and setbacks Agatha could not face head-on. She had taught herself to soften the cruelest blows by closing her attention down to a narrow beam and training it on a topic unrelated to the matter at hand. Later, little by little, she would absorb this outrage, she would ponder its ramifications and examine her injuries, but here in the window of the Hub Cafe she would shut Myron Kleinschmidt's betrayal out of her mind for the moment.

"I used to think it was worse in cities. I used to hear about senators and entertainers behaving like alley cats in Washington and New York and Hollywood, and I would thank the Lord for situating me in the Middle West where vows were sacred and standards were holding firm. I should have known it would all break down eventually. There's a kind of gravity at work in the moral life of this nation, Myron, a tendency toward the bad and away from the good, standards crumbling and sliding downhill, and do you know the reason for it?" Her eyes were moving left and right, trained on the cars going by.

"California," he ventured.

"Original sin," she said.

"Yes, I suppose," he sighed.

"It goes way back."

"To the very beginning," he agreed.

"Cain killed Abel." She was still facing outdoors, her eyes still fixed on the cars and pedestrians. "What can you expect when your ancestors get off to a start like that?"

"Indeed."

"Betrayal is what you can expect." Her voice was soft and dreamy-sounding. "Betrayal and worse."

"If there is worse." He spoke quietly and cautiously. He was fitting his responses neatly into the dialogue, so as to lull her, not rouse her.

"Oh, there is worse," she mumbled. "There's murder."

"Yes, of course," he said. "Murder is worse."

"Murder is killing someone."

"So it is," he said, verifying the obvious.

Slowly she turned her eyes on him. They were empty of expression, empty of all vitality. Her voice, when she spoke, was raised slightly. "Murder is taking a life."

He rose from the table, straightening his tie and buttoning his suit coat. "It's my career on the line, Agatha." He reached out for her hand. "I'm due to give a luncheon speech in Berrington, so I'll have to be running along. All I can say is how sorry I am."

Withholding her hand, she pierced him with her small blue eyes. "I suppose I should be thankful you didn't murder me."

At this, he grimaced as though in pain. He turned and strode out the door, his ears a lurid shade of red, and she watched him march down the street to his car.

She sat there a long while, stirring her tea and contemplating her next move. What move? She didn't seem to have one. At least not in this town, where her name was soiled and her usefulness had come to an end. All that remained here were years of tedium stretching ahead God knew how long.

So frightening was this prospect of living out her old age in idle solitude that she decided then and there to leave Staggerford.

She left her tea and hurried home, where she spoke on the phone to French and Janet and then called a travel agency in Rookery. An agent named Verna quoted plane fares to Dublin. She then went to her desk in the sun room and wrote a lengthy letter to James, stating in part, *A month-long separation will be good for both Staggerford and myself. We've been married for seventy years, this town and I, and like a lot of old married couples we've suddenly taken it into our heads not to like each other for a while, so I'm packing my bag and leaving home. Can you find me a room in Kilrath?*

She pictured, as she wrote, an Irish assembly hall with an amber globe over the door. This was the hall that had appeared to her in a vision that day in Assisi when she was sitting with James and listening to his plan to become an evangelist for peace. It was a building she'd never seen in real life, and yet the image in her head was full of vivid detail. It was a rainy evening and she and James were entering the hall, where his audience awaited him. In the distance, before the door closed behind her, she could hear ocean waves pounding ashore in the dark.

PART 4

38

THE TALL, ELDERLY O'HANNON brothers fitted themselves into the little gray Austin parked behind the pub, Matt behind the wheel, James on the passenger side.

"Rain's a pity, today of all days," said Matt, starting the engine and switching on the windshield wipers. "Her first time, I mean."

"We'll leave it to her if she wants to drive at all," said James. "I can take the bus if I have to."

"Or the sun might show itself, the radio was saying earlier."

"Hard to imagine," James replied crossly. He couldn't remember one entire day of blue sky in the two months since his return from America. Rainiest spring ever, the farmers said in the pub. He was not much affected by weather himself; it was Agatha he was anxious about. He feared the rain might drive her home before her month was up. Agatha liked sunshine, the hotter the better.

Matt drove the car out from behind the pub and turned left on High Street, following its downhill curve to the line of two-story row houses beyond the shops. He parked with the left-hand wheels up on the curb because the street was narrow.

James, getting out, said, "I'll just see if she's ready."

"Will I drive first, to demonstrate?" asked Matt, switching off the engine and setting the hand brake.

"We'll leave that up to her."

Pebbly rain turned the windshield quickly opaque. Through his side window Matt watched his brother cross the street and rattle the knocker on number 12, Katie Bromley's house. Katie Bromley was their first cousin on the O'Hannon side. Matt saw Agatha's face appear at one of the small upstairs windows

365

and quickly disappear. The door opened and James was admitted, ducking his head under the low lintel. The door closed.

Matt thought the door very handsome with its fresh coat of blue paint and its brass knocker gleaming like gold. He must ask Katie if she had any paint left over; he'd like the door of the pub that color. He noticed the shade of blue had been applied to the two window frames flanking the door. These windows were hung with lace curtains. On the sill of the left window a potted geranium bloomed. A statue of the Sacred Heart stood in the other window, looking out at the rain. He'd better paint the pub's window frames while he was at it. They were in desperate shape, as Agatha had pointed out, weathered and splintering from neglect.

Matt turned the key in the ignition in order to hear the radio. Having no ear for music, he fiddled with the dial until he found a discussion program. The topic, it seemed, was the eccentricity of foreigners; some woman with a fast delivery was phoning the station to say she'd lived in Germany for a time and the fussiness of Germans was unbelievable. She said her neighbor used to call her up to say the clothes on her clothesline needed straightening, and the moderator, a man with a mellow, agreeable voice, said yes, he believed it. Next, a woman from Galway rang the station to tell a joke about emotionless Norwegians. Had the moderator heard about the Norwegian who loved his wife so much he told her? No, laughed the agreeable moderator, he hadn't heard that one. His laughter was interrupted by a message advertising a certain brand of butter and cream from Limerick.

This message was interrupted by silence. Matt pounded the dashboard with his fist and the voices returned, but only for a few moments. By striking the dashboard repeatedly, he was able to listen for another minute, but then he gave up and turned off the ignition. He'd been putting off the expense of having the radio looked at, which, like the car itself, was eighteen years old. He was able to maintain the engine in good running order, but he didn't understand radios.

Agatha and James emerged from the blue door and hurried across the street. Matt clambered eagerly out of the car and swung his finger to his cap in respectful salute.

"Good morning, Matt," she said. "Get in out of the rain."

"Will I drive to start with?"

"Goodness, yes, you'll have to show me how everything works."

She got into the front seat. James got into the back.

Matt demonstrated the starting, the shifting, the lights, the wipers. He did so patiently, enjoying the opportunity to teach the schoolteacher. He'd never finished school himself, having dropped out to help his widowed mother in the pub. One son for the pub and the other for the Church, his mother was fond of saying, and a daughter for grandchildren. But Marion had never married.

"Let's go over that again, if you don't mind," said Agatha, memorizing the gears.

Matt didn't mind in the least. He treasured every moment he was allowed to spend with this woman who'd turned up in Kilrath as unexpectedly as sunshine in winter, a volunteer aide to his brother in his ministry of peace. Matt, since the death of his mother and sister, had been praying for a female presence in his life without actually believing that God could figure out how to make it happen. Marriage was surely out of the question. Who'd marry a shy old bachelor whose only two skills were fixing Austins and pouring drinks? How clever and unforeseen of God to send this dear soul all the way from America, with her flat way of talking (James said everybody in Minnesota spoke that way), and her ideas for sprucing up the pub (like his mother and sister, her talk was full of wax and paint and soapsuds), and most amazing of all, her American driver's license. His mother, of course, had never driven, nor had his sister Marion. Nor had his brother James, for that matter.

When Agatha judged she was ready, Matt moved the car slowly along High Street, depressing and releasing the clutch as she worked the gearshift and James said encouraging things from the backseat. "Isn't she doing wonderfully well, Matt, her first time out?"

"She's a powerful driver, I tell you. She'll be spinning along on her own in no time."

"Let's not get ahead of ourselves," cautioned Agatha. "Wait till I get behind the wheel."

"You'll do a grand job behind the wheel," said James with

tension in his voice. To him, driving seemed as complicated as piloting a plane.

"You'll do powerful," said Matt. He was sincerely impressed, this being her first experience with four on the floor. Their progress was not excessively jerky and she hadn't once ground the gears.

He brought them to a stop at the edge of town before turning onto the motorway. "Will we change places, Agatha?"

"Yes, I believe I'm ready." She got out and went around to the driver's side.

James said, "Remember now, we stay to the left."

"Thank you," she said, securing her seat belt. "I'll need to be told over and over."

She edged out onto the motorway, Matt guiding her through the gears.

"Left," said James.

"You're doing a powerful job," said Matt. "Just pick up your speed a bit now."

Oncoming traffic was straddling the center line, passing a tractor.

"They shouldn't be over the line when I'm coming toward them," cried Agatha.

"We do that in Ireland," said Matt apologetically. "Just hover along the edge till you get to feeling more confident."

"The left edge," said James.

"You might increase your speed a bit," said Matt. "We've got trucks on our tail."

She pulled over into a side lane and stopped. Trucks hurtled past in a swirl of rain. She took a minute to summon her reserves of willpower, for she was determined to learn to drive this English car on these Irish roads, determined to be of use to James in return for the lifesaving accommodations he'd arranged for her in Katie Bromley's house.

She couldn't have asked for a better place. Katie Bromley, a widow with a doting son in the next town and two daughters in Dublin, kept a meticulously clean house and made it her business to see that Agatha was provided with every comfort and every last piece of Kilrath gossip. Katie loved to visit over tea, which she served in her kitchen before a peat fire on rainy days, or, on dry days, on folding chairs out the back door on the patch of grass she called her garden. Katie was a wonderfully congenial housemate in all ways but one: like nearly everyone else Agatha had met thus far in her four days in Kilrath, she had very little enthusiasm for James's ministry of peace. Even Matt seemed skeptical of his brother's mission. A man of seventy ought to settle nicely into retirement and not be stirring up trouble—that was the implication.

After several deep breaths and a prayer to St. Christopher, Agatha set her jaw and pulled out onto the tarmac again. She shifted handily and picked up speed.

"Oh, you're doing a grand job of it," said James, bouncing excitedly on the backseat. "Isn't she, Matt? Isn't she a marvel?"

"Lovely," Matt agreed.

"Just keep left and you'll be grand," said James, beginning to believe, at last, that she would indeed learn to master the Austin, and be of use to him. Only by feeling useful, he knew, would she remain in Ireland for the full month she'd specified in her proposal. It was the answer to his prayers, her living just down the street.

Already their days were fitting a pattern. He and Agatha on their morning walk, rain or shine, after Mass. The two of them eating their midday meal with Cousin Katie, sometimes at Katie's table, sometimes in Peter Donohue's pub at the other end of High Street, where the turkey à la king was superb and where there was a great deal of kidding about James, the pub keeper's son and brother, patronizing the competition. Another walk in the afternoon, often followed by tea before the peat fire in Katie's kitchen. He hoped that Agatha would come to frequent his own place more often, but so far, much as she and Matt seemed to hit it off, she acted very uncomfortable in the pub. True, O'Hannon's wasn't the gleaming, carpeted, paneled showplace Peter Donohue's was, but give her time and maybe she would gradually come to discover that the room at the back, with its hearth and its soft chairs, including the chair his mother had lived out her old age in, was as cozy as any room in town. Was it the cigarette smoke that repelled her? There was a lot more smoking in the pub, now that business was picking up. Nothing could be done about that, short of an impossibly expensive ventilation system.

And it wasn't only Agatha's companionship James was relishing as he was carried down the rainy motorway in the backseat of the Austin. He relished, too, the thought of being dropped at the door of his lecture halls. No waiting for buses, no walking miles through the rain. Not, at least, until mid-June, when Agatha would return home to tend to some library business.

Astonishing and frightening, at seventy, to have the bottom drop out of your life, she'd said in her letter, *but that's what happened when the congressman gave me the brush-off. I have no place or purpose in this town anymore, and so I'm coming to Ireland for a transfusion of your purpose, James, hoping that you can find me a warm room to rent and a useful role to play in your ministry of peace.* It was a letter he'd read over and over, pondering the irony of having his prayer answered so ruthlessly by Congressman Kleinschmidt.

"Now up here on the left there's a lay-by," said Matt. "We could drive in there and work on the reverse gear."

Parked in the lay-by were two young women eating sandwiches in a Ford Escort. They watched, perplexed, as the gray Austin backed up and came forward eight or ten times with a priest smiling at them from the backseat. Finally the Austin halted and they watched a consultation between the priest and the other two old folks.

"Superb driving, Agatha."

"Powerful driving."

"I do seem to be getting the hang of it," she purred with pride.

"What are you thinking, Agatha? Can you drive me to Farlington?"

"Of course she can drive you to Farlington. She's a lovely driver."

"Let her decide, Matt. We're not forcing her into anything."

"If the road's not a motorway, I think I can do it."

"No motorways," said Matt. "Small roads entirely, here to Farlington."

"The motorway is so busy with trucks," she explained.

"Lorries are terrible," Matt sympathized.

"And the oncoming traffic ignoring the center line," she added.

"Yes, isn't it shocking."

"In the States they'd be jailed."

"Extremely shocking," James agreed.

"How far is it to Farlington?" she inquired.

"How far, Matt?"

"An hour and a half, more or less, depending if you're held up at the border."

She looked surprised. "I thought you said Farlington was in the South."

"It is," said Matt, "but the road bends into the North on the way, and then bends out again. The odd day you'll find the border blocked by the Queen's army, but it's a lazy old road and mostly there's nobody there to stop you."

"And your talk is at three?" she asked James.

"Three," he said. "We could leave at one and have plenty of time."

She said, "We could leave at twelve and make sure."

"Twelve will be grand. If we're early we'll walk by the sea."

"Farlington's by the sea?"

"Oh, yes. A beach you can't see the end of."

She put the car in gear and crept out of the lay-by, then gunned it toward Kilrath. At the crest of a hill James shouted, "Left!" and Matt shouted "Holy Christ!" as Agatha swerved to avoid a car coming toward her over the center line.

"A madman!" said James.

"Entirely deranged," Matt agreed.

"It would be a snap driving on the left if the *Irish* would drive on the left," she scolded.

French was dreaming about his mother and his stepsister Rae when the phone rang.

Much thinner and less easygoing in his dream than in reality, and bearing a marked resemblance to Miss McGee, his mother came back from the dead to inquire if he was living a useful life, whereupon he donned his Indian headdress and leather vest for her. Then he showed her the room in Miss McGee's house she could live in if she decided not to return to the cemetery. He made this offer without consulting Miss McGee. It seemed a forgone conclusion that the two women would make congenial housemates, related as they were by blood.

But then his stepsister showed up, the one from Duluth who lived hand-to-mouth and was accident prone, and there was suddenly a lot of nasty feeling in the air. His stepsister was temperamental, and she was accompanied by a sour-looking man. She and the man complained about the layout of Miss McGee's house while setting up housekeeping in the last available bedroom. They demanded that Miss McGee install a telephone upstairs. The sour-looking man turned out to be Grover.

An upstairs telephone wasn't a bad idea, thought French, sleepily descending to the kitchen. If his residence here proved permanent (he was putting off this decision as long as possible, even while sensing there would be no alternative), he'd propose running a line across the ceiling of the kitchen and up through the heat grating to the hallway above. This was the third time in four days that the phone had roused him out of bed in the morning. Amazing how many people, upon learning that she'd slipped out of town and left him in charge of her house, were calling up to inquire about her. Marsha Skoog yesterday. Congressman Kleinschmidt and Theodore Druppers the day before. Sister Judith and Father Finn and Lillian Kite the day before that. Sylvester Juba at least twice every day, sober in the morning, looped later on. Apparently the flap caused by Imogene's tape had run its course. Everybody wanted to know where Miss McGee had gone, and for how long. French detected an undertone of anxiety in their inquiries, as if they feared she might never return.

This morning it was Lillian again. "Will she be home by the twelfth, French?"

"I don't know."

"Well, the reason I'm asking, Flossie Granum at the nursing home turns eighty on the twelfth, and I thought Agatha might like to pick her up and bring her over to my house for cake if she's home by then."

French said as much as he knew: "No idea when she'll be home, Lillian. She went East on business."

No one but Janet Meers had been told of her destination or the duration of her trip. When Janet came to pick her up and take her to the airport in Rookery, Agatha had instructed him,

"Tell anybody curious enough to ask that I'm going East on business. If they want to know when I'm coming home, just say I'll be back in time for the next library board meeting. I don't want every Tom, Dick, and Harry to know my business. If you need to reach me for some emergency, Janet will know where I am."

"East on business," he'd echoed, committing it to memory as he lifted her two suitcases into the back of the Jeep Cherokee.

"I hope you don't feel insulted, Frederick, not knowing my whereabouts, but surely you understand that after what happened with Imogene, you'll have to earn my confidence all over again."

He didn't feel insulted in the least. By not telling him her secret, she spared him the responsibility of keeping it. The less you knew, the simpler your life.

Lillian was going on about the birthday party. ". . . and I thought what I'd do is to make a Duncan Hines spice—it's Flossie Granum's favorite kind—and maybe give her a birthday balloon, one of those silver ones with a funny picture pasted on. I'd invite some of her old friends, but if Agatha isn't home, it won't work out, because a lot of them need rides."

"East on business," he repeated regretfully, wishing he could tell her more. He understood why Agatha hadn't confided in Lillian—she was weak-willed when it came to keeping secrets—but still it seemed a shame to leave your best and oldest friend in the dark.

"How far east?" Lillian probed.

Recalling the second part of Agatha's instruction, he said, "She'll be back for the next library board meeting, whenever that is."

"Oh dear," said Lillian mysteriously, and then she said good-bye.

He was in the living room tuning in to "Donahue" when the phone rang again.

It was Janet. "Hi, French. Everything okay?"

"Everything's cool."

"I talked to Agatha yesterday. Her property tax comes due

at the end of the month, and she's sending me a check to pay it, but I'll have to come over to the house and get the statement out of her desk."

"Fine, come anytime."

"She also asked me to ask you to look at her water heater. She says sometimes her hot water isn't all that hot."

"Can do."

"Great. Well, I'll be over later on."

"Let me know when, so I'm not downtown."

"That's okay, French, she gave me a key."

"She did?"

"You know, just in case." In case of what, she didn't say.

"Hey, Janet, when's the next meeting of the library board?"

"They meet once a month."

"Yeah, but when?"

"Sometime around the middle of the month. I've got to go now, French. You're sure everything's okay at the house?"

"Everything's cool."

When "Donahue" ended, the phone rang again. It was Grover.

"You watch it this morning?"

"Yup," said French.

"Could you believe it?"

"Couldn't believe it."

"Me neither. You can't tell me none of those guys care if their wives are lesbians."

"Say, Grover, when does the library board meet?"

"What?"

"The library board. When does it meet next?"

"Why, they ask you to be on it?" Grover emitted a faint, huffing laugh.

"Never mind why, I just wondered."

"Say, French, did you ask her?"

"Ask who?"

Grover raised his voice impatiently. "Miss McGee!"

"Ask her what?"

"Goddammit, French, you know what I'm talking about." Grover was desperate for a place to live. The day of the wrecking ball wasn't far off.

"Go to Plan B, Grover. You can't live here."

"Did you ask her?"

"No."

"Listen, you said you'd ask her!"

"I never did."

"You did too. I said 'Ask her,' and you never said you wouldn't."

"Never saying I wouldn't isn't the same as saying I would."

"Don't give me the runaround, French. I need a room, not philosophy."

"One roomer's all she wants, Grover. Go to Plan B."

"What Plan B? There ain't no Plan B."

"Read the ads. There's rooms all over town."

He meant this to be helpful, but Grover apparently didn't see it that way. He said, "Jesus!" and hung up.

French, feeling sorry for him, dialed the hotel.

"Grover, what's the idea, hanging up on me?"

Grover, standing at the registration desk, delayed his answer a few moments, his eye caught by a pickup pulling up to the curb with BERRINGTON DEMOLITION lettered on the door.

"Jesus, here they are."

"Who?"

"The wrecking crew."

Two men got out of the pickup, one wearing a suit, the other dirty coveralls.

"Take a room at your brother's," said French.

"My brother's a farmer."

"So what?"

"I need to be in town."

"Why?"

"How would you like to be stuck out on a farm?"

French understood the problem. Grover needed a listening post at the heart of town. He ingested gossip like food and drink. "Well, couldn't you go live there for a while, not forever?"

The man in coveralls came in and asked to see the basement. Grover growled, pointing to the door leading down. The other man remained outside, studying the hotel's facade and writing in a little book.

"Just ask her, French."

French sighed. It would never work. Grover was addicted to

daytime television. He had fussy eating habits. He never changed his socks.

The plea came again, husky with desperation. "Just ask her."

What French didn't understand was the extent of Grover's attachment to him. Grover, though solitary by reputation, had valued their ten years of companionship much more dearly than had French, who was solitary by nature.

"How can I ask her if I don't know where she is?"

"Ask her when she gets home."

"That won't be for a while yet."

"How long?"

"It'll be into June."

"Jesus."

Grover hung up as the man in coveralls came up from the basement.

"She's a solid old building," said the man respectfully. "We'll be a week pulling her down."

"When do you start?"

"End of next week."

"Jesus."

Grover phoned French to say he had a week to clear his things out of Room 32.

French phoned Janet to ask if, when she came for the tax statement, she'd help him move his things. He told her that all his worldly belongings would fit into the back of her Cherokee.

Janet agreed to help him. Then she phoned Ireland and left word with Katie Bromley that French had decided to take up permanent residence in Agatha's house.

French phoned the post office and changed his mailing address. No, the postmaster said, they had no plans at present to hire new carriers, but maybe next Christmas they could use him as a sorter. He'd put his name down.

Grover phoned his brother the farmer and arranged to move into his spare bedroom.

39

*F*ARLINGTON, A WHITEWASHED TOWN clinging to the hilly coastline of the Cooley Peninsula, smelled of peat smoke and seaweed. A collapsed castle of moss-covered rock sat brooding over its high end, and at its low end, in a cove, a dozen brightly painted fishing trawlers leaned into one another, grounded by the outgoing tide. The rain was diminishing. Streaks of blue sky were visible far out over the roaring Irish Sea.

James directed Agatha to park the Austin in front of the needle-spired church that dominated the central street. "The gathering's over there," he said, pointing across the street to a windowless building of stucco with its name lettered over the entryway: FRIARS YOUTH CENTER.

"Friars?" Agatha inquired.

"Augustinians," said James. "They have several parishes in these parts."

A group of teenage boys dressed in school uniforms—gray trousers, black sweaters—were milling about the doorway. They stood aside to allow a number of elderly women to enter.

"I suppose we haven't enough time for a walk." Agatha was sitting behind the wheel, looking longingly out to sea.

James studied his watch. The drive had taken them much longer than Matt had predicted, delayed as they were by border guards and by a couple of wrong turns James had advised her to take. A lifelong rider of buses and trains, James didn't know east from west on a map.

He said, "We can walk afterwards, if you wish." He studied the ocean, its winking whitecaps. "If it's not too windy, that is."

"Oh, no, not too windy for me," she said urgently. She felt

377

the sea pulling at her heart, felt herself buoyed up and bobbing on a tide of adrenaline. "You've lived all your life near this coast, James. You can't possibly know the magic it holds for a landlubber."

They got out and crossed the street.

"Are you ever nervous beforehand?" she asked.

"A wee bit, until I get a sense of my listeners. It helps if I can look them over before I begin."

They found a mixed audience gathered in a chilly, dampish gymnasium. Thirty or forty boys from the local national school had been coerced into attending. A dozen or so elderly women represented the parish sodality, one of them bouncing an infant grandchild on her knee. A few idle old men drifted in, sheltering from the wind, and took seats directly in front of Agatha. One of them wore his long white hair in what Agatha considered a particularly repellant style; it was gathered at the back by a rubber band and hung over his collar in a ponytail. A carload of Presentation sisters arrived at the last minute from a neighboring town.

James, or rather his subject, was introduced by an Augustinian who stepped up to the lectern wearing a soutane and coughing into his handkerchief. A frail man with a gray beard, he spoke huskily from notes, presenting an overlong review of Ulster's troubles. By the time he let James have the floor, the baby was whimpering and the teenage boys were making their folding chairs squeak.

Then as James took his place at the lectern and was clearing his throat, the door opened on the howling wind and a pair of old ladies entered, followed by a youngish priest who directed them to seats next to Agatha in the back row.

"Did you take the keys out of the car?" asked one of the old ladies in a booming voice. She was very tall and angular. Her hair was dyed red.

"I did," whispered the young priest.

"He did," said the other old woman in a high-pitched cry. This one wore layers of sweaters and tapped the floor with her long umbrella, using it like a cane.

"He did?" boomed the first.

"Shhhhhhhhhh," hissed the other.

The priest, glancing at Agatha, smiled and flushed with embarrassment.

"Is this going to take long?" asked the tall one.

"We can slip out if he's tiresome," said the other.

Agatha closed her eyes and prayed that James would not attempt to speak until his audience had settled into perfect stillness. Half a century in the classroom had taught her that a stern glower was worth a dozen pleas for silence.

But she needn't have worried. Within minutes the teenagers and all the others were engrossed in the tragedy of Con Stitch. Even the baby fell silent. Everyone in Ireland, North and South, had a role to play in thwarting the terrorists, said James. Everyone must resolve never to aid terrorists, always to expose them.

This plea caused the old man in front of Agatha—the one with the ponytail—to moan softly and sit forward with his elbows on his knees and his eyes on the floor.

"Not likely, you say?" continued James. "The atrocities are carried out in the North, you say, and the odds are nil of your ever meeting a terrorist in Farlington? Well, you may be right. But don't you travel? Don't you now and again cross the border? Don't half the roads out of Farlington lead into the North? And you young lads, don't you expect your life's work as adults might someday carry you far beyond the town limits of Farlington? And you ladies of the parish, aren't you in touch with your family and friends all over this island, and can't you spread word through your letters and over the telephone that what this poor old divided nation needs more than anything else is a network of peace-mongers?"

The teenage boys and the sodality ladies alike gaped at James, the former as though he was the first to tell them they were bound to grow into adulthood, the latter as though they'd never imagined affecting anything so large as the national welfare.

"And look at it this way," he continued. "The terrorist thrives on secrecy and deception. He wants you to think he's got you outnumbered, outmaneuvered, outsmarted. He wants you to think there's a bomb in every mailbox, a sniper in every window. But the truth is that his numbers are very small and he's no smarter than you or I. He's probably much dumber, actually, for he's chosen the path of violence over the path of peace, and that requires a special kind of ignorance. Dealing in violence, he stands a fair chance of getting a hand blown off or an eye put out or being forced to turn traitor like poor Con Stitch, leaving his widow psychotic and all his relations in sorrow. I don't call that very smart."

Agatha saw one of the boys stare at his hands, imagining, she supposed, one missing. Another put his hand to his eye.

"And because his numbers are small, and because he's no genius, the terrorist has to depend on many innocent and less than innocent people to carry out his plans. Now my point is that if you ever in your life hear of, or see, or suspect terrorist activity and you don't report it immediately and try to foil the effort, you are less than innocent."

He bent intently over the lectern, looking from face to face. "Imagine this, if you will, my friends. Imagine that you hear in the roundabout way that gossip travels that one of your neighbor's nephews is in Belfast making bombs out of coffee jars. Are you going to wait till the next bit of gossip comes your way claiming he's blown up a Land Rover full of soldiers?"

The silence of held breath.

"No, yours is the anonymous voice the authorities are depending on. It's your duty to report what you've heard before the nephew finishes his next bomb. You must join the army of watchful informers this country requires if we're ever to live in peace. Now, I would like you all to stand and place your hand over your heart."

Agatha rose with the others—all except the long-haired old man—and repeated after him a brief pledge of resolve to work against the forces of terror. James than asked them to sit for his concluding story.

"I seldom take a nip anyway," said the angular woman with the dyed red hair. "I won't miss it."

"This wasn't the whiskey pledge," the young priest told her.

"Shhhhhhhh," hissed the woman in layers of sweaters.

"Not whiskey? What was it for, then?"

"For peace in the North," said the priest. "It was a peace pledge."

"*Peace* pledge, my word, I've never heard of a peace pledge."

"Shhhhhhhhh."

James concluded with the story of Mary O'Malley and the sniper who murdered a man from her sitting room window in Belfast. His emphasis today was on the grandson rather than the grandmother. Some unhappy new details had apparently come to light since Agatha had heard the story at Easter dinner. Bobby O'Malley, still living with his depressed and whimpering grandmother, was developing some serious problems. James called it misbehavior. Agatha recognized it as "acting out." The poor boy was defying his grandmother, defying his teachers, defying his father, who came home weekends from Glasgow. "If the boy is ever to regain his equilibrium," said James, "indeed, if the youth of Ulster as a whole is ever to regain its equilibrium, the environment must change, and change utterly."

The word "environment" put Agatha unexpectedly in mind of nine-year-old Stephen Meers, who lived with his mother and father and little sister on seven wooded acres overlooking the Badbattle River. A month ago Randy and Janet and the children had left the Morning Star Apartments and moved into their new split-level house with three bathrooms, two fireplaces, and a Jacuzzi.

"What a deleterious effect it must have on a boy's mental makeup to hear his grandmother scream every time a siren goes by."

The hardwoods would be just now leafing out, Agatha thought, and high in the swaying birches the orioles would be building their nests. The latecomers among the migrating birds—the flickers and bluebirds—would be arriving now, completing the chorus of bird song along the riverbank.

"How damaging it must be to a boy of seven to see his grandmother break down and weep every time she looks out the window and sees a soldier patrolling the street dressed in full battle gear."

The Badbattle, now in May, would be deep and swift. She pictured a brave canoeist sweeping downstream over the rapids below the Meerses' living room window. Upstream a fisherman was very likely visible from the Meerses' porch, wading out in boots and casting for pike.

James finished his address. Most of his listeners applauded. All of them looked thoughtful. There were a few questions, but Agatha did not hear them, for she was conceiving what seemed to her one of the best ideas of her life. What if Bobby O'Malley were transplanted to the Meers household for the summer? River and woods. Birds and sunshine. Janet his surrogate mother, Stephen his companion. Wouldn't ten or twelve weeks of fishing and climbing trees and sleeping in a peaceable house help to bring a seven-year-old back from the edge of delinquency or a nervous breakdown? Randy Meers would agree, surely, if Janet put it to him in the right way. She'd stress the importance of his role as a substitute father. Randy liked feeling important.

"No tea?" asked the angular, redheaded old lady as James stepped away from the lectern and his audience began filing out of the gymnasium.

"Nothing was said about tea," the woman in sweaters replied.

"Normally with talks of this type, they serve tea after." Dismayed, the tall redhead continued to sit on her folding chair, blocking Agatha's way out.

"Come along, Mother," coaxed the young priest, "come along, Auntie. We'll pop into the grill down the street."

By moving chairs, Agatha reached the aisle, where she joined James, congratulating him like the declamation coach she used to be. His persuasiveness, sincerity, and eye contact were superb, she told him; his audience could have listened longer.

"Leave them wanting more, and they'll ask me back someday," he said.

"James, I've just had a bright idea concerning Bobby O'Malley."

At this point the old man with the ponytail stepped rudely between them and put a question to James. "Isn't it your life you're risking, Father?"

"My life?" James was puzzled.

"By stirring people up." This man, whom Agatha had taken for a local idler wandering into the talk for diversion, spoke with inflections she'd not heard thus far in Ireland, a burr that put her in mind of Scotland. He thrust his face up close to James and added defiantly, "By criticizing the IRA."

"It's not the IRA alone I'm criticizing. It's the murders and maimings on both sides."

Agatha, full of her new idea, left them and stepped outside. The teenagers, their lessons done for the day, were scattering in several directions. A few of the women lingered at the entrance, discussing grandchildren as they passed the infant from hand to hand. The street was quickly drying in the sunshine and wind. Here and there a puddle rippled and glistened. Gulls were swooping over the seafront.

Approaching the Austin, reviewing the gears in her mind, she saw a fluttering piece of white paper tucked under the windshield wiper. An advertisement, she assumed, absently folding it small and looking about for a trash receptacle. Seeing none, she slipped it into her purse as James caught up with her.

"The world is filled with destroyers and builders, Agatha, and that man is one of the destroyers—I'm sure of it."

"That old man? A destroyer?"

"They give off a smell, as I said in my talk. It's evil they give the impression of. I'd wager my last pound he's one of them."

Agatha was stunned. "Not a terrorist, at his age." She scanned the street for another look at the elderly man, but he'd disappeared.

"If not one himself, then a strong supporter. You heard what he was saying?"

"He said what I say: be careful."

"No, you didn't catch the undertone, Agatha. 'Shut up, or else!' is what he was telling me. It's Belfast he comes from, you can tell by his speech."

"A warning." A shudder ran through her.

James nodded happily, his eyes alight with excitement. "That's the man's job, delivering threats."

Agatha looked frightened. "I told you there was risk involved, James. You told me I was wrong."

James looked delighted. "You know what this means,

Agatha? It means I'm making an impression. It's the break-through I've been waiting for."

"And if they kill you? What sort of impression will you make when you're dead?"

He laughed. "A martyr's impression."

Incensed by his breeziness, she started down the street toward the pier. James strode along at her side, speaking proudly of his breakthrough, his voice raised above the wind, his coattails whipping about his knees. Four and a half months he'd been at this business, he told her, and he'd antagonized the terrorists at last. His reputation was running out there ahead of him now.

Then, sensing her disapproval, he changed his tack. He explained that neither of them was at peril. "Think about it, Agatha, think of the public outcry if the IRA or the loyalists laid a hand on a priest. Every Catholic in Ireland would rise up in anger. And can you imagine the outrage in America if the likes of you, an American woman, were killed? The IRA would lose all those diehard zealots in Boston who've been sending them money for weapons. No, we're both guaranteed safe passage, Agatha. It's not only Providence we've got on our side, it's political expediency as well."

The sea sounded like an endless train at full throttle. The tide was low, leaving the wide beach hard-packed as pavement. Agatha, tightening the knot of her scarf, stood facing the roaring water, watching it leap and curl over itself and throw spume high in the air. The sea affected her heart as profoundly as love. The sea inspired her by doing what it pleased. It snatched up her soul and bore it to lands where her troubles couldn't follow. She felt confidence washing in on her, climbing up the beach on the advancing tide. The sea was saying a single word over and over, and the word was courage.

James stood a little behind her, not wishing to obstruct her view of the water. Nor, to be frank, did he wish to face her just yet. He was afraid he might have upset her. They were in accord about everything else; how tragic if they had a falling out over his mission. His mission was the one thing in life he could not give up, even for her. Just as she had become the joy of his old age, his ministry of peace had become its justification. He half expected her to turn from the sea and face him with an ultimatum. His knees grew suddenly weak as he imagined her saying, *Myself or your mission, James—you must choose.*

A minute passed before she turned from the crashing waves and smiled at him.

"I have a plan for Bobby O'Malley," she said.

40

T_{HREE} $_{WEEKS}$ $_{LATER}$ — $_{IT}$ was June now—
French steered the power mower into the shade of an elm, cut
the engine, and nodded at the postman approaching across the
grass.

"Hello, French. Not at the tourist center today?"

"I get Mondays and Tuesdays off."

The postman, a red-haired, sauntering man named Parks,
gave him a handful of mail. "There's your magazine there. It's
not the type Miss McGee would appreciate."

"She ain't home."

"I know, but I'm thinking you better tell me when she gets
back, so I don't deliver it. I'll save it at the post office for you
to pick up."

"Good idea." The mail included also the *Staggerford
Weekly*, French saw, as well as the *St. Anthony Messenger.*

Parks seemed in no hurry to be on his way. Lingering in the
shade, he said, "Nice out."

"Real nice," said French.

"When you figure she's coming back?"

Not a day went by that someone didn't ask him this. The
entire town was intrigued by the mystery. Drivers along River
Street examined the house as they went by, looking for signs
of her return. Her whereabouts was the talk of the Hub, and
none of the talk was bitter anymore. He'd overheard Marsha
Skoog and Theodore Druppers suggest a Welcome Home
party.

"It won't be long now," he told Parks. The library board,
he'd learned, would meet on the fifteenth. The library board, in
fact, demanded that French tell them the minute she arrived

home so that they could honor their chairlady with a bouquet of roses.

"Hope she's having a good vacation."

"Me too."

"She deserves it."

"You bet."

A consensus of those who felt guilty about snubbing Miss McGee had settled on "vacation" to describe her absence. It relieved them, French supposed, of admitting they'd driven her away.

"I never had her in school—I went to public—but they say she was a crackerjack."

"Knew her stuff all right," French allowed.

The postman ambled off across the lawn, and French took the mail up onto the porch, where he sat on the suspended swing and sorted through it. He paged quickly through his magazine, scanning the articles aimed at the young corporate male and the pictures of women wearing scraps of underwear. He'd decided to cancel his subscription. Someday Agatha, while cleaning his room, would find the magazine and there would be a scene. She'd make him feel horribly depraved. Of course it would be emblematic of his total loss of independence. He foresaw any number of rules going into effect, rules about making his bed and picking up his clothes, and she'd probably urge him back to church. She'd keep at him to quit being a fake Indian and find a real job.

But today, for some reason, all these rules and expectations didn't seem to be more than he could bear. There was something about sitting on a wide porch on a fine day in early summer that made him want to be more than he was. The bird song, the smell of new-cut grass on the breeze, the lovely shade under the elms along the riverbank—all of this seemed so clean and luxurious and heavenly after his decade at the Morgan that he seriously wondered if he was dreaming. And to think this house would be his someday. Why, it was enough— almost—to make him want to deserve it by amounting to something.

He put down the magazine, wishing he could sell the rest of his subscription, which had five months to run. Maybe Parks the postman would buy it, at a discount. He picked up the

Weekly and checked the help-wanted ads. Slim pickings this week. The Brass Fox wanted waitresses, the Hub wanted a chef, and Sure-Allure Cosmetics wanted a local sales representative. He should have asked Parks if the postmaster was planning to hire mail carriers anytime soon.

On the editorial page he read an article reprinted from the *Rookery Morning Call* concerning an election poll. The incumbent congressman was in trouble all over his district. Never before had Myron Kleinschmidt failed to carry his hometown and county, but now even that area was iffy. The experts were mystified, but French was not. The backlash against Agatha had reversed itself, and Myron Kleinschmidt, in refusing her employment, had made the biggest miscalculation of his career. Sister Judith, among others, was spreading the news like an evangelist. Kleinschmidt the chauvinist, Kleinschmidt the traitor. Come November, Kleinschmidt was likely to get creamed.

Hearing the phone ringing in the kitchen, he gathered up the mail and went inside. It was Janet calling with an amazing message. Miss McGee was bringing a child home from Ireland.

"Come again?"

Janet sounded ecstatic. "He's a boy of seven who's been through some terrible times and needs a stable home for the summer, or maybe longer. I mean, if it works out, maybe he can stay through the school year, who knows? His mother's dead and I guess he's seen a lot of awful stuff in Belfast, and it's made him pretty nervous. I'm sending Randy over to see you, French. Will you take him up in the attic? Agatha's got a youth bed up there she wants us to have. We're all so excited. Randy's all for it, and Stephen has always wanted a little brother."

French was enormously relieved by this last piece of information. He'd thought for a minute that the kid was coming to live on River Street. No telling what sort of upheaval a nervous Irish orphan might cause. The boy would want him to play catch. He'd climb up on his lap and spill soda pop. French got his fill of nervous kids at the tourist center.

"His name is Bobby O'Malley," added Janet. "Agatha's flying home with him. I'm picking them up in Rookery."

"When?"

"Next Monday night. I'm going to an orientation meeting that day at Rookery State."

"Can I tell people when she's coming? Everybody's asking."

"I don't see why not. Nobody expects her to miss Wednesday's library board meeting and pass up the chance to vote against Imogene."

"Vote against who?"

"Imogene Kite. Haven't you heard? She's applying for the job."

French shivered. "What job?"

"Librarian. Mrs. Kopka's leaving town. Didn't you know that?"

"No."

"Imogene's one of three candidates. Had her application in before Agatha left town. She wants to come back to Staggerford."

"She won't get hired, will she?"

"What do you think? Of course not."

"You're sure?"

"Hundred percent. Say, French, would you be insulted if I dropped in on Saturday to see if everything's shipshape?"

"Fine with me."

"I could do some last-minute straightening up."

"Could you vacuum?"

"Sure."

"I'll have the lawn mowed and the dishes washed, but I hate like hell to vacuum."

"Leave it to me. How about dusting?"

"I hate like hell to dust."

Resuming his yard work, French was troubled by the library news. He wished he could be a hundred percent sure that Agatha would withhold the job from Imogene. Her fellow townsmen apparently expected her to do so, and surely she'd be justified, and yet vengeance didn't strike him as something Agatha would permit herself to carry out. Vengeance was more in Imogene's line. Hard to say what sort of grief he'd be in for, for jilting her.

41

A N O T H E R   S P E A K I N G   E N G A G E M E N T.
Another coastal town, this one in Northern Ireland, thirty miles
from Belfast. Below the town a vast beach swept in a long
curve out to a headland that looked to Agatha, through six
miles of haze, like the silhouette of a crouching dog.

Steering the Austin left and right, she followed the crooked
road downhill from St. Patrick's School, where she had left
James to his audience of educators. She was adept now at handling the car, having delivered James to eleven engagements in
three weeks. This was the last of her driving assignments, at
least for this visit; and the last, but one, of her days in Ireland.

When she brought the Austin to a halt at the base of a sea-
side dune, Bobby O'Malley, in the seat beside her, lifted his
eyes from the book she had bought him—*Babar the
Elephant*—and said, "Oh, rubbish, do we have to walk?"

From the backseat came the voice of his father. "Now,
Bobby, behave for Miss McGee, or she won't take ye in the
plane with her."

Agatha addressed the seven-year-old. "We have to be patient with the elderly, Bobby. This old lady loves the sea, and
today is her last chance to walk beside it."

"Why can't I stay here and read while you walk?" the boy
whined.

"Because there are things about America you and I have to
talk over. Come along now."

"Oh, rubbish," he said, slapping his book shut.

His father thrust his huge hand over the seat to straighten
the boy's thick, unruly hair. "Now, Bobby, Miss McGee knows
what's best. Don't ye be making trouble, or there'll be no trip
to America." Mr. O'Malley was a ruddy, red-haired, hulking

man with small gray-green eyes and the thin, constricted sort of voice that got on Agatha's nerves. His tone was snappish, his touch rough.

Agatha turned and frowned reprovingly at the man. For all his good intentions, Liam O'Malley, the cement worker from Glasgow, was a nag. From the moment the two of them, father and son, stepped out of their car in front of St. Patrick's School, he'd been fussing and scolding and pulling at the boy's ears. She understood his motive. He wanted to seem a worthy, attentive father and present her with a worthy, obedient son. He was more eager than he could say—indeed, he was desperate—to transfer his troubled seven-year-old into Agatha's care.

Two weekends ago O'Malley had driven his son from Belfast to Kilrath, summoned there by James in order to meet Agatha and to discuss her plan for Bobby. The meeting had been a success. Today had been designated for handing over the boy.

Except for his voice, the boy in no respect resembled his father. The boy's features were delicate, his complexion very pale, with a saddle of freckles across his nose. His hair and his eyes were dark, almost black. He was small for his age, but more articulate than Stephen Meers had been at seven—indeed, more articulate than Stephen now, at ten. James said the boy took after his dead mother.

"Can't we talk about America in the car?" he whined. "I hate the sea."

O'Malley, again reaching over the seat, wrested the book from Bobby, and the boy's whining became a howl.

"Come along, Bobby," said Agatha, opening her door.

Bobby made no move to get out, but his father did.

"I'm sorry, but I'll need to go walking with Bobby alone," she told him. "I'll leave the keys, if you want the radio on."

"Right," the man agreed, "I'll just stand out and have meself a cigarette. Get along with ye, now, Bobby."

"Bring your book if you wish," she said to the boy.

She walked across the hard-packed sand to the edge of the water, tiny seashells crunching underfoot like broken Belleek. It was a warm, bright day. The tide was out. The sea was tame, the surface lazily shifting in various shades of green. Breezes were playing from several directions. Wavelets quickly lapped at the sand. She waited, her back to the car, for Bobby to join her. She knew better than to rush him. He needed a few minutes to establish his irritation at being ordered about by a woman the same age as his disturbed grandmother.

For all his willfulness, she was confident that Bobby would play into her hands, for she held the trump card—his airline ticket. And once in America, she was confident that he would fall into line. For one thing, he was intelligent, and intelligent children, in her experience, almost always straightened themselves out over time. For another thing, she'd discovered the perfect device for drawing him out of himself. He loved books. At some stage in his short life someone had obviously read to him. Books moved his mind away from his demons. She'd never known a book lover to grow up to cause trouble.

Liam O'Malley climbed a dune and lit a smoke. He stood looking inland, following with his eyes the crooked road up through the town and picking out his car parked in front of the convent school. That's where his old cousin James was regaling the teachers from miles around with his vision of the peaceable kingdom, the lion lying down with the lamb and all that. James and the woman from America had urged him to attend, but he hadn't come over from Glasgow to sit in a stuffy room for hours listening to a pie-in-the-sky sermon on peace and goodwill. On a day this fine, a man should be out in it, breathing God's clean air.

Inhaling deep, refreshing lungfuls of smoke, he turned around and looked down at the woman. She was facing out to sea, the inshore breeze lifting her white hair and tugging gently at the hem of her tan raincoat. She was a sprightly thing, sure of herself and quick with her tongue. He knew the type—opinionated, hardheaded, thin-skinned, conspiratorial, smart as a whip. Two generations removed from the old sod, yet Irish as Paddy's pig.

His mother had been that type in her day. Now his mother was a nutcase, her spirit broken and her mind permanently mangled. The more distraught his mother became, the more she clung to Bobby. She'd wept and raved this morning when she discovered her son packing her grandson's suitcase. The woman was a lunatic, plain and simple, driven over the edge by the atrocity she'd witnessed and by her guilt at not having shouted a warning to the man in the street who was shot. Mr. O'Malley's next problem was what to do with his mother. He'd have to start looking at institutions.

He watched his son get out of the car and slowly carry his book across the beach and stand beside the woman. The woman pointed in the direction of the hazy headland, and the boy nodded in agreement. Mr. O'Malley took another deep drag on his cigarette and watched the two of them set off in that direction, both of them turning to wave at him high on the dune. He watched them for a long time, the old woman striding over the sand with her purse hanging from her shoulder on a strap, the boy, book in hand, hopping over little rivulets and splashing through tide pools with his Sunday shoes on. At one particular tide pool, the boy and the woman stopped and bent over to inspect something. They remained there for several minutes, engrossed in whatever it was. O'Malley, suddenly jealous of the woman from America, had to turn and look away.

Fishing in his pocket for another cigarette, he strode along the crest of the dune, searching for a comfortable place to recline. He lowered himself into a grassy, hollowed-out place and lit the cigarette. He lay flat on his back, looking up at the sky, and imagined strangling his boyhood friend Tommy Feehan.

"What *are* the wee things?"

"I don't know, Bobby, we'll have to ask."

The boy's curiosity about the minuscule, swarming creatures in the tide pool was another good sign. She must make sure that Janet and Randy kept him challenged, kept him supplied with books from the library, taught him the names of birds and trees and stars. The world was a feast for the inquiring mind.

Leaving the pool, she asked him kindly to walk around it instead of through it.

"Why?" he whined, one foot in the water, one out.

"For the sake of your shoes. Wet shoes don't last very long."

"Me dad will buy new ones. He makes lots of money in Scotland."

"But you'll be in America. You can't expect the Meerses to buy you new shoes."

"Why not? You said they'd be like a mum and dad to me."

"Yes, and like all mothers and fathers, they have certain rules, and that's what we need to talk about."

"Me real mother didn't have rules."

"You were four years old when she died, Bobby. She'd have made rules by the time you were five."

He drew his wet foot out of the pool and walked around it. "Me granny hasn't got rules."

"But your father has, I'm sure."

Bobby stopped and squinted up at the bright sky. "Nothing about shoes. He only says don't go playing with Prods."

"That's another thing we have to talk about, Bobby. There's no fighting between Catholics and non-Catholics in America."

"Why not?"

"There just isn't. Stephen plays with Protestant boys and never gives it a thought."

"Soccer?" asked Bobby, his eyes lighting up.

"I'm not up on my games. He may play soccer."

"Will I play with him?"

"Of course you'll play with him. Why wouldn't you?"

"He's ten, you said."

"Ten last New Year's Day."

"Nobody ten ever plays soccer with me."

"Stephen will."

This prospect, after a moment's thought, struck Bobby as wildly amusing. His laugh was a joyous, hysterical screech, repeated over and over.

Agatha walked on ahead, letting him work off this fit of nerves. She was far down the beach when Bobby came running after her, his wet shoes squelching, his book clutched tightly to his chest.

"How many friends does Stephen have?"

"Quite a few, I should think. You'll have to ask him."

"What does he watch on the telly? Does he watch 'Dallas'?"

"I hope not. 'Dallas' isn't for children."

"I watch it with Granny. It's her favorite. Will I have my own bedroom?"

"Yes, I've told you Janet and Randy expect you to keep it picked up."

Bobby stopped in his tracks and howled at the sky, "I don't *want* my own bedroom. I want to sleep in Stephen's bedroom."

And so they proceeded, Agatha striding steadily onward, setting the pace, and Bobby stopping here and there to register his approval or disapproval of life, and then running to catch up. She noticed with satisfaction that he was avoiding the tide pools. Indeed, she saw him bend down once or twice to wipe the wet sand from the toes of his shoes.

They had walked half a mile when she noticed that the tide was turning, each wavelet creeping up the sand and erasing the line of foam left by the last. Bobby's tide of discontent was turning as well, as she'd known it would, his noisy protestations becoming less frequent as his nervous energy waned.

By the time they'd gone a mile, he was trudging along at her side, listening patiently to her recital of rules and regulations in the Meers household. At a mile and a half she was carrying his book and his blazer and he was holding her hand for support.

"Can't we ever have a sit-down?" he asked, pulling at his necktie with his free hand.

"Good idea, Bobby. Find us a dry place, and we'll have ourselves a rest."

He scurried up into the dunes and called to her from a height. She climbed to him and sat in the grass. Bobby curled into a ball, laying his head on her lap.

"I never take naps," he told her dreamily.

"I seldom do either," said Agatha, amused to see his eyelids already drooping. She changed her position so that her shadow fell across his face, which was already flushed with sunburn.

"Tell Janet I never take naps."

"I'll do that."

He was asleep in less than a minute.

Bobby's father, asleep in his hollow of grass near the car, was awakened by voices, young-sounding, snickering voices—teenagers, he thought, down to kick a ball back and forth on the beach. He sat up and fished for a cigarette as he waited for them to come into view, but instead of emerging from the dunes, they continued to babble in the vicinity of the car. He heard one of them ask, "How many will I jab?" and a second one answer, "All four—the whole job."

"The old lady's not looking?" asked the first.

"They're miles down the beach," the second replied, and then explained, "Goddammit, I dribbled paint all over my shoes."

O'Malley tucked away his cigarette and quietly crept along the ridge of sand. He looked down at the Austin in time to see the first young man stab one of the rear tires with an ice pick, while the second, with a brush and a small can of white paint, drew the letter P on the front door.

Because they both had their backs to him, and because the whistle of escaping air was high-pitched and loud, O'Malley was able to rush down on them and knock their heads together before they knew what hit them.

Upon concluding his talk in the auditorium of the convent school, James O'Hannon was surprised that the applause should be so tepid and that no one asked questions. Were educators always this lukewarm in their responses, or was it his less than brilliant delivery, hampered as he was today by a cold in the head? Or maybe it was the weather, everyone longing to be outside and enjoying one of the few fine days of the summer.

Or was his audience simply saturated with lecturers? In accepting the invitation, he hadn't realized that he was one of several speakers on the agenda of a daylong teachers' conference. He learned this only now, the hard way, by being shouldered away from the lectern by the man who had introduced him, and the next speaker was already cracking his opening joke before James was quite gone from the room.

He descended a narrow, creaking stairway to the ground floor and let himself out into the warm afternoon. The sky was gauzy white, the sunlight diffused and harsh from all directions. He looked at his watch and saw that he was a half hour early for meeting Agatha and the O'Malleys down at the seafront. He would find the car in some secluded spot, he knew, for Agatha said she required an unpopulated place to confer with Bobby. He hoped Cousin Liam knew enough to keep his nose out of their business. Cousin Liam wasn't known for his sensitivity.

Next to the school was a church, a small new building of whitewashed pebbledash, and James was drawn to it. A granite St. Patrick, larger than life, stood in the middle of the parking area, clutching his bishop's crook in one hand and a shamrock in the other. James tried the door and found it unlocked. The interior was so bright that he had to squint, the windows being of a plain, opaque glass that seemed to intensify the daylight. The walls were white and the woodwork was light oak. Candles flickered before the tabernacle. He had the place to himself. He knelt and folded his hands and brought up to God a full agenda:

That Bobby O'Malley's summer in America might set him on course with a fresh and happy outlook on life.

That Bobby's grandmother in Belfast might recover her senses.

That *Belfast* might recover its senses.

That Agatha might be showered with blessings for her three weeks of driving him so ably along the countless miles of his ministry, every one of them a crooked mile and most of them uphill; that she retain for the rest of her life the wholesome state of mind she seemed to have recovered in Kilrath; that she never again be brought low by depression.

He shifted his weight from one knee to the other and continued:

That nothing might stand in the way of Agatha's plan to return in September, and that he himself might someday, somehow, find the wherewithal for another airline ticket to Minnesota. (It obviously wouldn't come from the sale of spirits, poor Matt doing his best and yet the pub scarcely breaking even.)

That Matt, God bless him, might enjoy a long life as the agreeable housemate he was discovering him to be.

And speaking of housemates, that Agatha McGee and Frederick Lopat might take particular care of one another—an odd relationship, certainly, but a sound one when you thought about what each of them brought to it.

James then shifted from supplication to thanksgiving. "For

my trinity of blessings," he murmured under his breath. "One, for sustaining me in good health, never mind this head cold.

"Two, for inspiring me to be useful in my old age, for guiding me to my listeners, and for providing me with something worthwhile to say to them.

"Three, for Agatha, my dear soulmate. For picking the two of us out of our separate hemispheres and our separate preoccupations and bringing us together. For sustaining us year after year in Your—and our—love.

"Amen," he added, genuflecting before the tabernacle. He left the church and strolled down to the sea.

"Oh, the sea, the sea," sang Agatha under her breath. With the boy asleep in her lap and the sun falling warmly across her back, she gazed out over the water and realized that even without James in the picture, she'd periodically have to pack up and go somewhere to reacquaint herself with the sea. She loved the woods and rivers and meadows of home, of course, but more than those, she loved the level and rhythmical sea. In September, returning with Bobby O'Malley to Ireland, she would spend another month as Katie Bromley's lodger and James's driver. She would encourage him to schedule as many of his September talks as possible along the coast.

The thought of three months deprived of James did not make her heart sink—not as long as they had a definite date set for their reunion. It was only indefiniteness that caused the agony. In September they must not fail to plan their next visit. Would it be Kilrath or Staggerford? That would depend, she supposed, on their comparative finances. Most likely it would be Kilrath. Besides the mutual funds and government bonds inherited from her parents, Agatha had managed to put aside a good bit of her meager teaching salary over the years. In Staggerford National she had $85,000 in savings and $4,600 in checking. She also liked to keep her household currency, which was hidden in a coffee can in the linen closet, topped off at an even five hundred.

Her expenses were about to rise a bit. She'd be sending James enough to cover the fee charged by Donal O'Donnell for driving the Austin whenever he was available, and for James's bus tickets when he wasn't. When Agatha discovered how inconvenient the bus schedule was, the hours he'd been waiting beside country roads in the rain, she'd pressed him to take on a driver. Donal O'Donnell was a seldom-employed young folksinger who hung around Kilrath between engagements. It was Katie Bromley who lined him up as a driver, she being related by marriage to the girl Donal was engaged to.

There would also be expenses surrounding Bobby O'Malley's summer in Minnesota. Bobby's father was covering the big items—airfare, clothes, a certain amount to the Meerses for room and board—but she knew there would be many things, books for instance, she could hardly ask either Mr. O'Malley or the Meerses to pay for.

And then there was the house and yard on River Street. For three years—two in the principal's office and one down in the dumps—she'd neglected her house, but now with her spirit restored and her nephew Frederick in residence once again, she would start sprucing up the place. The trim needed to be painted, the screens repaired, a dying tree removed, the water heater and the downspouts replaced. Sooner or later she'd have to put on a new roof and have the foundation sealed. She would redecorate her dining room. She would search for a twelfth dinner plate to match her set and ask Frederick to install a lock on her china closet. That way, she needn't confront him about its disappearance, but he'd know she knew it was gone.

The sea, in the distance, was deep jade. The shallow waves edging up the wide beach were pearly and blue. Gulls, soaring and diving, were flashes of white against the gray-green horizon. What an incredible blessing, she thought, that there should be room in an old lady's life for both the ocean and James O'Hannon. It was James, primarily, who had restored her spirit—his sense of mission had proved contagious, as she'd expected—but the sea had helped. All that power contained in the cup of its coastline. All that expanse. All that timeless washing up the beach and washing back down. The tide was climbing gradually nearer now, the foamy wavelets reaching halfway up the beach. Soon she must wake Bobby and set off for the car; otherwise her shoes would be as wet as his.

But first there was the meeting of the library board to think about and savor. The board, appointed by the mayor, numbered five. Having been appointed by eight consecutive mayors, Agatha was currently serving her thirty-fourth year. During twelve of those years, like this one, she'd been its chairperson. She pictured herself on the fifteenth of June, seated at the head of the rectangular table between the card catalogue and the newspaper rack. On her left would be sitting Sister Judith Juba and Flossie Granum; on her right, Dora Druppers and the new member, a high school teacher she didn't know very well. Agatha had two plans for the library, one for the short term, one for the long. It was hard to say which one gave her more pleasure to think about.

The short-term plan she would carry out on the fifteenth. It required swaying only two other members to her way of thinking. Three votes against Imogene Kite, and vengeance was hers. Sister Judith would be easy. Nothing had changed for Sister Judith. Thus far, according to Janet's latest phone call, there'd been no call from another parish, no directive from the bishop. The nun was still stuck at St. Isidore's, still tending to the needs of her capricious father, and still feeling guilty about the tape recording. What better way to atone than by blackballing Imogene? -

Of the remaining three members, Flossie Granum was a cinch. Flossie Granum, appointed to the board twenty years ago, was now nearly eighty and beset by ill health and vagueness of mind. Having recently moved into the nursing home, she'd let it be known that Agatha's wishes were her own where the library was concerned. Soon the mayor would have to replace poor Flossie—she'd brought her purse full of underwear to the last board meeting—but not before Wednesday's vote. Let Dora Druppers and the high school teacher vote as they wished, Imogene's goose was cooked.

As for Agatha's long-term plan, she foresaw Janet Meers taking over the library. On Monday, Janet was scheduled to attend an orientation session at Rookery State College designed for older students who were resuming their education after dropping out for a time. In the fall she planned to embark on her degree in library science. It might take her five years to finish, given the long commute to campus, but Agatha could wait. Then, once the job was secured for Janet, she might feel like giving up her seat on the board. She'd be seventy-five.

How gratifying to be looking ahead as far as that. Or even as far as autumn, for that matter. For the past year, trying to envision her future, Agatha had been unable to see beyond the next half hour in the TV log. Yet now, concentrating on events of immediate concern—James preaching peace, the little boy sleeping in her lap—she saw the years opening up before her. Well, she shouldn't have been surprised. There'd been that principle of surveying in her sixth graders' arithmetic book— you measured distances by taking your bearings from things close at hand.

Descending to sea level, James saw the trunk of the Austin standing open and a young man kneeling on the ground, changing a tire. Cousin Liam O'Malley was standing over him, watching him work. Drawing closer, he saw an ice pick in Cousin Liam's hand, its point lightly touching the back of the young man's neck.

"Caught these two Brit sons of bitches tampering with your car," bellowed Liam, his face fiery with excitement, sweat standing out on his brow and upper lip. "Caught them before they punctured the second tire, otherwise we'd be in a fine fix."

James looked warily about for the second Brit. Was he hiding in the dunes?

"The creature ran away, the dirty weasel, but our friend here decided to stay and get us back in running order. Didn't ye, my friend?"

The young man squirmed and muttered something foul as Liam traced a line from the top of his spine to his ear with the ice pick. His long bleached hair fell over his eyes as he tightened the last of the four nuts with the tire wrench. He wore a black T-shirt. His blue jeans and sneakers were spattered with white paint.

"Looks like more than tampering," said James, stepping around to the driver's side and seeing the paint on the driver's door and the spilled paint can lying beneath it. He made out the letter P carelessly and crookedly applied, with two thin rivulets of white running down from its base.

"A sign painter he is, the bloody bastard, but he won't tell me what it would have said if I hadn't caught him at it. Something bloody dirty, no doubt of it."

"Priest," said James. "Maybe he was trying to write 'priest.' "

"Was that it?" Liam asked, pressing the point of the ice pick into the young man's hairline. "Was it 'priest' ye were trying to write?"

"Something like that," muttered the young man, cautiously getting up off his knees.

"Mothera God, what would that be for, now? What's the good of writing 'priest' on a car?"

"So the enemy sees me coming," James explained to Liam.

"Was that it? To make me cousin James a target for all your bastard friends? So they can spit on him as he drives by? Was that what ye had in mind, ye bloody bastard?"

The young man's answer was to fling the tire wrench into the trunk and slam down the lid. Then he stood stock-still, looking out to sea, waiting to be released.

James had never seen Liam so worked up. In other circumstances his red face and his bulged eyes would have been comical. As it was, he seemed to be straining against the impulse to drive the ice pick into the base of the young man's brain.

"We'll turn him in, Liam," said James.

"Of course we'll turn him in. We're driving him straight up into the town and turning him over to the garda. Here, since you don't drive, you'll have to sit in the back with this." He handed James the ice pick. "Let him feel it on his neck and he's tame as a pussycat." Liam laughed as he roughly steered the young man around to the passenger side.

"And we'll buy some paint remover," said James, desperately hoping that the incident might go unremarked and unnoticed when Agatha returned to the car. Although she spoke resolutely of his cause, and had proved a stalwart companion on these eleven speaking trips, he lived in fear of her losing faith in him. After all, she was not an Irish citizen. She was an elderly lady living a settled and comfortable life in America. How long could he expect her to support him if the way became rough? What if her heart was suddenly turned by fear? This was his one misgiving, this suspicion that in recruiting

Agatha to his ministry, he was asking too much of her. "And not a word of it to Agatha and Bobby," he added.

"As ye wish," said Liam, getting in behind the wheel.

James went weak in the knees as he climbed into the backseat with the ice pick. He didn't have the heart for this sort of thing, but of course it was his duty. In his lectures on peace, didn't he require others to report anyone suspected of treachery? He must follow through, then, despite his trembling hand and queasy stomach. How easy it was to preach at a lectern. How hard it was to keep the ice pick from shaking as he held it up behind the young man's head while Liam started the engine.

They climbed the road into town, and by inquiring of an old man on a bench in front of a pub, they found the police station. An officer in full battle dress, but without his automatic weapon, stood in the doorway, taking the sun. Liam beckoned him over to the car and told his story, describing the young man's accomplice and pointing out the direction in which he'd made his escape.

The officer was heavyset. He'd evidently just come on duty, for he was freshly shaven and smelled of skin bracer. "I know the blokes," he said with a flash of anger in his eyes, and after glancing at the evidence—the paint on the driver's door, the punctured tire in the trunk—he took the young man into custody and asked Liam to come inside and sign some papers. James went across the street and bought a can of turpentine.

Liam returned in a few minutes, complaining, "Mothera God, what they don't put ye through as a witness. They expect me back to give testimony."

"You'll do it, surely," said James.

"And give up a day's pay?" Liam O'Malley, starting the engine, laughed at his cousin's innocence. "Not on your life."

"But they'll serve you a summons."

"Not me, they won't. I made up a false name for meself and gave them a false address."

James frowned, laying a hand on his arm. "Liam, that's wrong entirely. We have to testify against these creatures if we're to get any peace in the land."

"You testify, Father James, I'm a working man meself."

"All right, I will," he said. "Stop the car." He went inside and registered his name.

Returning to the beach, they saw Agatha and Bobby a quarter of a mile away. They were standing near a rock at the water's edge, facing one another. Agatha appeared to be holding a hankie to the boy's nose.

"Handkerchiefs," said Liam O'Malley. "I forgot to pack the lad's handkerchiefs."

"Come on," said James. "Lend me a hand."

Using the rags Matt O'Hannon kept in the trunk for polishing the car, they worked feverishly to eradicate the paint. It didn't come off clean. A ghost of the letter P remained.

"I was hoping we could do better than that," said James, standing back from the door and wiping his brow with his shirtsleeve. "I was hoping Agatha might not see it."

"I should have stuck him like a pig and left him dead," seethed Liam. "I should have stuck the both of them and be done with it." He dropped his rag on the sand and lit a cigarette.

James turned to look down the beach, to see if he had time for more work on the door. Agatha and the boy had not advanced beyond the rock. Agatha was standing at the very edge of the water and flinging a handful of what looked like confetti into the waves.

"Oh, did the garda tell you what the bastard was writing?" asked Liam, blowing out a cloud of smoke.

"It wasn't 'priest'?" asked James, wetting his rag with paint thinner and bending to the job again.

"The garda got it out of him in the station. Popemobile."

Needing Kleenex for Bobby's runny nose, Agatha had searched the pockets and crannies of her purse and come across the folded paper she'd found on the Austin's windshield three weeks ago in Farlington. At first she didn't remember; then she recalled removing it from under the windshield wiper just as James had come up behind her with his observation that the old man with the ugly white ponytail was sinister. She'd assumed it was an advertising flyer, and folded it into her purse without reading it.

She unfolded it now, and read it.

Priest's woman McGee.
Go home to America.

She shuddered to think that even then, her first day out with James, they had known her name. She shuddered again, to think they might have been watching her ever since. She was afraid.

"Come on," whined Bobby. "I'm hunnnnnnnngry."

Her first impulse—to show the paper to James—was followed immediately by the impulse to destroy it. If she showed it to James, she couldn't possibly conceal her fear, and her fear might very well compromise his mission. Not that he'd give up his ministry of peace for her sake, but his resolve might be weakened ever so slightly, and his was no job for the faint of heart. Nor was hers. He must work with an undivided mind. So must she.

"Come onnnnnnnnnnn, they're waiting," cried Bobby, pointing to his father and James standing next to the car.

"I'm coming, Bobby," she said, tearing the paper into very small pieces and casting it into the sea.

42

*D*EAR JAMES,

Apologies for not writing sooner. I was laid low first by jet lag and then by a cold, which developed into bronchitis. It's now ten-thirty of a muggy, overcast morning, and I'm outside for the first time since I got home, attending to unanswered mail on my front porch while scaring away birds with my cough.

Frederick emerges from indoors every so often to replenish my supply of Kleenex and hot lemonade. It's his day off at the tourist center. He asks to be remembered to you, and wants to know what you did about your drainage problems at the pub. You were very kind to him, James—few people are—and the other day he asked me how much it cost to fly to Ireland. I suspect he dreams of showing up in Kilrath and helping you dig down to your sewer pipes.

Illness kept me home from the June meeting of the library board, at which it was my intention to oppose Imogene Kite's candidacy as our head librarian. In my absence there was a 2-2 deadlock, Sister Judith and Flossie Granum knowing my wishes and voting against her, Dora Druppers and the other member, a young man on the high school faculty, voting in her favor—both of them intimidated, I suspect, by Imogene herself, who, upon learning I was indisposed, drove up from St. Paul to plead in her own behalf. Her application will be taken up again at the July meeting. She won't attend, says her mother, not if I'm present, because she's sure to go down to defeat.

Well, now I'm wondering. She is qualified. She held the job once before, you see, with an unblemished performance record. Am I justified in voting no simply because I despise her? What

_would that do to my friendship with Lillian? And what if I go
to my grave with this hatred on my conscience? How would
that affect my eternal reward?_

_I haven't seen Bobby since the Meerses took him in, my ca-
tarrh possibly being contagious, but I've been on the phone every day with Janet. She says the boys are inseparable. They've
been given permission to build a treehouse in the lower
branches of a giant white pine, and they pass their days busy
as monkeys and smeared with pitch. Bobby has taken to Janet
as well, who reads to him every evening, but he remains wary
of Randy and has yet to acknowledge the baby's existence.
Janet is going to turn the reading duties over to Randy, in
hopes that that will win him over._

_As for his whining, Janet says he becomes insufferable only
in the presence of Baby Sara. I suppose the baby uses up a
good bit of the attention he feels is rightly his. His social instincts, if he has any, will be put to the test next week when he
accompanies Stephen to a friend's birthday party._

_My maternal instincts, if I have any, were severely tested on
the flight home. Bobby had a seven-hour case of the fidgets.
The flight attendants were extremely kind and our seatmates
long-suffering, but despite their help, I lost control of him. At
one point over the North Atlantic he entered the cockpit, and
there, having gorged himself on peanuts, was violently sick all
down the navigator's leg. . . ._

July 8

Dear James,

_It sounds as though you and your folksinging driver make a
marvelous pair. I'm not surprised that your audiences have
doubled in size. Who wouldn't drop everything to hear a talk
by James O'Hannon sandwiched between a few folk melodies
delivered by someone with (as you describe it) a sweet tenor
voice and a subdued guitar? Did you invite him to join your
program, or was it his idea? Or do you suppose your cousin
Katie Bromley had this partnership in mind all along when she
recommended a musician as your driver? I hope he's still with
you when I return in September. With him behind the wheel,
I'll have to find some other chore to make myself useful._

Two items from this week's Weekly: _Congressman Klein-_

schmidt is lagging far behind in the polls (the pleasure I take in this is surely a sin), and the Jubas' house is advertised for sale. Sister Judith, at last, has been invited to minister to a priestless congregation in the remote northern reaches of the diocese, where the Faith under her direction is sure to evolve quickly into something grotesque and unrecognizable. Her assignment there begins in August. It's not clear, says Lillian whether Sylvester is going or staying. Who would have him if he stayed?

I'm gratified to report that next week, following our July board meeting, I am to be the guest of honor at a library tea. The entire town is invited. Ostensibly it's in recognition of my lengthy service on the library board, but I suspect it's actually in reparation for the dishonor I've been done. You see, I've come home to nothing but smiles and good wishes. Oh, I still encounter a trace of embarrassed eye-avoidance now and then, but I sense no malice anymore, none of that horrible resentment that dogged my footsteps for months after Imogene went public with my letters. It may be, as you predicted, James, that everyone's indignation simply ran its course and died a natural death. On the other hand, it may have been hastened on its way by Bobby O'Malley.

Bobby's on everyone's mind. Janet and I get a dozen calls a day from people curious about Bobby and offering to do him favors—and not only people from Staggerford. Sister Judith published an article about Bobby in the Weekly *(enclosed), and it was picked up by the dailies in Rookery and Berrington. I've heard from a family in each of those cities wanting to know if they too might host an Irish child.*

As for Bobby himself, he grows more robust and freckled by the day. He's oblivious to all the attention he's attracting, Janet sees to that. She sees to much else besides, such as swimming lessons and dental and eye exams. (Glasses are recommended; I've written to his father about it.) He's going through an imitation phase, and Stephen, of course, is his model. That is all to the good. Stephen likes his stepfather and is attentive to his baby sister, and so Bobby, finally, is beginning to warm up to them.

Father Finn has gone to Montana on vacation. His replacement is a boy-priest from the cathedral named Father DeSmet, who says the most insipid things from the pulpit and wears tennis shoes at the altar.

Did I tell you whom the congressman chose as his local campaign manager? Marsha Skoog. She's sold her dress shop. The campaign office is a gloomy cubbyhole with crooked blinds in the windows. They say she sits in there nipping on a bottle of bourbon.

It is rumored that Sylvester Juba has intensified his search for romance. He's asked nearly every widow in town for her hand in marriage. It's been six months since he asked for mine, thank the Lord. . . .

July 14

Dear James,

Poor Mary O'Malley. If the institution her son has put her into is truly as gloomy as you say, then let's hope she's truly as deranged as she seems. This leaves Bobby without a home, does it not? Or without an Irish home, I should say. His home is here.

Poor Sylvester Juba. I haven't heard yet whether it was a stroke or congestive heart failure, but his respiratory system seized up, and when the medics arrived at his house, he was near death. Today he's conscious and off the respirator, but it's doubtful he'll ever be the same. Dr. Maitland says if he survives the hospital, he'll doubtless go to the nursing home. All of which seems Providential for his daughter, who found a buyer for their enormous ark on Juba Street. Or, rather, Randy Meers found the buyer—a couple moving here from Rookery who plan to turn it into a halfway house for recovering alcoholics. Ironic, what?

I will be thirty days in Kilrath, beginning September 20. Low airfares for autumn were advertised in yesterday's paper, and so I put my money down. I'm writing Katie Bromley to secure her spare bedroom again. Will Bobby be with me? You must help me decide.

I am fascinated by your insight concerning your so-called bias against the IRA. As often as I heard you speak, I didn't sense that you were being more critical of the freedom fighters than the loyalists, but if your audiences keep bringing it up, it must be true. And, if true, I find your explanation very *convincing—your desire to exorcise your lifelong hatred of the English. Our childhood impressions are the most vivid and durable of all, and you were scarcely seven when your father died at the hands of the British soldiers. Therefore, if hatred can ever be said to be justifiable, then surely yours was justified.*

More justifiable by far, for example, than my bitterness over Imogene Kite. Your letter has me questioning my grudge all over again. I'm still undecided how to vote at next week's board meeting. Your need to atone for your sixty-three years as an Anglo-hater tells me that a grudge leaves permanent scars. Your efforts to overcome yours strike me as wonderfully honorable, and makes my little snit with Imogene seem so petty. On the other hand, I sense my fellow Staggerfordians waiting for me to lower the boom. . . .

43

"*B* UT WHY?" *SISTER JUDITH* asked urgently as the meeting adjourned and the other board members got up from the conference table and left the library. "Flossie and I voted no because we thought you wanted us to." The nun looked hurt, betrayed.

"I voted yes for Lillian's sake," replied Agatha with some emotion. "Call it the power of friendship."

"Wow!" Sister Judith's expression changed to one of admiration. "I have to say, you are one great friend."

And not only that, thought Agatha, I saw an opportunity to give this town a lesson in forgiveness. I may no longer have a classroom, but I can still teach by example. Standing up from the table, she buttoned the jacket of her sky-blue suit and repinned the corsage of white rosebuds that had been delivered to her house earlier in the day. "Anyhow, it's over and done with, and this room is very stuffy."

"You are one tough woman," said the nun, falling back in her chair as though stunned. "I mean, what an example of virtue and forgiveness, wow."

Agatha left her there, wowed. She straightened her hair in the mirror behind the circulation desk and then stepped out into the heat of the summer. She found only a very few of her fellow Staggerfordians gathered under the two monumental old maples shading the library lawn. The long serving table was covered with a lace cloth belonging to Dora Druppers. The china cups and saucers had been lent by the Buckinghams, the Meerses, and Marsha Skoog. The silver tea service was Agatha's.

There was a slight spatter of applause as she descended the steps. Nodding to these few friends, she crossed to a patch of shade, where Lillian, assuming the worst, came up to her and said, "I can see why, Agatha. Sister Judith said if I prayed about it I could see why, and I do. Imogene hurt you too much, it's that simple."

Another guest or two arrived, bringing the total to perhaps a dozen. They stood at some distance from Agatha, waiting politely for Lillian to finish what appeared to be a message of some urgency. They guessed what it was about.

"I don't know why she did what she did with your letters, Agatha. I'm sure she's sorry and all, but it was simply too bad a thing for you to get over right away, and Sister says we have to honor that."

Agatha tried to interrupt, but Lillian wasn't finished.

"Do you think there'll ever come a day, Agatha, when you'll be friends with Imogene again, and the three of us can go back to having our Christmases and Easters together? I dearly hope so, but now it's a little too soon for you to get over it, and I understand that. Her job in St. Paul pays better anyhow."

"She got the job, Lillian."

Lillian gaped. "You mean . . . ?"

"She's been hired."

"Really and truly? You were outvoted?"

"I cast the deciding vote."

Lillian looked incredulous. "For Imogene?"

Agatha nodded. "Wisely or not."

Lillian was silent for a long moment, as though afraid of breaking a spell. Then she squinted thoughtfully and said, "I never wanted to move to St. Paul anyhow."

"Why don't you call her, Lillian? You can use the library phone."

Lillian, pressing a tear of happiness from her cheek, stepped back and gazed at her fondly. "What a friend you've been to me all these years, Agatha."

"And likewise."

Watching her stiffly climb the steps and disappear into the shadowy interior, Agatha wished she could feel something of Lillian's tenderness. All she felt were misgivings. It was true, as she'd told the nun, that she'd cast her vote partly for Lillian's sake and partly for Staggerford's sake, but more than that, she'd done it for her own sake. Following James's example, she'd done it to redeem herself, to test her largeness of heart, to prove that she was above grudges and acts of retribution. But she didn't feel as virtuous as she'd expected. She was full of worries. What if Staggerford misinterpreted her vote, saw it as a sign of an old lady's weakening will? What if Imogene was the sort who never learned from her mistakes, never overcame her habits as a detestable ferret, proved incorrigible, proved to be her lifelong nemesis? What if, despite being efficient, her chilly personality discouraged library patronage? What if she refused, five years hence, to take Janet on as her apprentice? Heavens, what a lot of trouble you let yourself in for when you tried for sainthood.

A few of her well-wishers stepped forward, then stepped back as a jogger came running up to her and shook her hand. He wore shorts and a T-shirt with FIGHTING IRISH stenciled on the front.

"Lovely here under the trees, isn't it, Miss McGee?"

"A heavenly day, Father," Agatha agreed, looking with disapproval at Father DeSmet's hairy legs and high-top running shoes.

"Congratulations, I'm told it's been thirty-five years."

"Actually thirty-four, but they seemed to need an excuse for a tea party."

"No word from your pastor," said the young priest, lifting his leg to scratch the inside of his thigh. "I hope he's finding good weather out west."

"I received a postcard," said Agatha. "It was raining in Helena."

"Oh," he sighed, visibly hurt. Older priests were always ignoring him. He turned and cast his eyes over the guests. "Well, you've got a very nice turnout," he said falsely.

"Yes," she sighed, trying to conceal her disappointment. By this time there were perhaps fifteen souls in attendance, most of them standing at the refreshment table where Dora Druppers was pouring tea. Mrs. Daniel Buckingham, Jr., was at the other end, dispensing punch in cups of clear glass lent by the Lutheran Ladies Aid. Addie Phelps was in charge of the cookies and bars.

A delegation from the nursing home pulled up at the curb,

and Sister Judith hurried across the lawn to help unload two old women from the van and into their wheelchairs.

It was well-known that Father DeSmet admired Sister Judith. "Judy's going to be missed in this town, isn't she?"

"Indeed," said Agetha vaguely.

"It looks like she could use a hand with those wheelchairs," he said, striding off to help her unload. "Many happy returns, Miss McGee."

She looked at her watch. One-forty. She had imagined throngs of people turning out to wish her well. She had imagined hearty handshakes and forgiveness and good conversation. Perhaps it was too soon after lunch.

In order not to appear as neglected as she felt, she crossed the grass to greet the seven guests from the nursing home, who were being deposited along the shady north wall of the building, two in wheelchairs and five on library chairs. Six of them, all widows, were women she'd known all her life, three of them her own age or younger. The seventh was a large man she'd never met. He had food stains down the front of his bib overalls. The two women in wheelchairs were sisters, Rhoda and Mona Cashman, both afflicted with some sort of nerve deterioration in their legs. Mary McClure, the nurse's aide from the home who was watching over them, said, "Wow, thirty-five years, Miss McGee. I wasn't even born yet."

"You missed some good years, then, Mary."

"Did I?" said the young woman skeptically, leaving to fetch drinks for her charges.

Gently patting the twiglike, arthritic fingers thrust up at her, Agatha thanked the oldsters for coming. The large man, sitting last in line, told her he used to farm near Berrington; he'd come to this nursing home because the homes in Berrington were full.

"And how are you finding it?" she asked.

"Had a better bed at home, but the food ain't bad."

She then inquired about certain of their fellow residents.

"Lorraine McGrane has dropsy," reported one of the women on wheels. "And Mildred Smith is down with pleurisy."

Her sister spoke up brightly. "Opal Stockman's getting over the shingles and Sylvester Juba's emphyzema is better."

"It's worse," said the large man in overalls. "They put Sylvester back on oxygen this morning."

"Lordy, Lordy," said the Cashman sisters together. Rhoda added, "The poor man." Mona said, "We heard he was better."

"He's worse," said the large man emphatically. "He's my roommate and he can't get his air."

"Can't *expel* his air," Rhoda Cashman corrected.

"Can't *get* his air!" the man insisted. "Ain't you heard him try to breathe?"

"Can't expel!" snapped Mona Cashman. "Can't *get* is asthma."

"Women!" lamented the man, appealing to Agatha for sympathy. "I'm living with too many women."

"I believe these women are right," she instructed him. "Emphyzema affects your breathing out, asthma your breathing in."

"What's the difference?" cried the man despairingly. "Sylvester can't breathe."

"Of course, what's the difference?" said Agatha apologetically.

"Sylvester Juba's a creep," exclaimed Mary McClure, returning with a pitcher of coral-colored punch and a stack of paper cups. "None of the aides want to go in his room. First time I went in his room, he didn't even have his first pill swallowed before he had his hand up my dress."

"Oh, he's the limit," said Mona Cashman sourly.

"Horrid man," her sister agreed.

Agatha heard her name called and turned to see Janet Meers arriving with Bobby O'Malley and Stephen and Baby Sara. The two boys went directly to the refreshment table, while Janet joined her on the north side of the building.

"Sorry we're late. We were out at Dad's farm, and you know how hard it is to get the boys away from him."

"I suppose he gave them rides on the tractor." Agatha pictured the softhearted, improvident Francis Raft in his overalls and flannel shirt, driving them over his hardscrabble acres.

"They took turns, one sitting on his lap and steering while the other one rode behind in the wagon."

"Your father's a dear man."

Agatha gathered the baby into her arms and displayed her to

the old folks, all of whom, even the large man in overalls, were instantly enlivened, making motherly noises in their throats, leaning forward to touch the soft cheek and lift the tiny hand. The baby snatched Mona Cashman's glasses off her face.

"Oops, sorry," said Janet, replacing them on the old lady's nose. "She's got this thing about glasses."

The baby reached for Rhoda Cashman's glasses as well, but Agatha held her back.

"We're going to have a real problem at our house when Bobby gets his glasses."

The two boys came tearing around the corner of the building, their mouths full of cookie. Surprised by the curious lineup of old people, they halted and stared.

Agatha presented them. "This is Janet's boy Stephen, my godson. And this is Bobby O'Malley. Bobby's visiting from Ireland."

Again the seven elderly bodies were drawn forward in their chairs, magnetized by youth.

"Stephen, Bobby, shake their hands," Agatha ordered.

Stephen dutifully went down the row, briefly touching each outstretched hand, while Bobby, shying away from the women, stepped up to the man in overalls and asked, "Do you have yourself a tractor, then?"

"A tractor?" The large old man chuckled. "*Had* a tractor. A John Deere."

"Where is it now?"

"Wore out. Like me."

Bobby frowned. "We're going to be farmers when we get big, Stephen and meself."

"Not much of a living in farming these days. Not around here."

"Aren't we, Stephen? Going to be farmers."

"Sure," said Stephen, who had come to the end of the line of handshakes.

"Well, if you want to be farmers, I can't stop you. Just make sure you keep the thistles out of your soybeans."

"Come on," said Stephen. "Let's get some more Kool-Aid."

"Thistles?" said Bobby seriously. "Why?"

"Come on," Stephen repeated, hurrying away.

Bobby followed him, but slowly, looking back at the old

farmer, who called after him, "Once they get in your beans, they spread like wildfire."

"He's growing," said Agatha.

"He's trying his hardest to be everything Stephen is," said Janet, laughing. "Even his size."

"He seems calmer."

"He still has his spells. But have you noticed how he listens to people? He loves to be spoken to, even if it's a reprimand. He'll stop what he's doing and take in every word, concentrating with all his might. It's so amazing."

"It's so Irish. Their sensitivity to language."

"Well, I wish Stephen would be more like that. Half the time Stephen doesn't hear what I say, but I can have whole conversations with Bobby."

Agatha lowered Sara to the ground. They said good-bye to the old folks and returned to the front of the library, the baby waddling between them, gripping their hands. Many guests had arrived, including Editor Fremling of the *Weekly*, along with his wife, his mother-in-law, and his camera.

"Half the summer is over," said Janet.

"So it is," said Agatha.

"Bobby can't go home. There's preregistration next week at school, and I'm going to register Bobby."

Agatha was surprised, less by the message than by its unequivocal tone. She was seeing more of herself in Janet with each passing year.

"I mean what home does he have to go to? He's got a dead mother and a weekend father and a grandma losing her wits. I can't stand to think of him going back to Belfast, Agatha. The poor little scamp belongs to us more than to anybody else." She stopped walking and frowned darkly, pleading with her eyes for Agatha's cooperation. "Isn't it obvious how he's getting over his nervousness? How he's developing? How much he loves Stephen?"

"And what becomes of your plan for college?"

"Oh that. I postponed it. I was doing it mostly for your sake anyway."

Agatha was taken aback. Janet pressed on. "I'm getting pictures reprinted that show Bobby making his bed and eating breakfast and fishing and climbing trees and helping Randy rake up birch twigs. One look at the pictures and you can see how much better his life is with us."

"I don't need convincing, Janet. It's his father who needs that."

The young woman nodded earnestly. "Will you . . . ?"

"I'll write him as soon as the pictures are ready." Agatha looked shrewdly at the two boys coming away from the refreshment table. "I'll write James, too, and put him on the case."

Janet then saw a pained or confused expression suddenly come into Agatha's eyes, and she asked, "What's the matter?"

"Nothing." The expression, quickly fading, was replaced by a smile. "There was a moment there when I thought I'd have no reason to go back to Ireland in September, if Bobby stays here."

"Oh, you've got a plenty good reason."

"Yes, I can help James in his ministry."

"No, I don't mean that. Your simply wanting to go is reason enough. It's okay to indulge yourself, Agatha."

The smile then turned into an expression Janet had never before seen on her old teacher's face. It was a shy smile, with a glint of conspiracy in the eye, a flush of pleasure in the cheek. A vulnerable look, yet satisfied. A happy look, yet timid. And she uttered no words to go with it. Typically, thought Janet, whenever Agatha was on the verge of vulnerability, she became fluent, burying her uneasiness under her clever way with language, but now she seemed strangely mute. How un-Irish, Janet thought.

By now there were perhaps a hundred people gathered on the lawn. Behind them they heard a man inquiring in a loud, forceful voice, "Where's our guest of honor? Where's our queen for a day?"

It was Congressman Kleinschmidt, making his way through the crowd, grasping at hands that were offered to him and hands that were not. "Ah, there you are, Agatha. I wouldn't have missed this for the world. I've driven all the way from Rookery, where I was speaking at Rotary, to tell you what a gem you are."

And to rehabilitate your reputation, Agatha guessed, as he

called to Editor Fremling and asked that his picture be taken with Agatha.

"With your permission, of course," he said to her deferentially, removing his dark glasses and replacing them with untinted lenses.

She considered withholding her permission. A hundred days ago this man hadn't wanted her on his premises; now he was intruding into her day of triumph, hoping that some of her honor would reflect on him. "One picture only," she said, picking up Baby Sara. "I'm not photogenic, but she is."

"Oh, what a cutie," he said, chucking the baby under the chin. "Ready when you are," he called to Editor Fremling. "I hope you'll put this on the front page."

Baby Sara, lunging for his glasses, smacked him in the face as the camera clicked, whereupon Agatha scooted away, the congressman calling after her, "But, Agatha, one more. That one won't turn out."

She ignored him, handing the baby to her mother as she faced a number of people waiting in line to wish her well.

Lillian was first.

"Imogene's all shook up, Agatha. You threw her for a loop."

"You mean she's disappointed."

"No, no, I mean she didn't see it coming. Says she was blindsided."

"Whatever that means."

"She'll move up Labor Day weekend. She has to give her boss and her landlord thirty days. I'll talk to you later, I've got to go wash teacups."

The line of well-wishers grew longer and longer. "Think of it, thirty-five years," they said, and Agatha replied, "Yes, half my life on the library board." Theodore Druppers closed his grocery store for an hour in order to come with his staff, all in aprons, and wish her well. Daniel Buckingham, Jr., did the same. Frederick Lopat came from the tourist center—without his feathered headdress, thank the Lord—and Marsha Skoog came from the campaign office. "Think of it, Agatha, thirty-five years," said Dr. Maitland. "My, how time flies," said Mrs. Maitland. "Congratulations," everyone said.

By which they meant much more than they said. Their platitudes, repeated over and over, were meant to say, Thank you,

Agatha, for being the person you've been to us. Thank you for being our teacher in school and our teacher in life. Thank you for coming home to us and taking up your life where it left off a year ago when St. Isidore's closed. "It's a wonderful thing you did," said a great many, "bringing that Irish boy over for a vacation."

"It may be more than a vacation," said Agatha.

The most surprising face to turn up in the line of well-wishers was that of Lisa Berglund, Agatha's pretty young companion from the Italian tour, who had learned of the occasion from Janet and drove down from International Falls with her fiancé. Because the line was lengthening, Agatha felt pressed to keep it moving and therefore spoke to Lisa only briefly, but nonetheless was able to gather a great deal of information. Lisa was worried about Paula the pixy, who was out of the hospital and back in Minneapolis, attending family therapy with her parents, who spent the sessions squabbling and fuming. Lisa was told this by Paula's friend Betty Lou, who also said that Paula was soon to leave on a tour of Alaska for the secret purpose of finding a job up there and never coming home.

As for Betty Lou, she had been hired, as she'd hoped, by the Department of Natural Resources, but instead of analyzing lake water, she was assigned to vehicle headquarters, where she was cleaning out, washing, and checking the engine fluids of the department fleet.

Dr. Finn was busy campaigning for one of his colleagues, a professor running for Congress against the incumbent. Trish and Darrin had dropped out of classes soon after the tour. Trish was a waitress. Darrin was selling vacuum cleaners. Lisa herself would be married within the month. "This is Larry," she said proudly, and Agatha shook the hand of a tall, balding young man who looked as if he couldn't imagine a greater waste of time than standing in line to greet an old lady at a library tea.

From all directions people drifted onto the library lawn, where they found the crowd abuzz with the news about Imogene's return. More punch and cookies were sent for. Ernie Shaw the postmaster showed up with his wife, and so did John Handyside the retired baker, and Larry Kelly the retired auto mechanic. Doris Bertram the seamstress brought her husband.

Mr. and Mrs. Harrington of the Orpheum Theatre brought their summer visitors. By three o'clock the proprietors of all the businesses on Main Street, following Theodore Druppers's example, had closed up shop and brought their employees. At three o'clock Editor Fremling counted 445 people on the library lawn; at four o'clock 708. He stood off to one side shooting pictures as the line inched along. The librarian's high swivel chair was carried out on the grass for Agatha to sit on.

"My, how nice you look, Agatha, your vacation must have agreed with you." "Congratulations, Miss McGee, we missed you when you were gone." When you disappeared so abruptly (their greetings were meant to say), we had the terrible fear that we'd done you some permanent harm. Not that you didn't deserve our displeasure, Agatha. You truly injured us in your correspondence with your Irish priest. But we weren't nearly so shocked or scandalized as we pretended to be—you've always been candid in your opinions and a little on the testy side—and we never meant to do you permanent harm. "Just think of it, Agatha, thirty-five years."

"Yes, half my life on the library board," she smilingly repeated. She looked deeply into the eyes of each well-wisher, and there she read fondness and goodwill. She saw how much she meant to them, and she felt how much they meant to her. Last winter she had witnessed, at the Vatican, the two-way current of love running between the Holy Father and his admirers, and that's what she was feeling now, that same powerful surge connecting heart with heart.

Dear James, she thought, it's too bad you aren't here to share this outpouring of goodwill. And then, thinking this, she suddenly realized she was feeling quite all right without James. Not that she could do without him forever, not that she didn't love him as she'd loved no one else in her life, but it seemed clear that James would no longer be her only inspiration. Now she could go back to drawing on this other, older source of strength, this hometown connection that had been short-circuited for a year or more, the nourishing goodwill of these dear friends and neighbors who one after another were stepping up to her—some of them smiling a bit wryly—and saying, "Congratulations, Miss McGee."

Their wry smiles were meant to say, It was sort of exhilarating, conveying our displeasure the way we did, with averted eyes and cold shoulders. It was like getting away with pranks in school. But pranks grow tiresome after a while, and we've come here today to say that just as you've given Imogene Kite your vote of forgiveness, we hope you'll forgive us for treating you badly. "Just think of it, Agatha, thirty-five years. Congratulations."

"Thank you, thank you," she went on saying all afternoon. By which she meant, You are forgiven, dear friends, and don't let it happen again.

Coming in August 1995 to
bookstores everywhere!

ROOKERY BLUES

by

Jon Hassler

Published in hardcover by Ballantine Books.

Read on for a sneak preview from this
compelling novel . . .

I F LELAND EDWARDS WAS known for anything beyond his slavish obedience to his mother, it was for his talent at the keyboard. He was the only youngster ever to
perform at twelve consecutive recitals of Miss Carpentier's
piano students. These recitals, held each year in the gymnasium of Paul Bunyan Elementary on the first Sunday in
May, were occasions of such cultural importance in Rookery that they attracted people who weren't even related to
the musicians. Clergymen brought their congregations, the
sewing circle brought their husbands, and the overseer and
his wife from the Poor Farm drove into town with a carload of codgers smelling of tobacco and urine.

The recital of 1952 marked Leland's final appearance.
He was eighteen years old. He sat head and shoulders
taller than the rest of the performers waiting their turn in
the front rows of folding chairs. Next to him sat his mother,
Lolly Edwards, a doting widow. She kept turning to her son
to make sure he wasn't taking the crease out of his pants by
crossing his legs, and now and then she reached up to pat
his unruly cowlick into place.

At precisely two o'clock, Miss Carpentier, a pale, bony
woman whose age was unknown and whose legs were
acutely bowed, welcomed the audience, handed out cough
drops to those in need, and introduced her pupils.

First on the program were the seven- and eight-year-olds playing pieces of nine or ten measures and striking eleven or twelve wrong keys. It seemed to Leland, a keyboard perfectionist, that he was witnessing a lot of sloppy fingerwork this year, and he wondered if Miss Carpentier was growing careless with age, or if talent was generally less plentiful since television had come to town. He recalled, with chagrin, his own first performance, at seven, when three-quarters of the way through "Anchors Aweigh" his fingers forgot what he'd memorized and he fled from the stage in shame. But he had not, as he recalled, struck even one wrong note up to that point, a fact that remained, to this day, a consolation.

Next came the intermediate students, who ranged in age from nine to fifteen and in height from four feet to five and a half. The range of talent was vast as well. Leland could tell by their applause that the audience had no idea who was good and who wasn't. He knew Rookery judged performance artists not by their art but by their demeanor. If a youngster approached the piano with a sure step and acknowledged the clapping with a smile and a bow, there was no telling what a great artist he might become. On the other hand, it took but a glance at Carl Henderson to convince these untrained ears that he was pursuing music down a dead-end road. Carl trudged over to the piano as if the floor were a miry field, and he played with his red face hidden behind one of his shoulders. His fingers trembled on the keys.

Why didn't Mr. and Mrs. Henderson relent and free poor Carl from the piano? they asked one another during intermission. Couldn't his parents see his shame? Didn't they understand how wretched was his playing? Mingling with the audience at the refreshment table, Leland heard these comments and held his tongue. He was too shy to point out that Carl Henderson, though a victim of stage fright, actually loved the piano and that his playing, far from wretched, was improving every year, right before their ears. They didn't know, as Leland did, that Carl hoped to major in piano or organ in college and go on to become the music director of some big Lutheran church somewhere.

As an only child and chronically lonely, Leland had hoped Carl might be his friend. Throughout Leland's boyhood, friends had been in short supply. There had been a neighbor girl when he was little, and a couple of boys in grade school and junior high, but after his father's sudden death, Leland had become more or less reclusive, taking pleasure in solitary things like fishing and coin collecting, and he became very serious about his music, practicing long hours in preparation for jivy jam sessions that existed only in his head. At one point, he'd asked Carl, three years his junior, to work up a duet with him for this recital, say a Gershwin medley, but Carl's taste ran to the sort of moody compositions that Miss Carpentier loved so dearly and Leland couldn't stand. Carl wasn't the least bit interested in the jazzy showtunes Leland liked to play.

After the punch and small cookies of intermission, Miss Carpentier presented her prize pupils, five in number. Shirley Pribbelow was first. Shirley, like Carl, was still completely under her teacher's power, which meant she was still playing the convoluted melodies Leland loathed, written by Debussy and other sleep-inducing Frenchmen. There was langour in Shirley's stride as she approached the piano, her playing was faint and dreamy, and the movements of her wrist and head were studied, hypnotic. The audience, who at the beginning of her piece had been shifting gingerly in their seats and loosening their elastic and buttons and exploring their teeth for morsels of cookie, fell gradually into a trance so deep that the applause Shirley got when she finished was as faint and scattered as the notes she had played.

Then it was time for the Skoog sisters. These three small, high-tailed blondes could be counted on to play the audience awake with lively melodies arranged for six hands on two pianos. Brisk bundles of nerves, Judy, Trudy, and Cecilia Skoog went rushing at the pianos with their hair flying, and they bounced on the benches as they pounded out pieces with clowns and stampedes and shooting stars in their titles. Every year they played their encore number, "Qui Vive," with such gusto that listeners were known to leap to their feet and whistle and cheer—such gusto this year that Cecilia, the youngest Skoog sister, midway through the crescendo, broke her index finger.

Perhaps it was the commotion of three girls wailing, one in pain, two in sympathy, as their father and mother and aunts and uncles rushed them out of the gym and across the street to Mercy Hospital that destroyed the audience's concentration and left them restless during Leland's performance. Or perhaps it was his own fault, for his rendition of "Slaughter on Tenth Avenue," though technically perfect, seemed to lack heart or soul or whatever it was that had made him such a hit in the years past—indeed had brought his mother to the piano more than once during this past week of practice to clap her hands with delight because the loud parts were so thundrous and the soft parts so tender and moving. But this afternoon all the parts were level and uninteresting. What a shame, thought his mother, something's got into the boy, maybe the flu bug; she must take his temperature.

But it wasn't the flu, it was reverie. Leland was dreaming while he played, imagining himself a member of a small jazz combo or dance band consisting of drums, a bass fiddle, a trumpet or two, his piano of course, and perhaps a trombone. The players were men he would meet next year in college, or perhaps later when he became a teacher of English. The group already had a name—The Icejam Quartet or Quintet or Sextet, depending on their number. This vision had been occurring to him more and more often the closer he came to the end of his schooldays, and now, this being his farewell appearance, these fellow musicians joined him on the piece he was playing and made it much livelier in his head than it sounded in the gymnasium of Paul Bunyan Elementary.

Not that it mattered much to the audience after all, for he stood up and took his bows with such aplomb and received Miss Carpentier's kiss and his mother's kiss with such a handsome smile that everyone knew they must have heard something fine.

Jon Hassler

"A WRITER GOOD ENOUGH TO RESTORE YOUR FAITH IN FICTION."

—The New York Times